A KISS FOR CHRISTMAS

Love is special all year round, but it's more special than ever at Christmas time. Sparkling snow — enticing presents under the tree — church bells and Christmas carols — and a sprig of mistletoe in case anyone forgets that Christmas is the season of love.

Invite six of your favorite Zebra authors into your home this Christmas. Here are six Christmas tales, each with a very special love story to read and remember, to save, perhaps to read again *next* Christmas. Six Christmas stories to cherish — written just for you by Caroline Bourne, Phoebe Conn, Kathleen Drymon, Wanda Owen, Patricia Pellicane, and Victoria Thompson.

Happy Holidays!

FEEL THE FIRE IN CAROL FINCH'S ROMANCES!

BELOVED BETRAYAL (2346, $3.95)

Sabrina Spencer donned a gray wig and veiled hat before blackmailing rugged Ridge Tanner into guiding her to Fort Canby. But the costume soon became her prison—the beauty had fallen head over heels in love!

LOVE'S HIDDEN TREASURE (2980, $4.50)

Shandra d'Evereux felt her heart throb beneath the stolen map she'd hidden in her bodice when Nolan Elliot swept her out onto the veranda. It was hard to concentrate on her mission with that wily rogue around!

MONTANA MOONFIRE (3263, $4.95)

Just as debutante Victoria Flemming-Cassidy was about to marry an oh-so-suitable mate, the towering preacher, Dru Sullivan flung her over his shoulder and headed West! Suddenly, Tori realized she had been given the best present for a bride: a night of passion with a real man!

THUNDER'S TENDER TOUCH (2809, $4.50)

Refined Piper Malone needed bounty-hunter, Vince Logan to recover her swindled inheritance. She thought she could coolly dismiss him after he did the job, but she never counted on the hot flood of desire she felt whenever he was near!

A Christmas Kiss

CAROLINE BOURNE
PHOEBE CONN
KATHLEEN DRYMON

WANDA OWEN
PATRICIA PELLICANE
VICTORIA THOMPSON

ZEBRA BOOKS
KENSINGTON PUBLISHING CORP.

CONTENTS

HER HEART'S DESIRE
by Caroline Bourne 7

A GIFT OF LOVE
by Phoebe Conn 53

A REBEL CHRISTMAS
by Kathleen Drymon 103

MELISSA'S MIRACLE
by Wanda Owen 157

GOLDEN ANGEL
by Patricia Pellicane 215

MERRY
by Victoria Thompson 281

Her Heart's Desire

by Caroline Bourne

Boston, 1777

"Dear Lord . . . I realize I am remiss in speaking with You on a daily basis, but I do hope You might open Your heart to me now. I don't ask for much — surely You must remember that I don't — but now I have wishes thrice over. Please, dear Lord — oh, this is Your humble servant's first wish — allow my beloved Willie to come home for Christmas — he does so love to decorate the tree and eat the popcorn. My second wish is that this humble girl shall prove worthy of true love, and my third wish — please Lord, I realize You are gracious and very generous with the snow, but so seldom does it fall when it would be most welcome. This year, please, let it snow on Christmas morning."

The coldness of the ground now penetrated the fabric of her gown and froze her knees, prompting Susannah to rise. Then she dropped again — despite the discomfort — to add, "In the event You might have forgotten — and I certainly understand if You have — but this is Susannah Warren of Boston speaking to You this night. You should remember me . . ." she continued hastily, though she was aware of the haughty tone she had now affected, "for on the night I was born You brought my dear mother into the fold of Your most cherished angels. I know she must be one of Your favorites . . . Aunt Emelyne says that

7

surely she must be." Then she heard her name being called and with a hastily added, "Amen," scooted up from her knees. The Great Dane, Bruno, moved to her side as she turned to exit the clearing.

As she trod the icy ground toward the stark, graystone house overlooking Boston, a twig snapped very close by. Spinning around, fear freezing her slender form, her emerald gaze attempted to pierce the knobby darkness of the hedgerow. Bruno growled, though the old boy did nothing more threatening beyond that and stood firmly at her side. Only the wind moved there and she began to relax, reassuring the Dane, "It must have been a rabbit, boy." She directed her chastisements toward herself: "There is enough fear without you inventing it, Susannah Warren." Then she turned and began to walk again. "Come along, Bruno," she ordered, picking up her pace as she tried not to look behind her.

She was fairly certain that if she had, something dark and ugly would have dropped a threatening hand to her shoulder.

Though he heard not a single word spoken, her prayers had awakened him. Clutching at his bleeding leg, Alan Duncan had tried desperately to pull himself to his feet and make his presence known before she disappeared into the night. The thorns of the hedgerow tore at what remained of his battle-scarred clothing. Pain rippled through his leg, and as his face fell heavily to the freezing earth, he watched the wide hems of Susannah Warren's skirts merge into the darkness.

"Susannah . . ." He tried to speak her name, but the gentle sound of it was little more than a harsh whisper. "Help me, Susannah . . ." *Blasted dog!* he thought with stronger inflection. *It is getting too old! A younger one would have rooted me out and dragged me to her feet!*

Sick, feverish, and delirious, Alan retained enough of his good senses to realize he didn't know how much more pain and disappointment he could tolerate. He had stood firm with General Nathanael Greene at Chad's Ford on the Brandywine, and had spent the last three months trying to make it home. Pressing his hand to his thigh, he could still feel the British musket ball he had taken there, deeply imbedded in his inflamed flesh. He really wasn't sure how he had stayed alive this long; sheer will . . . perhaps luck . . . probably fate. Now, having found his own house half a mile away burned to the ground, and summoning from only God knew where the strength to make it to the home of Willie, his childhood friend, he watched his last hopes of salvation become part of the December darkness.

The foggy silence washed over him once again, and Alan Duncan knew that he would die within an arm's reach of rescue. "Father . . . Mother . . . am I destined to join you this night?" Then he uttered, "Susannah . . ." with his final conscious breath.

Evening twilight draped its heavy veil over the lawns, though a rather weak moonbeam did manage to light her way through the overhang of red oaks and tangled, winter-barren vines. By the time Susannah reached the porch of her father's house in the hush of the night, Aunt Emelyne had taken up a patient vigil at the top of the steps. As a cowardly Bruno skulked past her, Susannah lifted softly sheened emerald eyes and peered at her aging relative from beneath the heavy fabric of her hood.

Light tumbled from the open doorway, betraying at once Susannah's crumpled appearance. "Where have you been, girl?" asked Aunt Emelyne in a tone both stern and loving. "Look at your dress . . . heavens forbid, have you been wallowing on the ground?"

Dragging up her skirts in two slender hands, to save her hems from further destruction, Susannah quickly traversed the steps and touched a brief kiss to Emelyne's cool, dry cheek. "You old dear. Always worried about me! I'm a big girl now, Auntie . . ."

"Come in and prepare for supper," ordered Aunt Emelyne, her tone softening with love for this precocious niece who was no longer a child. "And do apologize to your father for your sassy tongue."

Susannah pressed a full, petulant mouth, recalling instantly the argument with her father that had sent her out into the cold December night. He was staid, foreboding, unforgiving, and generally an old bear when his shallow viewpoints were contradicted by logic. The very idea that Susannah — his daughter and a mere wisp of a girl — would presume to state her observations in regard to the Revolution was, to Frederick Warren, an outrage and an unforgivable disrespect. She loved her father dearly, always, but most of the time she didn't like him very much. He'd been especially nasty, short-tempered, and quick-tongued these past few months.

"Are you coming in, Susannah?"

Startled by the growled query of her aunt, Susannah felt a coldness jerk through her shoulders. Turning, dropping heavily into one of the rocking chairs on the porch, she replied, "I'll be along presently," and did not meet her aunt's disapproving gaze as she reentered the house.

From the stately, columned porch of her father's house, Susannah could see the pale outlines of ships on the quiet waters of Boston Harbor. Usually the harbor was thick with ships, their masts and lines resembling a thick stand of pines, but most were off dogging or being dogged by the British. In the spring, when the world bloomed anew, she could not see the harbor from her special perch, which was one of the reasons she favored the winter season. She liked to know what was going on all around her.

The war with England had taken its toll on all their nerves; she tried to remember that when she allowed her father to anger her. She knew he had a lot on his mind, since they hadn't heard from her brother Willie since mid-September. He had been with Mr. Washington's troops at Chad's Ford on the Brandywine, and though all of Massachusetts, indeed, all of the colonies, knew that the Americans had been soundly defeated and lost a thousand good men, their brave Americans tenfold had survived. Susannah's daily assurances that Willie was among the survivors had been ignored by their pessimistic father, and she would do almost anything to prove him wrong. She had taken the little money she had saved over the years and paid a man to learn of Willie's fate, but to date he had not returned to Boston. Susannah suspected the nefarious fellow had absconded with her meager funds and would never again be seen.

The porch was uncomfortable this night; a frigid wind tried its best to whip back her hood and bare her to its treachery. But was it nearly as treacherous as her father's voice, now droning from within the house, and the almost hostile manner in which her name fell from his lips? She shrank within. These past few months had been almost unbearable.

Anger grabbed at her insides. She remembered the day in early August that Willie had left the house. Their neighbor, Alan Duncan, Willie's childhood friend, had waited outside, holding the reins of both their horses. Even from the distance of a hundred yards, the tall, handsome, dark-haired Alan must have heard the heated argument between Willie and his father. Willie had closed up his bookstore in town to join Washington's troops, and their father, who had financed Willie's enterprise because of his great love of reading, had been vehemently opposed to his involvement in the war. Let the other men fight . . . it's no business of yours. *I am an American!* Willie had bellowed in a tone not truly meant in disrespect . . . the same Willie who had never even raised his voice to their father, and had always honored his wishes. The same Willie who wanted to be a soldier . . . and who was lost somewhere in the carnage of battle —

"Susannah, come in at once!"

Memories bored into her as she remembered being a young girl standing in awe — and fear — of her father's booming voice. She jumped up, turning to face him. Then she caught herself, narrowing her gaze and pressing her mouth into a rebellious line so quickly that he might not have noticed her moment of apprehension. Easing past his tall, bone-thin form, she mumbled, "Yes, I was just coming in."

"Don't talk as though you have rocks in your mouth, daughter!"

Now, the rebellion ignited. Spinning, tossing off her cape, which immediately covered a good part of the foyer floor, Susannah drew her slim hands to her hips. "I'm nineteen . . . not nine, Father. I'd appreciate it if you spoke to me as an adult . . ." Impudently, she added, "and as an equal!"

Those were Willie's words, mused a now frowning Frederick Warren, who often found nothing but exasperation in the family appellation "Father!" Willie had always spouted "women's rights" with the zeal of a Patrick Henry, and condemned man's tendency, throughout the ages, to label them as private property, servants, nursemaids, and domestic whores. *Women can do anything a man can do!* he had bellowed into any conversation on the topic of women, *And they can do it better!*

Drawing in a long, deep breath, Frederick Warren said, "Do come in, Susannah. Our supper is growing cold."

Oh, how exasperating he could be! He knew she would not argue when he used that rare tone of voice, soft, almost affectionate . . . and overly polite. Susannah moved to skirt her father with enough distance that he could not drop that familiar hand to her shoulder. His overbearing nature had driven their gentle Willie away . . . Susannah would not allow him to chase her away as well. At least, not until her second wish had been granted.

At the supper table, conversation was virtually nil, and Susannah picked at her food with little appetite. She did not think about her father, always commanding and authoritative, or Aunt Emelyne, sitting opposite her, too subservient to argue with her brother. She did not think about Willie, away at war and being inconscionable in his failure to send word to them of his safety. Her thoughts were of her second wish . . . and she wondered if she would ever be worthy of true love. Across Aunt Emelyne's shoulder, the mirror reflected her image. Instinctively, she drew her hand up to tuck back a lock of honey-colored hair, then drew her finger across what she was sure was a tear glistening at the corner of one eye. She was slim, her heart-shaped features winter pale, her mouth rosy, and her emerald eyes large and almond-shaped. Her brother, when he hadn't been teasing his "funny little muffin," had claimed to have the comeliest sister in all of Massachusetts, for whom he would "fight off the lot of beastly suitors until one proved worthy." But comeliness was not what Susannah saw in her reflection; she saw only a woman who did not deserve true love . . . a woman who would wither and die without ever having experienced love, beneath the roof of her father's house in sixty-odd years, if the war did not claim her first.

"What are you thinking, daughter?"

Absently, Susannah dropped her hand to the wide space be-

12

tween Bruno's ears as he picked himself up from his usual spot beside her, expecting a handout. Offering him a bit of beef, Susannah met her father's steady gaze, trancelike. He had the kind of features that could intimidate without flinching a muscle. For that reason, she quickly dropped her eyes and said, "Nothing."

"Nothing? You appeared to be a million miles away. Surely, you have something on your mind?"

Susannah would not be goaded into an argument. The tone of his voice and the narrowing of his eyes were certainly familiar warnings. "May I be excused, Father? I'm not very hungry."

"You ate scarcely a bite," interjected Aunt Emelyne.

Susannah shrugged, cutting her polite glance from Emelyne to her father, where it immediately hardened. "May I be excused?"

He nodded, the lack of a verbal response almost as deafening as his critical gaze. Susannah retired immediately to her bedchamber, forgoing the usual hour of needlework she would have enjoyed with Aunt Emelyne in the back parlor. She had been working on a sampler as a Christmas gift to Willie, to take to the warfront for good luck. Ordering Bruno out of her bedchamber with a hasty "Go, boy, rest by the fire downstairs," she soon threw herself upon the bed, deciding to make up the lost hour of work on the morrow.

Her room was the largest in the house . . . its flocked blue and white wallpaper bordered in a deep royal blue around the fringes of the ceiling. A crystal chandelier magnified the light of a dozen candles, spilling upon the walls in gentle hues of gray and gold. Easing her fingers over the double arched headboard of her Sheraton bed, she looked absently at the treasures she had accumulated since her childhood: a rare clock from Medici Palace in Florence, which had been her mother's; the highly ornate miniature house with its wrought-iron and gothic trims, dominating the right front corner of the chamber; a collection of boxes in a glass cabinet . . . lacquered woods, silver, and glass, the small one of champlevé enamel that Willie had given her last Christmas. That one she had placed upon a rose-colored doily she had crocheted, set apart from the rest like a shrine.

"Oh, Willie . . . Willie . . . I do so miss you. And Bruno misses you, too. I've taken care of him for you as I promised I would." Then with a long, deep sigh, she asked, "When will you come home?"

When no answer was forthcoming, except for the howl of the wind beyond the long window, Susannah drew forward, and began her regimen of preparing for sleep. She brushed her hair, though not with the same enthusiasm as usual, cleaned her teeth, and drew on a comfortable bedgown. When she finally slipped into the soft down of her bed, she drew up the covers and lay quietly for a while, watching the change of ominous colors beyond the window, and an occasional flash of lightning far across the horizon.

A light series of taps echoed from the door, followed by the maid, Maggie, peering in. In her usual soft tone, she said, "I'll snuff the candles now, miss?" Following Susannah's almost imperceptible nod, the petite, pink-and-white-frocked girl, scarcely more than Susannah's age, loosened the ropes to lower the chandelier. Maggie was in charge of all aspects of domestic service in the house, except the actual preparation of meals. Emelyne had insisted on doing that herself, though she graciously allowed Maggie to clean up the mess afterward.

When Maggie used wet fingertips to extinguish the candles, Susannah asked, "Why aren't you using the candle snuffer?"

To which Maggie replied, "I've misplaced it, Miss Susannah." And in a softly persuasive tone, "You won't tell the master, will you?"

Susannah could scarcely hide her annoyance as she said, "Of course, not. Good night, Maggie."

When the maid had withdrawn, Susannah felt the anger filling her once again. Everyone was afraid of her father, and it sickened her, making her want to escape, as Willie had.

When at last sleep claimed her, she dreamed, as she always did; and as always, the one illusion she most wanted to enjoy eluded her. Willie was as far away in her dreams as the physical distance separating them; not once did she hear him call her the nickname he had long ago given her . . . his funny little muffin. Rather, her dreams were of casual things . . . the snow, which she loved, the first robin of spring, which always

14

thrilled her, and the tall, gentle man who would one day be her true love, and whose features were a strange blur of light and shadow that did not gain clarity before the morning rudely awakened her. He was there, she was sure of it, waiting for her to notice him . . . waiting for their gazes to meet —

A knock at the door chased away the early morning silence. Sitting forward, Susannah called, "Who is there?"

The door opened. Emelyne, carrying a silver tray, approached the bed, then set it on a small, claw-footed table. "I know you well enough, Susannah Warren, that you will not venture into the dining room for your breakfast. I've brought fresh, cold milk and eggs scrambled just the way you like them." Dragging her thick, gnarled hands to her hips, the older woman warned, "And you'll not leave the house this morning until the tray is empty."

Without malice, Susannah mumbled, "Oh, all right . . . you're becoming an old bear, just like Father." As her aunt double-checked the tray to make sure it was perfect, Susannah took the moment to notice the dear woman's wide, weathered features and tired, dark eyes that seemed bottomless in their depths. Emelyne's position as lady of the Warren household had proved a thankless job for as long as Susannah could remember. Because she, too, had taken her aunt for granted, she said quietly, "Have I ever told you how grateful I am, Aunt Emelyne?"

Suspicion narrowed her eyes. "Grateful? For what, girl?"

"That more than being my aunt, and a mother to me for these nineteen years, you have also been my friend."

Clasping her fingers, Aunt Emelyne cleared her throat. "Nonsense!" But her smile was as soft and sincere as the love she bore in her heart for Susannah. "And I'd not be comparing me to your father, if I were you, Susannah Warren! God forbid!"

Then she quietly withdrew.

Within the span of half an hour, Susannah had eaten her breakfast, luxuriated in the hot bath Maggie had drawn for her, and readied herself for a venture outdoors.

Perhaps she would make new discoveries this morning.

She was certainly in a mood for something new, strange, and

15

wonderful.

Dawn was a thinly veiled scattering of muted lights across the horizon. As Susannah closed the door and turned to the porch and steps, she suddenly felt the bitter cold penetrating the threads of her cape and flowing in painful gasps into her lungs. Hugging herself beneath the cape, she said to Bruno, "Do we really want to be out here, boy?" and the immediate resounding of her father's voice from within quickly answered that question. She might freeze to death outside, but no matter how warm the parlor might be, she would freeze much more quickly beneath the glaring scrutiny of her father's deep-set eyes.

As the December wind pierced her through, she reassessed her preference for the outdoors. Taking a moment to be thankful for her good health, for scarcely had she suffered so much as a cold in her nineteen years of life, she moved down the steps, her fingers closing over the bannister for support. When at last her shoes touched the icy ground, she tucked her hands into the warmth of her cape and moved toward her favorite spot with the Great Dane at her side.

While Bruno began his usual morning hunt for the old ground squirrel that had been teasing him for years, Susannah skirted the rotting boards of the gazebo floor and found a safe perch. Though she could see both the somber gray house above her and the harbor below, her gaze was upon her immediate surroundings as she now noticed the gazebo's sad state of disrepair . . . a broken arch, the paint flaking off all around, the extent of rot throughout the planked floor, and a brick fallen away from the side of the steps, exposing the crumbling mortar.

Mumbling her complaints, Susannah did not at first see the figures of two men emerge from the bend in the road. She heard the carriage that had preceded their appearance, and as she continued to mumble, she listened to the irritating clatter of its wheels upon the shell and rock. Her wave toward the driver, Mr. Pettigrew, a neighbor, was accomplished with absent duty, since he had waved first, and now her gaze returned to the slowly moving figures for lack of anything more exciting to hold her attention.

From beneath the darkness of her hood she watched them close the distance . . . one thinner and a little taller, his arm across the shoulder of his companion, his other hand wrapped firmly around the knobbed head of a walking stick. "Poor wretches," she uttered with sympathy, "coming home from the war," and continued to watch, pity and regret thickly imbedded in her heart as she thought of the horror of the young Americans being killed and maimed. She wondered if they had left the American forces at Valley Forge and thought about all the food her father had ordered to be sent to the camps.

She might have glanced away, but a rare ray of sunlight glimmered upon the shorter man's hair . . . which was wheat-colored, like her own. Then she noticed the familiar build, and as the distance closed, iron-black eyes suddenly lifted to meet her gaze. Mesmerized, disbelieving, she rose to her feet, uttering, "Willie?" and finding the tight constrictice of her throat almost painful. "Willie?" she repeated, her fingers closing over the gazebo's railing for support. Then the man grinned, winking in an oh, so familiar way, and Susannah's feet began to move, slowly at first, then breaking into a run across the icy earth. As she threw herself into her brother's arms, prying him away from the taller man leaning upon him for support, she laughed and cried, "Willie . . . Willie, dear Lord, can it truly be you?"

Willie Warren hugged his sister tightly, the laughter merging into an affectionate reply. "It is me, my funny little muffin! And look who I have brought with me!"

Wobbling against the cane that was now his only support, Alan Duncan made a feeble gesture of lifting a nonexistent hat. "Glad to see you again, Muffin," he greeted, and instantly began folding to the ground.

Grabbing for him and pulling him up once again, Willie informed her, "Alan said he was here last night, that he saw you. But by the time I found him, he had made it halfway back to his own —" He hesitated to add, "house," since the Duncan place was nothing more than a burned shell.

The British had burned the Duncan home, though no one was really sure why. Alan's life had been especially tragic these past few years, since his parents had been killed in a freak accident in Pennsylvania when a heavily loaded coal cart had

17

struck their carriage.

Susannah made a bold assessment of the tall, dark-haired Alan Duncan. She remembered the times he had come to the house to see Willie during their breaks from William and Mary College in Williamsburg, Virginia. The two had been inseparable, sharing pranks, honors, and eventually, their enthusiasm for the American cause, which took them into battle together. Now, the badly injured rogue was looking at her with deep-set gray-black eyes, scarcely able to stand and yet still accomplishing that silly, half-cocked grin she'd grown so accustomed to during her childhood.

"Well, how about it, Muffin, are you going to help him to the house?"

Her gaze, mesmerized by Alan Duncan's bold one, now returned to her brother. "Yes, I'll help you, Willie."

As she took Alan's cane and tucked her shoulder beneath his arm, Willie said, "I'm not going to the house—"

"Why not?" Surprise stiffened the two short words. "You must, Willie!"

"I cannot," he said. "I'll stay elsewhere."

"No! No!" Her vehemence, indeed, her horror, almost compelled her to leave Alan standing alone, but she maintained enough of her good senses to realize he would collapse without her. Willie, now facing them both, started to turn away. "Father will want to see you, Willie."

Without turning, Willie said, "No, he will not," then quietly added, "I can only stay until Christmas morning, Susannah. I'll see you around . . . I promise."

Tears filled Susannah's eyes. She was in a quandary, not wishing to leave Alan Duncan in his weakened state, but wanting to throw herself into Willie's arms and implore him to stay. "Willie . . ." Suddenly, the protests would not come. Rather, she asked, "Where can I find you?"

Now, he turned back. "There'll be no need. I'll see you every day."

Susannah cut her tearful gaze from Willie to Alan, and when she looked back to him, he had disappeared into the hedgerow. She wanted to call out to him, but she understood how he felt about their overbearing father. Perhaps tomorrow,

18

when he'd had time to think, he'd change his mind.

As she turned with the injured soldier, feeling the weight of him against her, she spoke. "Alan Duncan, you rake and you rogue. What are you doing here? Why aren't you in hospital somewhere?"

Alan smiled. He had always been enamored of the youthful Susannah, but the years separating them in age — as well as the omnipresent and very vocal disapproval of her father — had quelled his desire to call upon her. "You're glad to see me and you know it," he eventually responded, dropping his cheek against the tawny tresses of her hair to enjoy its softness. "Thank God for Willie. If he hadn't come upon me, I'd be dead for sure."

Willie! Dear, dear Willie! Susannah realized she couldn't let him go like this! Her pace increased so that she was almost dragging Alan along. At the steps to the gazebo, she compelled him to sit. "Wait here for a moment. I must try to talk some sense into my brother." Then she turned and fled toward the hedgerow where he had disappeared. Many years ago her grandmother, not wishing to be a burden on her family, had occupied a small cottage on the grounds, an occupancy that had lasted until her death last year at the age of ninety-one. Susannah was sure that was where Willie had gone.

Susannah pushed her way through the tangled hedgerow, oblivious to the thorns that ripped at her cape and the icy ground that threatened to unfoot her. When, at last, she pushed the creaking door to the cottage open, she stood for a moment, attempting to see into the darkness. The windows were covered by vines on the outside, allowing very little light. "Willie?" She stepped in, feeling the cold deepen and grab her tender flesh through the thickness of her cape. Another step and another quietly spoken, "Willie?" finally compelled him out of the dim niche in which he'd tucked himself. The familiar loving of her brother's eyes lit the room.

"Why aren't you with Alan?" Admonishment rested behind his tone. "Surely you haven't seen him to the house already?" At that moment, Bruno moved to his master's side and dropped to his haunches.

Susannah was a little surprised by the dog's obeisance. She'd have thought he'd be pouncing on Willie in his excitement at seeing him again. Perhaps her father was right; Bruno was getting old.

Moving toward Willie, then taking his hands in her own, she replied, "I simply couldn't let you walk away like this. Won't you at least come to the house and give Father the opportunity to apologize?" She moved into his embrace and quietly implored, "Oh, please, Willie. It's Christmas . . . a time for forgiveness . . . a time for love." She hesitated to add, "a time for family."

"It isn't as simple as that, Susannah."

She stood back now, as dismayed with him as she was happy to see him. "What do you mean? What is there to consider?"

Shaking his head sadly, he replied, "You just wouldn't understand, my funny little muffin. I am here for you. That is all that matters—"

He was as stubborn as their father, though that was something she knew in her heart he would not want to hear. She would give him time. Once he was alone in the cold solitude of the cottage, he would think about the hearth in their parlor, good food in his stomach, and shared family memories. Then he would change his mind!

So, touching her mouth in a tender kiss to his cheek, she smiled as sincerely as was possible. "Well, I mustn't leave poor Alan sitting on the gazebo steps."

"You'll take care of him, won't you, Susannah?"

"Me?" She managed a small laugh. "Your little muffin who drags home wounded puppies and kittens and triggers Mr. Beall's traps so he can't have rabbit for his supper? Of course, I'll take care of this latest stray . . . and you knew I would, you rascal, for surely that is why you dragged him home!" Dropping her smile, she looked down at the dog and asked, "Are you coming, Bruno?" And when he stood his ground at Willie's side, she said, "No, I suppose not."

Then she turned, moved into the light of morning, and looked back to wave at the dark form of her brother. She didn't want to leave him, and before she returned to Alan, tears were stinging her downcast eyes.

As she coaxed Alan to his feet, he asked, "Is Willie going to be all right?"

"Yes. He's much too stubborn for his own good." Then with some hesitancy and doubt, "He'll come around."

As weak as Alan was as she again tucked herself beneath his arm, he was aware of the light, floral fragrance of her skin, of soft, silken hair against his cheek, and the strength in her slight form as she carried the brunt of his weight against her. And he was aware of other things . . . soft, womanly curves where he could remember none before, and the sensual undertone of her voice as she coaxed him toward her father's house. He had stolen little more than glimpses of her during his frequent visits to the Warren household . . . and Willie had explained that their father didn't want the young men gawking at her, ruining her reputation and making her unsuitable for marriage.

Just as they reached the steps, Alan almost fell, and in her efforts to steady him, she was fully in his embrace, their mouths separated by a mere breath of space. Then, as their eyes met, Alan's mouth dipped and claimed her own in the softest of kisses.

Stunned, not by his boldness but by the fact that he was strong enough to accomplish it, Susannah did not at first respond. Though it was not an altogether unpleasant experience, she knew that it was something she should not have allowed. And if her father were to be watching at the window— God forbid!

With that thought in mind, she found the moment to end Alan's naughty assault . . . an assault that had betrayed to her the full extent of his illness as she'd felt his fevered features against her own. Standing back from him, then dropping her eyes as she tucked herself beneath the wing of his arm, she whispered, "If you weren't injured, Alan Duncan, you'd feel the sting of my palm." Then she looked toward the house and called, "Aunt Emelyne . . . Maggie . . . anyone . . ."

Scarcely had a moment passed before Maggie was easing down the steps toward her. "Master Duncan . . . my Lord, what has happened to you?"

Soon, with Aunt Emelyne now looming in the doorway, the two young women managed to get Alan Duncan into the foyer. Then her father, in response to the "Godawful noise," made an

21

appearance from his study at the back of the house. Although the women had been managing just fine on their own, Frederick Warren now began to bellow orders.

"Take him into the parlor. Maggie, bring some towels, then take the mare into town and fetch Dr. Haversham."

Maggie paled visibly. Susannah knew that her father was well aware of Maggie's fear of horses, even the gentle old mare who drew their carriage. "I'll fetch Dr. Haversham . . . if you won't," Susannah said to her father. "Maggie is needed here."

Frederick Warren pursed his mouth into a thin line. Susannah's offer had been solely intended to make him appear unchivalrous, should he allow his daughter to brave the weather and the icy roads to fetch the doctor. That alone infuriated him.

"I'll fetch Haversham myself," he grumbled, moving toward the foyer and his heavy coat upon the hall tree. "Women are better suited to these nursing duties."

Then, with a resounding thud as the door was being closed, he was gone. Susannah's heart went out to their groom, Joseph, who would bear the brunt of her father's anger as he saddled the horse for him. Were it not for Joseph's failing eyesight, he would be aiming the horse toward Haversham's home instead of Frederick Warren.

Alone with the women now, Alan said, "Still a bear, isn't he? I understand Willie's reluctance now —"

"What's this about Willie?" Aunt Emelyne's voice was little more than a whisper.

As she made Alan comfortable upon the divan, Susannah replied, "Willie wouldn't come to the house." Then in a quieter voice, "Because of Father. He's at Granny Gert's cottage. Oh, and if you missed Bruno, he chose to stay with Willie —"

Drawing a handkerchief from her panier to catch the first flood of tears, Aunt Emelyne turned and fled from the parlor, leaving the gaze of a surprised Susannah following after her. Asked Alan, "Did I say something wrong?"

Susannah returned her eyes to his gaunt, masculine features, and she thought at once that he needed to recapture the twenty or so pounds the war had taken off him. "It isn't you, Alan Duncan. Aunt Emelyne is as distressed as any of us that these tensions exist between Willie and Father. She'll probably prepare a plate of beef and potatoes and buttered biscuits to take out to him."

"And for me," said Alan. "I'm starving."

"For you, also, though I imagine you won't have much of an appetite until your fever has broken. I think we should worry about your wound first. Your stomach can wait."

Silence. Alan eased his head onto one of the plush pillows covering the divan. "That was good."

Susannah had retrieved a pair of scissors from her embroidery basket that was within reach of the divan and was cutting the material away from Alan's leg. "What was good?" she asked absently.

"The kiss."

The movement of the scissors suddenly ceased and Susannah cut disapproving eyes to the grinning features of the man who was at her mercy. The shadow of a beard half hid his angular good looks. His black hair, which she remembered always being drawn back neatly in a dark ribbon, hung limply to his shoulders . . . broad shoulders . . . her eyes lowered . . . to the wide expanse of his chest exposed through the ragged shirt he wore . . .

Remembering the last thing he'd said, and allowing his reminder to add color to her winter-pale cheeks, a frowning Susannah ordered in a hushed tone, "I'd forget that if I were you, Alan Duncan, because it will never happen again."

Instantly, her attentions moved to the muscular thigh, now exposed by the work of the scissors, and the blood-soaked bandage hanging in rags . . .

Her ministrations again ceased. Suppose the wound were gangrenous? Suppose his leg would have to be —

She caught a breath. No . . . she would try not to assume the worst for this rogue who made the blood run both hot and cold through her veins.

"You're a lucky young man, Master Duncan," announced Dr. Haversham, dropping the misshapen musket ball into a tin bowl. "There is no gangrene. The wound should heal nicely now."

Standing near the doorway when Dr. Haversham made his announcement, Susannah breathed a sigh of relief. Now she moved toward the divan and looked down on a grinning Alan Duncan, whose features still carried the pain of the surgery. Thank God, the musket ball had not been as deep as he'd thought. "Hear that, Miss Warren? The good doctor says I shall live."

Dr. Haversham, a close friend of the family who was usually much more casual, continued in his professional tone, "You should stay off the leg for a day or so. And if you ask politely, I'd imagine our Susannah wouldn't mind taking care of you." The short, stocky man looked up, his friendliness returning, then winked at Susannah. "It won't be so unpleasant, will it, having a young man around for the holidays?"

Upon his arrival at the house, Susannah had told him that Willie was at old Gran's cottage, refusing to come all the way home. That information had elicited no response. She wanted to again remind Dr. Haversham that another young man lurked about the premises, but knew the problems between her father and her brother were not the kindly doctor's fault. That was something she would have to work out with her father. "If it was any young man besides Alan Duncan," said Susannah, forcing a teasing tone, "perhaps it *wouldn't* be so bad."

"Aw . . ." An exaggerated frown drew Alan's features downward. "I've been fighting for right and liberty and the American way," he teased in turn. "And I might have died last night. You might have been attending my funeral, rather than hearing Dr. Haversham offering you the thankless position of private nurse." Then more seriously, "You will be my nurse, won't you?"

"Of course Susannah will aid in your recovery."

Startled by the sound of her father's voice, Susannah felt steel sabers tear through her shoulders. She looked up; Frederick Warren's profile was stark, unfriendly, and unsmiling. She suspected that he'd rather Alan Duncan—or any man for that matter—was anywhere else in the world than in their parlor. He had said many times these past few months that she was "much too young for men to be leering at her with lusty eyes." And somehow, sensing that, she found great pleasure in look-

24

ing back to Alan, then leaning slightly over the divan and brushing a thick lock of hair back from his forehead with the tips of long, tapered fingernails. "I'll never be farther away than the whisper of my name," she almost cooed, feeling her father's scorn bore into her. "Perhaps you and I and Willie —"

"None of this, daughter!"

Again the fear shot through Susannah. She straightened so quickly she might have fallen if her father's gnarled fingers had not twisted around her elbow. "You're hurting me, Father —"

"I'll hear no more about Willie. Do you understand?"

Her mouth pressed; quietly, she peeled Frederick Warren's tight, controlling grip from her arm. "I'll fetch a plate for Alan. He has already complained of hunger."

At that point, her father's gaze turned to Haversham, motioning him into the foyer. As Susannah moved toward the kitchen at the back of the house, she could hear their muted voices and, occasionally, the almost venomous fall of Willie's name.

She was furious with her father. How could he treat his only son so despicably? How could he be happy in the comfort of their large house, knowing that Willie was at the cold, dank cottage where a year had passed since occupancy had lent even a grain of warmth to it? Even Aunt Emelyne was acting with peculiar detachment. Every time Susannah mentioned Willie, she sniffed, began to cry, and left Susannah alone wherever they happened to be.

So now Susannah moved about the kitchen that Aunt Emelyne had just left and heaped roast beef, potatoes, and a healthy helping of custard onto two of their good china plates. Taking Alan his plate, with little more than a perfunctory apology for her tardiness — since her father was still with him — she now moved into the bitterly cold outdoors, caring not a whit that her cape was hanging in the foyer. She thought only of her dear Willie waiting for a meal to be brought to him . . .

But that was not quite true. She also thought of Alan Duncan, lying upon the divan in their parlor, wounded, feverish, and yet still able to exhibit that boyish humor she remembered so well in the many moments she had spied upon him from a dark recess of the house. Weren't men strange, wonderful creatures?

Except her father. He was self-serving, self-centered, self-righteous, and the most unforgiving man she had ever known.

She hurried along the walkway, entered the clearing, and absently scanned the gazebo as she entered the path to the cottage. She did not hesitate to push open the door, which creaked on its ancient hinges. Immediately, Bruno bounded toward her with the agility of a pup.

A coolness wrapped its fingers around her shoulders. Instantly, she wondered why Willie had not built a fire in the hearth, for on her earlier visit she had seen resin and brimstone and a healthy stack of logs that had been left in the brick grate. Putting the plate upon a small table, she dropped her hand to Bruno's head. His tail wagged so enthusiastically that his entire body was like a pendulum.

"Where is your master?" she asked, bending to rub the small black ears between her fingers. "Why don't you find him for me?"

At that point, Willie stepped from a dark corner. As she looked up, the gossamer at the window floated around him like a veil. The look in his eyes startled her and she immediately straightened, her hand lifting to the pale skin above her bodice. When her gaze cut across his shoulder to the window, Willie laughed sheepishly, "I'm afraid the window pane is broken and a good gust of wind whistled through. What did you think, my funny little muffin" — now he approached, his fingers lifting to her warm cheek — "that a bugbear had entered the room?"

Susannah smiled, thinking of the horrendous monster of her childhood, the ever-lurking "bugbear" that gained its strength from the dark, that Willie had said was always "sneaking about, waiting to gobble up unsuspecting little girls who wander away from the protection of an adoring brother." He had used the imaginary threat to control her when he'd found himself in charge of her at the most inopportune of moments, such as the hours that the local tavern was open and he and Alan had made plans to "swig the beer and soothe the wenches."

In that moment, she hugged Willie tightly, glad that he was nearby to dispel her childish fears.

"I do so love you, Willie," she said, stepping back so that she could gain a full view of him in the light now permeating the room from the open door. Then she turned, tugging him toward the small table that Bruno was now sniffing at. "I've brought you a good meal. Come . . . eat."

Willie took her hand and turned her back, giving her a brotherly look that thoroughly melted her heart. "I'll eat later. First, we must talk."

Her heart leaped in anticipation. "About Father? You and Father will make your amends so that you can return to the house?"

"No, it's not about Father."

"Then what?" She immediately regretted her angry tone; she continued with haste, "Of course, you know, Willie, that anything you have to say I am more than willing to hear."

"It's about Alan."

Again, her heart turned over, but this time she was not certain what had caused the physical reaction. She knew only that were it not for the tension between Willie and her father that was keeping him away from the house, she would be with Alan right now, tending him and nursing him and enjoying every moment she spent with him. But she could not let Willie know how she felt inside, lest he be as protective of her as their overbearing father. Her voice hardened as she replied, "Oh? What about that ragamuffin soldier? He's as worthless today as when the two of you were schoolboys."

"I want you to take care of him. I—" Lightly, Willie shrugged. "I lost sight of Alan during the battle at Chad's Ford and I didn't know until I heard—until I came upon him in the snow that he had survived. Perhaps if we hadn't been separated he wouldn't have been wounded."

Willie! Always the hero! Susannah was instantly sorry that his words prickled her so thoroughly, though it didn't soften the tone of voice she now used on him. "And you might both have been killed!" she argued. "Why must you always feel responsible for everyone, Willie?" She turned away now, her hands spanning the space before her. "Even when we were children you felt responsible for Father's ugly moods. You felt responsible for Aunt Emelyne's tears. And remember the time"—she spun back, her fingers now closing over her slim hips and press-

27

ing down her skirts — "that I fell and skinned my knee so badly when you were off at school? When you came home a few days later, you said that if you hadn't been away, perhaps it wouldn't have happened! I just don't understand you, Willie! Why don't you let those around you be responsible for themselves!"

Willie gave her a moment to still her rapid breathing. So pretty was his little sister when the fires of anger deepened her eyes to the color of a twilight forest. So flushed was her skin that he was sure an angel had touched it. Quietly, he replied, "Are you finished with your little tantrum?"

Slumping, dropping her hands, Susannah moved toward him and touched her forehead to the expanse of his chest. "Forgive me. I don't know what came over me." She looked up, a coy smile gracing her ample mouth. "Now, what were you saying about Alan at Chad's Ford?"

"I don't even remember." He chuckled, his hands now gripping her shoulders. "Just take care of him . . . for me," he asked quietly, "because he is my very good friend."

Aunt Emelyne's voice cut through the distance separating her from the house. "I must go," said Susannah and, lifting her skirts, moved quickly toward the door. Looking back, she entreated, "You will think about making amends with Father, won't you?"

To which Willie replied, "All in good time, Muffin. All in good time."

Willie's noncommittal answer did not elicit one of her cryptic replies. She was much, much too relieved to see him — alive and well — to argue with him if it wasn't absolutely necessary. Thus, she said, "Don't forget to eat your dinner before Bruno digs into it," then, smiling, pulled the door to. In just under half a minute she was hurrying up the steps to her father's house.

Days passed. Each evening, after Frederick Warren and Aunt Emelyne had retired to bed, Willie came to the house where he and Alan engaged in their favorite pastime, a good game of chess. Tonight, as the two young men mulled over a particularly challenging game, Susannah trimmed the tree old Joseph had erected in the parlor. "I can't believe you two lazy men won't help me with this," she chided.

Willie laughed, "You're holding the box of freshly cut mistletoe. I believe this is a job for Alan."

"Mistletoe?" Alan immediately took up the old cane Emelyne had found in the attic. "Sounds like a challenge to me." Looking to Willie, he grinned, "A break from the game, old boy, while I do the normal things one does beneath mistletoe?"

While Susannah fussed beneath her breath that "the boys" were acting very immature, Willie stood away from the game table, arched his back to relieve the tension, then moved toward the bay window. There he sat, watching Alan and Susannah work on the tree together.

Susannah draped the tree with garlands of popcorn and silk ribbons, laughing when Alan jokingly put the popcorn in his mouth and pretended to eat the hard work she had done just that morning.

Soon, balls of holly tied with ribbon, lace sachets, glass angels, and a hundred tiny candles graced the tall, narrow tree. The only decoration left was the mistletoe, and as Susannah put her hand in the box, so did Alan.

She froze, feeling the warmth of his hand upon her own. Their gazes met; Susannah felt overly hot in the cream-colored gown Aunt Emelyne had picked out for her that morning. She noticed only then the bronze tone of Alan's skin, the deepening shade easing into his sharp cheeks. She noticed then the black halocs surrounding the rich gray of his eyes, the tiny scar at the corner of his right eye, still a little pink, as though it were a fairly recent wound. She noticed the full, ample mouth untouched by even the slightest emotion . . . and then his fingers closed over hers, snapping her from her moment of bold scrutiny.

Embarrassment suffused her features; her mouth parted as though she would scold him. Then she saw the smile thin his mouth and all thoughts of scolding him were lost to the evening. She became unaware of Willie sitting silently at the bay window; for the moment, she and Alan were the only two people in the room.

His movements grabbed her attention. When his right hand slowly came up, holding one of the larger sprigs of mistletoe, he whispered, "Shall we keep with tradition?"

She did not react; her features were strangely void of emotion. When he let the cane fall, so that his left hand could ease around her tiny waist, she did not protest the distance closing between them. Now, she was against him, his breath whispering hotly against her cheek, his mouth parting, dipping, claiming her own trembling one in the gentlest of kisses. But when he attempted to gain more intimacy with a deeper kiss, she spun away from him, her cheeks so hot she thought they would explode. Instantly, her cool palms covered them, attempting to quell the dizzying warmth that might any moment unfoot her.

When she suddenly rushed from the parlor, her footfalls instantly heard ascending the stairs to her bedchamber, Alan looked toward his friend. "I think the comely lass likes me."

Willie, one leg drawn up and his linked fingers wrapped around his knee, merely smiled.

The cold wind bruised Susannah's cheeks as the sleigh moved silently over the icy road. Her father had shipped the sleigh, a romantic gift for his wife, from a small village near Copenhagen during one of his many foreign excursions several years before Susannah's birth. To her recollection, this was the first time it had been removed from the carriage house and its years of sitting idle had lent it a series of soft creaks and groans. As a girl she had settled upon its upholstered seat to watch Joseph work in the stables and pretend that the charming vehicle, pulled by a dapple-gray mare, was gliding over the first snows of the season. Now, she was almost sure she was enjoying its first saunter upon American soil. The large bells on the harness provided music without rhythm against the backdrop of comfortable houses and the harbor lying in the distance.

Susannah looked toward Alan, gaiety twinkling in his smoke gray eyes as he coaxed the mare along at a casual pace. This was their first outing in the fortnight since he'd come to the house and nothing, save a British invasion, was going to ruin it.

A yoke of ermine framed her winter-pale features, which were hidden deep in the recesses of her hood. Thus, Susannah hardly felt the needles of ice prickling her skin and she was as oblivious to the fierce howling of the wind as a dreamer was to reality. She knew only that she'd never been as happy as when she was with Alan.

In her tender ministries over the course of the fortnight, he had recovered sufficiently to allow this excursion into the outdoors. Though he still walked with a limp, the wound was well healed and he carried the cane simply for reassurance rather than as a crutch. In those moments that he walked with his arm across Susannah's shoulders, drawing her close, she often noticed that he carried the cane at midlength, swinging it back and forth as they moved along. And in those wonderful moments, when his mouth dipped to claim her own in the gentlest of kisses, the cane usually fell to the earth with a dull thud.

Willie had journeyed to his bookstore that morning, giving them the privacy of the cottage. There they would return and enjoy each other's company, without the glaring scrutiny of Susannah's father. He had journeyed to Concord on business; Susannah was sure he'd not have allowed the sleigh to leave the carriage house, and Joseph had let her take it out only because she'd promised that they'd return before her father.

"What are you thinking, little muffin?"

Susannah smiled at how easily Alan employed her brother's nickname for her. "I am thinking how wonderful it is to be outdoors, away from the parlor Aunt Emelyne keeps as warm as a cell in —" She stopped short of the rhyme, smiling up to Alan as he cut a feigned look of disapproval.

He did not verbally chastise her though. Rather, he pulled off the slick dirt road onto a smaller road dead-ending at a gate. In the meadow beyond, Mr. Pettigrew's milk cows stood beneath the bare branches of an elm, their backs to the icy wind. Halting the mare, Alan now turned to Susannah, his fingers traveling along the thick cape, then tucking into the opening where her hand was hidden. She did not protest its immediate capture between firm gloved fingers.

Grinning, he said, "Now, tell me how one so fair can utter such vulgarities three days before Christmas."

She peered coyly at him from beneath the fringes of pale, copper-colored lashes. "Vulgarity, sir?" She fought the smile playing upon her mouth. "Do tell me what vulgarity I have employed, that I may be careful to avoid it in the future."

"Don't play the innocent with me, Miss Susannah Warren. I'll have none of it." The playfulness suddenly ceased. Withdrawing his hand, he now moved to encircle her and drew her close. "I don't know what it is about you, Susannah. I've known you all my — or should I say *your* life — and I never really knew you." Drawing slightly back, so that he could see her pale features and rich emerald eyes, his tone grew serious once again. "Forgive me, but if you knew the thoughts I have of you . . . the dreams I wish would become reality, you would slap my face." He chuckled, though without humor. "Or worse, perhaps . . . you might tell your father how I feel about you and gladly watch him run me through on the field of honor."

Though she'd not intended it — or had she? — her gaze flashed an undeniable invitation. She leaned into him, and when she felt his clean-shaven chin graze her forehead, she lifted her trembling mouth to his. When his hands slipped beneath her cape and circled her tiny waist, she drew slightly away. Though she wanted only to be back in the confines of his strong arms, she found the sense to say, "The cottage is warm right now. Willie started a fire for us before he went into town." And without dropping her sensual gaze, "Shall we go there now? We might enjoy being alone."

Touching his cheek to her passion-warmed one, Alan now directed his attention to the mare. Within moments the sleigh was gliding the same roads in its return to the hill.

Aunt Emelyne had seen the two young people leave in the sleigh. Joy filled her that, at last, her dear niece was finding happiness. She was pleased that young Master Duncan was drawing her out of her shell of brooding silence and solitude. Susannah had other things to think about now; perhaps she would cease to dwell on the problems between her father and her brother that had sent Willie off to war.

Tears glazed Emelyne's eyes. The house had been sad these past few months. She did not want to think about what had been, and what could have been . . . if only. Her brother Frederick was suffering in his own private hell, and she was not helping matters by allowing his moods to blacken her own as well. There was Susannah's happiness to think about now.

Which was why she'd made one of her rare ventures from the house to make sure a healthy fire burned in the cottage's hearth. She'd have sent Maggie, but she'd been given a week off from her domestic duties to spend the holiday with her own family in Lexington. Emelyne had taken a basket of sweet rolls and freshly churned butter to the cottage—giving Susannah and Alan no excuses to return to the gloomy house on the hill—and she hoped the two young people might enjoy some time alone when they returned from their sleigh ride. It was much too frosty to be out and about, and Emelyne watched the window, hoping for their hasty return.

She did not have long to wait.

Susannah requested that Alan draw up to the front porch so she could ask her aunt's permission to spend time with Alan at the cottage. Unchaperoned! Would Aunt Emelyne glare at her with sternly narrowed eyes and swear, *Not while I still draw breath, young lady!* Well, that was a chance she would have to take.

When she started to alight, Aunt Emelyne was immediately at the door, shooing her with one pale hand. "Go on . . . you two young people need time to yourselves without me gaping about. The cottage is warm . . ." As an afterthought, she added, "And your father won't be home 'til well past dark." When Susannah's gaze questioned her, she continued a little roughly, "Go on . . . do as I say, Susannah."

Susannah smiled, reseating herself beside Alan. As he flicked the mare into action, he called back, "I'll take good care of our girl."

Neither heard Aunt Emelyne affectionately reply, "You'd better, young whippersnapper . . . harumph!" then retreat into the house.

Turning the sleigh and mare over to Joseph at the carriage house, Alan and Susannah retreated to the cottage, whose windows glowed in the overcast morning light. As they entered the warm interior, Susannah remarked that it was thoughtful of Willie to build a fire.

As he peeled off the thick coat and gloves her father had given him, Alan turned to Susannah and said, "Do you want to hear something very strange?"

"And what is that?" she replied, turning her back to him so that he could help her out of the cape.

Though his hands covered and affectionately massaged her shoulders, his voice was strangely detached. "Before Willie found me in the snow that night and helped me, I'd thought he'd been killed at Chad's Ford."

Susannah drew a short, quick breath, her heart skipping a beat as she drew instantly away from Alan. "Why ever would you think that?"

"Major Montgomery told me." Seeing the ashen horror upon her lovely features, Alan again took her shoulders. "Thank God for mistakes, Miss Susannah Warren. I thought I'd lost my best friend. Rather, I have found—" He stopped short; was it too early to tell Susannah how very much he loved her? That he always had—and always would . . .

Susannah wanted to hear him say it. *Say it please . . . love . . . you have found love. Dear, sweet, Alan . . . I love you, too.* But he had hesitated, and now the sentiment might rest on the tip of his tongue and he might be wondering how receptive she would be to such a commitment.

She could not press him, nor could she confess her love before the man had properly confessed his own. Oh, how stifling was convention! For mercy's sake! Who had made these ridiculous rules . . . and how many centuries ago? How she hated tradition and male dominance!

So, shaking away her angry thoughts, she stepped into his embrace and whispered, "Yes, thank God for mistakes. I would imagine there is a great deal of disorganization in war, and mistakes will be made. After all, they let you walk away without the surgery you needed, didn't they?"

A slim masculine finger rose to gently touch her mouth, though it was almost as instantly replaced by a sensual kiss. The fire burning in Susannah's cheeks was not fueled by the hearth only a few feet away; rather, it radiated from her heart, and from a deep, alien feeling that made her feel limp and yet filled with her with life and wonder . . .

She heard the cane drop as his hands moved to capture her waist, then slowly . . . oh, so slowly, they began to fold together to the thick, braided rug covering the planked floor. She wasn't sure what was happening to her; she knew only that the way she felt was more wonderful than she'd ever imagined.

Alan compared her beauty to a radiant rose. Her soft mouth trembled, her sea-green eyes glazed with innocence, vulnerability . . . desire.

Susannah wanted only to be with him, to be held by him and loved by him . . . she wanted this wondrous assault of her senses . . . the awakening of passions never experienced. She dared not open her eyes as they shared their deepening caresses, dared not allow him to see the wants and expectations lingering there.

This is not what Aunt Emelyne expected when she said we needed time alone . . .

What a time to think about her maiden aunt! thought Susannah, instinctively drawing her hands across Alan's broad shoulders.

Her body molded to his own, shared the passion with his own; though a moment of apprehension of what she had never experienced rose within her, she could not escape the prison of his arms, nor did she wish to. She wanted to be there . . . she wanted to know what it was like to be with a man she loved . . .

A man she was sure loved her . . .

And as the barriers of clothing — and apprehension — were slowly peeled away, the wild intense desire flooded her, begging for him, wanting to be held and loved and desired by him . . .

Magic moved upon them, taking them away to a far, distant place. There was no dusty rug over a planked floor . . . only the clouds . . . no fire pulsating within a brick hearth . . . only the liquid passions molding their bodies together as one . . .

He was much gentler with her than she was sure was necessary. Though his masterful hands scorched her flesh with passion, she wanted something more . . . though she had only her imagination to rely on as to what that *something* was. When, at long, long last, their passions became a tantalizing joining, Susannah knew that she wanted to stay forever in his arms.

The lusty gaze of his eyes offered promise . . .

And Susannah, as wild and free-spirited as a naughty wind, knew that what she shared with him today, she would share with him for a lifetime . . .

In those last two days before Christmas, a flurry of activity touched Boston. Men, exhausted by the war with England's merciless troops, began coming home for the holidays. Aunt Emelyne had prepared codfish cakes, meat pies, brown bread, and tea cakes, and had gone into her hoard of apple cider stored in the cellar to feed those poor souls hoping to reach homesteads farther to the west before Christmas was upon them. Her father had also ordered a large shipment of food items from Virginia and had been busy preparing it for its final journey to Washington's troops at Valley Forge.

Seeing very little of Willie these past two days, Susannah began to worry about him. With Alan engaged in mundane, and obligatory, conversation with her father over a goblet of brandy, she now sought her brother out at the cottage.

He was sitting upon a windowseat, reading from a book of poetry, when she knocked at the open door, then peered in. "Willie?" A smile lit her face as she saw his silhouette against the approaching darkness. When a chill invaded her shoulders, she said, "You do keep it cold in here."

"It feels good," he remarked, coming to his feet and laying the book aside. When she approached, then moved into the circle of his arms, he asked, "And what is this for?"

"I just want to thank you, Willie."

"For what?"

"If it hadn't been for you, Alan would have died, and I wouldn't have known what it was like to . . ."

"To what?" he asked at her hesitation.

She stepped slightly back, studying a brother whose features were warm and loving, whose eyes smiled as they returned her gaze. Softly, she responded, "I wouldn't have known what it was like to love, and to be in love. Oh, Willie, I love Alan with all my heart and soul, and the very thought of the future without him . . ."

"And have you told him this?"

She turned away now, picking at the buttons of her dark blue dress. "He hasn't said he loves me, willie. But . . ." She blushed, remembering the expressions of love — without verbal confes-

36

sions — they had shared just two days ago, only a few feet from where she stood with her brother now. What if he knew? Could she turn and face him?

She didn't have to. Willie sauntered slowly, deliberately, around her, his fingers linked behind him, his gaze searching her dropped one, then his fingers easing beneath her chin to force eye contact. "It isn't absolutely imperative that the man make the first confession. Have you thought that, perhaps, he might not feel worthy of you?"

"Who is not worthy?"

Susannah spun about, both her hands flying up to cover her mouth as Alan hovered in the doorway. So much color rose into her cheeks that she was sure he would notice and tease her unmercifully. But he did not. His eyes held her lovingly, admiringly.

Willie skirted his sister to approach Alan. "You, Alan Duncan, you scoundrel. I am wondering if you are worthy of my sister."

Why had he said that? Alan would know they'd been talking! Susannah thought she might faint right there; she could not lift her eyes to Alan. When he approached, then drew her limp frame against his own, he whispered, "And I am not worthy. No man, since the beginning of time, has been born who is worthy of such a treasure." Then, with teasing affection, "But I plan to make myself worthy, Susannah. This I promise you." As he held her close, feeling the softness of her pale hairline against his cheek, he said, "Your aunt has dinner prepared and wants you home." To Willie, "Are you sure you won't join us?"

Willie shook his head, then moved slowly toward the window to retrieve his book. "I don't think so. Come Bruno." The great black dog, heretofore unseen, moved from the shadowy corner of the sitting room. "Go up to the house and eat your dinner, too."

But he shook his head, as though he understood, and chose to disobey. Quietly, he turned around and returned to the corner.

Alan asked, "See you later on for a game of chess?"

Willie, returning to his chair with the book, said, "Glutton for punishment, eh, old boy?" and elicited a laugh from his old friend.

Susannah tucked herself against Alan for the short walk to the house.

Christmas Eve. Again, Susannah let the two words echo through her mind, *Christmas Eve.* Will my final wish come true in the morning? She moved slowly, gracefully, to set down the silver tray upon which rested a large pitcher filled with Aunt Emelyne's specially mixed eggnog and crystal goblets for each of them. This year, for the first time, her father was going to allow her to add a little extra brandy to her eggnog.

In just over four months she would be twenty years old . . . about time, she thought, that her father began treating her as an adult.

Father had already brought a decanter of his favorite brandy to the table, where the tray now awaited their attentions. Dr. Haversham pulled his bulbous frame up from the Queen Anne chair beside the hearth and loudly cleared his throat. "Emelyne's eggnog! I've waited a whole year for this time to come around again! Emelyne's eggnog and your fine aged brandy, Frederick Warren."

"I scarcely believe you've waited a year," said her father with indulgent affection. "I know for a certainty that you've raided our cellar since then. And after I gave you six bottles last Christmas!"

Winking, the friendly old bachelor responded, "Were it not for my housekeeper, Mrs. Higgens, the initial supply would have made it through the year. The woman is a swill!"

Then they all laughed, and Susannah began filling the goblets.

Is it the proper time to bring it up? thought Susannah, watching the merriment of her father, Aunt Emelyne, and Dr. Haversham as they sipped the eggnog. She looked to Alan for some kind of support, since she had mentioned the source of her present worry to him earlier. He nodded, the look in his silver-gray eyes saying, *The time will never be better.*

So Susannah drew in a small breath, set down her goblet, then smoothed down a wrinkle in her gown. The pace of her heart increased, and she was sure a tremble visible to everyone

38

was rocking her slender shoulders. Moving toward Alan, she linked her arm through his, then caught her father's attention with slightly raised eyebrows and her gaze full upon his own.

"What is it, Susannah?"

"Father, I am wondering . . ." *Oh, be still, heart. Stand straight, legs! Don't fail me now!* "I am wondering if Willie could join us for eggnog this evening. It is Christmas Eve, after all."

The blackness fell upon his features like gossamer at a funeral. His eyes narrowed, his mouth pressed into a thin line; why did he then cut his gaze to Haversham, and why did the short, stout man nod slowly, deliberately, silently, as though the two of them, without speaking a word, were engaging in some Godawful conspiracy?

Twisting his mouth into a wry grin, Frederick Warren calmly replied, "Yes, of course, Susannah. You may fetch him to the parlor . . ." He hesitated to add, "With my blessing."

She gave an impulsive, gleeful cry, then took Alan's hand. "Will you come with me," she asked, then moved hastily toward the foyer, lest her father change his mind.

Out-of-doors a brittle wind rubbed her skin raw, but with Alan holding her elbow as they moved along, she kept her footing on the icy path and soon entered the cottage. Tossing back her loose, disheveled hair, she called, "Willie!" and when he did not answer, she called with more urgency, "Willie, please, Father says you can come to the house." An oil lamp at the table where he always sat to read illuminated an open book. Approaching, closing the book over one of her fingers stuck between the pages, Susannah saw that Willie had been reading verses by the German poet Christian Gellert. Then she opened the book again, noticing at once that a section of the pages had come loose and fallen away somewhere. Her heart fell; Willie must have ridden to his bookshop in town to search for the missing pages.

Alan approached and gently closed his fingers over her shoulders. "He'll be back soon. We can wait."

"I know Willie." Emotion caught in her voice. "He'll find something interesting on the bookshelves and won't return until the predawn. I know our Willie so well." Then she turned in Alan's arms, a smile touching her full, pouting mouth. "At

39

least Father has opened the door. I feel in my heart, Alan . . . I feel that our Willie will grace us with his presence on the morrow. After all, if the ice has begun to melt from father's heart, perhaps by the morning it will be completely thawed. Perhaps, then, Willie will not leave as he said he would have to." Lifting her gaze, she smiled sweetly for him. "Imagine that! Having to leave for the war on Christmas morning! I can hardly imagine that a man would issue such an order!"

Laughing, Alan took her in his arms and held her warmly. Staring into swirling green depths surrounded by long, curled lashes, he said, "And I am sure that if anyone disobeyed the orders of a mere general, it would certainly be Miss Susannah Warren. For I'll wager, fair maiden, that our Willie will not! If he is told he must leave on Christmas morning, nothing on this earth can hold him back."

A chill traveled the length of Susannah's spine, propelling her more tightly into Alan's embrace. When she rested her cheek against his chest, she felt his fingers tangling through her hair. She stared into the dark distance beyond the open door, feeling tears well behind her eyelids, and yet not understanding the reason for them. Just when she might have shed them, Alan's curled index finger moved beneath her chin, coaxing her mouth up to his own. Then he noticed the glaze of tears and raised a quizzical eyebrow.

Explained Susannah, "It's Christmas Eve. Willie will leave on the morrow and I didn't finish the sampler I was making as a Christmas gift for him."

"That is my fault," said Alan. "I have monopolized your time. And since we have mentioned gifts . . ." Stepping back, Alan removed a small velvet pouch from an inside pocket of his coat. "This is for you. I hope you like it."

She felt a little awkward, even as her heart fluttered with joy that he had thought enough of her to buy her a Christmas present. Except for her father and her brother, she had never received a gift from a man before, and so hesitated, looking to him and expecting him to coax her into opening it. When he said nothing, but smiled that familiar crooked smile, she asked, "Shall I open it now?"

"Please . . ." He watched, delighted with her childlike excitement as she loosened the drawstrings, then poured the contents of the pouch into her hand. Then he picked up the necklace from the warmth of her palm and began to untangle its delicate gold chain. With tears again brimming her lower lids, she turned away so that he could fasten the lovely jewels around the slim column of her neck.

The gold heart with its single diamond surrounded by a dozen pear-shaped rubies gleamed against her pale skin. She touched her fingers to it softly, carefully, as though it were the most fragile crystal. "It's beautiful, Alan. But how — when — ?"

"This afternoon, while you were napping," he said, holding her close once again, "I rode into town and used my charms — and my wits, by God — to get Mr. Manton to open his shop and grant me a line of credit."

"I will never take it off," she promised, her eyes closing as he claimed her mouth in a deep, searching, passionate kiss.

Christmas morning dawned bright and cold. Susannah could hardly force herself to perform her usual regimen and slip into her dress of shimmering green brocade with a panel of white satin shaping the front that she'd been saving especially for this special morning. Her father's icy stare when she'd returned to the house last evening without Willie had metamorphosed into an ugly climate of sullen silence, and when he'd retired to bed soon after Haversham's departure, she'd wept openly in Alan's arms.

Then, just before ten o'clock, Willie had made his promised appearance for the game of chess with his good friend. He'd offered no explanation for his absence from the cottage, except to say that "I only stepped out for a moment."

Now, Christmas morning had arrived; Susannah's feelings were mixed, and she was rather tired. Her father was angry, Willie would leave, and the sky beyond the window was clear, gray, and cold. If her third wish was to be granted, it would certainly have to be a miracle. If anything, it would sleet and add an extra layer of danger to the already hazardous roadways. She did not foresee snow this day.

She was just exiting her chamber when she encountered her father. Surprised to see him up so early, she raised a quizzical brow. "Father? Is something wrong?"

"No, daughter. You remember Major Montgomery, don't you?"

"Of course . . . he's Willie's commanding officer. Will they travel together this morning?"

He ignored her question. "The major expressed his wish to see you. Will you come downstairs." As she dutifully took her place beside him, he said, "You look lovely, Susannah. The dress becomes you."

Again, she was surprised; her father rarely gave a compliment. "I am flattered that you noticed," she said, and was immediately sorry for the edge of sarcasm in her voice.

Traversing the stairs, with her father one step behind and slightly to the right, Susannah soon entered the parlor. Aunt Emelyne sat in her favorite chair, her hands twisting over the smooth wood as though she would peel away the varnish. Major Montgomery, resplendent in his blue and white officer's uniform, turned from the hearth to greet her. The tall, distinguished man looked unusually tired; war did that to a man, she supposed.

"Major Montgomery," she greeted him.

He bowed grandly, taking her hand to hold it gently and briefly. "I have brought a letter to your father. He wants you to hear it."

Though she didn't know why, she didn't want to hear anything Major Montgomery had to say and she certainly wasn't interested in any letter. Something deep in the recesses of her mind told her that this man was a conspirator, like the members of her family — like Dr. Haversham — and yet she could not quite remember what that conspiracy was. She knew only that the people she most loved had hurt her deeply, that she had fled, and that she was still angry with them. Dear Lord, she couldn't remember why.

"What letter? From whom?" came her rather indignant response, the gentle glow of her cheeks suddenly reddening. "And why today have you left your family?"

"I have yet to reach my family, Miss Warren. I stopped here first."

"Who is this letter from?" she demanded, lifting her hand to

42

the ruby and diamond necklace Alan had given her.

Major Montgomery raised a sharp, black eyebrow, as though it would suddenly take flight. He had no doubts that before him stood a young woman who had stepped into a private little world to shield herself from pain. He didn't like being the monster at the door who would drag her out; he was furious with Frederick Warren for putting him in this predicament. He cursed the timeliness of his visit. "Miss Warren, I have brought to your family the letter your brother was writing the night before he was killed at Chad's Ford."

"No! No!" The horror of his words flooded her like a bad dream. "You're mistaken. Our Willie is out at the cottage. You're mistaken. I'll fetch him."

When she turned toward the foyer, Frederick Warren bellowed after her, "Willie is dead, Susannah! Why can't you face it! He is dead!" Anguish burned in her father's heart as she turned to flee across the foyer and into the cold December morning.

The tears stinging Susannah's cheeks turned to ice as she traversed the steps, oblivious to the slippery mirror of frost and sleet clinging there, threatening to unfoot her. The clumps of green brocade of her Christmas dress were crushed in her palms as she lifted her skirts, allowing for a faster pace. The folds felt overly hot and she wanted to tear the garment from her slender frame before it burst into flames. Shortly, she rushed beneath the overhanging limbs of the red oaks, the icicles glistening like diamonds beneath the scant morning sun, and entered the clearing where the gazebo's shabbiness and state of disrepair stood stark against the winter morning.

"Willie . . ." The call of her brother's name squeezed through the tight emotion of her throat. "Willie . . ." she called again, hugging her waistline, feeling the mad thumping of her heart that surely would not be contained beneath the tight fabric of her gown.

The clearing was a scattering of frost and ice, clinging to the winter-barren trees, hanging in slim fingers off the thick, leathery leaves of rhododendron; a single red rose clung precariously to the thorny twine wrapped around one of the gazebo's six slim columns. And there, sitting serenely with his head

43

bowed, as if in prayer, was dear Willie, his right hand upon Bruno's dark head. Relief rushing into her features, she called out his name once again.

Quite before he could come to his feet, she had thrown herself into his arms to hold him with sisterly affection. Tears touched the cool fabric of the jacket he wore. "Oh, dear, dear Willie," she gently sobbed. "I — I could not find you . . ."

"Why these tears, little muffin? It is Christmas morning . . . a time for happiness . . . a time for family."

Linking her fingers at his back, her pert chin pressed into his shirt as her tearful gaze lifted to him. "Major Montgomery is at the house. The foolish man believes you were killed at Chad's Ford, and he has brought a letter he claims you wrote. Oh, Willie . . . Willie." Now, she stepped back, and both her hands closed over his right one. "You must come to the house and show the major that you aren't dead. Please, come now."

Rather than allow her to maneuver him toward the house, Willie gathered her to him. A sad, regretful smile turned up his mouth. "My funny little muffin . . . you asked for three wishes for Christmas . . . and you have gotten only two . . ."

Susannah's features paled to the color of snow. She had been alone that morning . . . only God could have heard her prayer. "But . . . how . . . you couldn't know . . ." Her gaze wide, touched by bewilderment, was suddenly rewarded with a mischievous masculine smile.

"No matter how," laughed Willie, hugging his dear little sister to him. "Now . . . close your eyes. I have yet to give you my gift this Christmas morning."

Alan sank deeply into the plush fabric of the divan. Major Montgomery hovered over the liquor cabinet, his trembling hand accepting still another goblet of brandy from the elder Warren. Dr. Haversham, who had just arrived, stood silently by the window, his arms crossed, his gaze narrowed as he watched Susannah's rather strange movements in the vicinity of the gazebo.

"What do you mean Willie is dead?" asked Alan again, having received no answer to his first inquiry. "He's been here for the past two weeks. Surely you've seen him." His gaze cut across the stifling warmth of the room where Susannah's father stood, then to Emelyne, her rueful, dark-clothed form rocking back and forth in the worn chair beside the hearth. "For God's sake! Are you telling me that I'm mad?"

Now, John Haversham pivoted from the window. "No one is saying any such thing, young Master Duncan. Things we cannot understand manifest themselves in the minds of a grievously wounded soldier. And, I have recently learned, you are very fond of the young lady. Of course, you would be inclined to indulge her fantasies and perhaps adopt them yourself."

"Fantasies, bah!" Alan shot to his feet, feeling a sharp, though momentary, pain in his right leg. "I have seen him. I have been with him. He has come to the house at night; we've played chess." Then in an accusing tone, "What is your motive . . . all of you? And why today, on Christmas, the holiest of all days?"

Tears flooded Alan's darkening eyes as he recalled the words spoken by each of these people in turn over the past few minutes . . . how word had come in October of Willie's death, how they had grieved, how Susannah had refused to believe the news brought firsthand by the soldier in whose arms Willie had died, how John Haversham, in his role as physician, had directed that she not be forced to admit her brother's death until she made the choice herself, and how they had indulged her when she'd spoken of him as though he were alive.

But . . . Dear God! He had seen Willie himself! He had brought him to Susannah that morning. He had kept him alive through a very cold night, had given him the incentive to return, and over these past two weeks had so patiently encouraged the love he had claimed was inevitable between his sister and his childhood friend. They'd played chess together in the parlor each evening after the others had retired . . . and Willie had won nine out of ten games! And now they were saying he'd been dead for three months? It couldn't be true. Why were these people denying that Willie had been here . . . as alive as any of them?

"I must find Susannah," he said on a quieter note. "She will need me. I don't understand why you are doing this . . . but I will find out!"

Taking up the cane with its engraved brass head, Alan moved toward the foyer, the heavy mahogany door soon separating him from the others of the household. He stood for a moment, attempting to still the tremble that ricocheted through his shoulders. The weakness in his legs made it almost impossible to keep his footing. Feeling his breathing relax, he moved into the cold morning.

With a coy look, Susannah smiled. "What are you up to, Willie?"

"I want you to close your eyes," he repeated, cocking a pale eyebrow. "And when you open them . . ."

Gently, Susannah's palm assaulted his chest. "Do you think I've forgotten what you used to do, Willie Warren? The last time you did this I was nine and you were nineteen, and when I opened my eyes you were gone! It took me all of two hours to find you quietly reading in the library!"

"Close your eyes," he laughed. With a playfully pressed mouth, she obeyed, and Willie's hands closed over her shoulders to turn her from him. "I promise you, my funny little muffin, that when you turn, you will meet the gaze of a man who loves you very much."

"Do you promise, Willie?"

"I promise," he responded, touching his cheek to her pale hairline. "Remember, little muffin, for all time to come, how very sad I will be if you grieve for that which is predestined. Remember how I love you . . . and remember that if you ever need me, I will be close by. There is no such thing as death if you remember life and happiness." Before she could question him, he stepped back and said, "Now open your eyes . . ."

A warm glow flooded Susannah's features; slowly, her eyes crept open. The clearing was the same, and yet different somehow . . . sun glistened upon the ice embracing the red oaks, breaking into a thousand blinding rays, like the tears of angels blessing the solid earth. Then, upon the flaming warmth of her cheeks touched a delicate coolness. As the snow spiraled, featherlike, all around her, she laughed, a soft, musical laugh, her arm's lifting to the rapturous day . . .

"Oh, Willie, Willie . . . snow on Christmas morning." And

she turned, the glow of surprise instantly transcending into one of the purest, sweetest love.

For there, an arms length from her, stood Alan, tall and proud, his smoke-gray eyes tear-moistened, holding her sadly, and yet lovingly, his broad-shouldered frame trembling with emotion. Susannah rushed into his arms, her tears spreading into the cool cotton fabric of his shirt. "Alan, Alan, my beloved, my darling . . ." And when his muscular arms moved to claim her shoulders, she whispered, "Our Willie *is* dead, isn't he?"

Stunned by her question, and before he could offer some semblance of an answer, a penetrating silence dropped over the clearing, like a haunting veil. From the misty ground there rose a single light, glowing, growing . . . rising into the morning mist and into the sky. As Bruno whined, dropping to the ground to rest his chin on an extended paw, Susannah and Alan watched, too mesmerized to utter words, so in awe that they could only hold each other . . . and Willie, charming, gentle, soft-spoken Willie, lifting a hand in final farewell, slowly ascended into the clouds.

Then . . . only then . . . did Alan softly cup Susannah's features between his warm palms. When their gazes met, he responded, "Either we are both quite mad, or we have shared in a beautiful miracle."

"We are not mad," she murmured, pressing herself to him. "Say something, Alan . . . anything . . . some explanation, if there is one."

Tenderly, he began, "Love is never dead, Susannah. A heart is never stilled . . . it merely enters a higher, more satisfying existence. And I promise you, we will see him again."

Susannah's cheek pressed more firmly to the wide expanse of his chest. "He wanted us to love each other, Alan. He heard my wishes . . . and he brought you to me."

"I have a confession," said Alan, a warm palm caressing her shoulder through the thick satin fabric. "I have always loved you."

"Even when I was ten, and you were twice my age?"

"Even then," he managed to laugh, though emotion moved within his tone. "Yes, even then."

47

"And Willie knew it, didn't he?"

Alan drew in a short, shallow breath. "Best friends tell each other everything." A slim, masculine finger moved beneath Susannah's chin, lifting her gaze to his own. His mouth lowered to claim her trembling one . . . gentle, caressing, then with a controlled need that flooded their entwined forms like a river of fire . . . the coldness of the snow touching their features scarcely felt . . . their passions as bright as the morning . . . and their love as strong as the angel's embrace — the Christmas miracle — that had brought them together.

Then Alan allowed a breath of space to separate them. "And now, Miss Susannah Warren, it is time for *my* Christmas gift."

Instantly, her hand rose to her throat, her fingers closing over the heart-shaped locket he had given her the previous evening. "But I am wearing your gift, Alan."

Allowing the cane to fall to the earth, Alan tucked her fingers between his own and coaxed her to the gazebo. "Go, Bruno," he ordered of the dog already moving toward the house, "We need some privacy." Outstretching his hand, he waited for Susannah to settle upon one of the benches, then dropped to his good knee and took her hand once again. "Susannah . . ." The coolness of gold slipped onto her finger, and as her emerald gaze fell upon the perfect, pear-shaped diamond contained within a cluster of golden filigree, Alan entreated, "Will you be my wife, my lover, my friend, and my companion . . . will you allow me to spoil you and pamper you, provide for you and love you . . . for the rest of our lives . . . and onward into eternity?"

Her slim fingers forging a loving path into his dark hairline, Susannah whispered with poignant emotion, "I will, Alan Duncan. I will give you forever," and sealed her promise with a kiss.

For a long, long while they sat there, enveloped by the warmth of their love, watching the flurries of snow — Willie's Christmas gift — flirt with the wind before settling upon the winter-barren earth. Then the glowing spirit of the century-old house beckoned to them, like arms opening in welcome. The young lovers arose and, arm in arm, moved toward family and home . . . to share the tender, rapturous love they had for one another.

As she and Alan approached the steps, Susannah looked back, lovingly, longingly, and for a moment, the sky seemed to brighten, like the luminiscent aura of a star on the clearest of nights . . . like a star that might encourage wishes in rhyme from the lips of a hopeful child. A sad smile touched Susannah's mouth, and through her heart echoed the words, *Farewell, my precious Willie — we shall meet again.*

When she turned back, she saw her father, a familiar woefulness molding his aquiline features, awaiting them at the top of the stairs. She understood his pain now, the harshness, his fury whenever she had mentioned Willie as though he were alive . . . as though he were here among them. She understood her father's agony and she knew that all along he had loved Willie, and that his heart broke for the loss of his only son. She understood now the agony she had caused him these past few months. The way he'd handled it — though his patience had worn thin at times — told her that he must love her deeply to have put up with her reluctance to accept that Willie was gone.

With a new and overwhelming love in her heart, Susannah tucked herself into her father's arms. When, at last, his embrace surrounded her shoulders, she spoke, "This will be a happy, happy Christmas, Father. Alan has asked me to marry him and—" She looked up, seeing a tear settle onto his gaunt cheek. "And our dear Willie would want us to be happy, wouldn't he? He is gone, Father, but he will live forever in our hearts and our memories. Do tell me that Willie's last letter confessed his love and forgiveness."

"Yes, yes, it did, my blessed child. And my dear boy knew how very much I loved him. It was a wonderful letter!"

Hugging his daughter, Frederick Warren wept openly. Then he gathered to him the man who had won her heart. They turned into the house glowing with love and warmth . . . a house touched by the miracle of Christmas.

Christmas morning, the following year

Susannah lay in exquisite exhaustion. In the corridor beyond the heavy oak door, her husband's nervous pacing suddenly ceased. While Frederick Warren went off to make joyful announcements, Alan eased into the large bedchamber, his dark eyes cutting across the shadows to see his lovely wife snuggled down into the warmth of the covers. Grinning proudly, Alan Duncan approached the bed, then gazed down on the loving features of his wife and the cherubic ones of his newborn child.

Oblivious to the retreat of Dr. Haversham and Emelyne, who had assisted with the birth, Alan had eyes only for his family. He smoothed the damp wisps of hair from Susannah's forehead, then touched the warm cheek of the infant.

"My Christmas gift to you, Alan," whispered Susannah, fighting the sleep she had certainly earned following these long, laborious hours of giving birth. "A son . . . a strong, healthy son."

Alan lifted into his arms the fragile, blanketed bundle now being offered to him. When his son locked tiny fingers around one of his own, he exclaimed in a father's proud tone, "The boy's got a grip! I do believe he's put a dent in my flesh!" Then, when the new life opened his mouth as if to wail, a nervous Alan quickly returned him to the crook of his mother's arm. Settling into the chair, he took Susannah's hand and held it tenderly. "And who is this little one who will look to us for love, protection, and guidance?"

A smile graced Susannah's mouth just before she touched a kiss to their son's little forehead. "I present to you William Charles Duncan . . . our little Willie." Looking to him, she asked, "Do you approve?"

"Do I approve? It is as I hoped, my precious wife." Then his gaze moistened as he looked again to his son. "Welcome to the world, little Willie, and to the hearts of your mother and your father. How loved you will be!"

This past year, serving as local liaison for General Washington, Alan had been able to live with his wife in her father's home and watch her body nurture this new life growing within her. Every day she had been more beautiful, and never once had she complained of being miserable, though he had frequently noticed her weariness these past few weeks. Nor had she complained about living in her father's house when she dearly wanted a home of her own. They were building a fine house now, on the land where he had grown up. There, where he had been happy with loving parents, he and Susannah would raise their own family. The war would end soon; he felt sure of it. They would settle down to domestic life and, grow as a family.

"What are you thinking, Alan?" asked Susannah, stirring him from his moment of reverie.

Covering her slim hand, which had risen to touch his cheek, he leaned into the warmth of it. "I am thinking how happy I am, and how much I love you and our little Willie."

Just at that moment, the sun, hidden for the past week behind an overhang of gray clouds, made an appearance upon the wide, spotless window. Fingers of sunlight filtered into the room, then shyly touched upon Susannah's pale features. Quietly, hypnotically, her eyes turning away from her husband and son, she watched the magical waltz of light and shadow upon the smooth, clean panes of glass. She knew what was coming, just as surely as she knew her own heart.

"Look . . . it is beginning to snow."

"I imagine," whispered Alan in reply, "that you knew it would."

She smiled. Then, unable to fight her exhaustion a moment longer, her eyes began to close. As sleep washed over her, she felt her husband's hands ease beneath the blanket and lift their son from the crook of her arm.

Alan's lips touched her forehead. "Rest, my darling, my wife."

And as sleep covered her in its warmth and glow, the exquisite world of dreams opened its arms to welcome her in. Susannah was sure she heard a familiar voice say, *Well, my funny little muffin . . . what have you gone and done . . . and done so well?*

She did not see her child, lovingly cradled in his father's strong arms, ball his tiny fingers against a pink, cherubic cheek kissed by the angel who was his namesake.

Wrapped within the warmth of her husband's love, she dreamed on —

Of Christmases past —

And Christmases future —

And their special angel watching over them, keeping them safe for all eternity.

From the realms of her sleep, she cooed, "I love you, Alan
. . . and little Willie—"

Alan Duncan approached the bed and looked down upon
the loving features of his wife who had spoken endearments
from her dream. Touching his mouth in a soft caress to her
forehead, he murmured, "And we love you, wife . . . and
mother—"

For all eternity.

Had the room itself whispered the promise? Alan looked toward the window and the flakes of snow floating down from the
heavens.

Settling onto the edge of the bed, he brought Susannah's
hand against his heart. His gaze reached beyond the window,
beyond the snow and the hill upon which the house stood . . .
reaching into the clouds and beyond.

"I'll take good care of our funny little muffin. For all eternity,
Willie. I promise you that."

Willie wasn't at all worried.

Angels—especially Christmas ones—have very good instincts when it comes to sincerity.

And love.

A Gift of Love

by Phoebe Conn

Northern Mexico, December 1887

Belle stood braced against the balcony railing, her red hair whipped by the wind, her long ruffled skirt sculpted to her legs. When she and Coyote had first come to his grandfather's *hacienda* in June, they had been inseparable, but now her handsome Apache husband preferred to spend his days with the *vaqueros* tending horses and cattle. She could ride as well as any of the men, so it wasn't a lack of skill that kept them apart, but rather the growing restlessness which drove Coyote to follow a separate path. At least they still shared the same bed, but when he shut her out of his days, how long could the devotion he showed her at midnight possibly last?

She brushed a stray curl from her eyes, then clutched her shawl more tightly. Coyote was a superb horseman, but as she watched him now, pride failed to lighten the throbbing ache in her heart. A lone Apache brave and his American bride, their lives had once been closely entwined, but with each new day Coyote was becoming more distant and Belle's feelings of abandonment were growing more painfully acute. He was too far away to see the tears streaming down her cheeks, and she made no move to brush them away.

Approaching the house, Don Antonio Beltran observed his granddaughter-in-law's silent vigil with a worried frown. The bedrooms on the second floor all opened out onto the balcony, and once upstairs, he quickly passed through his room to join her. Distressed by her tears, he withdrew a fine linen handkerchief from the hip pocket of his heavily embroidered black suit. Although 'n his sixties, he had retained a lean build, and with obvious pride he wore the stylish short jackets and flared pants favored by Mexican *rancheros*. A handsome widower, he adored Belle and rejoiced in the love and laughter she had brought to his home. Her sorrow was also his.

"My grandson neglects you shamefully. I will speak with him this very afternoon."

Belle readily accepted the handkerchief, but nothing more. "Thank you, Antonio, but no, he has too many problems as it is. I'll not be an additional burden to him."

"My grandson has the best of wives in you, *querida,* but you deserve an equally thoughtful mate. A gentle reminder may be all that's required."

While she was grateful for Don Antonio's affectionate welcome to his home, Belle would not allow him to interfere in their private lives. "No," she repeated more emphatically, "he gives me what attention he can, and it would be demeaning to beg for more."

A proud man, Don Antonio readily understood her reluctance to plead for attention. "I have no intention of dropping to my knees to beg," he assured her. "I will merely point out that a beautiful woman who is ignored by her husband cannot be faulted for welcoming the attentions of other men."

Coyote bore a slight resemblance to his grandfather, who was still a remarkably handsome man. His black hair was only lightly flecked with gray, and his dark eyes danced with a flirtatious gleam. Despite the more than forty-year difference in their ages, Belle had always found him attractive, but he posed no competition for her husband.

54

"You'd try and make Coyote jealous?" Belle smiled for the first time that afternoon, but she did not want him to misunderstand how little she thought of his idea. "Issuing such a threat would not simply be a foolhardy mistake, it might even be dangerous."

Don Antonio's expression filled with dismay. "It is no threat," he countered. "It is the truth. There are many wonderful parties during the holidays with music and dancing. All of my neighbors will be eager to entertain you. Some might even be described as too eager."

Untutored in the art of flirting, Belle did not realize her glance held a subtle invitation. "You were speaking of your neighbors just now, not yourself?" she asked.

Thrilled that she would even imagine that he had more than a grandfatherly interest in her, Antonio began to laugh. "I'm flattered that you think me capable of making my grandson jealous, but no, I was not referring to myself. However, if you insist . . ." He held out his arms to offer a tempting embrace.

"Don Antonio!" Belle scolded, but she stepped close and hugged him to end their teasing exchange. Cheered for the moment, she left the balcony for the warmth of his gracious home.

Glancing toward the house, Coyote saw Belle and his grandfather hug and leave the balcony arm in arm. He was glad that they liked each other so much for he could not have borne his own pain had Belle been unhappy there too. He knew he ought to be grateful they had this haven in Mexico, but he could not overcome his sense of outrage at having been driven to it. That he had once served as a scout for the very army which had swept the Apache from their native lands in the Arizona Territory was a deep source of shame. He might have escaped the final betrayal of being sent to Florida with Geronimo and the rest of his tribe, but he could not shake the numbing sense of loss that had engulfed him ever since.

His work finished for the day, he turned his black stallion toward the foothills of the Sierra Madre Mountains and urged him to a gallop. The horse responded with a burst of speed and ran for the same pure joy of exertion his master sought. Coyote raced only the wind, but eager for the win, he sped on until the last of his horse's considerable energy was spent.

Coyote turned back then and surveyed his grandfather's ranch with an anguished gaze. It would belong to him one day, but would another army come to take it away simply because he was as much Apache as Mexican? His Apache father and Mexican mother had been such a devoted pair that he had never considered himself less than whole. Now he felt split in two, half fugitive Indian, half respectable *ranchero*, and it was the most painful sensation of his life. He told himself over and over again that this was now his home, that this was where he belonged, but his heart refused to believe.

He had brought Belle to Mexico thinking this was where their future lay, but as his longing for the past became more desperate, his dreams for their marriage had begun to blur and grow faint. He nudged the stallion, still as nameless as his hopes, and returned to the house at a meandering pace that left him barely enough time to clean up and dress for supper.

Belle greeted him with a smile that tore his soul, but from somewhere deep within, he found a loving smile for her.

In his youth, Coyote had made frequent visits to the *hacienda,* and Don Antonio had done his best to instruct his grandson in not only the art but also the business of ranching. However, it wasn't until Belle had arrived that he realized just how little Coyote cared for his lessons. The daughter of an Arizona rancher, she did not merely listen in a distracted silence as her husband did, but always had something valuable to contribute to their conversations. She was a skilled horsewoman, and also possessed the financial expertise Coyote lacked, but Don Antonio thought it best not to point that out to either of them for fear it would create more problems than it solved.

He watched the pair as the three of them shared the evening meal. Rather than tears, Belle's pretty brown eyes reflected the glow of love that shone in her husband's admiring glances. They were an exceedingly attractive, if unusual, pair, and Don Antonio dismissed the memory of Belle's sorrow as an example of the fleeting moods common to women. He still thought she needed more attention, but when it was obvious Coyote intended to give her plenty that evening, he decided to follow Belle's wishes and not comment on any failures his grandson might have as a husband.

When Don Antonio excused himself at the end of the meal, neither Belle nor Coyote offered an objection. They strolled out on the patio, but the coolness of the night air soon chased them back indoors. Coyote took Belle's hand as they climbed the stairs.

"It's been a long while since we heard from your cousin," he remarked absently.

"Three weeks isn't that long," Belle replied. "Besides, Edwin is probably too busy running our ranch to have time to correspond more frequently."

Coyote opened the door to their room. "This is our ranch," he reminded her.

Warned by the caustic edge to his tone, Belle hurriedly closed the door to ensure their privacy. Coyote was a soft-spoken man but she did not want anyone to overhear his comments regardless of his mood. She had left her home willingly to be with him, but the fact was, while her cousin might be managing the ranch now, she still owned it.

"This *hacienda* will be ours someday," she agreed, "but I'd like to think your grandfather will live to be a very old man."

"He is already an old man," Coyote argued. He yanked off the jacket Don Antonio insisted he wear to supper, unbuttoned his shirt, and sat down on the side of the high feather bed to remove his boots. Except for the length of his hair, when he dressed as a Mexican *ranchero,* he looked convincing.

"This is our home," he stressed in another vain attempt to convince himself rather than her.

Belle knelt in front of him and rested her arms on his knees. "My home is with you." She meant that with all her heart, and yet even as she spoke, her words echoed with a hollow ring. "I want so much for you."

Filled with bitter longings he couldn't describe, Coyote nodded. "For us."

Belle saw a brief flicker of fear, or was it dread, cross his gaze, but as he drew her into his arms, the love flavoring his kiss blurred all thoughts save those of him. The loneliness that marred her days was forgotten in her eagerness to share the splendor of the night. As he rose, Coyote pulled her to her feet, then clasped her waist even more tightly and deepened his kiss. His mouth was hot, eager, demanding, but Belle's seductive surrender urged him to take even more.

With a matador's grace he peeled away her gown, one of the many his grandfather had provided. The deep russet hue was only slightly darker than her glorious red hair and provided a superb complement to her creamy complexion. He stepped back to catch the ruffled silk before it fell to the floor and then tossed it over the foot of the bed.

The intricacies of her lingerie still eluded him and he waited with growing impatience as she saw to the beribboned garments herself. Each piece was scented with fine French perfume, another of his grandfather's expensive gifts. He fondled the lacy bits of silk and savored their exotic fragrance before adding them to the growing pile.

The first time they had made love, Belle had been dressed in male attire and he had not had such an agonizing wait. Now more than a year later, his passion for her was undimmed. If anything, he wanted her more. She was the only perfect thing in his life and he loved her with a consuming hunger he made no attempt to disguise.

Now clad only in her chemise, Belle reached for Coyote's belt buckle. He caught her hands and drew her close, pressing the fullness of her breasts against the hard planes of his bare chest. Her impatience to make love thrilled him, but he could not resist teasing her by pretending an indifference he did not feel. His feigned resistance lasted no more than an instant, however, before the absurdity of the ploy forced a deep chuckle from his lips.

He wound his fingers in her flowing curls, and striving to assuage his need, he captured her mouth with a brutal abandon. Her taste was sweet, and he was enchanted by the way she molded the contours of her supple body gently against his muscular frame. Like tendrils of flame, desire licked at his belly, and scorched by the heat, he broke away only long enough to cast off the last of his clothing while she removed her chemise.

He drank in her loveliness then doused the lamp to prevent the other men who lived on the ranch from sharing in that same privilege. They already envied him, and needed no sultry silhouettes to encourage their admiration of his bride's charms. The darkness increased his pleasure, giving added meaning to taste and touch and leading him ever deeper into the madness of desire. He caught her hand, brushed her fingertips down his chest, and then pressed her palm against his hardened shaft, silently pleading for the magic of a fevered caress.

Belle was all too willing to fulfill his unspoken demand. She then moved close, ground her hips against his, and when he moaned in response, she guided him onto the bed, where she moved astride him with a practiced ease. The ends of her curls brushed across his chest, taunting his senses while her fingertips kneaded the knots of tension from his broad shoulders.

Coyote shut his eyes and let the magical motion of her hands bring him the first glimmers of tranquillity he had felt all day. With increasing pressure she coaxed the current of energy that had always flowed between them until, like the endless quest of a river for the sea, he could no longer delay his need to lose himself deep within her. He rolled to the side, bringing her down with him in a playful confusion of giggles and tangled curls.

He drank in the sound of her laughter, letting the musical trills overflow his heart before smothering it with his lips. Hunted and alone, he had taken refuge on her ranch, and touched by her courage and beauty, he had returned to claim her heart. That prize was still his, but for how long? he agonized. How long could they escape the cruel fate that decreed they ought not to be together?

Clasped in his arms, Belle felt only the strength of Coyote's love rather than the depth of his despair. He entered her slowly, with shallow penetrations that teased her senses until she could bear no more of the delicious torture. "Please," she urged in a husky whisper.

Understanding her need was as great as his own, Coyote gave in to the passion that drove him to take all she could give. Forceful, determined, his tempo now kept time with the thundering beat of his heart until, awash in the roiling rapture that threatened to drown them both, he shuddered, and finally lay still. He was dimly aware that he ought to speak of love, but his feelings were too precious to risk bruising with words, and he fell asleep without offering his undying devotion aloud.

Equally sated by pleasure, Belle cradled Coyote in her arms and combed his long, ebony hair through her fingers. It was only late at night, when he came to her full of desire, that she felt as though she were truly his wife. She savored the moment, testing the limits of the fleeting bliss, then closed her eyes as a single tear rolled down her cheek. At dawn the loneliness would return, but there was no way to make the night last as long as her love.

Late the next morning, Belle awoke alone in the wide bed. Coyote's scent clung to the bedclothes, and rather than rise, she stretched, languidly drinking in the comforting traces of his presence. Until they had come to the *hacienda,* she had also gotten up with the dawn, but with so little to do, there was no reason to begin the day early. The first weeks had been a marvelous vacation from the responsibilities her father's death had imposed, but now, so much leisure time had grown numbing.

She slid her hand over the silken hollow of her stomach and wondered how long her prayers for a baby would go unanswered. The desire for a child had led her mother to desperate lengths, but Belle felt no such compulsion. She would welcome Coyote's child, but as yet the longings for motherhood were no more than faint stirrings.

Reluctantly, she sat up and brushed her hair out of her eyes. Antonio had mentioned holiday parties, and she should have been more thoughtful and asked if she could help plan whatever festivities he wished to host. Not that she had any experience in entertaining — her father had been reclusive — but she could at least try. Just the prospect of having a project to fill her days brightened her outlook immediately and she left her bed singing softly to herself.

After having bathed and dressed, she found Antonio in his study. She waited at the doorway until he noticed her and then summoned with an impatient gesture, she approached his desk. "I didn't mean to disturb you," she greeted him. "I just wanted to offer my help with the parties you mentioned yesterday."

Antonio lay down his pencil, and pulled another chair up beside his. "Ah yes, parties, they will be splendid, but first I need help making my accounts balance. You are a smart girl, can you find my mistake? I have been working on these figures all morning and I haven't gotten the same total twice."

Belle sat down and reached for another pencil. "After my father's death, I kept the books for our ranch, but I don't claim to be a proficient bookkeeper."

"I think you are being too modest. Here, add up the expenditures for last month, if you would, please." Fearing he would distract her, Antonio moved away from the desk and went to the window which provided a clear view of the yard. *Vaqueros* were clustered around the corral, eagerly vying for the chance to ride a pinto mustang that was equally determined not to be ridden. He saw Coyote seated on the top rail, watching the others with a slow smile, but apparently content to let someone else break the rebellious horse.

Having failed in his attempt, a disheveled *vaquero* picked himself up off the ground, brushed himself off with his hat, and limped out of the way of the next man brave enough to take a turn. Antonio envied them their youth and stamina, but not the bruises they'd suffer. There were certain comforts which came with age, and he was grateful he no longer had to compete with his men to gain their respect.

"I think I've found your mistake," Belle called to him. "Six times two is twelve, not fifteen. That's what threw your totals off."

"Fifteen?" Antonio winced. "How could I have made such a silly error?" Before he had taken the first step toward the desk, a shout went up from outside and he turned back to the window. The *vaqueros* were rowdy by nature, but when he saw them standing unnaturally quiet and still, he knew something was wrong. "Excuse me, *querida,* I fear there's been an accident."

Belle rose, and when a quick glance out the window assured her Coyote was safe, she followed Don Antonio outside. The dozen *vaqueros* grouped around the corral were shaking their heads, and murmuring to each other, but no one was tending the man lying in the dirt. She went to Coyote who was still seated on the top rail.

"Go on back to the house," he ordered in a harsh whisper.

"But why? I've seen more than one man get thrown and knocked unconscious."

Coyote stared down at her, his dark eyes as cold as obsidian. "His neck's broken. He's dead."

"Dead?" Belle grabbed her husband's wrist to steady herself. The fallen *vaquero* lay with his arms and legs jutting out at comical angles. His head was tilted back, his eyes staring up, his expression one of shocked disbelief. Had he known, she wondered, that this fall would be his last?

"Oh, how horrible," she murmured.

Don Antonio chose a couple of men to carry the deceased to the bunkhouse to await burial, and then shaken by the senseless tragedy, he joined Coyote and Belle at the side of the corral. His men were watching him with narrowed eyes, speculating among themselves as to how he would handle the pinto that pranced with uneasy steps along the far side of the corral.

"Shoot him!" a man cried, and a cheer went up from his companions.

Don Antonio sighed unhappily, then looked up at Coyote. This was a perfect opportunity for the Apache to gain experience in handling a difficult situation and he had no qualms about giving it to him. "A good man is dead because of that mustang. The men want him destroyed. What do you say?"

Coyote's posture was still relaxed, his hands resting easily on the top rail. He eyed the spirited horse a long moment before he spoke. "The pinto did not ask to be ridden and he is not to blame for your man's lack of skill," he advised. "He is a fine horse." Bent on proving the validity of his opinion, he slid off the top rail and started toward the pinto. The mustang's ears lay flat against his head, and he pawed the dusty earth in a silent dare Coyote simply ignored.

As the Apache moved closer, he sang an ancient chant that praised the oneness of all creation. His words were lost on the morning breeze, but the calmness of his manner soothed the agitated horse. The mustang raised his head and answered with a rumbling whinny but did not back away when Coyote grabbed his reins. Standing close, the Indian again spoke to the horse. The others present strained to overhear, caught a word or two of Apache and ceased trying to understand what grew to be a lengthy conversation. The pinto, however, nodded approvingly as though he agreed with Coyote's every word. Several minutes passed before the Apache leapt upon the animal's back.

"Open the gate!" he shouted, and immediately two men ran to fling it open wide. The mustang did not buck this time, but instead galloped away with a long, graceful stride that swiftly carried his agile Apache rider from view. Their fallen *compadre* forgotten, the *vaqueros* sent up a wild cheer and, hooking elbows, danced around in tight circles kicking up dust in billowing flurries.

Caught up in the thrill of the moment, Antonio gave a loud whoop too, but when he turned and met Belle's incredulous glance, he instantly felt ashamed. "Forgive us," he begged, "but it is unusual for triumph to race so closely on the heels of tragedy."

"It was only a horse," she reminded him. "Everyone knows Coyote is an expert horseman, but that scarcely makes up for the death of a *vaquero*." Sickened by the shortness of the men's memories, she turned away and started back toward the house. Then knowing she would never be content inside, she veered away toward the hills and followed her husband.

Coyote did not ride far before dismounting and unsaddling the pinto. He removed the bridle and slapped the horse's rump. The mustang surveyed the open plain with an anxious glance and then finally realizing he had been set free, bolted and fled without giving the Apache so much as a grateful nuzzle. Expecting nothing from the horse, the Indian shrugged, slung the saddle, blanket, and bridle over his shoulder and started back toward the *hacienda*.

The morning was cool, the trek not unpleasant, and when he saw Belle in the distance, he dropped the saddle and sat down to wait for her to reach him. He plucked a sprig of dry grass and chewed the parched stem. "You're a long way from home," he called to her.

The breeze cruised over the valley with a gentle hum carrying her husband's voice, but leaving her worries hovering near the ground. The scenery was lovely here, and the mountains little more than a violet haze in the distance. Belle stopped a few feet from Coyote and turned around slowly but the red mesas and cliffs of home were nowhere to be found. The man she loved was here, and she had not expected to be homesick for the iron-rich earth of the Oak Creek Canyon, but the painful longing tore at her very soul.

Coyote made a playful grab for her ankle, and hiding her sorrow, she sat down facing him. "What did you do with the horse?" she asked.

"I set him free." Coyote cocked his head and watched closely as he waited for her reaction. When she pursed her lips and glanced away, he could see she wasn't pleased, but prodded her for a reason. "What would you have done?"

"I'd have wanted to show the men they're more important than the stock." Belle paused briefly, then looked her husband in the eye. "I'd have shot the pinto. It wouldn't have brought the dead *vaquero* back to life, but it would have demonstrated clearly that a man's life is more precious to me than a horse's."

Coyote nodded, then broke into a wide grin. "I am the Indian," he mused slyly. "The *vaqueros* expect me to be cruel, but you, you are far more dangerous because you can justify your actions with logical excuses."

Insulted, Belle started to rise, but Coyote reached out to stop her. "The pinto is free, you needn't be angry with him, or me."

The silence of the valley was broken by an occasional birdcall, otherwise, their isolation was complete. Feeling lost in a strange land, Belle was quick to defend her principles. "Do you really regard me as cruel?" she asked, then continued without giving him a chance to respond. "Perhaps I am, but you must remember that I was tutored by an expert and learned my lessons well."

Stunned that their conversation had led to her father, a man Coyote had shot rather than watch murder his own daughter, he drew her close and rested his forehead against hers. "I did not mean to hurt you with old memories," he apologized. "It is only that you stop to think things through, while I must follow my feelings."

Belle doubted that was the true difference between them. "If I lacked a heart, I wouldn't be here, Indian."

Coyote relaxed his hold, stroked her cheek, and then captured her mouth in a long, tender kiss. "It is all right for us to be different," he assured her.

"Until the moment we disagree on something important," Belle forecast darkly.

Coyote curled his lip in a mock snarl. "I know how to make you agree with me," he bragged, and before she could elude him, he pushed her down into the grass. He caught her hands in one of his, and blocked her attempt to scramble away by sliding his knee between her legs. "You have no way to fight me now," he whispered against her lips. "No way at all."

She was caught, unable to move her arms and legs but still not without a potent weapon. "Why would I want to fight such a charming man?" Belle responded in a seductive purr.

"Good, you learn quickly."

"You can let me go," Belle coaxed sweetly, and when Coyote leaned down to kiss her, she slid her tongue over his in a welcoming thrust that clouded his senses so completely he did not realize what she was after. He released his hold on her wrists to caress the tip of her breast with his thumb. Distracted by her delicious kisses, he relaxed under the warmth of the sun and in the next instant Belle broke away and leapt to her feet.

"You see," she taunted him, "it's a wise woman who can think as well as feel."

She sprinted away from him then, but Coyote was enjoying himself far too much to allow her to get away. He overtook her in half a dozen strides, slid his arms around her waist, and lifted her off her feet. He spun her around, making them both dizzy, but when they sank to the grass-cushioned earth, they were laughing harder than they had in weeks.

Without releasing her, Coyote unfastened his belt buckle, and gathered up her long skirt. She was wearing pantalettes, and despite his lack of experience with her lingerie, the ribbon ties came loose with a single tug. He lifted her hips slightly and yanked the lace-edged garment down to her knees.

"Is this what you want?" he asked in an enticing whisper. "To be taken in the pasture like a . . ." When no suitably derogatory term came to him, he smothered her giggles with such passionate kisses she offered not a single word nor slightest gesture in protest. As alluring as she was in their bed, she drew him into an embrace whose only purpose was shockingly clear.

Wild as the mustang he'd set free, Coyote accepted her bold, if unspoken invitation, and moved with a series of deep, savage thrusts to bring her quickly to the brink of rapture. He halted then, balancing on that divine precipice until any further delay was absurd. With ecstasy within his reach, he plunged to her depths, and felt it roll through him as it rocked her. If this was the only way to create harmony between them, he vowed to travel the path to pleasure so often they would know the way by heart.

Lulled into a passion-drugged sleep, the uncomfortable awareness of another's presence jarred Belle from her blissful dreams of love and she sat up so abruptly she woke Coyote, who lay sprawled beside her. Not three feet away, a handsomely dressed *ranchero* sat on a fine white horse. His back was to the sun, his face was obscured by a deep shadow, but his voice held a warm ring of humor.

"I was on my way to deliver this invitation to Don Antonio," he confided, "but because it includes you two as well, I'll leave it with you. I will be as honored to welcome you to my home, *señora*, as your husband obviously is to welcome you to Mexico."

He sent a white envelope sailing into Belle's hands, and then after touching his broad-brimmed hat in a mock salute, he rode away.

Belle was relieved to find her skirt lay modestly draped

around her ankles, and that Coyote had pulled his clothing back into place before he had fallen asleep, but she was still badly embarrassed. Her hands shook as she tore open the invitation. "That must have been Don Emilio Alvarado. Is he a friend of yours?"

"I think we are all good friends now." Coyote rose and offered his wife a hand.

"Oh Lord, you don't think he was watching us, do you?" Once on her feet Belle hurriedly brushed the grass from her skirt and then removed her combs and attempted to restore a flattering order to her curls.

Coyote glanced up to judge the angle of the sun. "It's just past noon now. We couldn't have slept more than a few minutes. But we are married, and this is our land, so if anyone was behaving badly, it was Don Emilio for trespassing."

Belle bit her lip. She had been looking forward to the Christmas parties, but she certainly didn't want to attend Don Emilio's and find everyone gossiping about how she and Coyote enjoyed making love on the prairie where anyone riding by might see. This was her home now, but had her reputation already been irrevocably ruined?

She clutched the invitation in a frantic grasp as Coyote went back to pick up the saddle. When he returned to her side, she tried to smile, but failed to hide her distress. "I'm sorry, it's just that I want everyone to like us, and I'm worried about what Don Emilio might say."

Coyote gave his head a rueful shake. "If you were worried about gossip, Belle, you shouldn't have married an Indian. Now come on, if we hurry, we'll get back in time for dinner."

Shaken that what had been a spontaneously joyful interlude might have the worst of repercussions, Belle hurried to catch up with him, but whether it was her lively mind or her feelings that had betrayed her, the *vaquero*'s death now seemed a very bad omen and she was desperately afraid.

Belle fidgeted nervously all through dinner. Coyote seldom joined them for the noon meal, and while she was pleased to have his company, his sly glances and teasing winks made her fear he might at any moment begin a colorful description of their morning's romantic interlude and she could scarcely catch her breath, let alone enjoy the deliciously prepared *pollo con arroz.* Chastened by her earlier rebuke, Don Antonio was uncharacteristically solemn. Apparently fond of the dead *vaquero,* one of the girls serving their meal was sobbing openly. All in all, it was a miserable hour. Belle didn't attempt to encourage conversation, and could barely control her apprehensions when Coyote did.

"Give Grandfather the invitation, Belle," he urged.

It had lain beside her plate all through dinner but Belle hadn't wanted to explain how they had come to have it. She sent Coyote a pleading glance. Ordinarily she admired his directness, but she did not want him sharing their most intimate secrets with his grandfather. Reluctantly, she handed Antonio the envelope.

When they made love, Belle never showed any shyness, but now she was so delightfully demure Coyote had no wish to embarrass her. "We saw Don Emilio this morning," he explained simply. "He said the invitation was for all of us." He smiled at Belle, hoping that she would be impressed by his discretion but her anxious glance was now focused on his grandfather rather than him.

Antonio scanned the artfully penned invitation, and his mood lifting, he smiled with genuine pleasure. "You two discouraged my desire to host a reception for you last summer. Emilio's party will be a wonderful opportunity for you to finally meet all of our neighbors."

"We had no need to celebrate our marriage with strangers," Coyote announced proudly. "It was enough that the three of us knew."

Obviously disagreeing, Antonio shook his head. "They would not have been strangers after the reception, but we needn't repeat that argument." He turned to Belle. "I must

69

confess that this morning's reminder of how swiftly death can overtake us has quite natually dampened my enthusiasm for entertaining, but I am going to insist that we all attend Emilio's party Saturday night. I imagine that you were very favorably impressed by him, weren't you?"

Too panicked to explain why she had gotten no more than a brief glimpse of the man, Belle looked to her husband for a response. She held her breath, hoping that he would not make light of the appalling incident to amuse his grandfather. A slow smile tugged at the corner of his mouth and she could see he was tempted. While still wearing the most innocent of expressions, and with the table hiding her move, she stretched slightly and kicked him in the shin. He did not even flinch.

Amused by his wife's unnecessary burden of shame, Coyote broke into a broad grin. "He seemed very friendly. Wouldn't you say so, Belle?"

Mortified by the erotic display she feared Don Emilio had observed at length, Belle nodded, then hurriedly attempted to change the subject. "Yes, and he rides a splendid white horse."

Always eager to discuss the breeding of horses, which was his passion, Don Antonio immediately took her bait. "His stallion may be fine looking, but he lacks the stamina of a true champion." He continued to compare the stock raised on Don Emilio's *hacienda* unfavorably with his own until they were ready to leave the table. Coyote excused himself to attend to the running of the ranch, but Antonio asked for a moment of Belle's time.

"I want to thank you for your help this morning," he began. "I don't know what to blame, perhaps my eyesight is not what it once was, or my attention wanders, but keeping my accounts has become a troublesome chore. I would ask Coyote to assist me, but he has such little interest in business matters that I fear I would only bore him. Do you suppose that you could help me? It would take only a few hours each week, and I would be most grateful."

Like her husband, Belle would also rather round up

strays than total columns of figures, but after the way Antonio had opened his heart and home to her, she did not see how she could refuse any reasonable request. "I'd be happy to help you," she replied. "In fact, I'd welcome having something more to do. If you'd like to host a Christmas party I can help with that too."

"Let's see what other invitations we receive. If my friends are all eager to entertain this year, we can wait for another occasion. Would you like to familiarize yourself with my books this afternoon?"

Too restless to nap, Belle agreed, and their discussion became so involved they ended up perusing Antonio's accounts until it was time to dress for supper. The *hacienda* was a prosperous one but, compared to her father's rigorous management, very sloppily run. While Belle was loath to make such a comment, she did offer a subtle suggestion or two for cutting costs which Don Antonio greeted with such ready enthusiasm she knew he had not been insulted. It was unnerving to think of herself as a practical businesswoman, because it reminded her of the father she would sooner forget, but she was grateful for the opportunity to be of use.

That evening, when Don Antonio failed to mention how they had spent the afternoon, she assumed he had done so out of consideration for Coyote's feelings. She understood that his concern for keeping the ranch's books would be an onerous task for an Apache brave, and since he'd had little in the way of formal schooling, she wasn't certain he could successfully do it. Believing the matter was of little consequence, she did not reveal it either, but two mornings later Coyote returned to the house unexpectedly and found her working at his grandfather's desk.

"What are you doing?" he asked.

Her husband was so seldom at home during the day that Belle was startled by the sound of his voice. She looked up, and as always greeted him with a smile. She then dropped her pencil and dismissed her efforts with a casual shrug. "I'm just doing a bit of bookkeeping for your grandfather."

Coyote remained in the doorway. "If he needed help, why didn't he ask me?"

Attempting to be tactful, Belle rose and went to him. She spoke softly, her tone intimate, coaxing rather than pleading for his understanding. "I believe he had a couple of reasons. First, you prefer working with the stock, and second, I doubt he wants to admit that keeping the accounts accurately has become difficult for him."

Unconvinced, Coyote regarded her with a menacing frown. "He's said so often that I would one day own the *hacienda* that I had no idea he doubted my ability to run it."

Belle reached out to grasp her husband's arm, but he pulled away. "Antonio has nothing but praise for you," she insisted, "You mustn't be insulted." She was tempted to relate her gratitude at finally having something useful to do, but fearing that would merely confuse the issue, she kept her feelings to herself.

Coyote pushed past her and went to the desk. He ran his fingertip down the column of figures she had been adding and silently totaled them in his head. He then wrote the sum on a scrap of paper and, folding it, kept it in his hand. "Come back and finish this," he ordered brusquely.

"I don't want any argument over this with you or your grandfather," Belle replied.

"We're not arguing," Coyote denied. "Now come and add it up."

He was a man whose feelings were so close to the surface they were easily read. No matter what Don Antonio's reason, Belle knew he had made a grave error in requesting her help with the books rather than Coyote's. She could not only see her husband's disappointment in his sullen expression, she could feel a deeper sense of betrayal as well. The United States government had broken all of its promises to the Apache, and he had expected better from his grandfather.

"Please don't make so much out of this," she begged. "Keeping the books is a very small part of running the

72

ranch."

Coyote stared at her coldly. "If it is so small, so unim-
portant, so insignificant, then why couldn't I be trusted to
do it? Now come here and finish your work. What's the
matter? Are you afraid my total will be wrong and that I'll
die of shame?"

Belle approached the desk slowly. He was a proud man,
and she knew she could not refuse to do as he'd asked
without making it appear that she did indeed doubt his
competence. His hair was blown by the wind, his shirt
open at the neck, showing off a broad expanse of deeply
bronzed skin. He was so handsome, but she truly believed
he belonged astride his stallion, not behind a desk doing
routine bookkeeping, but to say so dismissed his fine
mind, which had been Antonio's mistake.

She returned to her seat, picked up her pencil, and began to add up the figures. She toyed briefly with the idea
of making an error, just in case he had, so neither of them
would appear to have any talent for bookkeeping. But believing that would be a stupid ruse, and not treating him
with the respect he deserved, she did her best to provide
the accurate total. She wrote it at the bottom of the
column.

"There," she exclaimed. "What did you get?"

Coyote tossed the scrap of paper bearing his answer on
the desk and walked out. Fearing that he had been humili-
ated when their totals hadn't matched, she unfolded it
slowly. She was the one who felt ashamed then, for he had
written the identical figure. Not only had he come up with
the right answer, he had done it much less time.

"Coyote, wait!" she called, but he had already left the
house.

Coyote did not return home for two days. Then rather
than bathe and dress in one of the fine suits his grandfather had given him, he simply brushed the dust from his
riding clothes and took his place at the supper table. He
nodded toward his grandfather, then ignoring his bride, he

focused his attention on his plate. The cook had prepared barbecued beef, one of his favorite meals, and he proceeded to eat with a hearty appetite.

Belle was so happy to see her husband she would not have complained, but aghast at the rudeness of his grandson's behavior, Don Antonio took exception to it immediately. "In the future," he demanded, "you will inform me whenever you plan to be away from the house for extended periods. No one knew where you were, and we feared for your safety."

Coyote looked puzzled. "Really? Why?"

"Why?" Don Antonio sputtered. "The *hacienda* is large, and the dangers are many. You could have been thrown from your horse and seriously injured, or perhaps bitten by a rattlesnake. Do not pretend you don't know what hazards exist."

Coyote fixed his grandfather with a steady stare. "You and Belle can run things so well without me that I didn't think you'd even notice I was gone."

Hurt by his grandson's sarcasm, Don Antonio sent Belle an anguished glance before responding. "You are behaving like a spoiled child," he scolded. "It matters not at all who does the books here as long as they are done."

Coyote finally looked up at his wife. "I knew you'd go to him. It is a blessing our family is so close."

"Coyote, please," Belle pleaded. "No one is shutting you out."

Rather than acknowledge her request for a more reasonable attitude, the Indian kept on eating. He had spent the last two days on the range with *vaqueros* who squatted around the campfire at mealtimes and he had felt far more at home with them than he did now. He had missed Belle terribly, though, and she was the reason he had come home.

"Don Emilio's party is tomorrow night," Antonio reminded him. "I have already sent an acceptance, and I expect you to accompany us."

Coyote had forgotten the *ranchero*'s invitation, and was

sorry he had not stayed away longer. "I have been looking forward to it," he lied between bites.

"Not only will you be there," Don Antonio continued, "but you will be handsomely groomed and dressed and on your best behavior."

"I do not usually wear a breechclout and feathers."

Belle shook her head, and Antonio swallowed an equally hostile retort. She understood, even if the older gentleman didn't, just how badly Coyote had been hurt. It wasn't simply a question of who did the bookkeeping, either; he carried a much deeper sorrow, and while she was moved by his despair, she didn't know how to relieve it. When he left the table abruptly, she feared that he might again be absent for several days, but he came up to their room while she was still brushing her hair.

Coyote closed and locked the door. "No accusations or apologies," he ordered as he drew her into his arms. "Only this."

His bruising kiss made any comment impossible, but as unable to describe her emotional turmoil as he, Belle welcomed his ardor. She had missed him, and not merely his body beside hers at night, but the warmth of his presence in her life. She slid her arms around his waist and held him close, but he did not soften his approach.

He had shown her many ways to make love, from teasing and playful to deeply passionate, but tonight his mood was one of unrelenting domination. There was no tenderness in his touch, merely possessiveness, and while he sated his desires, for the first time she failed to share in his pleasure. Frightened, she lay cuddled against his back listening to his slow, even breathing as he slept and fearing that while he had returned to her bed, she had nevertheless lost him in every way that mattered.

She tried without success to remember exactly when the once tightly woven fabric of their marriage had begun to unravel. The change had begun with such subtlety that it had gone unnoticed until one day she suddenly realized they had begun spending more time apart than together. It had not been her choice either, but his. In the last few weeks, she had watched Coyote's growing detachment with mounting dread, and feared his anger with her and his grandfather over who did the bookkeeping was further evidence of the resentment festering in his heart.

She had thought it impossible to feel lonely while lying next to him, but the sad, hollow ache kept her awake for hours.

Having scarcely slept, Belle tried to nap Saturday afternoon, but as she dressed for Emilio Alvarado's party, she had to fight not merely physical fatigue but emotional exhaustion as well. Despite her best efforts, their marriage just wasn't working, and if Coyote continued staying away for days at a time and then treated her with the harsh indifference he had shown her the previous night, she would no longer call herself his wife. She had seen too many women with pinched lips and bitter eyes to remain in a troubled marriage herself.

When she looked in the mirror to style her hair, she saw not a beautiful young woman but a terrified child who longed for the love she had known all too briefly. She had expected to have a lifetime with Coyote, not a fleeting six months, but maybe they had simply been too different to ever find lasting happiness and he would no longer pretend a love he did not feel. She had too much pride to beg if he no longer wanted her, but when he came through the door, and regarded her with a familiar, admiring glance, renewed hope for their future lit her smile.

"Turn around," Coyote asked, and as she obeyed slowly, he walked in the opposite direction. She was dressed in red, her gown a confection of ruffles and lace that was perfect for the holiday season. "You look very beautiful," he complimented her sincerely.

He was dressed in black, his short jacket and flared pants adorned with swirling braid and silver buttons. "So do you," she replied.

"Grandfather would like me to cut my hair. What do

you think?"

Belle chose her words with care. "You wear his clothes, live in his house, isn't that enough? Does he want you to give up all that is Indian?"

"Yes," Coyote assured her. "He would like me to be exactly what he is, but I am not."

Belle moved close. "I love you as you are."

Coyote took her hand and brought it to his lips. "For how long, *querida?*"

"Forever," Belle responded easily, for regardless of his waning interest in her, she would always love him.

Coyote stared down at her, a dark cloud of confusion marring his gaze, but rather than respond with an equally devoted vow, he led her toward the door. "We mustn't be late."

That he hadn't spoken of love confirmed the worst of Belle's fears, but she preceded him down the stairs with her head held high. Even if this were the only time Antonio's neighbors saw them together, she wanted them to remember what a handsome couple they were.

Antonio was pacing anxiously by the front door, but he relaxed when they appeared. "Ah, there you are. You are lovely as always, Belle, now come, let us hurry." He kept up a running commentary as they traveled by carriage to Don Emilio's *hacienda*. While he strived to provide a brief background on the other guests, Belle was too distracted to recall the details of his friends' lives. She appreciated his attempt, but by the time they reached the party, she knew no more than when she had left home.

As splendidly attired as Antonio and Coyote, Don Emilio met each of his guests at the door with a personal word of welcome. Six feet tall, and wickedly handsome, he had saved his most charming smile for Belle. "I'm so pleased you could join us," he enthused. "I've been most anxious to see you again."

His glance swept her exquisite gown, lingered overlong at her bosom, and then locked with hers. If there had been any doubt in Belle's mind as to whether or not Don Emilio had seen more than he should have on the morning they had met, his heated gaze had just removed it. More compelling problems occupied her now, and she no longer cared how much he might have enjoyed being a voyeur.

"Thank you," she answered, and quickly withdrawing her hand from his, she followed the other guests into the spacious home. While built of adobe like Antonio's, it was a one-story structure with a large open patio in the center which provided ample room for entertaining. The weather had again turned warm, and a hundred candles gave the sultry night a magical golden glow while the fragrance of roses filled the air.

With Coyote close by her side, Belle easily returned the welcoming smiles as Antonio made the introductions. Families had been invited to bring their children, so there were a great many people to meet. Coyote repeated the name each time someone new approached them, but other than that small courtesy, he took no part in the conversation. While most had not met him before, all were aware Don Antonio had a half-Apache grandson, and although some were merely curious, others were apprehensive, but none were rude.

When everyone had arrived, the traditional Mexican celebration of *Las Posadas* began. In a reenactment of Mary and Joseph's search for lodgings in Bethlehem, the guests formed a line. With the children carrying small wooden figures of the Holy Family and the animals that had shared the stable where Christ was born, they made their way through Don Emilio's house singing carols, but whenever the leader stopped at a door, they were told the inn was full and refused entry.

In the middle of the line, Belle moved along with Coyote's hands resting lightly on her waist. She had vague memories of *Las Posadas* from parties when she had been small, for the Arizona Territory had many families of Mexican descent. Her father had not been a religious man and their observance of Christmas had entailed little other than a fine dinner, so being able to take part in such an

78

enthusiastic celebration was a rare treat, or at least it should have been.

Longing to join in the joy of the occasion, Belle turned to smile at her husband, but he wore a preoccupied frown and was merely shuffling along silently to please his grandfather rather than enjoying himself. Their first Christmas together should have been such a happy time, but Belle felt none of the good cheer which lit the faces of the other guests. She wanted to drop out of the line, but was swept along and had no chance to break away. This wasn't how she wished to live: wearing a gorgeous gown, attending a lavish party, but barely able to hide her tears.

At last the revelers reached the parlor and were welcomed inside. Then in a delighted awe, the children arranged the carvings they had carried to form a Nativity scene on an awaiting altar. Everyone then returned to the patio, where musicians were ready to entertain the adults, and children crowded around a candy-filled star-shaped *piñata,* eager for the chance to be blindfolded and swing a stick to break it. Their squeals and laughter carried above the lilting sounds of the guitars and violins.

Having been separated from Antonio at the beginning of *Las Posadas,* Belle stood alone at her husband's side. They had never danced together, but she certainly wanted to try. "Would you like to dance?" she asked.

Coyote shook his head. "The Apaches dance, but for a purpose, not like this."

"This has a purpose," Belle pointed out, "to have fun."

Couples were dancing *La Jota,* a lively Christmas favorite, and observing them from the sidelines, Belle envied them terribly. She saw Don Emilio approaching, and his appreciative grin made it plain he wished to dance with her even if her husband didn't. It wasn't his company she craved, however, and she turned, hoping for a way to avoid him, but the patio was too crowded for her to escape him easily.

Don Emilio greeted Coyote with a mock bow. "May I have permission to dance with your lovely wife?"

"I doubt that's all you want," Coyote replied under his breath.

"I beg your pardon?" Don Emilio inclined his head.

Coyote took Belle's hand and placed it in their host's. "Go right ahead," he suggested, "and this time I will be watching you."

Amused, Don Emilio's smile widened. "I shall strive to be equally entertaining."

To have to listen to her husband and a man who was little more than a stranger exchange insulting innuendos embarrassed Belle badly. She had absolutely no desire to dance with Don Emilio, but his fingers tightened on her hand and she couldn't get away. It wasn't until he had drawn her into the swirling throng that she dared look up at him, but there was no flirtatious sparkle in her gaze.

Enchanted by her beauty and challenged by her chill indifference, Don Emilio skillfully maneuvered Belle through the crowd to the opposite side of the patio. Forcing her into a secluded corner, he pulled her close. "I know you enjoy being with a savage, but have you ever had a gentleman?"

Belle put her hands on his chest in an attempt to break free. For a man with a slender build, he proved to be surprisingly strong. His back was to the dancers, and no one saw her struggling against him. "Surely you don't consider yourself in that category!"

A sudden crescendo in the music covered Don Emilio's hearty laughter. Not content to hold her close, he ducked his head to kiss her. This time Belle tried to squirm free, but he had caught both her wrists and held her fast.

A thousand stars sparkled overhead. Children, not twenty feet away, were shouting out directions to a boy striving mightily to slug the *piñata* but missing on every swing. The dancers' hushed conversations floated above the dance tune aiding Emilio in smothering Belle's cries with a series of impassioned kisses meant to enslave her desires but instead arousing only a furious anger. In a desperate bid to elude him, she slackened her resistance a moment,

80

and then catching him off guard, bit his lower lip until she tasted blood. He released her then and, raising his hand, would have struck her a fierce backhanded blow had Coyote not stepped between them.

"I told you I would be watching," the Apache said with a deceptive calm but in the next instant his fist slammed into Don Emilio's chin, snapping his head back with a cruel twist. The Mexican staggered, then caught himself and came at Coyote but the Apache was too quick for him and avoided his widely swung punches. He pushed Belle toward the dancers to clear a path, and then struck Emilio a brutal blow that knocked him off his feet.

The *ranchero* sat down hard on the rough brick of the patio, and dazed, his chin drooped to his chest. Blood gushed from his broken nose and dripped down on his white shirt in gruesome blotches. Rather than come to his defense, all around him his guests ceased dancing and backed away, but unaware of the fight, the musicians continued to play with delirious dedication and the next child took a wild swing at the *piñata*.

Coyote adjusted the fit of his jacket and braced his feet, but none of Don Emilio's friends wished to continue the fight in his place. Don Antonio broke through the edge of the crowd, and horrified by his grandson's handiwork, he gestured for several men to help him raise Don Emilio to his feet. He then pointed them toward the house and they obediently carried their battered host inside. His face flushed with anger, Antonio waved to the guests to continue dancing, then reached for Belle's hand.

"Come, we are leaving."

That was all Belle wanted, and she hooked her elbow through Coyote's to bring him along. No one tried to delay them, and once they left Don Emilio's house, they hurriedly entered their carriage. Taking the seat opposite Don Antonio's, Belle pulled Coyote down beside her and kept her hand in his.

"Thank you," she whispered before kissing his cheek.

"You cannot be serious!" Don Antonio exclaimed. "Your

husband chooses to behave like an outlaw at a Christmas party attended by families with young children, and you thank him? I expected better of both of you, truly I did. I will send my apologies to Don Emilio in the morning, and pray that he does not wish to pursue the matter."

"Don Antonio, you're being very unfair," Belle insisted. "Had Coyote not struck Emilio, he would have slapped me for refusing his kisses. It is Don Emilio who owes us the apology, not the other way around."

Don Antonio's expression was hidden in shadow, but his tone of voice remained bitterly hostile. "You must have encouraged him," he argued.

"I did no such thing," Belle argued, but when Coyote squeezed her hand, she supposed that by making love outdoors, she had indeed encouraged the advance of any man who might have ridden by. "Well, not intentionally, I didn't."

"Shameful," Don Antonio muttered. "A disgrace. I introduce you to my friends, and this is the way you behave? I dare not accept another invitation, not that we will receive any!"

Coyote had not said a word in his own defense, and Belle ceased to try to justify his actions when she feared the more she explained the worse she would make things sound. So much had gone wrong for them of late, that she now wondered why they had ever agreed to go the party. Not that Don Antonio had given them any choice, but perhaps that had been part of the problem. When they arrived home, he did not wish them a good night, and Belle and Coyote climbed the stairs in a strained silence.

Coyote closed their door, and then leaned back against it. "I need to get away for a while. I'm going hunting."

Fearful he was leaving her forever, Belle made fists at her sides. "You'll be home for Christmas, won't you?"

"Christmas holds no meaning for an Apache."

"Perhaps not, but it means something important to me."

Coyote nodded to concede the point, and stepping away from the door, he removed his jacket. "I'm leaving tonight, as soon as I can gather my things."

Not trusting her shaking knees to hold her upright, Belle sat down on the edge of the bed. "You sound as though your plans are all made."

Coyote examined his jacket, and finding it undamaged, he replaced it and the matching trousers in the wardrobe. He pulled on one of the worn pairs of pants he wore for riding, and his old moccasins rather than boots. Never having cared much for clothes, he picked up a warm coat and considered himself ready to go.

"No," he finally answered. "I have no plans other than to hunt."

Belle closed her eyes for a moment in a valiant effort to summon the resolve for what must be said. When she looked up, the lingering seriousness of his expression broke her heart. "Must you leave tonight? There are so many things we need to discuss."

Coyote walked over to her, leaned down, and brushed a light kiss across her lips. "No, I need to get away."

Her heart breaking, Belle watched him go. Tears stung her eyes and a sob tore her throat as an all too familiar ache bound her chest in a constricting knot. She loved Coyote with all her heart and soul, but it just wasn't enough for him. He needed more, but she had no more to give.

She had no hope anything would be different when he came home either. She sat there for a long while, miserable and alone, before it finally occurred to her that there was something she could do. She could save them both any further torment, and with a calm determination born of abject despair, she vowed that by the time Coyote returned, she would be gone.

Belle slept poorly. She had the same scant regard for apparel that her husband had, and after dressing in comfortable riding clothes, she packed one small bag. She gathered up the Christmas presents she had ready for Don

Antonio and his household staff then did not tarry in the room she had shared with Coyote, for with him away, it was unbearably empty. Past tears, she went downstairs and for the last time slid into her place at the dining room table.

Don Antonio's mood had not improved overnight and he barely glanced up from his breakfast. "Coyote left a note saying he was going hunting. Did he tell you?"

"Yes, but I wanted to speak with you personally before I left."

She had finally captured Antonio's attention, and his head bounced up with a startled jerk. One of the serving girls came in to pour coffee and bring Belle a plate of fresh fruit and *pan dulce*, and he was forced to hold his tongue until she returned to the kitchen.

"Where are you going?" he then inquired.

Belle sighed very softly. "Home."

"For a visit while Coyote is away? I think that's a fine idea. I'll send several men along as an escort."

"Thank you, I'd appreciate having some company on the trip, but this isn't a visit. I'm going home for good."

Shocked, Antonio sat back, and regarded her with a sorrowful gaze. "You can't mean that, *querida*. Perhaps I was too harsh last night, but I did not mean to drive you both away."

Belle leaned over to take his hand. "You've been wonderful to me, Don Antonio, and you mustn't blame yourself, for my decision had nothing to do with you." She paused momentarily and then continued before her courage deserted her. "I simply can't stand by and pretend nothing is wrong when each day Coyote grows more miserably unhappy. He's suffered too much, and I won't add to his sorrow. I know he doesn't celebrate Christmas, but perhaps he'll appreciate that his freedom is the best gift I could ever give him."

Choked with emotion, Don Antonio had to swallow hard, and even then he had difficulty speaking. "You are making a dreadful mistake, *querida,* for Coyote will never interpret your action as coming from a wonderfully generous heart. He will simply feel deserted and be enraged. I beg you to reconsider. Coyote won't go after you; the anger that will fuel his pride won't let him and you will be foolishly ending a marriage that could bring many years of joy to you both. The days when the Apache could roam the land at will are over. Believe me, Coyote knows his home is here now. Even if you have doubts, I am convinced that you are all that makes his life worth living."

Tears Belle had thought she was past shedding filled her eyes and she shook her head. "You're very kind, but mistaken. Coyote doesn't belong here, and neither do I."

Before Don Antonio could offer further argument, his housekeeper appeared. "Don Emilio Alvarado is here. Shall I ask him to wait in the parlor?"

Antonio issued his directions with an impatient wave. "No, please ask him to join us." As the housekeeper turned away, he leaned toward Belle. "After last night's disgrace, let us pray he does not challenge Coyote to a duel. I have sent no apology."

Belle had no wish to remain, but fearing Don Emilio might threaten her husband, she wanted to be there to defend him. Bracing herself, she turned toward the door. The room's whitewashed walls reflected the sun's bright promise for the new day, but she was certain it would number among the worst of her life. She could hear Don Emilio approaching, his boots striking the plank floor with an ominous ring, but his stride was uneven, creating a syncopated beat. When he limped into view, she understood why. He was dressed in gray and the solemn color made his badly bruised face all the more pathetic.

"Don Antonio, señora, it is good of you to see me."

Amazed he had not been greeted with a string of vile curses, Antonio shot Belle a quick glance and her slight frown warned him to be cautious. "You have always been welcome here," he reminded the young man.

Turning his wide-brimmed hat in his hands, Don Emilio looked down at the toes of his boots and mumbled, "I have come to apologize."

"I beg your pardon?" Belle asked.

While he raised his voice, Emilio still could not bear to look at her. "I have come to apologize for my behavior last night. I treated you in a most ungentlemanly fashion, señora. Your husband had every right to be angry and to punish me for it. Is he here? I wish to beg his forgiveness as well."

"You want to apologize to my grandson?" When Emilio nodded, Don Antonio was so relieved he began to gloat. "Unfortunately, he has gone hunting, but I will convey your apology when he returns. Would you care to join us for breakfast?"

Mortified by the whole wretched experience, and most especially by his battered appearance, Don Emilio declined the invitation, begged to be excused, and hurriedly went on his way.

Don Antonio waited until he heard the front door close before he released the laughter welling up inside him. "I don't know why I am so amused, when I fear I am as much at fault as he. I also owe you and Coyote an apology. I should have known better and believed your explanation for the altercation last night. Perhaps if I had been more understanding, and Coyote had known how sorry Emilio would be today, he would not have left."

Belle wouldn't give him false hopes. "No, the trouble with Don Emilio didn't create a crisis. It was just further evidence of how poorly we fit in."

"But you've only been here a few months, surely in time—"

"No. More time will only deepen the estrangement. I want to leave now, before Coyote begins to hate me." She slipped her hand into her pocket and withdrew a gold crucifix suspended on a fine chain. "When he gave me this, Coyote said it had belonged to his mother. Will you return it to him, please?"

Don Antonio accepted the necklace reluctantly. He clutched the crucifix tightly but let the chain drip through his fingers. "I gave this to my daughter at her first communion. It was precious to her, and to Coyote as well. If he gave it to you, you should keep it."

Belle had treasured it as a token of the love she was sure was lost, and had to refuse. "No, it should stay in your family. As for all the beautiful clothes you've bought me, it would make me too sad to wear them now. Please give them to the servants, or charity. Do whatever you think is best. I've left Christmas presents for everyone on the table in the front hall."

Drawing their sad exchange to a close, Belle pushed herself to her feet. "I'd like to go as soon as the *vaqueros* you've offered to send with me are ready."

Devastated that he had been unable to change her mind, Don Antonio rose to embrace her. He memorized the glorious shade of her hair, the delicate perfection of her features, and the heartbreaking sorrow of her expression. Had she been his wife, he would never have caused her this pain. He reminded himself she was Coyote's responsibility, not his, but he thought his grandson a great fool for losing such a jewel.

"I will never forget you, *querida*."

"Nor I you." Belle stepped close, and with a tender hug bid him farewell.

Coyote had ridden to the foothills before stopping for the night. In the morning, he followed an ancient trail into the Sierra Madre Mountains, but escaping his troubles at the *hacienda* failed to bring the longed-for sense of peace. The wildness of the terrain challenged his endurance as well as his mount's, but the physical demands did not touch his mind and he was plagued by bitter memories.

His father had taught him the mountain trails and he had learned them so well he had been able to lead the Army after the renegade bands he should have joined. Right and wrong, peace and war, he had weighed the options with a childlike faith until after helping to defeat Geronimo he and the other scouts had also been treated as criminals. Riding the paths the renegades had traveled in a fruitless search for sanctuary, he felt haunted by the spirits of the warriors he had tracked. A lone hawk circled overhead, but unlike the handsome bird, Coyote cursed the fact he had not been wise enough not to prey on his own kind.

The sun rose high above them; the trail shimmered with reflected light and the black stallion lost his footing on the rocky path, sending a hail of jagged stones into the deep gorge below. The life-threatening mishap caught Coyote by surprise. For a brief instant he wavered between fighting to survive, or simply letting go and diving off the mountain with a headlong plunge. His death would be lamented as a tragic accident rather than ridiculed as an act of cowardice, and burdened by guilt he was sorely tempted to hurl himself into eternity.

He shut his eyes against the pain, but as Belle's dear face filled his mind, he felt a rush of pleasure so intense any choice save that of life would have been lunacy. Awakening from his melancholy stupor, he threw his weight toward the mountainside in a forceful attempt to help his mount regain his balance. He shouted to the terrified horse, exhorting him to be strong.

Precariously suspended on the edge of the precipice, the stallion's hooves slipped and slid into the air where his steps formed a frantic, grotesque dance, but inspired by Coyote's determination, he gave a mighty lurch, and again found solid footing on the trail. The danger was past as quickly as it had appeared, but to Coyote, it had been an epiphany. He patted the stallion's sweaty neck and praised him, feeling for the first time that such a fine animal deserved an impressive name.

Believing they both needed a rest, he dismounted when the trail widened and led the stallion out onto a small plateau. Surrounded by the mountains he had loved as a boy, he sat down and rested his elbows on his knees. A gentle wind began to blow and the pine trees on the slopes below swayed with a dancer's grace that hinted at the delights only a woman could bestow. A delicate fragrance clung to the breeze, teasing his senses like Belle's perfume as it caressed his cheek with a feminine touch that brought a delicious heat rather than a refreshing coolness.

A slow smile curved across his lips, and along with it, the realization that in choosing life he had also chosen to make it worth living for Belle. She had been remarkably patient while he had mourned a way of life that was gone forever, and tragic mistakes that could not be undone. She had wanted him to be home for Christmas, and he could manage that easily. He glanced over at the stallion grazing on the sparse yellow grass.

"Because you are a Mexican horse, I'm going to call you *Navidad* rather than Christmas. What do you think of your name?"

The horse snickered softly, and looked very pleased indeed.

Coyote sat there awhile, then led the stallion into the peaceful glade where he had planned to spend the night. He built a small fire, and imagined his bride's brilliant curls in the dancing flames. It wasn't until then that he recalled how sad she had looked when he had kissed her goodbye. He had selfishly thought only of himself, and he had not realized how badly he had failed her as a husband. Ashamed of the way he had taken advantage of her loving patience, he hoped that when he returned home, it would not be too late to apologize and make everything right.

Don Antonio sent five *vaqueros* with Belle, but even without knowing the reason for her trip, they sensed the seriousness of her purpose from the solemnity of her mood. Her every gesture was filled with a languid grace rather than her usual lively energy. Taciturn by nature, the *vaqueros* respected her need for privacy, and did not pry or intrude, but rode silently in her shadow. No princess ever had a more loyal, admiring, and respectful private guard.

Born and raised in the Arizona Territory, once across

the border Belle led the way north at a brisk pace, stopping to rest only when their mounts grew weary, and delaying making camp each night until after dark. They had brought along beans to simmer over the campfire, and spices to make them flavorful. One of the men could make passable tortillas from corn meal, and while his companions teased him, they let none go to waste. Belle sat apart as the men enjoyed the simple fare, and hid just how little she ate. She was given the place closest to the fire each night, and while her dreams were never sweet, surrounded by devoted companions she felt safe.

She rose each morning with the dawn, stiff and sore from sleeping on the rocky ground, but nonetheless eager to continue their journey. They skirted the silver mining camps near Tucson, then followed the stagecoach trail north to Phoenix. Filled with prospectors and gamblers, the bawdy town held no appeal to the small caravan and they quickly passed it by.

As they gradually gained altitude, the temperatures cooled, the soft sandy soil of the southern deserts took on a reddish cast, and at last, the towering mesas that ringed Belle's home came into view. Awesome in their spectacular strangeness, their bright colors were muted by the pale winter light. To be greeted by their familiar beauty at the end of such a sad trek brought small comfort to Belle's troubled soul. They had made the journey from northern Mexico in slightly less than a week, but it wasn't the arduous trip that had caused the strain marring her features; rather, it was the heavy burden of sorrow she had carried each step of the way.

Her parents had built a pine and sandstone replica of the stately columned mansions of Virginia. It was painted white each year, but the area's red dust always lent it a subtle pink tinge. Sad memories of a lonely childhood as the unwanted daughter of a widowed Confederate major prevented any feeling of elation from lifting Belle's mood as she and her escort neared the elegant home. She had been away six months, and in that time her cousin had planted more fruit trees and shrubs near the house. Come spring, their foliage and blossoms would soften the starkness of the mansion's lines, but now it still looked as dreadfully unsuited for its site as it always had.

Astonished, the *vaqueros* stared, and exchanged puzzled glances, for none had ever seen another dwelling even remotely like it. They were used to the charming warmth of the unassuming adobe houses most ranchers built. But Donovan Cassidy had been fiercely independent, even in his choice of architecture. Belle knew she had inherited her father's stubborn independence, and it had given her the courage to wed an Apache brave, but it certainly hadn't prepared her for this joyless homecoming.

Seeing a small riding party approaching, the ranch's foreman, Kenneth MacKenzie, waited by the corral, but when he recognized Belle, he rushed out to meet her. He helped her dismount and enveloped her in a boisterous hug that knocked her hat askew. "Why didn't you send word you were coming home? We would have had the whole place decorated as fancy as that tree Win has in the parlor."

He scanned the faces of the men accompanying her, and recognizing none, he lowered his voice. "Where's that Indian of yours? Didn't he come with you?"

Belle had been dreading that question all the way home, but she still had no ready answer. She didn't want to blurt out right there in the yard that she had left Coyote, but she didn't want to lie either. "He's still in Mexico," she explained simply, then felt guilty for telling one of her oldest friends such a small part of the truth.

Kenneth was a perceptive man who saw more than fatigue in her veiled gaze. "I won't keep you. Just go on in the house and tell Win you're home. He'll be real tickled. I'll take care of your men. We've room in the bunkhouse and plenty of food for them."

"Thank you." As Belle turned toward the house, a chill wind bit through her coat and she glanced up at the sky. Usually a brilliant blue, it had taken on the dismal gray that heralded snow. They had been lucky to have good weather on their trip, but it obviously wouldn't hold. That was such an ominous sign, Belle stood on the porch for a full minute before finding the strength to open the door.

Edwin Pierce had just added a log to the fire in the parlor. A Virginian who had dropped out of medical school, he had come out west to find adventure, and had gotten more than he had bargained for when his uncle's death and Belle's marriage had left him in charge of a prosperous cattle ranch. He heard the door, straightened up, and hoping his visitor would ask a question he could at least understand, if not competently answer, he set the poker aside. When he turned and found Belle at the doorway, his mouth fell agape.

"My goodness, Win, do I look that bad?" she asked.

Win let out a delighted whoop as he crossed the room. Thrilled to have Belle home, he picked her up and whirled her around in an ecstatic circle before replacing her on her feet. Then he stepped back and really looked at her. She was lovely still, but thinner than when he had last seen her, and she looked tired to the bone.

"You're gorgeous as always," he replied with a Southerner's natural talent for flattery. "Why didn't you send word you'd be home for Christmas? Never mind now, you needn't provide excuses. I'm so glad to see you I don't care if you wished it to be a surprise. Where's Coyote? We've plenty of men to see to your horses. He needn't do it himself."

Again Belle braced herself for the questions she didn't want to have to answer. Her cousin was a good-natured young man with blond hair and startling blue eyes, but while she had missed him, confiding in him was still difficult. "Coyote stayed in Mexico," she finally admitted.

When Belle immediately glanced away, Edwin placed his hands on her shoulders. "There's more to it than that, isn't there? If he mistreated you in any way, by God, he'll have to answer to me." Six months earlier that boast would have been ludicrous, but running the ranch had toughened not only his body, but his resolve as well. "Now tell me the truth. What happened?"

Hearing Belle's voice, Aurelia Calderon, the housekeeper who had raised the young woman, rushed into the parlor. "You've come home for Christmas," she exclaimed. "Why didn't you let us know? We would have been baking for a week."

Belle shrugged off Win's hands and turned to embrace Aurelia. "It was a sudden decision," she replied. "But I'd really like to have a bath and change my clothes before I explain. Are any of my things still upstairs?"

"Well, of course, your things are just as you left them, *querida.*"

Belle started toward the stairs with Aurelia, then paused to look back at Win. "There will be plenty of time to talk later," she promised.

Impatient, Win nodded, but he heard Aurelia asking about Coyote as she escorted her mistress up the stairs. He hurried to the doorway, hoping Belle would confide more in the housekeeper than she had in him, but all he heard was the sound of the women's footsteps retreating down the hall. The impression conveyed by Belle's downcast mood and hesitance to confide in him was that she had not merely left Coyote in Mexico, but that she had left the Apache for good. Win could scarcely contain his joy at that prospect, for he had missed her very badly and hoped she was home to stay.

Belle had managed to maintain her composure on the trail, but when she stepped into the warm, soapy bath Aurelia had prepared, huge tears began to roll down her cheeks. Aurelia knelt by her side, and stroked her hair as though she were still comforting the little girl who had been left in her care. She knew only that Coyote wasn't there, and was certain his absence was the cause of Belle's distress.

"All couples go through difficult times, *querida.* You mustn't carry on so. Here, let me help you wash your

93

hair." Hearing no objection, Aurelia began shampooing Belle's dusty curls. She kept up an encouraging patter until she realized no amount of cheerfulness on her part would lift Belle's despair.

"You are exhausted," she murmured. "Come, let's get you out of the tub before you become chilled." When Belle rose, the housekeeper quickly wrapped her still dripping body in a large towel. She then rubbed and patted her dry.

Belle sat with her eyes closed as Aurelia towel-dried her hair. She had hoped being home might relieve her heartache, but being surrounded by old friends and familiar things didn't help. She still felt as wretchedly lost and alone as when she had left Mexico.

Aurelia took one look at Belle's slouched pose and went to fetch her a nightgown. "You will never stay awake through supper, *querida*. I'm going to put you right to bed. Would you like me to bring you something to eat on a tray?"

Certain she would become ill if she tried to eat, Belle shook her head. She obediently donned the nightgown, shuffled down the hall to her bedroom, and climbed into bed. She was asleep before Aurelia could tuck her in, but her lashes were still wet with tears.

The attentive housekeeper found Win waiting at the bottom of the stairs. "Belle was exhausted, and I put her to bed. I'm sorry, but you'll have to dine alone again tonight."

Badly disappointed, Win walked along with her to the dining room. "Tell me what she said about Coyote," he urged.

"Nothing, she just cried." When Win's face lit with a triumphant grin, Aurelia was tempted to slap it off, but she controlled the impulse and scolded him instead. "Stop looking so pleased, or Belle will think you're very unsympathetic and you'll ruin your chances to become her second husband."

Believing in the value of her advice, Win grew contrite. "I'm sorry, but I'm so glad to have her home, I doubt that I can keep my feelings from showing."

"Well, you must try."

Win nodded, but all through supper, he wore a delighted grin.

Aurelia let Belle sleep until noon, and then certain she needed nourishing food more than further rest, she went upstairs and woke her. She pulled back the curtains, but the day was overcast, with the scent of snow hanging in the air, and her gesture brought little cheer. "I wish that I had some pretty flowers to decorate your room, but springtime is a long way away."

She fussed with Belle's pillows, but her heart fell when Belle looked no more rested than she had the previous evening. If anything, her tear-swollen eyes now made her sadness more pronounced and there wasn't even a trace of a smile in her expression. Aurelia placed a tray with a bowl of soup, and freshly made flour *tortillas* across her lap. "The *albóndigas* was made just the way you like it."

Belle picked up her spoon and stirred the meatball-filled vegetable soup before raising a tiny sip to her lips. "It's delicious," she complimented without enthusiasm.

Belle had once been effusive in her praise, but Aurelia considered her mood and tried not to be insulted. Rather than remain at her bedside, she moved around the room, tidying up a bit here and there, although there really was no need for it had been immaculately kept in Belle's absence. While Aurelia had not admitted it to Win, she was elated to have Belle home and prayed that she would remain there. She could understand a young woman running off with a handsome Apache, but she thought Belle had shown far more sense by returning home.

"Win is so anxious to talk with you that he is nearly beside himself. When you have finished eating, would you like to see him?"

"No, but I will anyway." Belle rolled one of the warm *tortillas*, took a small bite, then laid it aside. "I'm sorry, but I can't eat any more. Will you please take the tray?"

Belle had eaten most of the soup, and pleased with that accomplishment, Aurelia did not press her to have more.

She carried the tray over to the dresser, and returned with a hairbrush. "Let me brush out your curls so you'll look pretty for your cousin."

"I don't know what to say. I know I did the right thing," Belle explained softly, "but it still hurts."

Aurelia waited for her to add more, and when she didn't, the housekeeper agreed. "Sometimes doing what is right can be very painful. Life presents us with many difficult choices, *querida*, and I am sure you have made the right one."

Belle looked down at her hands. She hadn't left her gold wedding band with Don Antonio, and even now, as she gave it a twist, she could not bear to remove it. Perhaps it was merely too soon. "I feel as though someone has died."

In an effort to soften the anguish in Belle's face, Aurelia fluffed out the ends of her curls so they rested on her shoulders and then stepped back. "Your marriage is over then, you will not go back to Mexico?"

"No, I've come home for good." It didn't feel good, though, and Belle would have closed her eyes and gone back to sleep had Win not rapped lightly at her open door. "Come in," she called to him.

Aurelia swept by him as he entered, and the housekeeper's warning glance provided another reminder to show the proper consideration for his dear cousin's feelings. He sat down at the foot of her bed. "How are you feeling?"

Belle had no reason to lie. "Wretched."

"Well, you look very pretty. Tonight's Christmas Eve. Janet and her husband are having a party. All your friends will be there. We needn't stay long, but I think it would really do you good to go and see everyone."

Not understanding how he could make such a suggestion, Belle regarded him with an incredulous stare. "I've left my husband, Win. That's not a cause for celebration."

"You've left Coyote for good?" Win did his very best to look shocked, and then deeply concerned. "I had no idea you'd come home for such a serious reason. Forgive me if mentioning a party seemed insensitive. I'm so sorry, Belle.

96

I know how much you loved Coyote. I'm sure this isn't your fault."

Touched by his sympathy, Belle relaxed slightly. "Thank you. I tried to be a good wife, but perhaps I had unrealistic hopes. I'd become used to running a ranch, and in Mexico, there just wasn't much for me to do. Coyote's grandfather managed everything, and his staff had been with him for many years. Everyone was very sweet to me, but I felt more like a guest than at home there."

"And Coyote?"

Belle shrugged sadly. "He wasn't happy either. Now without the bother of a wife, he can do as he pleases."

"Oh Belle, surely the man didn't call you a bother."

"Not in so many words, but when he began finding excuses to stay away for days at a time, he didn't need to."

Not wanting to tire her, Win got up, and came close to brush her cheek with a light kiss. "Why don't you rest? Tonight we can have a quiet dinner here, just the two of us. It's going to snow any minute, and it will be too cold for us to go out anyway. We can sit by the fire and I'll tell you how we used to celebrate Christmas in Virginia. Would you like that?"

Belle glanced toward the window and thought she saw the first faint whispers of snowflakes. "Yes, that will be nice," she agreed.

Win waited until she had snuggled down into her covers before leaving her room, but he was very pleased with the way their conversation had gone. He hurried down the stairs and rushed out to the kitchen to make certain the cook was preparing something special for supper.

With Aurelia's insistent encouragement, Belle left her bed, and dressed in a yellow gown for supper. The roast chicken was delicious, but she felt full after a few bites, and then played with her food rather eating it. Win was the most charming she had ever seen him, and grateful for his efforts to lift her spirits, she did her best to smile. Inside, however, she was still filled with a numbing sorrow that made every thought and gesture a strain.

After supper they went into the parlor, and while the beautifully decorated tree delighted the eye, and both Win and the warmth of the fire were pleasant, Belle soon begged to be excused. "Thank you for everything, Win, but I'd like to go on up to my room now."

"But it's still early."

Brushing aside his objection, Belle kissed his cheek and left the parlor.

Discouraged the evening hadn't gone better, Win paced uneasily until he realized he had expected too much from Belle. She was a sensitive young woman who would recover her former joy in time, and he vowed to be far more patient. After all, they were living in the same house, and it was only a matter of time before she came to appreciate the fact that he would make a far more considerate husband than Coyote had.

Satisfied that Belle would eventually be his, Win sat down to finish the novel he had been reading. None of the servants slept in the house, and when close to midnight he heard the back door open, he was amused to think one of them had snuck in to leave presents. He sat up, expecting the sound of familiar footsteps, but heard nothing. Alarmed, he reached for a pistol from Donovan Cassidy's collection and walked quietly to the hall. He saw the silhouette of a man in the shadows, and his heart fell as he recognized him.

For a brief instant, he was sorely tempted to shoot, and explain later he had mistaken him for a robber, but making Belle a widow would only double her sorrow without bringing her an inch closer to his arms. He lowered the pistol and tried to get rid of him with words instead. "Belle's left you and according to her with good cause. What are you doing here?"

Seeing the pistol in Win's hand, Coyote approached him slowly. "I've come to spend Christmas with my wife. If she says I'm not welcome, then I'll go."

"You've broken her heart," Win argued. "You mustn't

98

torment her again."

Coyote stepped into the circle of light thrown by the lamps in the parlor. "Do you really think you can stop me from seeing her?"

Win's grip tightened on the pistol, then relaxed. "I don't know, maybe, but knowing Belle, once she's made up her mind about something, she doesn't change it. There's room in the bunkhouse. Sleep there tonight and talk with her in the morning."

Coyote laughed and slid past Win before the Virginian could block his way. "This is my wife's home, Win, and I don't sleep in the bunkhouse." He went up the stairs two at a time, and entered Belle's bedroom without knocking. He took the precaution of locking her door, then waited at the foot of the bed, thinking she would awaken as she had the first time he had come to her room, but she was sleeping too soundly to sense his presence. He had brought her a gift, but it could wait. Cold, he slipped out of his clothes and climbed into bed beside her. He pulled her into his arms, and snuggled close. She was all warm and smelled sweet, but he was tired, and if she wanted to sleep, he was more than willing to let her.

In the pale light of Christmas morning, the first thing Belle noticed was the snow sifting past her window; the second was the fact she wasn't alone in the bed. She tore back the covers, meaning to leap up and escape her uninvited guest, but Coyote encircled her waist and pulled her back down beside him.

"Merry Christmas," he greeted her.

Her heart pounding in fright, and now in recognition, Belle could barely catch her breath. She had not expected to see him again, and yet as she looked up at him, she could not imagine ever wanting to see anyone else. Her lips trembled slightly. "Merry Christmas."

Coyote nuzzled her neck with light kisses and then propped his head on his hand. "What am I going to do with you, *querida?* How could you believe that I would be happier without you? You are my heart. Did you think I could live without my heart?"

"You've cut your hair." Belle reached up to brush the soft waves off his forehead.

"Yes, my darling," Coyote mimicked in a feminine voice. "I've missed you too."

Embarrassed, Belle tried to pull away, but Coyote held her fast. "Please, we've got to talk."

Coyote focused his kisses on her lips this time. "Later."

"No," Belle pleaded. "Now."

Coyote leaned back slightly. "Grandfather told me what you said and I agree. Neither of us was as happy as we could be at his *hacienda*, but that doesn't mean we should part. It just means we need our own home, our own ranch. With my hair short and in a *ranchero*'s clothes, I can go wherever I like in Mexico, or the Arizona Territory and the army will never suspect I am a renegade Apache. I'll call myself Don Carlos Beltran, or would you prefer Ramon?"

Belle didn't believe what she was hearing. "But that's not who you really are."

Coyote placed a lingering kiss on her palm. "I am as much Mexican as Apache, *querida*, and now is a good time to try living like one. I am through mourning the past. I want us to have a future. Look there in the drawer of your nightstand. I brought you a present."

Curious, Belle sat up, and to her delighted surprise, found a small, brightly wrapped box. Coyote drew himself up beside her to watch her open it. When she withdrew a silver necklace with both a silver and a turquoise heart, tears filled her eyes. "This is so beautiful, and I don't have anything for you."

"No, you gave me my freedom," Coyote reminded her, "which was a very brave and noble thing to do, but I've come back to you."

His expression was so loving, Belle knew he had made the right choice for them both. She slipped the unusual necklace over her head and admired the two hearts. One smooth stone, the other bright metal, they were as different as she and Coyote and yet hearts all the same. "Do you think we can really find a place where we can be happy?" she asked in a breathless whisper.

A wicked grin lit Coyote's expression. "Oh yes, *querida*, and for now it is right here."

As he pulled her down into the pillows, Belle started to giggle. "I'll never forget this Christmas, Coyote."

"Carlos." he reminded her, "and all you need remember is me."

Later that morning, Win walked by Belle's room and heard soft sounds of contented laughter. He wanted to be angry but couldn't. After all, it was Christmas, and he couldn't begrudge his lovely cousin a happy marriage. He could, however, hope the new year brought him someone to love as passionately as Belle and Coyote loved each other.

A Rebel Christmas

by Kathleen Drymon

December 24, 1864

The excitement of the townspeople had been growing over the past two weeks, ever since the troop of Confederate soldiers set up camp outside Burnsville, North Carolina. They had been sent there to await their orders before traveling on to Raleigh.

The annual Christmas party was always held in the community center building on the outskirts of town, but this holiday season was special, for the entire township had turned out to honor their brave boys who wore the gray of the South.

Plump Ema Billings sat before a piano, which had been loaned by Reverend Silas Fletcher; her shrill, high-pitched voice carried beyond the community center and into town as she banged away on the ivory keys. Old and young alike joined in with the lively Christmas songs, but Ema Billings outsang them all!

"She has enough air in that large bosom of hers for her voice to carry all the way to Asheville!" commented

103

Abigail Strickland, who was dressed in a deep blue velvet gown with cream-colored lace edging. The gown had seen better days but still looked fresh; she had mended it with special care. The older lady whispered her snide remark behind her fan, which she was never seen without, and brought a smile to the lips of her companion and best friend, Maude Collier.

From where the pair of older women sat, in the high backed rockers that had been placed in the back of the building for their use, they could easily view all of the goings on at the Christmas Eve party. Maude nodded her gray head toward her dearest friend, in total agreement with Abigail's statement. Everyone in Burnsville knew that Ema Billings was having some sort of sordid affair with Pete Dansmith, the owner of the only mercantile in town, and all the ladies of the town were in total agreement that it was Ema's voluptuous figure that had caught the eye of the confirmed widower. Why, Pete's wife had died more than twelve years ago, but Ema's husband was in the grave no more than a year, and the two of them chasing after each other like a couple of school children! The idea of it!

"Isn't that your granddaughter standing over there with that group of girls, Maude? Why I just knew it was Shelby Lynn." Abigail Strickland answered her own question, which she had the habit of doing, to the annoyance of those who did not know her as well as Maude Collier. "She certainly has grown into a fine beauty, that one has!" Abigail went on. "With that burnt-rose-colored hair and those flashing dark-blue eyes, she'll soon be a handful for your Chester to watch after!"

"Let's pray that this war ends soon and our menfolk return home for just such jobs as that! I fear Chester is a mite too old to be chasing after his granddaughters and their beaux." Maude looked across the room, past the colorfully dressed young women standing around her granddaughter, Shelby Lynn. A soft smile settled over her lips. "I hope there will still be some young men in the South for my granddaughters after the war." Her words were spoken wistfully, as though the years of killing between North and South had taken its toll upon her as well as the entire country.

"I wonder why your Shelby isn't joining in on the singing and dancing like most of the young ladies? She should be taking advantage of all these nice-looking young soldiers while she can. It's for sure they might receive their orders to move out at any time now."

Maude nodded her head in agreement. "I am not sure what has gotten into the girl over the past few weeks." Maude studied her granddaughter, who stood quietly in the midst of the other young women, and remembered when not long ago Shelby Lynn would have been unable to wait for a party such as this one. Perhaps her attitude was also due to the war; its effects were probably troubling her as they were everyone else. "My Chester declares that the girl has her head in the clouds because of the winter blues. But it hasn't snowed now in days and she and her sisters have been coming and going much as usual. Why twice this week Shelby Lynn volunteered to go to town with Chester's eggs for Mrs. Rodgers. Beth Rodgers swears that Chester's chickens lay the best eggs she has ever cooked up for her boarders, and truth to tell, I can't be denying that the money from their sale comes in real handy now that Shelby's daddy and brother are off fighting and we have to make ends meet without the help of the field hands out at Rosedale."

As the two women carried on their conversation, the young woman they were speaking about stood nervously among the girls she had known since childhood. The conversations were of Christmas, and the war. One girl mentioned that she had not heard a word in over seven months from her fiancé, who was off fighting. Another spoke about fashions, but none in the group had an extra coin to waste on material for a new gown, nor even had any idea of what the latest fashions were. The Northern blockades had been doing their work well, and the years of fighting between North and South had laid the Southern states bare. There was some whispering about the soldiers that were in attendance at the Christmas Eve party, and when Annie Clideburn pointed to a young sergeant leaning against the far wall of the building, Shelby's attention instantly perked up.

Several times in the course of the past hour Shelby's violet-blue gaze had gone across the room and settled on the young man. Now as then, when he became the topic of the group's conversation, her eyes went back to him. She felt the wild beating of her heart as her gaze was met by the sable-eyed regard of Sergeant Seth Carlton.

"I would just simply die to have him spend the night under our roof!" declared Callie Mansfield.

"What a treat he would be, under my Christmas tree come tomorrow morning!" Sophie Livingston chortled, her lively rejoinder to her friend's bold statement receiving the laughs she had desired, as most of the young women in the group tried to cover their smiles with their fans.

There was no denying that the man in question was by far the handsomest in the building. He was tall, broad of shoulder, and had dark hair hanging around his shirt collar. His handsome features appeared to have been made lean by his years as a soldier, but not in the least did this detract from his good looks; in fact it seemed to add to his appeal. He seemed to stand out from the other soldiers around him.

"Let's go and get something to eat, before I am

106

tempted to go over there and gobble him up!" Callie grinned at Sophie and the two young women left the group and headed toward the tables which had been set up for the food that each family had donated for the occasion, and which coincidentally was surrounded by a group of soldiers.

Shelby was glad that the other girls had left. She had never before noticed how bold they were until now, but she guessed that their actions were entirely due to the lack of available young men here in Burnsville. If not for the war, all of them would be laughing and flirting with childhood sweethearts. But Sophie's beau had been killed shortly after the war had begun and Callie had promised herself to Stewart Boyette and he had reportedly been captured and sent to a Yankee prison; little had been heard about him over the course of the past two years, so it was no wonder that Callie and Sophie both tried to forget their losses with a teasing manner.

Shelby's thoughts were interrupted as her middle sister, Carrie Ann, grabbed hold of her arm. "Which one do you think will come home with us, Shelby? The reverend is going to start the drawing any time now! I heard him tell Grandpa Chester and Mr. Boatwright!" Thirteen-year-old Carrie Ann was flushed with excitement as she watched the soldiers from across the room.

Shelby tried to focus her attention on the strands of garland and popcorn with which she and her sisters and the other townswomen had decorated the community hall. She forced herself to look above Carrie Ann's blond head at a wreath fashioned out of holly. She dared not look her in the eye for her sister might somehow guess at the soldier she would pick.

As though Carrie Ann had been right on target, the Reverend Fletcher's voice boomed out above the singers and the piano player, Ema Billings. Within moments the music as well as the laughter and talk began to die

107

down, as everyone's attention was turned toward the front of the building and Reverend Fletcher.

"Ladies and gentlemen, I want to thank you for turning out once again for our annual Christmas Eve party." Reverend Fletcher, tall and overly thin owing to his pious belief in fasting at least two days a week, stood before the townspeople as though he were behind the pulpit in his church on a Sunday morning. He felt his importance — there were those under this roof who had not attended church in some time, and as his pale eyes went about the room, they touched upon each one of the offenders for an added second or two.

Several gentlemen, including Grandpa Chester Collier, squirmed where they stood before the condemning regard. But shortly, the reverend remembered that he still had to make the Christmas speech that he practiced each year for just this occasion. This year, however, the party at the community hall held a more festive atmosphere, owing to the troop of Confederate soldiers in Burnsville, and so of course he had also been forced to change his speech at the last moment. Two weeks was not much notice given to one who prided himself on his long-winded speeches. Clearing his throat, which forced his Adam's apple to bob up and down, he began again, "This year we have something extra special to be thankful for here in Burnsville."

At this point Shelby Lynn stole a glance across the room, but quickly her eyes went back to the preacher as she felt a slight flush touch her cheeks. The soldier seemed to be paying as little attention to Reverend Fletcher's speech as she was, and the dark eyes that looked in her direction seemed to charge the space of the building between them with an electrical current. Shelby wondered that Carnie Ann, standing next to her, did not feel the force of it.

"We have some of our brave fighting boys right here

in Burnsville with us, and no matter that they will only be here for a short time; we wish to welcome them with open arms!" Reverend Fletcher took a breath before continuing. "There's not a family here tonight that does not have a loved one or a friend off somewhere fighting in this war between North and South. With our belief that God is on our side, and because of the fact that the good people of Burnsville have volunteered to make this Christmas an extra special one for these boys who are here tonight and a long way from home, I propose that we get on with the drawing!"

A loud cheer rose up from the townspeople, as much from wanting the end to Reverend Fletcher's speech, as being anxious to hear what family name would be the first drawn from the bowl.

Sticking his slender hand into the large punch bowl that sat upon the table before him, Reverend Fletcher drew forth a small slip of paper. "The Sanders family!" he shouted aloud, then one of the soldiers standing near the table of food stepped forth and stood before the preacher. The entire Sanders family converged upon him. Mabel, little Sally and Daniel, the twins, and William Sanders welcomed the soldier as though he were a long lost relative. The young man was grinning from ear to ear as he was ushered away amid the promises of home-baked goodies and a present under the Christmas tree that the whole family had been working on for days and days.

"Oh, Shelby, I'm just so excited!" Carrie Ann whispered in breathless tones as the next family name was drawn.

Shelby could not answer Carrie Ann; in fact she could barely breathe as she felt the searching-dark eyes of Seth Carlton still upon her. *He had to be the one*. She told herself over and over. *He had to be the one chosen to go home with her family*. Without realizing it, her hands twisted nervously together in the folds of her skirts.

Another family name was called out by Reverend Fletcher, and then another. One by one the long line of soldiers were united with a family for Christmas Eve and Christmas Day, until at last the Collier name was spoken loudly. For a moment Shelby could not move as Maude made her way from the back of the building and joined her husband, Chester, and April, Shelby's mother, who was clutching the arm of her youngest daughter, Sara Elizabeth. Standing before Reverend Fletcher, they anxiously waited to see the young soldier step forward who would spend the holiday with their family.

"Come on, Shelby!" Carrie Ann grabbed her arm once again and pulled her along toward the rest of the family.

Everyone waited in excited anticipation until at last a young man wearing dun-colored trousers and high black cavalry boots, stepped forward. He had a gray frock coat draped carelessly over one arm and a yellow-trimmed cavalry hat held loosely in his hand. At his side a sword was buckled securely in its scabbard. Sergeant Seth Carlton had a refined, Southern drawl as he smiled warmly at the family that would be his host for the holiday. "I thank you kindly for your warm generosity toward me." He nodded toward Chester before bowing to the two older women, and as he straightened, his dark eyes glittered with unspeakable depths of warmth as they lingered for a brief second upon Shelby's flushed face.

Shelby thought for a second that she would surely swoon as she tried to draw in a much-needed deep breath of air.

Chester Collier slapped the young man on the back in good-natured greeting as he stated cordially, "Think of yourself as a part of the family now, young man. My

110

womenfolk have been counting the days until they could once again have another man around the house. The last we heard, my son and grandson were heading toward Raleigh with General Johnston. It's been some time since either one of them has been home. It's been lonely for me as well as for the ladies without our menfolk, but we do thank God daily that at least they are both still alive. There have been so many losses on both sides, at times I find myself shuddering when I think about it all!"

Seth Carlton willingly agreed with the older man's sentiments as the family dragged him away from the front of the building and bombarded him with questions about his home and family. At the same time the two youngest girls excitedly told him about all the preparations they had made for Christmas. His ebony gaze again and again went to the eldest Collier daughter. *Shelby Lynn* — the name played over and over in his mind. It had been well worth the gold coin he had slipped into the palm of Jason Wilcox, the soldier who had been standing in line before him and who would have rightfully been the one to go home with the Collier family for Christmas. Shelby was a rare, Confederate treasure, and well worth any price to spend time with her!

The Collier plantation was located only a mile and a half outside Burnsville. Chester Collier drove the pair of horses pulling the carriage, his excited family's chatter filling his ears, while Seth Carlton rode behind on his large, dun-colored stallion. The night air was chilled with a hint of snow, but pulling his coat closer about his neck, Seth kept his thoughts centered upon the lovely Shelby Lynn.

So far he had not had the opportunity to speak alone

111

with her. They had stayed awhile longer at the community hall after the name drawing. After each family had been joined with a soldier for the holiday, Ema Billings had once more taken up her position behind the piano, and the townspeople, in a festive mood, sang Christmas carols, ate the food that had been laid out, and visited with new and old friends. Seth had hoped then that he would have the chance to speak with Shelby, but that had not been the way of things. There was so much he wanted to know about her! They had spoken only a couple of times in town over the past two weeks and each time they had been forced to part company, he had felt somehow empty inside.

The long lane that ran off the main road from Burnsville was tree-lined on both sides. The drive, wide enough for two carriages to pass, ran into the lawns of the plantation home known throughout North Carolina as Rosedale.

The three-story mansion had been built over a century ago by the Hightowers, April Collier's ancestors. A wide veranda ran around the front of the house in a circular pattern. Four large, white pillars stood as evidence that at one time Rosedale had been a thriving, money-making plantation. Today there were signs of deterioration and neglect if one looked closely enough, as was true of most of the plantation houses in the South.

Chester pulled the carriage up to the stone steps before the walkway which made a path to the entrance of the front veranda. Hurrying down from the carriage seat, he presented his arm to each family member in turn, paying a great deal of attention over cautioning each one about their steps. "Watch you don't turn an ankle now, my dear." He fretted over Carrie Ann as he remembered the afternoon when she had slipped while descending from the carriage and the doctor had had to be sent for.

112

The older and younger females of the Collier family each smiled in turn at Chester's gentle fussing. It was Maude who took over once they were all standing on the walkway. "Now hurry, girls. Run along and make sure that Jerome and Hessy have a fire going in the front parlor and Hessy has something warm to drink."

Chester pulled the carriage away and Seth Carlton guided his horse to follow behind to the back of the house where the stables were located; the three girls hurried to do their grandmother's bidding.

Much of the house was not in use these days. It took many servants to run a twenty-one-room plantation house, and with only Jerome and Hessy left on Rosedale, it was easier to use only that portion of the house which was necessary for the family to live in comfortably; most of the third-story rooms were kept closed.

Pulling off their cloaks and hats in the foyer, the sisters made their way toward the back of the house to the kitchen area. There they found Hessy puttering about the large stove and worktable.

"He's here, Hessy. He's here!" Sara Elizabeth cried as she spied the rotund figure of the black woman who was humming softly to the empty kitchen.

"And he's simply beautiful!" Carrie Ann added as she fell into a chair near the worktable.

"Why, Miss Carrie Ann, you best be watching yer mouth. Yer momma hear such words coming from her child and she be thrown into a fit!" Hessy rebuked the middle Collier daughter as she shook her kinked gray head. This here girl child is going to be the life of us all, she told herself once again as she had been prone to do a lot of late.

"Oh pooh, Hessy! Why must I always be careful of what I say? Things are changing every day now, what with the North whipping the South and all! Why, you would be truly shocked if you had heard what I did,

113

only this evening, from Sophie Livingston and Callie Mansfield!" Of course Carrie Ann had better sense than to repeat a word of what she had overheard the older women saying at the community hall. She knew better! Hessy was not averse to reaching out and giving her a good-aching pinch, if she thought she was deserving of it!

"I jest bet ye I would be shocked!" Hessy agreed as she put the cider on to warm.

"Come on, girls, let's make sure everything is ready in the parlor. Hessy, do you need any help out here?" Shelby Lynn took charge of her headstrong sister and took Sara Elizabeth's hand into her own at the same time.

Hessy nodded gratefully in Shelby's direction. "I ain't be needing a thing for now, honey child." She smiled affectionately upon the eldest of the three. She could always count on Shelby Lynn, she thought to herself as the girls left her kitchen. Her humming instantly resumed.

Early that morning Grandpa Chester had gone in search of a Christmas tree, the one he deemed the most fitting to stand in the front parlor of Rosedale. The rest of the afternoon the family had decorated the full, fragrantly scented tree with the little treasures that had been passed down over the years for that purpose. The girls had popped corn and strung it along with cranberries to place in swags about the room and on the tree. Stirring the fire in the hearth to allow greater warmth, Shelby's eyes sparkled warmly as she took in the entire parlor. She hoped Seth would feel welcome here.

Maude and April were next to arrive in the parlor, and shortly the women could hear Chester's loud voice coming from the back of the house. Following closely behind the two men, Hessy entered the parlor with her hands filled with a tray of cups and hot cider.

114

Seth's dark gaze instantly sought out Shelby, and found her standing near the fireplace. His eyes brightened warmly as the firelight played within the auburn locks of her hair. Her deep blue eyes for the briefest second swept over him before quickly turning away.

"Oh, Mr. Carlton, wait until you see what Carrie Ann and I made you for Christmas! I can't wait until morning when we open our gifts!" Sara Elizabeth broke the silent spell that hung about the parlor with the men's entrance, and with her words everyone seemed to begin to speak at once. The holiday season brought cheer and laughter as the cider was passed out and Hessy hurried back to the kitchen to fetch the apple tarts she had made for the occasion.

It was a warm, festive family holiday setting here in the front parlor of Rosedale as the Collier family, along with their guest, sang Christmas carols, told stories of past holiday seasons when Phillip, the father, and Thomas Alan, the son, had been at home, and life in the South had been gracious and abundant. The refreshments offered and a Yule log burning in the hearth sent warmth throughout the room as a light snow began to fall outside.

April Collier was a woman of delicate sensibilities, who had been raised surrounded by Southern charm and gentry. Oftentimes and especially of late she was finding it harder and harder to face the reality of everyday life. All of the Rosedale slaves except Hessy and her husband, Jerome, had fled the plantation shortly after the Emancipation Proclamation, which had been issued in January a year past. Up until that time, April had fought to keep her senses about her, but somehow everything she had known throughout her life was slipping away. Her husband and son were off somewhere fighting for a cause she in truth did not understand. Her home held none of the grandeur that it had while

115

she was growing up, and now, as she looked about her parlor and her blue eyes touched upon the stranger sitting on her settee, wearing a gray uniform, for a minute she wondered why he was here at all. Only the fact that Maude, Chester, and her girls were also in the room kept her from jumping to her feet and fleeing the parlor. As it was, she slowly rose to her feet and tried to bring a smile to her pale features, as she looked at everyone in the room, including the stranger. "I do believe that it is time for me to retire to my chamber. Shelby Lynn, dear, please see to the girls."

Her lilting words were spoken with as much control as she could muster at the minute.

"I reckon as how you are right, daughter." Chester smiled warmly upon his daughter-in-law. They had all noticed that April was growing more unaware of her surroundings, and they had tried to adjust for her sake. It was hardest on the younger children, Chester knew, but he hoped that things would change once his son returned home. They could all use a good night's rest, he thought as he reached out to help Maude rise from her chair. "You ladies go on up, I'll carry Sara Elizabeth." The older man looked to his youngest granddaughter, who had fallen asleep at the foot of the Christmas tree. Turning toward their guest, he added, "Come along, Seth, after I tuck this armful in, I'll show you what room will be yours for the night."

Seth would have much preferred that the eldest daughter of the family show him to his bedchamber but as Chester stood holding Sara Elizabeth in his arms and the women left the parlor, he could only follow behind through the hallway and up the stairs to the second-floor landing. Before Shelby disappeared through a doorway down the hall, he glimpsed her looking one last time in his direction.

116

After the house had quieted, Seth Carlton lay stretched out on the fresh bedding, his eyes wide open as the light from the fireplace danced with lively images upon the ceiling of the room. It had been some months since he had been able to lay his head upon a soft pillow. His thoughts went to his own home, and he pictured his younger brother striving to keep up with the holiday traditions that his family had observed for generations. Steven would be hard-pressed, he knew, to carry on during the holidays without Richard, his next-to-youngest brother, and himself to help out. With two brothers gone to war, one fighting for the Southern cause, the other for the North, it had fallen to Steven to keep their own plantation, Land's End, going smoothly. All signs seemed to indicate that the war would be over soon. The Southern defenses were slowly crumbling away, the North proving the stronger of the two. The two brothers would return to Land's End and they would try and put away the reminders of the war forever. Seth could only pray that this would truly be the way of things, as they had promised the last time they had seen each other.

Sitting up and putting his feet on the colorful rag rug beside the bed, Seth felt the anguish of his position. The Collier family had welcomed him into their home without a thought of distrust about the man wearing the gray uniform of the South. He had always been a man of strong convictions, and throughout his life had fought hard for whatever cause he had believed in. The same had been true when this war had first broken out. But for some strange reason at the moment all of the death and destruction that he had witnessed over the past few years were focusing this night and playing havoc with his emotions! Always in the past he had managed to steel himself to the hardship and ruin all about him,

117

and had told himself that he was fighting for justice; tonight he was not so sure.

Leaving the bedside he silently stepped out of the bedchamber and into the dark hallway. On silent feet, he made his way back downstairs to the front parlor. He had felt a certain peace come over him tonight as he had sat in the parlor surrounded by the Collier family as they sang Christmas carols and sipped the warmed cider. He wanted to recapture something of the moment, if only for a fleeting few seconds.

Silently stepping into the parlor, Seth was instantly held immobile, his dark gaze going across the room to the Christmas tree. There, sitting beneath the decorated tree, Shelby Lynn was tying a bright-colored ribbon on a small package. He must have made some slight noise, perhaps his indrawn breath, for her gaze rose from the gift and went to him.

Her hands stilled upon the piece of ribbon that she had been fashioning. She had scrimped and saved the entire year to be able to get each member of her family some small trinket for Christmas, especially her sisters, who had gone without so much lately. As soon as the house had quieted, she had slipped away from her bedchamber to lay her presents beneath the tree. She had never imagined that Seth Carlton would also come downstairs. Her tongue ran over dry lips, the blue in her eyes sparkling warmly as she watched him approach.

Seth also had been taken by surprise. He had not expected to find himself fortunate enough to have even a single moment alone with Shelby. The Collier family always seemed to be about and he expected no less Christmas day. As he looked at her still sitting beneath the tree, his ebony gaze took her in in a single long glance. She wore a lacy pink and white gown and outer dressing robe. It was apparent, even with the dim lighting of the room, that the material had seen some wear, but upon Shelby Lynn it was a fetching creation. Her shimmering, copper-highlighted tresses hung freely over her shoulders and down her back, and as earlier this evening, the firelight played within the curls and brought about enhanced lights of glowing reflection in their depths. The creamy, smooth texture of her heart-shaped face looked up to him as he made his way to her and with her deep purple-blue gaze holding upon his own eyes, he felt his breath catch until he stood before her and was at last able to exhale. "Shelby." The name escaped him as though the simple word held the power of life and death over him.

Shelby knew in that moment that she should turn away from him. She should flee to the safety of her bedchamber. She should never have spoken to him those few times in town when he had approached her while she was delivering her grandfather's eggs to Mrs. Rodgers. This was all wrong! *But if it is so wrong, then why does it feel so right for him to be standing here before me?* The husky tremor of his voice when he spoke her name seemed to surround her as a silken caress, and she silently rose to her feet. "I . . . I was putting my gifts to my family beneath the tree." She at last was able to speak, but then silence returned and they both could only stand and stare at each other.

Her words seemed to hold the power to bring Seth back to his senses. His gaze shifted to the bottom of the tree where she had been sitting and then back to her beautiful face. "I also have a present that I would like to give to you, Shelby."

"You do? But how on earth could you have known that you would be spending Christmas with my family, here at Rosedale? How would you have known to bring me a present?" For some reason Shelby's tone never rose above a loud whisper, as though she feared that this moment in time would be broken forever if someone

119

were to hear them and enter the parlor.

From the moment his troop's captain had announced that the townspeople would be holding a drawing to see which soldier would spend Christmas with which family in the town of Burnsville, Seth had known that, come hell or high water, he was going to spend Christmas day with the Collier family. Of course he could not tell Shelby this, nor the fact that he had slipped one of his fellow soldiers a gold piece for changing places with him. Instead he reached out a hand and gently drew her along with him to the settee. "There was never any doubt in my mind that I would be here with you for Christmas. Fate would not dare to be so harsh as to deprive us of this time together!"

Shelby felt her heart skip a beat with his words, and at the same time she felt a light blush stain her cheeks.

It seemed the most natural thing in the world when Seth's arms drew her to him in a gentle embrace. His mouth slowly descending down upon her own also seemed very right. And as her lips parted and she felt the heat of his tongue lightly pressing between her teeth, she knew true paradise.

"Shelby . . . Shelby." His breath exhaled the sound of her name as his lips drew away from hers. "God, you don't know how long I have wanted to do that!" The shared kiss had been all that he had ever imagined, and much much more! She filled his arms just right, her sweet-flowery scent filling his nostrils even as his fingers lightly trailed within the strands of her glorious hair.

"I know." That was all Shelby was capable of getting out at the moment. Her heart raced wildly in her chest, her entire body trembling within his embrace as she was surrounded by his powerful masculinity. She also had dreamed of such a moment as this. From the first time she had set eyes on him in Mr. Dansmith's mercantile, she had felt the energy that flared up between them with only the slightest contact of their eyes meeting.

She appeared so innocent, so soft and loving to Seth at this moment. His arms tightened around her, her full breasts pressing against his chest. The hardened buds made themselves known even through the material of her gown and robe and the fiber of his shirt. Lord, she was all that any man could ever want! His mouth covered hers again. The kiss began as before, softly entrancing, his tongue lightly brushing her teeth and tongue, but soon the storm of this invisible thing that raged between them rushed to the surface. The branding flame of his mouth over hers sought out all that she was willing to give; and at that moment it was all that she possessed! The scorching heat of his moist tongue searched out each secret place in her mouth. He drank of her as though a thirsting man who had miraculously found a fountain of the sweetest ambrosia, and at the same time a deep-throated groan escaped from within his chest.

Shelby's own moan of awakened desire mingled with his, her fingers twining within his dark, shoulder-length hair as though she had to clutch on to something to keep her from being drawn forever into the searing depths of his passion.

"Ah, Shelby, if only I had the right to claim you for my own right this minute! If only this damn war were not between us! This North and South that has the power to pull men in two directions, to destroy families, and to keep apart those who truly love!"

Shelby Lynn Collier had been raised in the belief that one fell in love, married, and lived happily ever after. She saw no reason why the war, or anything else, should stand between her and Seth Carlton. She knew she loved him, had loved him in fact from that very first meeting in Burnsville. And if he truly felt the same about her, nothing could get in the way. She was

121

eighteen years old, well of an age to marry. Her family would surely welcome Seth with open arms. After all, he was fighting for the same cause as her father and brother. How could anyone wish for a braver or more honorable man than he? "But there is nothing that can keep us apart." She breathed aloud just before his mouth covered her lips once again.

For a time they both were held in the sensual assault that their joining lips produced upon their senses. Seth's hands lightly caressed the pale slenderness of her throat, his fingertips lightly toying with her collarbone above the ribbon tie of her dressing robe. He was at a loss. He wanted this woman more than he had ever wanted anyone before in his life. But just kissing her caused a stirring of guilt to rise deep within his belly. With a force much greater than his weak will, for it came from his heart, he tore his mouth away from hers; his arms drawing back from around her.

Shelby looked at him without understanding why he would hold such sweet pleasure from her.

"Shelby, you are far too tempting a little rebel for me to hold for any great length of time." He tried to make his voice sound light as his aching need for her ground within his vitals. His sensual lips drew back into a tender smile as his hand reached up and brushed back a tendril of auburn hair that had fallen over her eye. "I told you that I had brought you a present, remember, my sweet?" He clutched on to anything that would bring about some reason to the moment, and allow him to try and think about what he was doing here in this parlor. It would be far too easy to allow his desires full rein, but that was not what he wanted for Shelby. She was far too precious to be treated in such a fashion.

In truth Shelby had entirely forgotten about his mention of a gift. When she was near this man, all thoughts fled except those of him. He held some strange power

122

over her wherein she was helpless to fight off her attraction for him. She had no wish to ward him off! He was everything she desired: handsome, brave, and the man of her dreams. "Yes, the present." She forced herself to try and forget for a moment the power those lips had over her own and the way her body shivered with inner need when he held her in his arms.

Only yesterday Seth had gone to the mercantile in Burnsville and had carefully selected the gift that he would give to Shelby. A delicate lace handkerchief with pale pink roses embroidered over the edges had caught his eye, and he had had the store owner wrap it carefully in bright paper. The gift was in his coat pocket upstairs, but at the moment it seemed far too insignificant for this woman sitting next to him. He wanted to give her something that would speak of his inner feelings for her. Reaching up to the back of his neck, he loosened a silver clasp, and drew the length of a silver chain and locket out for her regard. "This belonged to my mother. I would be honored if you would wear it now."

Shelby gasped aloud as she held out her hand to inspect the antique silver locket. There was an intricately worked tiny rose on the facing; the rest of the locket was etched in delicate designs of leaf work. With a movement of her finger the locket sprang open to reveal a tiny sketch of Seth Carlton.

"My father brought the locket as a gift for my mother after returning from one of his many sea voyages. He had commissioned an artist to make portraits of them both. When my mother gave me the locket, she removed the portraits and told me to put my own inside and then that of my wife next to me." His dark gaze sought her out as she studied the locket in her hand, and as he told her that the empty space next to his sketch was for his bride, her blue eyes raised to his with

123

question. "There is so much that I must explain to you, Shelby, but I cannot speak of these things that torment me now, and in so doing I cannot appeal to you as I would like. I am bound on my honor as a soldier to keep my silence for the time being, but as a man of honor I cannot ask you to bind yourself to me without full knowledge of my life. If you would find it in your heart to wear this locket until the finish of the war, I will explain everything to you then, I swear." He only prayed that she would not return the locket to him when that time came!

Shelby had no idea of what he was talking about. If the locket was intended for his bride, was he in some fashion asking her to wait until the end of the war for him to request her hand in marriage? "I will wear your locket proudly, Seth," she whispered softly with the belief that it was much like a betrothal gift.

Though her words were of agreement, Seth still felt somehow as though they were both caught up in the unfairness of a cruel whim of fate. What more could he ask for, he questioned himself as he looked into her warm gaze, and at the same time he knew that if things were somehow different, he would be able to come right out and declare his feelings for her. They could as early as tomorrow have that skinny preacher from town marry them, and when he left Burnsville to continue on with his part in this damn war, he would be assured that Shelby would be here at Rosedale waiting for him, waiting for the return of her husband. But he was not free to experience such happiness. He remembered the day when his brother, Richard, had shouted at him that his sense of duty and honor would one day be his downfall, and as he looked at Shelby, he knew that that day had come upon him. "I swear to you, Shelby, it will not be long before the war is finished and then I will be free to claim you."

He fastened the locket around her neck. The creamy flesh on the back of her neck such an enticement, Seth's fingers lingered for a few seconds before he pulled her once more into his embrace. "You will love my home, Shelby. My father named the plantation Land's End because the blue-green sea appears to dash its breakers right at our back door."

"Then your home is not in Atlanta?" Shelby questioned, remembering that that was what he had told her family earlier in the evening.

Without replying, Seth's mouth covered hers once again. He dared not speak because he had been lying to her family earlier. His family home was outside Richmond, not Atlanta as he had stated.

With the reluctant end of the kiss, Seth insisted that he see Shelby back upstairs to the safety of her bedchamber. Safe from the likes of him, he thought as he turned from her door and went down the hallway to the room that her grandfather had shown him earlier.

Throughout the long night Seth tossed restlessly on his bed. His life had been consumed with this war between the states and now it even stood between him and the woman of his heart. Seth swore to himself at that moment that he would not let this happen! The two of them had every right to find happiness amid the raging destruction that was taking place all around them, and he would do everything in his power to ensure that they had a chance!

Shelby's sleep was much easier in coming. Snuggling within the down folding of her comforter, her hand caressed the silver locket hanging between her breasts. She thought not of war and destruction, but of the first fresh bloom of love. She reflected on the kisses she had shared with Seth, and even in the darkness of her chamber she could feel the blush stealing over her face and neck. She had found strength and comfort as well as passion in the embrace that had held her in the parlor. What more could any woman ask for?

By early morning, just as the first touches of dawn cast its dim light across the gray sky, Seth began to dress. He had reached a decision in the early hours of the morning. He had been reluctant to take on this mission to begin with, but he had gone along with his orders up until now. He would not return to Burnsville and to the troop of Confederate soldiers; instead he would head for Savannah to seek out General Sherman. He would once again let the general know that he was not suited to the life of a spy. He could better serve the Union by fighting face to face with the enemy. But that enemy was his own brother, and now he had to admit that it was also the family of the woman he loved. Perhaps he could beg the general for a leave of absence, and pray that the war would be over soon, he thought as he pulled on his boots and buckled on his sword.

The only other person awake at this hour of the morning was Carrie Ann. Sleep the night before had been as hard-won for her as it had been for the soldier sleeping down the hallway. At thirteen her body was just beginning to bloom with the first buds of her womanhood. She had put aside her childish ways and her dreams now were of young men and the prospect of falling in love. She had awakened early, and stoking the fire to get some degree of warmth in her chamber, she had wrapped herself in her robe and roamed about her room. Her thoughts again went to the Colliers' Christmas guest. She wondered how Seth Carlton had slept last night, and if just perchance he had thought about her right before he had shut his dark eyes. Perhaps he had even whispered her name, *"Carrie Ann,"* to the empty chamber before sleep overtook him. Wrapping her arms tightly over her small breasts, her steps took her to her chamber window which faced out over the stables.

It was still snowing, but as she looked toward the barn, she could just make out the shape of a man pulling the double stable doors closed. Had she imagined it, or had she seen the man for the slightest second look toward the house and up at her bedroom window? Perhaps Seth Carlton was waiting there in the stables for her to meet him! Her thoughts took excited flight, and at the same time she hurriedly began to pull on her boots.

There was not enough time for her to change clothes, she told herself. A blanket wrapped over her shoulders would have to be enough to keep her warm for the time being. She would just run downstairs and to the stables and wish her soldier a very merry Christmas!

Without thinking further on her actions, Carrie Ann was soon running down the stairs, her excitement causing a healthy pink flush to touch her cheeks. Passing through the kitchen, she noticed that it was still too early for Hessy to be up and about, and as she passed the side door that opened to her and Jerome's chamber, she took extra precaution not to make any noise. Without the rest of the house awake, she would have a few minutes alone with Seth Carlton. She had never been alone in such a man's presence before. Later, when his troop would leave Burnsville, she would be able to recapture this morning and cherish it in her dreams!

The snow seemed to have increased in just the few minutes it had taken her to leave her chamber and reach the stable doors. Silently she pulled the doors open; she knew that she would catch Seth Carlton by surprise. He had more than likely also noticed that the snow was growing heavier and had come to the stables to make sure his horse was well cared for. She took one step into the dimly shadowed interior and then another.

She searched around to try and see the man that she had followed into the barn, and in the dim recesses of her mind, she wondered why he had not lit the lantern which always hung ready upon a beam near the entrance way of the stables.

Grabbed from behind, Carrie Ann screamed at the same time as a hand was pressed over her mouth. Instantly fear gripped her and she knew that she had made a terrible mistake.

"Why looky here, Billy boy. I done caught myself a little rebel gal!" The laughter of two men followed the remark and nearly sent Carrie Ann into shock.

"I knew we done right by searching out this barn. Folks hereabouts have hardly been touched by the war. Why there's horses in here and I heard some chickens clucking toward the back of the stable. And now, by God, here we done got ourselves an extra special Christmas treat!" The man called Billy boy joked with his friend, his hand reaching out and jerking the blanket away from Carrie Ann as his grubby hand began to paw at the front of her robe.

Carrie Ann tried with all her might to fight the men off. She kicked out and tried to scream as she pushed against them for all she was worth, and at the same time a flood of tears poured from her eyes. She was just a girl, and knew little of what they were going to do to her, except that it would be terrible. "Please!" she cried aloud. The man's hand slipped from her mouth, but was instantly replaced.

"Oh, little gal, we aim to please you all right! Me and Sammy here aim to please you real good, little reb! And when we finish, we'll be pleasing you once again!" Billy laughed as he tore her robe and gown down the front with one yank of his beefy hand.

"Yeah, you'll be able to tell all your little galfriends that you had the pleasure of pleasing two damn fine

128

Yanks!" the one called Sammy added.

"Only you can be leaving off with the telling that we are deserters!" Billy slung her to the straw-littered stable floor, and before she could catch her breath, he was falling atop her.

Darkness descended upon her but would not last long enough to keep the horrible images of the man from assailing the darkest corner of her mind. As he fumbled with something between his legs, Carrie Ann tried one last time to scream for help.

"Cover her mouth!" Billy shouted at his friend and instantly her cry was smothered by Sammy's large hand.

Consumed with what they were doing, neither Yankee deserter heard the opening of the stable door, nor did they hear the loud click of a pistol trigger being pulled back. "I hate to interrupt this little party, but I think your fun's about to run out!" The voice was deadly, holding a chilling tremor that circled the interior of the stable.

"What the hell?" Sammy jumped to his feet first, forgetting for the moment that he was supposed to keep the girl quiet.

Whack! Seth Carlton drew back his hand holding the pistol and forcefully slammed it against the man's mouth, sending the large brute flying across the stable.

Carrie Ann, her mouth free and at last able to scream, let out a piercing wail that seemed to have no ending.

Billy, forgetting for the moment about his now limp manhood hanging half out of his breeches, jumped to his feet, his hand already going to the pistol at his hip. Seth was the quicker!

"Why, you son of a bitch!" Sammy shouted, coming to his senses upon the floor of the stable where he had landed after Seth had struck him, his bloodshot eyes going from his partner to their attacker. "You'll pay for

that, you low down Johnny Reb! By God you'll pay!"
Crouching low, he charged, his hand encircling the hilt
of his large knife.

Sammy, like his friend, had totally underestimated the
man they were up against. Within a split second, Seth
drew his sword from its scabbard and with a quick,
deadly movement found the mark of the man in the
center of his ribs!

Seth wasted no more time on the two men; his concern was for Carrie Ann. Gently he reached down to
her, her screams still filling his ears. Lifting her to her
feet, he pulled her against his broad chest. "You're all
right now, Carrie Ann. You are safe. They won't bother
you again." His voice was tender as her screams turned
to sobs of terror. He wished at that moment that he
could somehow make the pair of deserters pay even
more dearly for what they had put this child through.

Jerome had been awakened by the odd sounds coming
from the stables. Silently he stepped through the doorway of the stable, not knowing what to expect as he lit
the lantern overhead. At a glance he took in what had
taken place. "You saved the little missy, master sir!" His
words were a statement and his dark eyes brimmed with
gratitude. "I had best go and fetch Master Chester, he
be knowing what ta do with this white trash lying here
in our stables!" As fast as Jerome had entered the stables, he left it.

Seth silently bent down and drew the blanket back
around Carrie Ann's shoulders. Her slender body was
visible where the gown and robe had been torn away,
but with a gentlemanly manner he turned a blind eye as
he soothed her and began to lead her out of the stables
and back up to the house.

Seth was proclaimed the hero of that Christmas day

130

at the Collier plantation. The entire household had been awakened when Jerome ran through the back door calling loudly up the stairs for Chester. As the women and a sleepy Sara Elizabeth hurried to see what was happening, Chester raced after Jerome out to the stables.

Without any delay Chester Collier and Jerome put the bodies of the Yankee deserters into the work wagon, hitched up a horse, and drove them past the back pastures. There, they buried them. There was no telling how many more Yankees were in the area, so they decided to keep the morning's events to themselves. No good could come of spreading word throughout Burnsville about Carrie Ann's attack and rescue, Grandpa Chester declared as the family gathered around the dining room table and Hessy prepared a hurried breakfast.

The moment Carrie Ann was led into the house by Seth, she flung herself into her mother's arms as though she were little more than a child. And April, appearing for the moment to keep her wits about her, seemed to recognize that her daughter was in desperate need of mothering. Maude and April led the still whimpering girl upstairs and helped her to dress then tried to put her back to bed. But Carrie Ann was too emotionally wrought-up to be left alone. After a time she calmed down, and was once more escorted downstairs.

"Thank you so much, Mr. Carlton." She sniffed and wiped her nose on the handkerchief she had brought downstairs with her. "If not for you, I don't . . ." She could not continue for she could only imagine the horrible things that the two deserters would have done to her.

In turn each member of the Collier family thanked Seth for his heroic deed. Even little Sara Elizabeth threw her small arms around his neck and kissed him fondly on the cheek, her own gratitude given for his saving her sister.

Shelby was the only one who remained silently watching. She could easily see that Seth had won over the hearts of every member of her family. Her grandfather seemed not to be able to thank Seth enough for rescuing his granddaughter. Chester had seemed to take it personally that it had not been he who had rescued Carrie Ann, but he thanked God again and again that Seth Carlton had been at Rosedale and had gone out to the stables early that morning.

It was not until the family finished breakfast and decided to go into the front parlor for the opening of the Christmas gifts that Shelby had a moment to express her own gratitude to Seth for what he had done for her family. Her hand reached out just as the dining room emptied and they were the only ones left in the room. Silently she squeezed his hand, her eyes brimming with love and adoration.

No words were needed between them. Seth tenderly smiled at her, and if given the opportunity he would have bent his head to once again allow himself the sweet pleasure of partaking of her tempting lips, but at that moment Hessy entered the dining room, and Shelby's hand instantly fell away from his. An anxious laugh came from her lips as she caught hold of Hessy's hand and pulled her along with them to the parlor. "You can clean up later, Hessy. You and Jerome are as much a part of this family as anyone. Let's open the gifts under the tree!"

Jerome had arrived in the parlor before his wife, offering warm apple cider. As a special treat a pinch of cinnamon had been added to the cider for this Christmas morning.

"Where ever did you get the cinnamon, Hessy?" Maude questioned as she savored the flavorful drink.

"Why Master Seth, he gave me a small tin of it last night." Hessy was pleased to heap more praise upon the

132

young man they all now admired.

Seth was well aware that most of the households in the South were lacking in much-needed supplies. When he had entered the house the night before, after stabling his horse, he had set down a sack of food supplies upon the kitchen worktable. Among the items he had paid dearly for at the mercantile had been the tin of cinnamon. He had also brought coffee, tea, and an assortment of preserves, a small sack of sugar, and some spices that were hard to come by.

Once again he felt Shelby's warm regard upon him, and as the family sat around the Christmas tree, he felt at peace with himself—a feeling that had been lacking for some time now.

After the gifts under the tree had been handed out and everyone was thanked amid much hugging and kissing, Shelby was given a small package wrapped in shiny blue paper. Pulling the tie on the ribbon and opening the box, she found the delicate rose-edged lace handkerchief. Her blue gaze went to Seth and without thought her hand went to the locket around her throat, hidden for the time being beneath her gown. She would have voiced her thanks aloud, but she dared not speak with her family sitting all around. The warmth in his gaze as he looked upon her spoke volumes to her and left her feeling strangely emotional.

"Why, Shelby, dear, who ever gave you such a beautiful gift?" April had been watching her eldest daughter opening the beautifully wrapped present while Sara Elizabeth played with the rag doll Maude had fashioned for her and Carrie Ann was going through the assortment of hair ribbons Shelby had given her.

Shelby looked at her mother, for a moment unsure what she should say. She would not dream of implying to her family that there was anything between her Christmas guest and herself. It would be better for him

133

to make the first move in such a matter.

Sensing her thoughts, Seth quickly spoke out without any reservations. "The gift is from me, Mrs. Collier. I hope you don't mind."

"Oh" was the initial reply that escaped April Collier's mouth as she was once again thrown into confusion. How on earth had this young man known to bring Shelby a gift? Had he had time after the party at the community hall last evening to go and purchase something this nice? Well, perhaps he had left the plantation early this morning, and that could have been his reason for being in the stables, which again reminded her of Carrie Ann's rescue from sure death. And with the thought, her smile grew wide and her strained features seemed to take on a much younger look. "Well, it is certainly very pretty, Mr. Carlton. Shelby, let your grandmother see the stitch work, dear."

The moment had passed as quickly as it had come, and with its passing Seth Carlton had made it known to all that he held some interest in the eldest Collier daughter. Even Carrie Ann seemed pleased as the handkerchief was passed in her direction. For the time being she had sworn off all thoughts of men and adulthood. She would not again rush nature but would allow it to take its proper course, and she would grow to her adulthood without any premature help from herself. Seth Carlton was the man who had saved her life, and if he was attracted to Shelby Lynn, well and good! In her opinion her sister could not do any better than this brave man.

The rest of the morning and early afternoon was spent in the parlor in warm celebration of the holiday. More songs were sung after the opening of the gifts, and sometime during the late hours of the morning, before Hessy announced that dinner was ready, Grandpa Chester began to read from a story entitled "A Christ-

134

mas Carol," written by his favorite author, Charles Dickens.

The story had been written twenty-one years earlier and the Collier family had heard Chester Collier read from the pages of his book many times in the past. As he did each Christmas, Tiny Tim seemed to come to life before them through their Grandpa Chester's voice, as well as Ebenezer Scrooge and the Ghosts of Christmas Past, Present and Future.

Seth had also read the story; his father had a copy in the library at Land's End. There was also a collection of Dickens's novels and short stories which had first appeared to the public in print form as newspaper and magazine articles. But this morning, surrounded by the Collier family, and with Shelby sitting on a footstool not far from where he sat in a comfortable wingback chair, Seth found a desired peace in the old man's voice. The story itself reminded him that good usually triumphs and in the end happiness abounds. He could only pray that, like Tiny Tim and his family, he would share happy moments with the woman of his heart at the end of this war between South and North.

Sometime in the early afternoon when Hessy announced that Christmas dinner was ready in the dining room, Chester Collier lovingly set the novel upon the mantel. "For those who wish, I will continue later this afternoon." He smiled with pleasure at the nodding of heads in his direction. "For now, let us not make Hessy wait. That turkey I shot last week, I swear took a year off of my life, what with tracking him for the better part of a day, so I for one will be more than pleased to bite into him!"

"Oh, Chester, I do declare, how you do go on!" Maude smiled toward her husband, and as he took her hand to help her up from the settee, she was seen to give him an extra little squeeze on his hand right before he bent and kissed her on the cheek.

Holding out his other arm toward April, he announced to the entire room, "I am the most honored man, to have two such beautiful ladies to escort to Christmas dinner."

"You old fool," Maude jokingly murmured right before he led them out of the parlor. Carrie Ann and Sara Elizabeth followed closely behind.

Seth smiled at Shelby. Feeling as one with this warm family, he held out his arm to her. "May I have the pleasure, Miss Shelby Lynn?"

"Why of course you may, Mr. Carlton." Shelby felt her face lightly blush as she laid her hand upon his arm.

Seth placed his other hand for the briefest moment atop hers, and feeling her slight trembling, his ebony gaze looked to her in question.

"Thank you for the handkerchief," she said, and as his eyes met hers, they both felt the power of the glance and the flame that flared between them.

"It was my pleasure, Shelby." Just before they stepped through the parlor doorway, he bent and softly kissed her bow-shaped lips. "It is my deepest wish to be allowed to spend the rest of my life having just such small pleasures."

Before she could respond, he pulled her along with him to the dining room, and amid the great bustle about all the mouth-watering food Hessy had laid out to entice their appetites, no one seemed to take notice that the couple had lingered overlong in the front parlor.

The chair to the right of Chester Collier at the head of the table and the one next to that had been left vacant for Shelby Lynn and Seth. Shelby sat down next to her grandfather. Taking her hand in his, the older man waited for the entire family and their guest to do likewise.

"We have much to be thankful for this year, family. Though the South has been through hard times, at least those of the Collier family have not been brought low, and of course, I am including our special guest." Chester looked at the young soldier sitting at his table and his heart swelled with thankfulness.

Before he could speak the words that would tell all exactly how he felt about the young sergeant because of Seth's rescue of his granddaughter, the front door was pushed open and stomping boots could be heard in the front foyer.

Chester and Seth both jumped to their feet, not knowing what to expect of such an untimely intrusion. "Stay here, girls," Chester commanded, his gaze for a single moment going to his wife and daughter-in-law. And in the glance was the warning that this could well be more Yankees and that, above all, the younger girls should be kept safe from harm.

Everyone in the dining room anxiously waited for Chester and Seth's return. In each of their thoughts was what had happened that morning in the stables to Carrie Ann. The threat of Yankees in the area had been brought fully home to each, and as they heard the sound of voices coming from the foyer, Shelby and her sisters, as well as her mother and grandmother, all appeared to be holding their breath. It was not long before they heard the clicking of boot heels coming down the long hallway that led to the dining room. All eyes were fixed upon the doorway.

Sara Elizabeth was the first of the group seated around the dining room table to react to the two men who stood between Chester and Seth. A shout of excitement escaped her as she jumped from her chair and she fairly flew across the room. "Papa, Papa!" She threw herself into the arms of the tall, bearded man who wore a Confederate uniform, and whose blue eyes lovingly

137

went around the room as though to assure himself that all were there.

The rest of the girls, and Maude and April, circled Phillip and Thomas Alan Collier, their cries of happiness at such a reunion freely shared as they came together amid hugs and kisses.

April clutched her husband as though she would never let him go, her other arm reaching out and drawing her only son against her heart. It was some moments before she, as well as everyone else, could speak, and when she could gather her breath, she said, "You are both well? You have not been hurt?"

Phillip and Thomas Alan for the briefest second smiled warmly over April's head at each other, as though they had predicted just such a homecoming. "We are both fine, April." And Phillip included the rest of his concerned family as he said, "We were able to get a few days' leave, and wasted precious little time in getting here. We will have to start back the first thing tomorrow morning."

"Why, you boys must be near starving!" Maude declared in the motherly fussing way that her son remembered from his earliest childhood. With hurried motions she went out into the kitchen and quickly returned with two more place settings. Without a word spoken to her son or grandson, she began to pile their plates high with their Christmas feast.

At last settled in a chair at the opposite end of the table from Chester, his father, Phillip looked about the table at his entire family. It had been too long since he had had such pleasure, and that thought brought a long sigh. "I think in all the excitement that I misheard my father when he told me your name, young man." Phillip Collier directed his warm glance upon the man to whom his father had hastily introduced him, out in the foyer. A frown of worry marred his creased brow as he studied the Confederate sergeant.

"His name is Seth Carlton, from Atlanta way." Chester spoke up before Seth had the opportunity, and waving a plump turkey leg about in the air, he added, "Without this young man being here at Rosedale this morning, this Christmas Day might have had a whole different ending! Seth here saved Carrie Ann from two Yankee deserters out in the stables. Took them both on single-handed. Me and old Jerome buried them out in the pasture behind the stable."

Phillip did not say anything but appeared to study the young man even harder. It was Thomas Alan who stretched his hand out toward the soldier sitting at their table. "I want to thank you, Mr. Carlton, for saving Carrie Ann. I only wish that I had been here to help you!" Carrie Ann had always been Thomas Alan's favorite. He was well aware of her headstrong ways, but in the past it had drawn them closer. Even now, as he sat next to his middle sister his free hand took hers and squeezed it in reassurance. He as well as his father would have been devastated to have returned to Rosedale to find that Carrie Ann had been harmed.

Seth warmly returned the handshake, and before the meal was finished, Thomas Alan and he had become fast friends. The bond between them would be a strong one, for in rescuing one of the Collier sisters, Seth had earned a place in the family that no other outsider ever had.

"We are beholden to you, young man," Phillip finally stated as the rest of the family sampled all the savory delights that Hessy had concocted for the holiday.

"I am only glad that I was here to help, sir," Seth replied, feeling somewhat uncomfortable under the older man's regard.

Phillip Collier said no more, only shook his head. He, like the rest of his family, began to sample Hessy's

139

desserts.

"It sho' is good to have you and the young master back home again, Master Phillip." Hessy grinned as she cut out a big wedge of apple pie and set it before him. The next piece she put in front of Thomas Alan and then the next in front of Seth. "It be fur sure that it be one fine piece of luck that brought Master Seth out here to Rosedale, that be the truth of the matter!"

"Why, Hessy, it wasn't luck at all, but the drawing at the community hall!" Sara Elizabeth declared loudly.

Hessy lovingly ruffled the youngest girl's blond curls. "Yes, honey child, I's be knowing that it was the drawing that brought Master Seth to us. I's only thankful that it were him instead of some other soldier."

"Me too!" Sara Elizabeth grinned across the table at Seth before cramming a large piece of pie smothered in whipped cream into her mouth. "I'm glad it was Mr. Carlton, too."

As they finished dessert, Chester questioned Phillip and Thomas Alan about news of the war. "All we hear at Rosedale comes from the troop of soldiers camped outside Burnsville. Does it appear that things are changing any in favor of the South, Phillip?"

Before Phillip answered his father, his blue eyes went to his son as though they had already discussed what news of the war they would share with their family. Then, for the briefest second, Phillip's blue gaze touched upon their guest. Sadly, he shook his head. "There's not much of a change, Pa. You probably heard already about Sherman and his troop of devils who marched through Georgia. They pillaged and destroyed most everything they came upon. They finally arrived outside Savannah about December tenth; he and his troop entered the city December twentieth, only five days past. Thomas Alan and I were riding with General Johnston, as you know, but he was replaced by Presi-

140

dent Davis with General John Hood. Hood was defeated in Nashville in the early days of the month, and I tell you, Pa, there were so many deaths, I hate to think about it. It was only by the grace of the Lord that Thomas Alan and I made it without being wounded. We'll be returning once again to General Johnston when we leave Rosedale."

April's features had grown paler by the moment as Philip spoke. Maude, though, was the one who replied. "Let's save such talk for later when you men can talk in private. Sara Elizabeth, why don't you go and get that rag doll from under the Christmas tree and show it to your brother. I'm sure he would like to see everything you girls got."

"I reckon as how you're right once again, old woman." Chester smiled fondly upon his wife and pushed back his chair. "I guess it is time that I finished reading from my book. Would anyone care to join me in the parlor?"

The entire family began to step away from the table, all anxious to show Thomas Alan their gifts and to listen to the ending of Grandpa's story. As Seth Carlton made to join the others, Phillip signaled him out.

"Would you care to join me for a drink in my library? I would like to thank you personally for saving my daughter."

"I would be more than pleased to join you, sir. But I assure you no more thanks are necessary." Seth would like to forget the happenings of this morning, and he wished the Collier family would try to do the same. He felt uncomfortable being singled out as their hero.

As the two men turned away from the parlor door and went farther down the hall, Seth caught a glimpse of Shelby, her violet eyes seeming to seek him out from where she sat. Once again his heart ached with longing, and as he forced his glance away from the parlor door, his mind took flight. Perhaps this opportunity alone

141

with Shelby's father would be the perfect time to declare his feelings for his daughter and to request that he be considered as a suitor. Again his guilt over his part in this war swept over him. With a strong will, he tried to push it out of his mind.

The Rosedale library, like the rest of the plantation house, was clean and well tended, but on looking closely, one could glimpse that the interior of Rosedale had seen finer days. The velvet curtains were a little frayed where they were drawn back by tasseled ties to give the room sunlight. The Turkish carpet, which had been imported some years earlier, appeared dull and in certain places a bit threadbare. Entering the room he had always considered his one true sanctuary, Phillip Collier placed his saddle bags down upon his desk before going to the door and silently closing it behind Seth Carlton.

As the young man took a comfortable wing chair which faced the large oak desk, Phillip stepped around the desk and without speaking a word sat down in his red-wine leather-upholstered chair. His blue eyes, so much like those of his eldest daughter, glanced upward once before he pulled two glasses from somewhere in his top desk drawer. The drawer he left slightly open as he poured the glasses half full and pushed one toward his guest.

Silently, Phillip appeared to study the man across from him as he slowly drew the glass to his lips.

Seth also took a drink of the strong whiskey, feeling somewhat uncomfortable at the moment with the quietness of the room.

Setting the glass aside, Phillip Collier eased his hand into the top desk drawer. His blue eyes held on Seth Carlton as he wrapped his long fingers around the trigger and butt of his dueling pistol. "Now again, sir, what is your name?" The words hung ominously in the air.

The hard, cold look in the blue eyes looking across the desk at Seth told all. There would be no fooling Phillip Collier. He knew that Seth was not who he claimed to be. Slowly Seth set his glass upon the desk after downing the contents. He eased his large frame back in the chair, as though to say, All right, if I am to die, I will do so in a comfortable position. "Captain Matthew Dawson, at your service, sir."

For a full minute longer Phillip studied the young man, his finger lightly caressing the trigger of his gun. "You are a Union man?"

"As you are a Confederate one, sir," Seth responded, knowing that it would do him little good to try and lie his way out of this.

It was some time before Phillip nodded his dark head. The hand that was not in the drawer toyed with his mustache and then absently tugged on the edge of his beard. "You know, I knew Seth Carlton. He was a good man. Joined up with the Atlanta troop at the start of the war." Phillip Collier at that moment truly felt old. He had lived a lifetime in the course of the past few years. Killing and maiming made him old before his time, and now here was another name of an old friend to add to the long list.

"I can assure you, sir I had nothing to do with his capture."

"He wasn't killed?" Some flickering light of renewed humanity sparkled in the depths of the older man's eyes.

"As far as I know he is still sitting in a prison camp somewhere near Pennsylvania."

For a full moment Phillip appeared to digest this bit of information as he thought of the laughing, good-natured young man he had met years ago, known as Seth Carlton. "Why are you here in Burnsville?" It seemed to him that this young man, Yankee spy that he was, was gathering very little information for the Union so far from the action of the war.

"That is one question, sir, that I have asked myself time and again over the past couple of weeks." A rueful smile touched Seth's lips as he looked at the older man. With a small sigh, he continued, "General Sherman gave me my orders, and they brought me here. I think he believed that I would be able to send him back some information about the Southern troops around Raleigh. But I fear now that he will more than likely arrive there before I do." Seth was an honorable man and would never have divulged even this little bit of information to any other man, Confederate soldier or Union. But there was something in this man's look, a wariness that reflected his own, that allowed him the freedom to speak freely. After all, the results could only mean his death, he told himself.

"Can you give me one good reason, sir, why I should not kill you right here in my library?" He slowly drew forth the dueling pistol that he had been holding on to for the younger man's viewing. But even as he asked the question, he answered himself. He knew the one big reason that he should stay his trigger finger: This man had saved the life of his daughter, and there was no telling how many more members of his family could have been harmed by the Yankee deserters if not for this man sitting before him.

Seth silently shook his head, as though at a loss to give the other man a reason which could prove the value of his life. "All I can say, sir, is that I am tired unto death of all this fighting and spying. If left up to me, I would this minute be on the front porch of my plantation, Land's End, sipping on a goblet of brandy and scratching my old hunting dog's head."

Phillip smiled to himself at the picture the young man

had conjured up in his head. He admitted that he himself felt much the same, and ached in his heart for the time when he could return to Rosedale without having to leave again. He felt as though his duty had long ago been played out. His family needed him and he was unable to be here to protect and comfort them. Silently Phillip Collier placed the gun back in the desk drawer and eased it shut. Once more he refilled his drink and began to sip at it.

"If it will ease your mind, sir, I was on my way this morning to try and seek out Sherman and beg a leave of absence from this war. That is when I came across Carrie Ann and the two Yankees in the stables."

"I doubt very seriously that you will be granted such a leave, young man. If my predictions are correct, the South is running out of time. Your General Sherman will want all his forces intact for the final plunge to the Confederacy."

"I will still try," Seth replied stubbornly.

A year ago, if Phillip Collier had returned home to find that his family had been unknowingly housing a Yankee spy, he would have taken the act as a personal affront. He would have believed they held a viper in their midst at Rosedale, and without questions asked, he would have quickly put a bullet through the young man's heart. He realized now that a lot had happened over the course of this past year. If it were possible, he would put his guns down forever and never raise them up again. "I guess you can finish out Christmas Day here among my family. They already believe you their hero. I see no need to tell them different."

Seth was glad that he would not be exposed to the entire Collier family. It had been a memorable day for him, and he would not wish to see the hurt come over the face of the people he cared about. "I appreciate that, sir. But there is one more thing that I would like

145

to approach you about." Seth knew that his timing was a bit off, but he told himself that he should get all his cards out into the open now, for there might not be another chance.

Phillip waited for whatever it was the younger man had on his mind.

"It is about Shelby Lynn, sir."

"What about my daughter?" Phillip seemed to sit up a bit straighter in his chair as he set his glass of whiskey back down.

"I love her, sir. I request your permission to ask Shelby Lynn to be my wife when this war is over."

Phillip Collier leaned back in his chair, studying the face of the man before him. He felt as though the very breath had been knocked out of him by the other man's words. A Yankee spy was in love with his daughter, and was asking as boldly as you please for her hand in marriage! Of all the nerve! He opened his mouth to shout out something, his fingers itching once more to wrap around the butt of his pistol; but some inner calm prevailed. The young man had saved his Carrie Ann's life, and remembering what he had said earlier about sitting on the porch of his plantation, he questioned, "And does Shelby Lynn know of your feelings?"

The young man silently nodded his dark head.

"And does she also know of your Union loyalties?" If he said the word yes, Phillip at that moment was unsure how he would take it. For Shelby Lynn to have known that this man was a spy against the Confederacy and not tell her grandfather or someone else would certainly have been a betrayal of her entire family.

"No, sir! Shelby has no idea I am anyone other than who I have told her from the start. I have not even felt that I had the right to ask her to wait for me, or to tell her of my true feelings, because of my duties in this war!" Seth rose to his feet and began to pace around

146

the library. "I love her, sir, but I fear that she will not be able to return my feelings when she learns the truth."

The Southern accent in his voice and even the way he strode about Phillip's library lent the older man the feeling that he was conversing with a close friend. A Southern gallant perhaps, who had come to him with a heartfelt problem. Shaking his head, he reminded himself that the man was a Yankee spy and that he was declaring his love for his eldest daughter. "My suggestion, then, is that you immediately seek Shelby Lynn out, and tell her all that we have discussed here in my library." As the younger man looked upon him with some alarm, he added and not unkindly, "My daughter, sir, has always had a mind of her own. She will not judge you harshly for no reason. After she has been told of your sentiments, I will then talk to her and make my decision on the matter." For some strange reason which Phillip Collier could not understand, he could not just send the young man away from Rosedale. There was something about him, he admitted to himself, that he admired. Like the rest of his family, he found himself liking the man who was, in reality, Matthew Dawson!

The words he had said to Phillip Collier in the library — "*I love her, sir, but I fear that she will not be able to return my feelings when she learns the truth.*" — ate at Seth's heart as he waited for Shelby on the front veranda. Early evening was just setting in. It was no longer snowing but the chill of the night air could easily be felt. Seth, though, felt nothing except the anguish within his heart as he worried over what he would say to Shelby and what in turn she would say to him.

"Seth, Father said that you wanted to speak to me out here on the veranda, but why did you not come into the parlor where it is warm?" Shelby softly shut the front door, the warm glow in her blue eyes holding upon Seth Carlton's handsome face as she wondered what he and her father had talked about for so long in the library. When her father had sought her out and told her that Seth was waiting to speak to her on the veranda, he had kept his features impassive, and she had been unable to pry anything out of him.

Seth took her hand and pulled her farther out onto the veranda. "Are you cold?" he questioned, noticing the wrap about her shoulders which was draped over a high-collared blue velvet gown. He would be more than willing to wait a moment for her to go and fetch a cloak if she so desired.

"I am fine, Seth." She glimpsed the serious look in his ebony eyes and not for a minute did she wish to leave him. "You and my father spoke in the library?" She was unsure how to question him on the subject of his feelings for her because in truth he had not as yet truly expressed them to her.

Seth nodded. "That is what I want to talk to you about, Shelby." He led her over to a beautifully carved, high-back wicker settee, and waited for a minute while she settled her skirts before he sat down next to her.

Reaching out, he took her hand within his own. "You are sure that you are not cold?" And as she once again indicated that she was fine, he took a long, deep breath. Not knowing how or where to begin, he stared down at the soft, slender hand in his own. He tried to gather his thoughts as he felt the heavy hammering of his heart. He feared the worst. She would not be able to think of him as anything other than a traitor when he confessed his deceit. Perhaps his original plan to tell her all at the conclusion of the war was the best path for him to take. But with this thought once again the image of Phillip Collier came to mind, and he was forced to comply with the older man's wishes. "Your father is a very wise

148

man, Shelby."

"I am so glad that he and Thomas Alan were able to come home for Christmas Day and that you were able to meet them before you also have to leave Burnsville." Shelby felt the soft blushing upon her cheeks with her confession.

Seth's grip upon her hand tightened somewhat. He knew he had to tell her all. Get it out and be quick about it man, he told himself. "Shelby, there are some things that you don't know about me."

"As there are some things that you do not know about me." Once again her blush rose as she thought of the day when perhaps there would be nothing hidden between the two of them.

Seth smiled softly. "I am sure there are many things that neither of us knows about the other, but what I am speaking about now, your father thinks is too important to put off any longer. I was going to tell you when I returned to Rosedale after the war, but I only hoped that by doing that, I would have more time for you to think favorably upon me."

"I don't believe that that could be possible," Shelby softly replied, and as Seth looked into the blue depths of her gaze, he found himself utterly lost.

A deep-throated moan escaped his lips as without will he pulled her up against his chest, his lips brushing against hers and then settling more fully over her mouth.

She melted against him, lost to all but the sensations he stirred within her. The power she felt in the arms that embraced her sent her pulses racing wildly.

He could not bear to have her turn away from him. The thought of his having searched his entire life to find the one woman that could fill his heart, only to have her turn her back on him, sent cold chills of fear down Seth's backbone. God, he wished he could just leave her with this kiss and go back to the war, only to return to find her waiting for him with open arms! The resignation of his own fate, though, would not allow him such blissful peace. With a will that came from somewhere deep within, he pulled his mouth away, his dark gaze watching as her eyes flickered open, the thick lashes dusting lightly against the smoothness of her cheeks with the motion.

Shelby felt her senses drowning before his tender regard as he looked down at her. She loved him, she told herself once again, and with that thought she felt the wild racing of her heart within her breast.

Seth tried with an effort to put a distance between them, his hands holding her arms as though he would keep her at bay, when in truth he knew that if he allowed himself to pull her back into his arms he would be lost forever. "Shelby." He whispered the name aloud.

The sound of her name stole across her every fiber and a soft smile settled over her pink lips. "Yes, Seth. What is it you wish to say?" She could tell that there was something bothering him, and she knew that she was not making things any easier. Whatever he had to say surely could not be anything too terribly serious.

His entire future with this woman at his side depended upon what he said at this moment, and he was fully aware of the importance of making her understand. "I do not expect that what I am going to tell you will be easy for you to absorb quickly, Shelby. But if you will just hear me out, and consider my words for what they are, that will be enough for now." He still thought that perhaps with the passing of time the hurt might be lessened, and still he might have a chance to win her love. "I am not the man that you believe me to be, Shelby."

"Who else can you be, Seth?" She turned her head as though she were trying hard to try and understand him.

150

At that moment the thought struck that perhaps he was already married. Was this why he said that he was not the man she believed? "You . . . you are not married, are you?" Her voice trembled with the question as her greatest fear at this moment was that this man could never truly be hers.

Instantly Seth's hand once again covered hers. "No, Shelby, I am not married." Oh if only it were so easy, Seth told himself, but at the same time he knew that that would be one problem that would be even harder to deal with. "I have never found a woman I wished to marry, until I found you, Shelby."

Incredible joy leaped within her. Her eyes shone with all the tender emotions that his words had brought to her soul.

"It is not marriage though that I speak of at the moment. I am not Sergeant Seth Carlton. My true name is Matthew Dawson." For a full moment he allowed her the time to try and digest what he was trying so hard to explain.

"Matthew Dawson?" Shelby repeated, the name sounding alien to her tongue. "But I don't understand. Why would you be going by the name of Seth Carlton?" She was truly at a loss, not in the least understanding what he was trying to gct at.

Perhaps Seth had thought that somehow she would immediately understand his meaning. He was finding, instead, that there would be no easy way out for him. "I am a captain in the Union army, Shelby." He spoke the words softly as though they would be easier for her to swallow.

All but straining to hear his words, Shelby's beautiful blue eyes slowly began to fill with disillusionment. "The Union army? But you are a Confederate soldier! Your troop is stationed in Burnsville!" She fought to keep her life together as it had been only a few short minutes

151

previously.

"I never wanted this assignment, Shelby. All I wanted was to fight for the cause that I believed in. I never meant to become a spy for the Union, nor did I ever wish to hurt you!"

"A spy!" She gasped aloud. Until he had said the word, it had never entered into her thoughts. For a moment she felt herself growing dizzy.

"Are you all right, Shelby?" Seth's tone turned anxious as he noticed that she was turning pale. He feared that she might faint.

Shelby tried to pull herself together. *She was in love with a Yankee spy!* She loved a man that was fighting a war on the opposite side from her family and friends!

"I do not mean to hurt or upset you, Shelby. I did not even mean to fall in love with you! I guess everything would be so much easier if I just ride away from Rosedale and try and forget that I ever met you!" But God, that would be the hardest thing he would ever have to do in his life.

Shelby could not speak. She could not tell him that he should indeed leave Rosedale, nor could she say the words at the moment that would keep him at her side. She felt the instant stinging of her tears as they gathered behind her eyes. *Did love have to always be so painful?* Silently a tear fell and then another.

Feeling the dampness hitting the back of his hand where it lay in Shelby's lap, pressed over her own, Seth looked down at the great drops of liquid and his heart felt the swift pang of regret that he had hurt her so deeply. "Ah, Shelby, my dearest rebel. If only I could change things for us." His words were heartfelt as he gently pulled her back into his arms, thinking this might be the last time he would have such a privilege. His lips rained small kisses across her forehead and over her cheeks. "I cannot tell you even at this moment that

152

I regret my choice in siding with the cause that I most believe in, but I can say truthfully that I wish this war had never begun. I wish I could have met you under different circumstances, and had the proper time to woo you into falling in love with me. I would attempt to move heaven and earth for you if possible, but I cannot change the man that I am."

"Oh, Seth, I do love you, and would never want you any different than the man that you are," Shelby whispered softly against his throat.

Seth's heart took flight. Had he heard her correctly? She had said that she loved him and that she would not have him different than he was, but did that mean that she would be able to spend the rest of her life with him, knowing that he had fought against her beloved Confederacy? "And how will you feel when this war is finished?" He held his breath waiting for her answer, not willing as yet to release her or even to look down into her lovely face.

"My feelings for the man I fell in love with will not be changed. It may take me some time to understand, but I will still love you, Seth."

"Matthew," he corrected her right before he lowered his lips over hers and pulled her up tightly in his arms. "You will never regret your decision, Shelby. I will spend the rest of my life seeing to that!"

That promise of tomorrow was enough for Shelby Lynn!

April 9, 1865

General Lee surrendered to General Grant. No rancor or malice marked the occasion of the meeting of these two great generals. Each held the other in deep mutual respect and esteem. General Grant's terms were generous. Unconditional surrender came first, but officers and soldiers alike were to go on their way to their homes unmolested. No personal property was to be given up, and no swords were to be laid down. Each man was allowed to take his own horse or mule home for the spring plowing, and the starved Southern army was to be fed at once before disbanding forever. The war was over!

December 25, 1865

The front parlor of Rosedale was decorated with strings of popcorn, and cranberry swagged about the room and on the tree. A Yule log burned in the hearth, and not far away the Christmas tree stood decorated with all the little treasures that had been collected over the years by the Collier family. This year there was something new: a bride and groom stood before the Christmas tree as skinny Reverend Fletcher called aloud the words that would forever bind them as husband and wife.

"And do you, Shelby Lynn Collier," Reverend Fletcher addressed, "take this man as your husband, for as long as you shall both live?"

As the bride softly gave her reply, her thoughts went to the first time she had seen this handsome man now standing at her side, in Pete Dansmith's mercantile. She had fallen in love with him the very first time their eyes had touched and she loved him even more now.

They had gone through so much in such a short period of time; a full year to be exact. With the finish of the war, he had returned to her. When her father and brother had returned to Rosedale, Seth — no, Matthew, she once again corrected herself — had approached her father about joining him in his shipping business. Thomas Alan would leave next week for Richmond to begin learning the business. Her father planned a trip

154

along with the rest of the family after she and her husband were settled at Land's End. With thoughts of her husband's home, and knowing that they would soon be living together as husband and wife, Shelby felt chills of anticipation dance along her spine. Tonight would be her wedding night, and throughout the day, she had felt the heat of a blush each time her thoughts took this path.

"And do you, Matthew Brice Dawson, take this woman as your wife for as long as you both shall live?"

The squeezing of her hand brought Shelby back to the moment, and as Matthew's dark eyes looked into her own with the tenderest regard, he responded, "Yes, I do." A small tear of happiness filled her eye.

At the finish of the ceremony, shouts of good wishes, long life, and merry Christmas filled the parlor. And Shelby Lynn Dawson knew in that moment that this would be the very best Christmas of her life!

Melissa's Miracle

by Wanda Owen

Pascal and Christine Rocheleau had accepted the fact that their marriage was not going to include the children they yearned to have. Christine had suffered three miscarriages during the first five years they were married. Her doctor sternly warned her that she should not try again. "You'll never carry a baby, Christine," he'd told her.

So Pascal poured his energy into his haberdashery shop in New Orleans and Christine kept herself busy at home. Her only "baby" was a little black-haired puppy Pascal brought home, hoping it would give her pleasure. He was named Bébé.

The pup was a very pampered pet. Yes, Bébé was a good tonic for both of them. He gave them many happy moments over the next five years.

In the spring of 1846 Christine began to suspect she might be pregnant, but she said nothing to Pascal for the next eight weeks. At the end of the ninth week she could not restrain the joy she was feeling. "I'm pregnant and this time I will have our baby," she told Pascal. "I feel it right here." She gestured to her heart.

"Oh, Christine—you must go to your doctor immediately," he urged her. As thrilled as he was, he felt a deep concern for his beloved wife. As much as he wanted a child, he wanted nothing to happen to her.

But Christine adamantly refused to go to the doctor until she was well into her fifth month. By that time she was sure that this baby was going to be her and Pascal's miracle!

Doctor Gordon was amazed when she told him her news and he admired the young lady's courage and determination.

Pascal had always loved his little German bride, but over the next four months, his love and admiration grew stronger and deeper. Each day, as she grew larger and larger with their baby, he saw her unwavering determination.

On Christmas Eve of 1846, Christine gave birth to a beautiful daughter. It was truly a Christmas miracle for the Rocheleaus. They called their little girl Melissa, for that was the name of Christine's mother. Now their happiness was complete. Christine was radiant and glowing and Pascal could not have been a happier man.

The only unhappy one at the Rocheleau house was Bébé, who was receiving less attention than he was used to.

But by the time little Melissa was toddling around the house, she and Bébé were constant companions. Pascal and Christine got many laughs just watching the two of them.

Christmas over the next two years were joyous occasions, for it was a twofold celebration: the holiday itself and their daughter's birthday.

Thirty-three-year-old Pascal believed himself to be a

blessed man, for he'd come to America practically penniless from France. Now he had a business of his own which was prospering, a beautiful wife, and a precious little daughter. Being very frugal, he owed no man. His small house was bought and paid for. He worked long hours at his shop, for he had only one clerk. Christine attended to his ledgers.

Melissa was going on three in the spring when the epidemic of yellow fever invaded the city. No part of New Orleans was spared. Families living in fine mansions were stricken just as fiercely as those living in the shantytown of the city.

Pascal came home in a panic when he heard about the entire family of one of his patrons being stricken and severely ill. He sent his clerk home early, put a sign on his door, and immediately rushed to buy passage to send his wife and daughter out of the city to stay with his sister, Renée, until the epidemic had passed.

But when he got home, Christine was already desperately ill. Two days later she was dead and Pascal ended up taking Melissa to Natchez.

Once he got to Natchez and saw the wonderful care Renée gave to his daughter, he'd decided it would be best for Melissa if they lived here.

He'd never regretted his decision to sell his shop in New Orleans and open a new one in Natchez. Now, thirteen years later he had a very prosperous business here and he owned a comfortable two-story white frame house. Now that she was sixteen, Melissa served as the little mistress at their home. Even though Renée did not have to care for her as she once had, she and Melissa were very close and saw one another almost daily. Melissa filled a deep void in her aunt's life for Renée's two sons were married and she was a widow.

But Renée had discovered that raising a girl was a

159

different experience from being the mother of sons. All those years she'd tended to Melissa, while Pascal was working at his shop, had been a new experience for her.

Perhaps it was because she and her husband had had sons that now she felt Pascal was too protective of his daughter, so she allowed Melissa some liberties which he refused. After all, she was no child anymore. It seemed that Pascal was at his shop so many hours that he'd not taken the time to notice for the last year how his beautiful green-eyed daughter had blossomed.

Renée had been the one to tell her "the facts of life" for she knew that soon, whether Pascal approved or not, Melissa was going to have young men wanting to court her.

It was a wonder, with all of Pascal's pampering her, that Melissa wasn't spoiled. A couple of times Renée had tried to warn him about giving her so many extravagant gifts. No young lady Melissa's age wore finer gowns. She was the envy of her three best friends, Evelyn, Florine, and Marian.

Lately, when Renée and Melissa were together, Melissa had urged her aunt, "Tante Renée—please talk to Papa. He won't allow me out of the house unless I'm with you or him. All my friends go places I'm not allowed to go. Evelyn and Florine are always going to the concerts in the park on Saturdays and Sundays. What could possibly be the harm in that, especially if I went with them?"

"I'll see what I can do, ma petite. I promise," Renée told her. She agreed with Melissa that there was nothing wrong with what she wished to do. She also knew that sooner or later Melissa would slip out, if she was forced to, so that she could be with her friends.

But when she tried to approach her brother, she got nowhere. His comment to her was that the young girls went to the park to meet young men. "I'll not have

160

Melissa doing that," he declared.

"Whether you like it or not, Pascal, Melissa is going to be attracting young men. She's sixteen and she, too, will be eyeing young men, for it is only natural." But she wasn't able to persuade her brother to loosen the reins on Melissa.

The best thing that could happen to Pascal would be if some nice, middle-aged lady attracted him so he would not concentrate his entire life on his daughter and his shop. He was still a very attractive man with a trim figure and a dapper air, and jet black hair slightly streaked with gray.

Renée had never been able to persuade Pascal to attend any social affairs in Natchez. He shied away from them. However, he had allowed her to take Melissa with her the last two years.

Just a few months ago she'd met Justine McCall, a widow like herself, and she liked her very much. She was a very vivacious, earthy woman who had come here from Texas with her husband, James McCall. As Renée had helped Pascal raise his daughter, Justine had found herself in a similar circumstance when her eleven-year-old nephew had landed on her front steps.

Justine had laughed. "That was ten years ago so Lance is a big guy now but he still lives with me. He seems like my son."

Renée was thinking to herself that Justine and Pascal could have so much in common. She was a most attractive lady with a very voluptuous figure. Renée noticed at once that the gown she was wearing the day they'd met was expensive. But it was her vivacious manner that impressed Renée. It would be good for Pascal to be with someone like Justine McCall.

She told Pascal about meeting Justine, but he gave her no hints that he knew her nor that he was interested in knowing her. So Renée went home that evening after Sunday dinner thinking to herself that one day, sooner than Pascal realized, he was going to be roaming around his house alone. Melissa was going to be leaving him!

More and more, as the two of them went together on their little shopping sprees, Melissa voiced her discontent. Renée saw how the young men ogled her as their buggies pulled up beside her buggy when they traveled down the Natchez streets.

Melissa was a lovely sight to behold with that long, thick black hair of hers cascading down her dainty shoulders and those brilliant green eyes, so alive and sparkling.

It was on one of their jaunts out in the countryside that Melissa told her aunt that she didn't know what she was going to do if her father didn't change. "He tries to make me feel guilty, Tante Renée. I love him but I also want to be with my own friends. I don't want to be with Papa all the time. Is that so wrong?"

Renée knew that Pascal would have been upset if he'd heard her reply, but right then she didn't care what Pascal felt.

"You've no reason at all for feeling guilty just because you want to be with people your own age, Melissa," Renée had assured her. She could have tried to excuse her brother by telling herself that he just didn't realize what he was doing, but Renée knew better than that. He knew exactly what he was doing. She guessed why he had brought the fuzzy little white pup home to Melissa a week ago. He knew his daughter was out of sorts with him, and he hoped to appease her with the little dog.

She adored the pup and named him Snowball. That's what he looked like to her, for he was so chubby with his lavish coat of white fur. As Bébé had been her constant companion for the first ten years of her life, Snowball was to become her little shadow, following

162

constantly behind her wherever she went around the house or yard.

As cute and playful as the pup was, however, his company was not enough to content Melissa. So Pascal had not been as clever as he'd thought himself to be, and Melissa had been wise enough to suspect his little scheme.

The citizens of Natchez loved social gatherings where friends got together to visit and celebrate, no matter what the occasion. In the spring and summer there were garden parties out on the manicured lawns with the many magnolia trees in full bloom, along with the white and pink blossomed dogwoods.

The mild weather in Natchez provided a long season for the multitude of flowers, whether they were in the grand gardens of the palatial mansions or the more modest homes like those of Pascal Rocheleau or Justine McCall. Justine had never yearned for the impressive mansion that James McCall had wanted to purchase for her just a short time before he died. He could have well afforded it, but she'd told him, "Now what would we do with all that house, James? You'd get lost and I couldn't find you. Are you just wanting someplace to hide from me, James McCall?"

He'd given her a husky chuckle. "Just like to give you the world if I could, Justine. You've given me so much."

"Not half as much as you've given to me," Justine had told him. She had been born and raised in Texas and the men she'd known all her life were strong, masterful men like her father and brother, Jake. Until James McCall came into her life, most other men had seemed pale and lifeless.

Once, when her young nephew had quizzed her as to why she'd never remarried, she'd told him, "Never found a man who could stand as tall as your Uncle James, sugar."

James McCall's lawyer, Trevor Haywood, squired her to different Natchez affairs but there was nothing romantic about the relationship. It was at the last garden party of the summer season that he told her about some property coming up for sale the following week. He knew about the inheritance Justine had guarded over the years for Lance Avery, her nephew.

"Meadowbrook is up for sale, Justine. It could be a hell of a deal for Lance. He's got the money and more to purchase it. I know what old Bingaman thinks of him since he's been working out at his stables. Lance could make himself a heck of a stable at Meadowbrook. Don't have to tell you the proud name Meadowbrook once had before Curtis Brooks' son took over the stables out there."

Justine was filled with excitement by the time she arrived home and waited for Lance to get home from his job out at Bingaman's Stables. Colonel Bingaman admired Lance's natural skill and how he worked with his fine thoroughbred. Justine knew that this talent had been inherited from his father, Jake.

Lance knew about the vast sum of money left to him by his father, but he'd never asked Justine for any of it. He'd had all he needed for spending from the salary he made working for Bingaman.

When his aunt told him about Meadowbrook being for sale and what he could acquire it for, he didn't have to be urged to go see Trevor the first thing in the morning.

"You could still put in a few more months over at Bingaman's to draw salary and let Meadowbrook lay out for a while. I'm sure you'll find everything rundown — the house and stables. You've surely heard the gossip about what vast sums Duncan Brooks lost at the races

164

last year?"

"Oh, yeah. I've met him a few times around the tracks. Never liked the man, I can tell you. Doesn't surprise me that he's forced to sell the place. He thinks he's a real dandy. He'll have to catch himself a wealthy young lady or he might be forced to do an honest day's work," Lance told his aunt.

As he was turning to leave her kitchen, she asked him, "Can you take me over to Eugenia's Friday night? You don't have to stay but I would like for you to pick me up when the party is over."

"Of course, I'll take you, Aunt Justine," he said, giving her one of those grins that reminded her so much of her brother, Jake. "And I'll also pick you up!"

After Lance left the room and Justine was still puttering around her kitchen, her thoughts went back to her big brother, Jake. She remembered when her good-looking brother had brought his young English bride home to the ranch. Jake had rushed to get home for the Christmas holiday. It was a special occasion for he and his father always went hunting in the woods for wild turkeys.

Justine's first impression of Jake's bride was that she'd never survive the rugged Texas lifestyle. Her pale, flawless complexion could not take the hot Texas sun unless she constantly wore a wide-brimmed hat to shade her face. Her tiny, frail body could not do what she'd be forced to do there at the ranch.

Justine had been right, for she'd had only one son before she died. Jake had raised his son until he, too, died when Lance was only eleven.

When she dimmed the lamps in her kitchen, she also dimmed the memories of Texas and Jake. By the time she got to her parlor, she was thinking about what she might fix to take to her friend Eugenia's house for her daughter's party.

Eugenia had been distraught when she found out that her husband, John, was going to be out of town the night of the party and she was to have all those young people coming to her home. But John was the owner of a newspaper, the *Free Trader*, and he'd had business in New Orleans to take care of, so he could not be there with her.

Justine had assured Eugenia that she could be there to help her. Now that it was autumn, the parties had moved inside. Each gala and social gathering was given a special name. Young Evelyn's party was called the Harvest Moon party.

She'd invited all her friends, and Melissa was her dearest friend. Melissa had come to her aunt in tears for the only evening parties she'd been allowed to attend were those where Renée had escorted her. Her father would probably say no.

"I'll go if I have to crawl out my window, Tante Renée!" she'd vowed to her aunt.

"You'll not have to do that, Melissa," Renée told her.

As soon as Melissa left the house, Renée got in her gig and went to Pascal's haberdashery shop. She spared him none of her wrath when they sequestered themselves in his office at the back of his shop.

Her French temper exploded. "What a fool you are, Pascal! Your daughter is very upset, thanks to you! It is a respectable party given by one of Natchez's most esteemed families. John Thorton owns the *Free Trader* and Eugenia Thorton is one of the grandest hostesses in Natchez. Surely you can't find anything wrong with a party they are giving for their sixteen-year-old daughter. I can't believe how narrow-minded you are, Pascal!"

Renée was so irate that she didn't wait for any reply he might have made as she marched out of the shop.

She was delighted the next day when her niece paid her a visit and excitedly told her that her father had given her permission to go to Evelyn's party. Renée was convinced that her harsh words had made an impact on that stubborn brother of hers.

Melissa dressed with very special care the evening of the party. She chose her prettiest gown, an emerald green taffeta that matched the color of her eyes. This was a very special occasion for her since it was the first time she'd been allowed to go to an evening party without her Tante Renée. She was very excited.

Pascal had taken her in his buggy over to the Thornton mansion and Melissa could sense that he was apprehensive and tense about allowing her this liberty. She had been tempted to try to assure him that he had nothing to worry about, but she didn't.

He'd escorted her to the front door and told her he'd there promptly at ten to pick her up. She'd told him, "Yes, Papa—I'll be expecting you at ten."

Many of her friends had already arrived and the parlor was aglow with all the lovely colors of the fancy gowns the young ladies were wearing.

Evelyn broke away from her guests to greet her and tell her how gorgeous she looked tonight. Melissa had remarked to her, "Well, so do you."

No introductions were needed, for Melissa knew all the guests at Evelyn's party.

She accompanied Evelyn back into the parlor, which looked so lovely ablaze with vases of autumn flowers.

Her friends, Marian and Florine, were all atwitter as they stood there talking with the Brewster twins, Jeff and Josh. Evelyn's newest heartthrob, Devin O'Neal, was there. All the young men were seventeen or eighteen.

While Melissa liked all the young men there, none of them interested her as they did her friends, Florine,

167

Marian, and Evelyn.

She was thinking that her father had no reason to be concerned about this party. Eugenia Thorton was roaming around the parlor, greeting Evelyn's guests, and another very attractive lady stood in the dining room where a most elaborate table was set with huge crystal bowls of fruit punch and trays of finger sandwiches and little meatpies. A silver tray was filled with iced petit fours.

A couple of times Melissa noticed the lady in the dining room staring at her and giving her a warm smile. Melissa didn't know who she was, but she seemed friendly, so Melissa returned her smile.

The truth was that when Justine spied Melissa among the guests, she was struck by her breathtaking beauty. She made all the rest of the young ladies look pale and that included her friend's daughter.

She asked Eugenia, "Who is the pretty thing in the green gown, Genie?"

"She is lovely, isn't she? Her name is Melissa Rocheleau. You know her father, Pascal Rocheleau. He owns the haberdashery shop—remember?"

"Oh, of course," Justine drawled. "I've been in his shop from time to time to buy something for Lance. Seems like a very nice man but I've never seen him anywhere in Natchez except in his shop."

"And you won't. Melissa loves parties, but Pascal just won't attend any of the affairs. We've invited him a couple of times to our dinners or parties. Oh, he's always very gracious, but he declines the invitation," Eugenia told her.

Before Eugenia or Justine realized it, the first hour and a half of the party had gone by. Justine had told Lance that he could pick her up at ten.

It was about nine-thirty when Lance slipped in the back door leading into the kitchen. This was a party for "young sprouts," as he called them, so he had no intention of participating in the festivities.

He greeted Mrs. Thornton, who told him that Justine had gone to gather up her things in the bedroom. "Go and help yourself to some of the refreshments, Lance," she urged him.

"Oh no, ma'am. I couldn't eat a thing," he told her. When Eugenia excused herself to see one of her young guests to the front door, Lance moved to the dining room to survey the young crowd gathered there.

They all looked so young to him—the pretty little girls in their fancy gowns and the young dandies in their fine attire. As his eyes were scanning the spacious parlor, he chanced to see a young lady sitting by the fireplace in a green taffeta gown. She was like no other girl in the room, for her beauty was rare. She could have been the subject of a masterpiece portrait, so graciously was she posed in the chair. She was the most beautiful girl he'd ever seen!

His eyes could not leave her and he suddenly gave way to a wild impulse to go to her. He was drawn to her as a moth is drawn to a flame.

Justine came back into the dining room at the same moment that Lance began to saunter toward the parlor. She watched him with fascination. He was like a young man in a trance and she knew which young lady he was seeking out even before he reached her.

She saw him take Melissa's arm and lead her to a secluded corner of the parlor, away from the others. Justine was unaware that Eugenia was standing beside her until she softly whispered in Justine's ear, "God, he is a handsome young rascal, Justine!"

Justine turned to see her standing there. "You mean Lance?"

"Who else?" Eugenia softly laughed. "He would have turned my head when I was young, I can tell you."

They were both curious as cats as they continued to watch the young couple.

They turned to exchange glances when they observed the tall, towering Lance guiding Melissa out of the parlor. Eugenia smiled shyly. "Well, I would say that your nephew will have something more exciting to remember about the party than he'd anticipated."

Eugenia had to leave her, for some of her guests were leaving. Justine was left there alone. She was thinking to herself that her nephew could be a scamp for she knew exactly what was going on in his mind and why he was taking that pretty girl out on the dark porch.

Justine McCall was exactly right, for Lance Avery had wasted no time once he had the beautiful Melissa in the seclusion of the darkness. He'd led her around the south corner of the porch because he knew guests would quickly be coming out the front door to leave. His arms encircled her tiny waist and his dark head bent down to capture her half-parted lips in a long, lingering kiss.

Never had he tasted such sweet nectar from a woman's lips and never had a soft, supple body fitted so perfectly to his as he held her close. He pulsed with a wild passion that he'd never experienced before.

His kiss was the first she'd ever known and she felt giddy and breathless by the time he released her. Softly he murmured in her ear with his lips still lightly caressing her cheek. "Don't be angry, Melissa. You're just the most beautiful thing I've ever seen. Please tell me you're not cross!"

She tried desperately to sound calm when she told him, "I'm not angry, Lance. Why should I be?" She was just glad her voice didn't crack, for she was anything but calm. She was glad that he was still holding her, for her legs felt like jelly.

"I'm glad to hear you say that, because I want to see

you again. I can call on you, can't I, Melissa?" he asked her.

She dared not have him come to the house, for she knew how her father would react. But she certainly wanted him to call on her again, so she told him she was planning on going to the concert on Wednesday afternoon at Wilson Park between two and four. "Would you like to meet me there, Lance?"

"Oh, I'll be there, Melissa. Where will you be?"

"By the gazebo where the band plays," she told him, priding herself on how cleverly she'd arranged the meeting, for her father would be at his shop during those hours. He had flatly refused to let her go to the concerts on Saturday and Sunday, but she didn't have to ask his permission to go on a Wednesday afternoon.

She was glad that Evelyn had mentioned the concert tonight, or she'd not have known what to tell him. But she also knew, after what had happened tonight, that her father was going to have to give her more liberties or she'd be forced to slip around behind his back. This didn't please her, for it went against her nature.

She and Lance had no more time to linger, for buggies were lining up on the drive and one of those buggies belonged to Pascal. Melissa quickly recognized it.

"My father's here, Lance!" She was now the one leading him across the long porch. By the time they came around the corner, Pascal was out of his buggy and marching up on the porch. Just the sight of the tall young man walking beside Melissa and holding her arm was enough to put Pascal in a foul mood. He was already prepared not to like the young gent, whoever he was.

Melissa tried to be very gracious and calm when she made the introductions, but it wasn't easy. Pascal was very reserved but Lance Avery didn't seem to be intimidated at all. Reluctantly, she had to leave the two of

171

them on the porch to get her cape and tell Evelyn and Mrs. Thornton good night.

Evelyn rushed up to her as she was getting her cape. "You know you were the envy of every girl here tonight when that handsome Avery walked over to claim you. God, isn't he divine?"

"Oh, yes, he is that," Melissa whispered as she told her a hasty good night and mentioned that her father was out on the porch. She breezed out of the room, anxious to get back to her father and Lance, praying that her father had not acted obnoxious with Lance or he'd never want to see her again. She wanted most desperately to see him again.

One way or the other, she would, she vowed as she rushed down the hallway toward the porch. Things were going to be changing in the Rocheleau household.

She had no reason to concern herself. Lance could handle any situation he might be faced with where her father was concerned. Like his aunt, Lance had that warm, friendly Texas charm about him. He didn't stand there with Pascal all flustered and tongue-tied.

"I wasn't a guest, sir. I just came to pick up my Aunt Justine. She was helping out Mrs. Thornton, since her husband had to be out of town," Lance told Pascal.

Melissa was relieved to see that Lance was having an easygoing conversation with her father. At least, it appeared to be that way.

Pascal sought to say hasty farewell as soon as Melissa joined them. Their conversation on the way home was very casual; the subject of Lance Avery didn't come up. The same was not true when Lance and his aunt were traveling back to her home. He talked about Melissa Rocheleau all the way home.

Justine smiled as she sat beside him on the buggy seat, listening. Her nephew had finally found himself a pretty girl who'd caught his eye and his interest.

She was not prepared to hear him say what he declared, in that candid way of his, "I've met the girl I'm going to marry, Aunt Justine. I'm going to marry Melissa Rocheleau!"

In that similar candid way of hers, she told him, "Well, be prepared, Lance, that Pascal Rocheleau keeps a very tight rein on her from what Eugenia tells me. You have your work cut out for you."

Justine was thinking back in the past and she was to conclude that Avery men fell in love at first sight when they spied the lady who captured their heart. That was the way it had been with Jake, her brother and Lance's father.

Obviously, Lance had lost his heart tonight when he spotted Melissa.

The next morning Pascal went to his shop. He forgot about Lance Avery and the party over at the Thorntons, but Melissa had not forgotten. Her gay mood was due to the fact that she was anticipating Wednesday afternoon when she would once again see Lance Avery. If he didn't make an appearance at the park, she was going to be very disappointed.

Pascal was also in a very high-spirited mood. His business was thriving, for Natchez gentlemen were buying his finery for all the holiday affairs. He'd stocked his haberdashery with a huge selection of fine brocade waistcoats and linen shirts for the approaching holiday season.

He could not be happier about the sales mounting up daily at his shop, so Melissa found him to be in a grand mood when he arrived home in the late afternoon.

It seemed forever to Melissa before Wednesday morning arrived. When it was finally time for her to start getting dressed, she chose a pretty pink gown and the berry-colored short jacket which completed the ensemble. Berry-colored velvet piping trimmed the pink gown. She admired her reflection in the full mirror as she tied the bow of her bonnet to the side of her face.

What if Lance Avery didn't show up? She was going to be mortified, for she'd confessed to her friend, Evelyn, about her secret tryst. The sweet-natured Evelyn promised her, "We'll not intrude, Melissa. I'll tell Florine to do the same."

"Thanks, Evelyn. You know how it is with Papa. Any time I manage to spend with Lance will have to be when Papa is at his shop," Melissa reminded her.

"Sooner or later, he's going to have to let you have a beau, Melissa. He surely can't expect his beautiful daughter to be an old maid," Evelyn remarked.

Melissa laughed. "Well now, Evelyn, I've got a few years before I have to worry about that."

On Wednesday afternoon, promptly at two, Melissa strolled into the park and moved toward the gazebo. Some two hundred feet away, Florine and Evelyn had already arrived and were sitting on one of the many benches on the pathways of the park.

They didn't have long to wait before they saw Lance Avery pulling up to the archway entrance of the park. He eagerly leaped out of his gig to come into the park. The two girls turned and exchanged smiles for both of them were harboring the same thoughts about how good-looking he was and how his black twill pants molded to his firm-muscled body. His chest was so broad that it looked like the buttons could pop off of the gray chambray shirt he wore. Atop his head, tilted slightly to the side, he wore a black felt hat with a tan leather band.

Lance wasn't exactly happy about having to come straight to the park from the Bingaman's Stables and not be able to go home to change into the fine-tailored fawn-colored pants he'd worn the other night at the Thornton's party. He was rather embarrassed about the old gray shirt he was wearing instead of his best linen one.

He'd also had plans to stop at the flower stand to purchase a bouquet for Melissa, but nothing had quite worked out as he'd planned. He was certainly not going to arrive late and have Melissa think he wasn't going to keep his promise to her.

Melissa chanced to see him striding toward her and her heart began to pound wildly. His appearance was so completely different this afternoon than it had been the other night. The jaunty set of his felt hat and his tight-fitting pants gave him a rugged look which was just as fascinating to Melissa.

He rushed up to her and greeted her, apologizing that he'd not had time to change his work clothes, but she gave him one of her lovely smiles as she told him, "You look fine to me, Lance."

An instant smile came to his tanned face and he reached for her small hand. Bringing it up to his lips and planting a kiss on it, he said, "Thank you, darling! As long as I look fine to you then I'm satisfied."

Anyone observing the young couple would have considered them to be lovers, the way the young lady was gazing up starry-eyed at the young man. His eyes were adoring her as they danced over her.

They sought out one of the benches, for the band had begun to play. But Lance or Melissa were paying little attention to the music for they were too engrossed in one another. Lance knew that moments like this were going to have to be stolen and brief. Pascal Rocheleau was not going to accept him as a caller at his home, but that wasn't going to discourage him, Lance had already decided. He was going to win the love and heart of

175

Melissa Rocheleau!

Florine and Evelyn were not absorbing much of the concert either. In fact the two of them were so engrossed in watching Melissa and Lance that they were not flirting or encouraging the young men who were sauntering by the bench where they were sitting.

Evelyn was either nudging Florine or Florine was giving out a gasp. "Did you see that, Evelyn? He's kissing her! God, what a long kiss! How's she even breathing? I think I would be fainting."

"Florine, she's breathing!" Evelyn laughed. "I don't think you have to worry about Melissa fainting. I thought you knew so much about boys and kissing. Come on, Florine—the truth! You've obviously never been kissed like that."

A twinkle came to the impish Florine as she confessed to her friend, "Never like that but I'd sure like to be. That Melissa—she's the lucky one!"

Melissa hadn't spotted her two friends; she had eyes only for Lance Avery. The music had quit playing an hour ago and the crowd gathered to hear the concert had departed. There were a few couples strolling around the grounds now, but Melissa and Lance were in their own private world.

When Melissa suddenly realized how low the sun was in the sky, she told Lance, "Lord, I've got to be getting home. Papa could be home already. I lost track of time."

"Come on, I've got my gig. I'll have you home in five minutes, honey. Time stood still for me too but anytime I can be with you, Melissa, I'll be there. I want to see you again and again," Lance told her as he took her hand to walk her toward his gig.

All too quickly, Lance had pulled the gig in front of the gate and was leaping out to help her down. He walked her to the door, not caring if Pascal Rocheleau was staring out his window observing them. He restrained himself from kissing her as he said goodbye at the door, but once again he promised her, "I'll see you again, Melissa. Nothing will stop me."

He quickly turned on his booted heels and went back down the steps.

Melissa breezed through the front door, so overwhelmed with happiness it didn't bother her that her father had already arrived home. Gaily she greeted him, "Oh, Papa you're home!"

"I usually am at this time of the day, Melissa," he said, trying to control the anger seething within him for he had seen the two of them arrive at his gate and walk to the door holding hands. Young Avery was taking liberties!

He asked her where she'd been, and she flippantly told him that she'd been to the afternoon concert in the park. But before he could say anything to her, she was scampering up the stairs from the hallway. Halfway up the stairs, she called back to him, "I'll be back in a minute, Papa, to get our dinner going. I made a big pot of beef stew this morning, so all it needs is warming up and bread is already baked."

Pascal went back to the parlor to sit down in his chair to stare at the wall and think!

Melissa bounced down the stairs a few minutes later and marched into the kitchen to kindle the cookstove. Pascal could hardly speak to her when she was so busily moving around the kitchen after tying on the apron to protect her pretty gown.

She gave him a sweet smile and urged him to go to the parlor and relax while she got their dinner ready. She gave him no hint that she was aware of his displeasure with her. In fact, she seemed to shrug that possibility aside and that vexed Pascal even more. But he did as she suggested, for she was moving around the kitchen so fast. He hardly relaxed though. He didn't like this independent manner of hers.

Sitting in the parlor, making an attempt to read John Thornton's newspaper, the *Free Trader*, he blamed Melissa's association with Evelyn Thornton for this turn of events. The Thorntons gave their sixteen-year-old daughter far more freedom than he was going to give his pretty Melissa. But how was he going to criticize the Thorntons, one of the most respected families as well as one of the wealthiest? He'd look like a fool!

By six-thirty, Melissa had a fine dinner ready to serve her father and their table was bright with candlelight. She had a talent for putting a lady's touch to their home. His Christine always brightened their dinner meal by having candles burning as they'd dined.

The beef stew was delicious, and she'd baked his favorite fruit pie before she'd dashed off to the concert.

Utter frustration consumed Pascal by the time he left his dining table that night. His beautiful daughter had served him a most delicious meal. How could he rant and rave at her as he wanted to do? He had to have a talk with Renée, for he knew no one else to talk to about Melissa.

So he restrained all the fury churning within him as he rose up from the table. In that quiet reserved way of his, he told her that it was a very delicious dinner she'd served him. As she moved around the kitchen to wash the dishes and put the kitchen in order, there was an amused smile on her face, for she suspected that he'd seen her arrive home with Lance Avery.

She knew her father as well as Pascal knew her so she sensed his restrained tension. She'd handled him just right, she told herself. So when the lamps in the kitchen were dimmed, she did not linger in the parlor. She did as she always did in the evening when she was ready to

178

retire. She gave him a goodnight kiss on the cheek and called out to Snowball to come with her. Together, they mounted the stairs. Always following her, Snowball trailed behind her for his legs were short yet so he couldn't climb as quickly as Melissa did. Up to a few weeks ago, Melissa had carried him up to her room but then she'd decided to see if he could do it. The first time had been a struggle for the little pup, but he'd done it. The second and third trip had proved to be easier.

By the time he'd made it up the stairs, he was ready to curl up and go to sleep.

Sleep did not come to Melissa as quickly as it did for Snowball. She lay in the darkness of her room thinking about the afternoon she'd spent with Lance Avery.

Just one week after Lance had met Melissa at the park, Trevor told him that he was the proud owner of Meadowbrook. Justine McCall was elated, for she knew that her brother would have approved of how she'd handled the money he'd left his son. Land was the most important investment a man could make.

So they had a lot to celebrate this holiday. Since the year Lance had arrived at her house, when he was eleven, the Thanksgiving Day feast had always been the same menu she and her brother had had back in Texas. Jake and his father had always gone into the woods to shoot a wild turkey. When Lance was eighteen he'd gone into the woods just outside Natchez to get a wild turkey for them. This year, he'd shot the fine bird that would grace their table. Justine provided the rest of the meal, including a pecan pie which they both liked better than pumpkin pie. There would be cornbread stuffing for the big bird, and sweet potatoes. Like Jake, Lance loved baked apples lavished with butter and cinnamon.

179

All Texas men loved that rich creamy gravy they could put over their meat and dressing.

So different were the traditions of the Rocheleau family. Since the time Pascal had bought his little two-story frame home, Renée had come over in the late afternoon on Thanksgiving Day with her pot of bisque soup and the delicious pâté made from the liver of the goose Pascal would bake for the occasion. It was not a pecan pie or pumpkin pie that graced their Thanksgiving table, but delectable crocks of custard lavishly mixed with eggs and rich creams. Renée always made a delicious dish of rice laced with the herbs she grew in her herb garden. There were chives and savory seasoning the fluffy rice.

The Rocheleau family spent a lovely holiday together and for the day and evening of Thanksgiving, Pascal forgot about being so displeased with his daughter. At least, he did until he was escorting his sister back to her home at nine that evening. When he saw her safely inside her front door and the parlor lamps were lit, he told her that he needed to talk to her about Melissa.

Renée took off her shawl and asked him why not talk about Melissa tonight. But Pascal told her that it was too late. "I've got to open up the shop early in the morning. Besides, it's been a very pleasant day so I don't wish to talk tonight and spoil everything."

"Whatever you wish, Pascal. Come by anytime," she told him as she followed him to the door.

Renée knew what was troubling her brother. She'd tried to warn him about it months ago, but he'd shrugged her warnings aside. Melissa was beginning to show her desire for independence and Pascal was stubbornly refusing to accept the reality that Melissa was no longer a twelve-year-old girl. She was sixteen and a full-blossomed beauty.

The cloistered surroundings she'd existed in would no

longer satisfy her for she was ready to go beyond those restraining walls. Pascal was going to have to accept that, for it would happen whether he approved or not. Fathers had such a different attitude with daughters than they did with sons, Renée knew. Pascal would not have been so strict and rigid with a son as he'd been with Melissa.

Becoming the proud owner of Meadowbrook, Lance found it demanding every free moment he had after putting in a full day's work at Bingaman's Stables. For the last two weeks he'd spent his weekends over there.

He had surveyed the entire place and carefully checked out the barn and stables. All the outbuildings were sorely in need of repairs but the two-story house was in better shape than he'd expected. It was a beautiful house, or at least it could be made beautiful again with some care and cleaning.

Justine marveled how tenaciously he set in motion getting Meadowbrook restored as he wanted it. So like Jake he was!

He hired a black man and his wife that they'd both known for years to go out to Meadowbrook and stay until the house was in order. Old Thaddeus Tucker and his wife, Molly, were thrilled to be hired by Lance Avery for handyman jobs were not easy to find.

Molly's job was to clean the house from top to bottom while Thaddeus was to give it a new paint job along with some minor repairs.

Many of the lavish furnishings were still in the house; Brooks had not got around to selling them. All the fine paintings had been stripped from the walls and the fine collection of guns and rifles was gone. The mahogany gun cabinets in the study were bare.

The more time he spent there, the more intrigued

Lance became with the place. The house was coming alive after Molly and Thaddeus had been there a week. Molly had the parlor cleaned and smelling fresh with the aroma of beeswax. The rich woods of the furniture gleamed; there were enough nice furnishings left in the parlor to make it a very comfortable, livable room. Only the walls were bare and the same was true in the spacious dining room.

He told Molly, "Why you've transformed the rooms, Molly. Everything looks wonderful."

"Well, Mister Lance, I'm working on that kitchen now and don't inspect that yet. It's still got a lot of cleaning to be done. A lot of messy people must have been in there."

But the next time Lance rode over to Meadowbrook, Molly had the kitchen looking spic and span. The pantry had been cleaned, too, and the shelves stocked, for Lance had given Thaddeus money to buy the food he and Molly would need, as well as staples he himself would need when he took up permanent residence there.

Justine began to worry about Lance for he was putting in long days and nights and he was beginning to look weary. "Honey, it doesn't have to be done in just a few short weeks. You're looking worn out," she told him when he finally arrived home that evening.

"Can't help it, Aunt Justine. The more I'm over there, the more anxious I am to get it all fixed up. You know what I'm going to propose to Thaddeus? I'm going to offer him a deal I think he'll accept. I'll always need a handyman around there, and Molly could be my housekeeper. There are more darn bedrooms than I will ever need. I'm going to offer them a job and a home. I like those two and they're hard workers."

A warm smile came to Justine's face and she was to realize what a wonderful young man her nephew was. She had no doubts that the black couple would leap to accept such an offer. "Oh, sugar—you will certainly give them the nicest Christmas gift they could ever receive," she declared.

Lance was to find this out the next day when he made his offer to Thaddeus and Molly. He wasn't prepared for Molly's reaction as the three of them were sitting at the kitchen table drinking coffee. Tears started flowing down her ebony cheeks as she stammered, "You mean we can live here in this pretty place? It could be our home and work for you? Oh mercy, Thaddeus, you hear that? The good Lord is blessing us for sure!"

"I heard, Molly," Thaddeus answered her. His voice was cracking with emotion for they'd been told they were going to have to move in another month from their small, four-room shack.

"So I can count on you and Molly to help me here at Meadowbrook, Thaddeus?" Lance grinned.

"You can sure count on us, Mister Lance," Thaddeus assured him.

Molly picked up the end of her apron and wiped her cheeks. Lance got up from the chair, for he had to be getting on over to Bingaman's place. In another couple of months he figured that he might just be ready to tell the colonel that he was going to be quitting.

Molly got up from her chair and grinned as she began to speak, "Mister Lance, I ain't never kissed a white man but could I kiss you?"

Lance roared with laughter. "You bet you can, Molly! Come here!"

She gave him a kiss on the cheek. Lance couldn't resist teasing her. "See there, Molly, my cheek's just like Thaddeus's cheek."

It was a most marvelous day for the couple for they now had themselves a home. It was as if a miracle had happened for them. A broad smile came to Molly's face as Lance walked out the kitchen door and she looked down at Thaddeus to declare, "Oh Thaddeus—this is going to be the best Christmas we've ever had!"

Thaddeus gave his wife a warm embrace. Feeling as overwhelmed with happiness as his wife, he asked her, "Tell me the truth, Molly Tucker—that why you have been cleaning and prettying up that big back bedroom behind the study, eh? You been thinking that it might be ours?"

"An old gal like me can dream, Thaddeus," she giggled.

A week after the Thanksgiving holidays, Renée heard both Pascal's and Melissa's side of the story about what had happened between the two of them. Her sympathy went to Melissa. Pascal was fighting a losing battle. Melissa was in love and all Renée had to do was listen to her talk about Lance Avery to know that. And from everything Melissa told her about Lance Avery, he was not intimidated or threatened by the disapproving Pascal Rocheleau.

The day after she had her talk with Melissa, she ran into Justine McCall while shopping. It was obvious that both of them were tired from doing their Christmas shopping. Laughing, Justine said, "Lord, Renée, I'm finding it harder and harder to get it all done. Think I'll call it a day. I'm tired!"

"I was thinking the same thing. I have one more gift to buy and I find it so hard to shop for Pascal," Renée told her.

A serious look came to Justine's face. "Renée," she began, "you and I have always got along just fine and I don't know your brother Pascal that well. Can you soften him about his objection to my nephew? Lance is in love with Melissa and nothing will stop him from his quest. I can assure you of that! I think your niece is

184

just as much in love as he is."

Renée nodded in agreement. "I think you are absolutely right, Justine, but Pascal is a very stubborn man. I've tried to speak with him about his very strict rules."

"Well, Lance would like to court her in the honorable way but they've been forced to slip around."

"I know, Justine. Melissa told me all this just yesterday. She will see your nephew regardless of what her father's restrictions are."

"Well, good for Melissa! Lance is a fine young man if I do say so myself."

Before they parted company, Justine added, with a twinkle in her eyes, "You and I are thinking alike. My Lance and your Melissa were meant for one another."

Renée said nothing but smiled as she turned to walk in the opposite direction. Justine McCall was like no other lady here in Natchez. Perhaps it was her Texas heritage that set her apart. That certain drawl she had was so different, too!

But what Renée admired the most about her was her honest, open manner. Justine McCall would be the perfect lady for Pascal to meet . . . but she'd given up on that a long time ago.

What a whirlwind Lance had been caught up in over at Meadowbrook! It had been days since he'd last seen his beautiful Melissa but that didn't mean that he'd not been thinking about her when he finally lay down on his bed at night. She was in his thoughts nightly.

He was eager to see her, but after the long days he put in at Bingaman's place, it was too late to go to her house, for Pascal was home. He wanted to take her out to Meadowbrook this coming Sunday afternoon, but Pascal had refused to let her go.

Lance had few options open to him in his quest to

court his beautiful Melissa. Well, perhaps he could leave Bingaman's place a couple of hours early to go to the Rocheleau home before old Pascal arrived home. That way he and Melissa would have two precious stolen hours.

This went against his nature and galled him, but it was exactly what he did the next afternoon.

Melissa was thrilled to see him standing at the front door when she opened it. She gave way to the sudden impulse to fling herself into his arms. Only later she would realize how boldly she'd acted. But her eager response could not have pleased him more. He was hungry for her kiss and she obviously felt the same way.

As the two of them walked over to sit down on the settee, he told her, "Melissa—I hate this slipping around. It isn't easy for me to find a time to get over here when your father's not here."

"I know, Lance. I don't like it either," she told him.

"Two weeks away from you seems like forever but I've been putting in long hours," he said, explaining what he'd been up to the last two weeks. He told her that he was now the owner of Meadowbrook.

"Well, how wonderful! That is a beautiful old place. No wonder I've not seen you!" She smiled up at him. He did look weary. Privately she was thinking to herself that she could not wait to tell her father about this. Of course, she'd have to lie and tell him that Evelyn had told her the news.

"I'd love to take you out there to see what I've been doing, but I can't figure out how to arrange it," he admitted to her.

A devious twinkle came to her eyes and she declared that she just might be able to work it out. "If I could arrange to spend Saturday night with Evelyn, as I often do, then you could pick me up at the Thorntons. They are not ridiculously strict like my father."

186

Lance grinned and he reached over to plant a kiss on her lips. "What a conniving little fox you are, Melissa Rocheleau! But how would I know to arrive at the Thorntons' on Sunday?"

For a minute she fell silent, a thoughtful look on her lovely face. Suddenly her face glowed and her green eyes flashed as she asked him, "Your aunt? I could send Evelyn with a message from me if I'm at her house. She would give it to you, wouldn't she?"

"Oh, sure she would. Aunt Justine is great."

"Then we have a date for Sunday, Lance Avery, if I can get Papa's permission to spend the night with Evelyn. If you get no message from me by late Saturday afternoon, then you will know that the Thorntons had plans or that I couldn't get Papa's permission to spend the night."

"Sounds wonderful to me, honey, and I'm going to keep my fingers crossed that I get that message. I'll tell my Aunt Justine what we're about. I might as well confess to you that my aunt knows how I feel about you. We're close, Melissa—real close." He grinned.

"She seems like that kind of lady, Lance—so warm and friendly." Had the clock not begun to chime, Melissa would have completely forgotten about Pascal, who was due to arrive home early that afternoon. He had to go down to the wharf to pick up a special order being shipped in to him from New Orleans, so he was leaving his shop early to pick it up. He'd told Melissa when he'd left that morning that he'd come directly home instead of going back to the shop.

She told Lance this, and he didn't hesitate a minute getting up from the settee. "I don't want to cause any trouble for you, so I'll be on my way. I've got Sunday to look forward to now."

She went to the door with him and he lingered just long enough to kiss her one more time before he started

187

out the door, then he paused to look down at her. "This can't last too much longer, Melissa," he told her. "Somehow—some way I've got to convince your father to change his mind about me."

"He will, Lance." The expression on her face was as sober as his. Like Pascal, Melissa could be stubborn and determined.

She watched him mount his fine thoroughbred and ride down the street. It was quite a handsome figure of a man she saw sitting up on the huge beast. She figured that the fine horse was one from the Bingaman's Stables, for he'd not got around to tell her that he had purchased the stallion just the other day. He was the first thoroughbred of his Meadowbrook stable and he dreamed of having many such fine horses.

He had named the stallion Duke. He was a handsome horse of an unusual color which had caught Lance's eye. His coat was a deep rich roan with a black thick mane and tail. Lance was already envisioning the fine colts he'd sire for him.

Pascal was in a grand mood when he arrived home, for his order had arrived as promised and the day at his shop had been a very lucrative one. The Christmas season was bringing people into his haberdashery shop constantly, so Pascal could not have been happier. This order of fine brocade waistcoats would be sold within the next week or ten days.

Ironically, Justine McCall had put in an order for one of the waistcoats for her nephew. She'd ordered the black brocade, for that seemed to be the color Lance always chose. She had not yet come to his shop to inquire about the waistcoat. Although she wanted that black waistcoat for his Christmas gift, she felt like forgetting about it, leaving it there for someone else to purchase.

Her feelings for Pascal Rocheleau were not too kind right now. How dare he look down his snobbish nose at her nephew!

Melissa wasted no time in seeking out her friend, Evelyn, to help her out so that she might be with Lance on Sunday afternoon. Evelyn was more than willing to join in her little scheme. She found it all very intriguing.

As soon as Melissa had left her house, Evelyn rushed to seek out her mother, for she knew what close friends she was with Justine McCall. She wondered if her mother knew about Justine's nephew buying Meadowbrook. It rather surprised her that she hadn't known this news.

"Well, he did buy Meadowbrook, Mother," Evelyn told her. She did not hesitate to tell her mother about Melissa's plans for Saturday night and Sunday. Eugenia prided herself that her pretty daughter felt so free to talk honestly with her. She felt very sorry for little Melissa for she had no mother to turn to as Evelyn did. Oh, she knew that her Aunt Renée had been there for most of her life, but it was still not like having a mother.

"That is fine, Evelyn," she'd told her daughter, but she couldn't understand why Pascal Rocheleau was being such a stubborn man. He should have welcomed such a fine, hard-working young man as Lance Avery to call on his daughter. After all, she was now going on seventeen. If he was now the owner of Meadowbrook, then he wasn't coming to Melissa empty-handed. He had a magnificent home to offer her. Pascal had to be a fool!

The next day Eugenia paid a visit to her friend Justine and told her how the two of them were going to be involved in the lovers' scheme this Sunday. Justine listened to Eugenia tell all of her tale before she said, "That doesn't surprise me at all. Lance is just like his

189

father, Jake Avery. He sets his mind to do something then he does it. He told me weeks ago that he'd met the young lady he would marry and that nothing or no one would stop him. He knew that Pascal Rocheleau did not approve of him."

Eugenia laughed. "But Pascal would not approve of any man for Melissa."

"Then Pascal better be ready for a rude awakening now that Lance has Meadowbrook," said Justine. "If I know Lance the way I think I know him, he's not going to waste any time asking that pretty little girl to marry him."

His Aunt Justine indeed knew him well. When Lance left Melissa's house, he went directly to a jewelry store to purchase a gift to give her on Sunday. Never did he doubt that she would be coming to Meadowbrook on Sunday afternoon, for her knew she had a firm determination to match his own.

It was an exquisite emerald and diamond ring he bought for her. Her lovely green eyes were as brilliant as any emerald and the sparkling fire of a diamond reminded him of Melissa. He'd seen that this afternoon, when she'd suddenly become excited about how they could be together Sunday. Spontaneously, she'd had a solution. Never had he adored her more.

His spirits were soaring so high that late afternoon that he purchased gifts in the jewelry store for his aunt, and for Molly and Thaddeus before he finally left. The clerk waiting on him was never going to forget Lance Avery. Molly was to have a pretty brooch and Thaddeus a fine gold pocket watch. For his beloved Aunt Justine, he chanced to see a pair of ruby teardrop earrings and he was to remember how she always wore a brilliant red gown at Christmas. A ruby seemed right for his vital,

190

vivacious Aunt Justine. Lance had a theory that ladies should wear gems that reflected their personalities. Melissa's would always be emeralds and his aunt's should be rubies. He well remembered that his own mother's most precious, cherished pieces of jewelry were deep blue sapphires.

Perhaps it was because he was so young when his mother died that Lance's memories of his mother paled beside the memories of his father, who'd been around until he was eleven. He'd truly never gotten to know his mother. A much deeper impact had been left with Lance by the death of that rough, rugged Texan who was his father. He towered some four inches over six feet and he was a formidable figure of a man. It was an image that Lance had etched in his mind that he wanted to be. He admired no one more than Jake Avery!

He was in the highest spirits when he arrived at his aunt's home late that afternoon.

Justine McCall decided that if she was to pick up that black brocade waistcoat for Lance, she'd better do it the next day. After this weekend she might not wish to go into Pascal's haberdashery.

When she arrived at the shop to inquire about the waistcoat, Pascal greeted her in his usual gracious manner and told her it had arrived. For the first time, she noticed that Pascal was a very attractive man with fascinating eyes. It was too bad he was overly protective of his daughter, but then Eugenia had told her that he'd raised Melissa alone.

Justine paid him and picked up her package. "I wish you and Melissa a very happy Christmas, Pascal," she told him as she turned to leave the shop. She had no inkling that he was trailing behind her. She was almost to the door when he called out to her, "Madame Mc-Call—I need to speak with you."

She whirled around to face him. "So—let us talk, Pascal."

"I don't know a delicate way to put this, Madame McCall," he told her, slightly stammering.

She gave a laugh. "So don't put it delicately. Just say what's on your mind."

"Well, it's my daughter and your nephew I wish to speak to you about, Madame McCall."

"For pity's sake, call me Justine if we're to have such a personal talk."

"All right, Justine. I think your nephew is taking too many liberties with my young daughter, Melissa. She is only sixteen and your nephew is much older. So I resent it," Pascal said.

Justine knew that Melissa was almost seventeen—the same age as Evelyn.

"Your daughter is almost seventeen and my nephew is not that much older than she is. More to the point, Lance is a very honorable young man and your daughter is ready to be courted! Ask your daughter if Lance takes any liberties *she* disapproves of." She angrily turned to leave but she took only three steps before she whirled around to face him with fire blazing in her eyes. She shook her finger at him and told him, "Don't you dare look down your snobbish nose at my nephew, Pascal Rocheleau! Face the truth that no young man would be acceptable to you. You want to keep Melissa a child. Well, you are a fool, Pascal!"

She marched out of the shop and got into her gig, traveling at a very fast pace as she headed toward her house, giving vent to the fury flaming within her.

Back at the haberdashery, Pascal's young clerk had overheard everything and he had to turn around to go to another part of the shop for he was about to break out laughing. That Mrs. McCall was a real firebrand who'd certainly minced no words to tell Mr. Rocheleau off. But what she'd said was true. Clarence, like everyone else, knew how overly protective the boss was of his daughter.

Pascal was shaken by the tonguelashing he'd received from Justine McCall, and he was embarrassed that his clerk had overheard. All afternoon he kept thinking about the fiery Justine McCall and what she'd accused him of. He'd certainly riled her temper and she'd proven to be quite a hellcat! Closing his shop and traveling down the street toward his house, Pascal had to privately admit to himself that Justine had spoken the truth. He was basically an honest man so he could not lie to himself.

That evening was the perfect time for Melissa to ask permission to spend Saturday night with Evelyn. She was a little stunned when her father said without any hesitation at all that she could.

Excitedly, she rushed over to give him a hug before she went upstairs to her own bedroom. She couldn't wait until tomorrow so she could tell Evelyn the great news. Now there was nothing to stop her from keeping the Sunday date with Lance.

As soon as Pascal left the next morning, and she could get herself dressed, she hurried down the street to the Thorntons' house.

Evelyn gave a shriek of wild delight. "This is such fun, Melissa—all this plotting and scheming you and Lance are having to do to be together. Far more intriguing than if he were politely coming to your house, I think."

"Oh, Evelyn!" Melissa laughed. "I can't say I enjoy it. Papa surprised me last night. Guess he must have had a good day at his shop. Normally, he would have given me an argument."

"Well, I've already told my mother and she understands," Evelyn said.

Melissa shook her head as she pointed out to Evelyn what a lucky person she was to have a mother like Eugenia Thornton. "If my mother had lived, I'm sure the two of us would have been close, too. I'm sure a lot of things would have been different."

Evelyn agreed with her about the wonderful mother she had. "At least you have your aunt," she reminded Melissa.

"Oh, I don't know what I would have done without Tante Renée, but it's still not like having a mother."

But Melissa didn't linger, for she'd done nothing to straighten the house before she left so she had to get home to do her daily chores around the house. "Can't rile Papa right now so that he'd change his mind about Saturday night. I'd just die!" she declared as she made a dash for the door with Evelyn trailing behind her.

After she arrived back home, she put in a very busy day cleaning the house and polishing the furniture. She fixed boiled beef and vegetables, one of Pascal's favorite dinners. She also baked a pie. Only then did she take some moments to sit in the parlor to rest as the dinner simmered slowly on the cookstove.

What a very long day she'd put in! The clock on the mantel told her that Pascal would be arriving home in another hour.

She was thinking, when she leaned back in the chair, that she would go to bed early tonight so she could be rested and refreshed when she went over to Evelyn's tomorrow afternoon.

Melissa knew that she and Evelyn would stay up late tomorrow night, as they usually did when they stayed overnight with one another. But over at the Thorntons' she could sleep late on Sunday morning, for they always had a late Sunday breakfast.

That would give her plenty of time to be ready by the time Lance arrived at one to take her out to Meadowbrook.

Madder than a hornet was the way Justine McCall would have described herself by the time she arrived back at her house. She vowed that Pascal Rocheleau would not see any more of her money flowing into his haberdashery shop.

She had wanted to slap Pascal's arrogant face and it had taken all her willpower to restrain herself from doing just that.

Once she was inside her house, she calmed herself. She was determined not to do or say anything to let Lance know what had happened at the haberdashery shop. She wanted nothing to spoil this next Sunday for him.

She applauded herself later, when she was retiring, for she'd managed not to mention anything about her upsetting afternoon and the stormy encounter with Pascal.

Lance had told her good night early, for he had a very long day to put in tomorrow.

Early the next morning, when Lance was pulling away from his aunt's house, Pascal was mounting his buggy to open up his shop for this would be a big day for Christmas shopping.

Something was bothering Pascal this morning as it had last night after Melissa had gone upstairs. He'd always prided himself on being a well-mannered, polite man, but he hadn't been gracious to Justine McCall yesterday. She'd probably never come into his shop

195

again. She was a respected matron here in Natchez and she was certainly the most attractive lady he'd seen since he'd been here. He could still see the fury on her pretty face and the fire in her bright eyes. He had to admit that she'd ignited a strange feeling within him. This morning he was still consumed with guilt that he'd not been courteous to her.

He had a busy day from the minute he unlocked the front door, but the shop became ghostly quiet by four. Apparently, people were through shopping and heading for home. It was not Pascal's nature to act impulsively, but this late afternoon he did just that. He announced to his young clerk that he was leaving early; the young man could lock up the shop.

"I've got a couple of errands to run for myself," he told Clarence as he went toward the back of his shop. A few minutes later he was rushing out.

The young clerk was dumbfounded by Pascal's announcement, but gave him a nod of his head. Pascal said nothing else as he prepared to leave his shop. He made two stops along the way to purchase a lovely bouquet of flowers and a bottle of the finest white wine.

It was almost four-thirty when Pascal pulled his buggy up to the front of Justine McCall's white-framed house. It wasn't easy for him to make this gesture but he was driven to do so. He felt the need to ease his guilty conscience and apologize to Justine McCall.

She was hardly prepared to have a guest at this time of the late afternoon, and she knew it wasn't Lance, for he never knocked at her door. Having just put two pecan pies into her oven, Justine had an apron tied around her waist and straying wisps of hair were out of place. There was even a smudge or two of flour on her cheek where she'd brushed her straying hair from her face a few minutes earlier.

She was busily wiping her hands on her apron when

196

she opened the front door. Pascal Rocheleau, with a sheepish expression on his face, was the last person she expected to see standing there.

Unlike Pascal, Justine always gave way to responding impulsively. "Good Lord—Pascal!" she cried. "What the hell are you doing here?"

In one arm he cradled a basket of colorful flowers, and the other hand held a bottle of wine. "May—may I come in, Madame McCall—Justine?"

"I suppose so," she stammered, backing up from the door to allow him to enter.

"For you, Justine," he told her, holding out the flowers and the bottle of wine. "Call it a peace offering if you will and a way to say I'm sorry for what happened yesterday."

Justine took the bottle and the flowers. She was bedazzled by the overture, for she would not have expected this from Pascal.

"Have a seat, Pascal," she said, taking the wine and flowers. "The flowers are very beautiful and this is very nice of you." She gave him a slow, hesitating smile, then left the parlor as Pascal was seating himself in one of her comfortable chairs by the fireplace. When she returned from the kitchen, she had removed her apron.

Like Pascal, she was feeling a little awkward, for she was not as neat as she usually was when company came to call. But Pascal saw her as a very different lady in this setting from the one who came into his haberdashery from time to time in her fine, elegant attire. Nevertheless, he thought she was just as attractive in her pretty sprigged muslin gown. He liked her simple hairdo, which was slightly tousled with little wisps curling around her face. In some ways she looked younger.

He would not have dared tell her that she had some white smudges of flour on her face. But he did quickly tell her that he felt urged to call on her. "I'm not usu-

197

ally so rude and I felt I must make my amends to you. I was wrong, Justine!"

She took a seat on the settee. "Always takes a big man to admit that, Pascal. I can admire you for that. You see, I love my nephew just like you love your daughter."

"I understand that, Justine. I admire you for that. I—I gave a lot of thought to what you said in my shop and last night privately I said to myself that you'd spoken nothing but the truth, so I was not to rest until I came here today. I apologize for coming here unannounced. I know it isn't proper."

She gave a gale of laughter. "Oh, Pascal—you're talking to a lady born and bred in Texas. Back there, friends and neighbors drop in all the time unannounced, shall we say."

An amazing thing happened that next half hour as the two of them sat in Justine's parlor, sharing coffee and talking. Pascal found himself telling her about his and Melissa's life and how he'd happened to settle in Natchez after his wife had died from yellow fever.

She told him how she'd come to be the adopted mother of an eleven-year-old when his father, Jake, suddenly died in Texas.

Justine was easy to talk to. Pascal had not felt so relaxed around a lady for many long years. Had he not chanced to glance up at the clock on the mantel to see that it was five-thirty, he might have lingered longer than he did. Melissa would be gone by now, he realized.

Justine didn't hesitate to tell him as she was walking him to the door, "I wish you didn't have to go, Pascal. I've had no one to talk to like we've talked in a long, long time."

"I know, Justine. I know that feeling very well." He dared to take her two hands in his, but he fought the urge to kiss her. That was a desire he'd not known since Christine had died almost fifteen years ago.

"Come again, Pascal," she urged him.

"I'll come again, Justine. I promise you."

Justine closed her front door and rambled around her house in a rather giddy fashion, like a young schoolgirl, for she'd not felt that way since she'd first met Jake McCall. It was a feeling she had never expected to capture again.

Did miracles happen after all? Only yesterday, she detested this man, and yet this afternoon she found herself stirred with sensations she'd thought were forever dead.

She was glad that it was an hour later when Lance arrived home. She'd had time to calm herself and take her pecan pies from the oven. It was when she went to her bedroom to put some order to her hair that she noticed the smudges of flour on her face. She realized that Pascal had obviously noticed this but had said not a word.

She said not a word to Lance about Pascal's visit. She wished to keep that her little secret for right now. Lance was not to know anything about the bottle of white wine, but he did notice the lovely basket of flowers and asked her, "Now where did you get those flowers, Aunt Justine?"

She didn't lie when she told him, "A nice friend of mine brought them this afternoon, Lance."

Lance retired to his room early that evening for he'd put in a long day. He wanted to have a good night's sleep so he'd be at the Thorntons' promptly at one to pick up Melissa. He had received the message that she was spending the night at the Thorntons', and that was enough to give him sweet dreams.

Justine lingered later in her parlor that evening, for she had no plans for Sunday as her nephew did. She could sleep as late as she wished. Tonight, she gave way

199

to private musings.

It was past midnight by the time she finally climbed the stairs to her bedroom. She was like a young girl anticipating Christmas and the New Year. She'd always known that she was a romantic and she somehow knew that this might be the most wonderful holiday she'd had for many a year!

It was a glorious December afternoon with only a slight chill in the air. Melissa had brought her green wool dress and matching short cape to Evelyn's house to wear on Sunday afternoon.

Evelyn couldn't have been more excited if she herself had been going out on the rendezvous Melissa was anticipating tomorrow afternoon. Melissa had drifted off to sleep with Evelyn chattering away for it was almost one in the morning. It took Evelyn a few minutes to realize that Melissa had not heard a word she'd said for the last five or ten minutes.

It was past ten when Melissa woke up, but she knew the routine at the Thorntons' on Sunday. They all gathered at the table at eleven-thirty to enjoy a delicious breakfast.

Melissa took special care in dressing and styling her hair so Evelyn left her in the room to finish dressing.

When she joined the family a few minutes later, Eugenia commented about how very attractive she looked. "I'll be very anxious to hear what you think about Meadowbrook, Melissa. There was a day when Meadowbrook was the grandest stable in Adams County. I think Lance Avery could make it that way again."

"I know he's very excited about it," Melissa said.

"He has a reason to be," John Thornton declared. "It would be wonderful to see the grand old place restored to what it was before Duncan Brooks devastated it."

200

At the appointed hour of one, Lance arrived in his buggy. A few minutes later, Melissa was in the seat beside him. Both of them couldn't have been happier as they rolled down the road together on this late December day.

Melissa was impressed by the fine old estate even before Lance ushered her through the front door. Molly had everything in perfect order and she'd placed vases of colorful asters in the living room and dining room. The flowers gave the rooms a warm, inviting look.

Molly couldn't resist leaving the kitchen door slightly ajar so she could sneak a peep at the pretty young lady Mr. Lance had brought here. An amused smile creased Lance's face when he saw the slight opening. That curious Molly wanted to get a look at Melissa.

As he took her on a leisurely stroll around the grounds and his stables, he told her of his many plans for Meadowbrook. All the time they walked side by side, he held her dainty hand. There was a boyish eagerness in his voice as he asked her, "Do you really like Meadowbrook, Melissa?"

"Oh, Lance—words can't describe it. It's beautiful!" she exclaimed, her eyes shining brightly as she gazed up at him.

"That means everything to me, honey. You see, Melissa—I want you to share Meadowbrook with me. I want you to be my wife—the mistress of Meadowbrook."

Melissa was so overcome with emotion she could hardly speak. All she could manage to say was, "Oh, Lance! Yes!"

"Yes, you will marry me, Melissa?" A slow grin came to his face. "Is that what you're telling me?"

"Yes, I'll marry you, Lance, and I'd love to be the mistress of Meadowbrook." She smiled up at him.

She found herself suddenly lifted up in his strong arms, then swung around. "Darn, Melissa—I am the

201

happiest man in Adams County. I—I love you so much!"

As he lowered her to the ground, he bent to kiss her honeyed lips. "Don't make me wait too long for a wedding," he pleaded.

She gave a soft, lilting laugh. "Oh, Lance, I wouldn't do that. I'm just as eager to be married as you are."

"So what would you think about getting married on New Year's Eve and spending our honeymoon right here at Meadowbrook? I can't think of a better way to start the new year. You've already made this the happiest Christmas I've ever known, Melissa Rocheleau."

"I think New Year's Eve would be perfect. And I can't imagine anywhere being more wonderful to spend a honeymoon than right here at Meadowbrook."

So it was settled. They both had a glowing radiance on their faces when Lance brought her to the Thorntons' front door.

Evelyn was beginning to get nervous when Melissa had not returned and it was almost five. She was at the house alone, for her parents were paying calls on some of their friends to exchange Christmas gifts. Evelyn had been sitting in the overstuffed chair by the windows in the parlor so she would have a view of the drive leading up to the front entrance. Her fear was that Mr. Rocheleau would come over to see why Melissa had not returned home.

Dear Lord, she didn't want to face him! What would she tell him? So she decided that if she saw his buggy rolling up the drive, she'd just not answer the door. If one of the servants answered it, then she'd just dash up the stairs to her bedroom.

She heaved a deep sigh of relief when she spotted Lance's buggy coming up the drive. She watched the two of them coming up the steps toward the front door. How adoring Lance's eyes were as he looked down at

Melissa! Evelyn didn't have to see through the carved front door that he was kissing her before he left.

She was impatient to hear from Melissa about the afternoon she'd spent. Only after she heard the door opening did she leap out of the chair to call to her, "In here, Melissa! I'm here alone. Gosh, I can't wait to hear everything."

Still bedazzled by everything that had happened, Melissa told her, "I don't know where to begin, Evelyn. It was a glorious afternoon and Meadowbrook is beautiful." While Evelyn was her dearest friend and she could not tell her all that had happened this afternoon but she did tell her that Lance had proposed and she'd accepted.

Evelyn gave a wild shriek. "I can't wait to tell Florine and Marian!"

Melissa chanced to glance up on the mantel to see that the clock was striking five, and she told Evelyn that she'd better be getting home. "Papa will be coming over here and making a scene. He was probably expecting me home almost a half hour ago." She got up off the settee to go upstairs to gather her belongings from Evelyn's bedroom.

In a few minutes, she and Evelyn were walking back down the hallway on the second landing and Melissa was telling her how much she appreciated her making this Sunday afternoon happen for her and Lance. "Without you, Evelyn—it wouldn't have happened."

"We're friends, Melissa. You'd have done the same thing for me," Evelyn remarked. "I just insist on being there when you and Lance get married on New Year's Eve."

"Oh, you'll be there," Melissa assured her.

It was twilight by the time Melissa walked through her front door; she'd already prepared herself to be greeted by a very angry father. But to her shocked amazement, the parlor was dim with no lamps lit, and

203

the house was ghostly quiet. She had to ponder where her father was for this was so unlike him. Their paths would have crossed had he been coming to the Thorntons' to look for her.

The truth was Pascal had forgotten about the time once he'd decided to pay a call on Justine McCall. Melissa would not be returning home for a few hours, he'd told himself, so he had impulsively decided to pay a visit on the very interesting Justine. He had at least two hours before he had to get back home.

When Pascal arrived at Justine's door she was sitting in her parlor surrounded by a myriad of ribbons and colorful sheets of paper, wrapping her Christmas gifts. It had been the perfect time for her to get her nephew's gifts wrapped and placed under her tree, since he was gone for the afternoon. She had to scramble over things to get to the door. "Now I wonder who that could be," she mumbled to herself.

Pascal stood there with a smile on his face and a huge tin of chocolates in his hands. "Well, Pascal—come in but ignore the mess in my parlor. I was wrapping gifts." She laughed, ushering him through the door.

"It's looking a lot like Christmas at your house, Justine," he remarked, glancing around her parlor. Her parlor was twice as large as his. Packages were lined under the Christmas tree and she had wreaths made of dried herbs and flowers which gave off a most pleasant aroma. There also the smells of pine and cedar permeating the room.

"Please sit down, Pascal, and let me get some of this stuff out of the way," she said.

"Oh, I'm not staying long, Justine. I just wanted to come by for a minute and bring you this little gift before I went back to work tomorrow."

She took the tin of chocolates and thanked him. All the paper and ribbons she piled to one side of the settee and then she asked him if he'd like a glass of sherry. Pascal accepted her offer and ended up having a second glass, even though he didn't really care for sherry.

His short visit became a rather long one; the clock was striking four and the two of them were still talking away like two magpies.

Justine knew that her nephew had gone to pick up Pascal's daughter at the Thorntons' to take her to Meadowbrook. She too noticed the clock on the mantel. The chances were that the two of them were out at Meadowbrook right now. Dear God, Pascal would be in a frenzy if he knew that!

Here the two of them were, thoroughly enjoying themselves as they talked and sipped their sherry. He was nothing like the stiff, remote person she'd first suspected him to be. He seemed to like her rather earthy, worldly air. This surprised and pleased her. Justine had learned long ago that she had stunned some gents around Natchez with her independent Texas ways, but this didn't faze her at all. James McCall had loved her. That was all that had mattered to Justine.

When the clock chimed five, Justine began to get nervous, for she wondered what Pascal's reaction would be if her nephew suddenly walked through the door — which he could do anytime now.

The truth was Justine didn't want to mar this nice, pleasant relationship she was now sharing with Pascal Rocheleau.

Her worst fear was realized just a short time later when her nephew came bounding in to greet her, suddenly stopping short when he spotted Pascal Rocheleau. Never had she witnessed her nephew so dumbfounded that he couldn't speak. It took him a minute before he could finally find his tongue and greet Pascal.

Pascal responded to his greeting, "Good evening to you, too, Lance."

The vivacious Justine came up with a most clever idea to help the two young lovers. She turned to Pascal to suggest to him, "Pascal, I have a wonderful idea! I've a huge beef roast baking in my oven. Why don't we send Lance over to fetch Melissa. We could all share a nice dinner. Ah, Pascal, don't say no to me. It is the holiday season, so let us celebrate."

Lance stood there, amazed, for he'd never witnessed his aunt use her wiles on a man as she was now doing with Pascal Rocheleau. He also saw that Pascal was succumbing to those wiles.

"You make it awfully hard to refuse a good roast beef dinner, Justine." He laughed. "I never expected this when I came to call on you today. Are you sure?"

"Pascal, I never say anything I don't mean," she declared. Both she and Pascal knew what she was talking about, even though Lance was in the dark about that. She referred to that stormy encounter at Pascal's haberdashery shop.

Lance was utterly confused as he got back in his buggy to go over to the Rocheleau house to fetch Melissa. He had had no inkling that his aunt and Pascal Rocheleau were on such friendly terms.

By the time Lance knocked at her door, Melissa had finished feeding little Snowball and was becoming more concerned about her father. To see Lance standing there at the door, after he'd just told her goodbye, put her in a state of shock. "Lance? What are you doing here?" she asked him.

He grinned. "I know I'm the last person you expected to see, and I'll try to explain, Melissa. I was sent to get you to bring you over to my aunt's house for dinner tonight."

"I can't do that, Lance. My father . . ."

"Your father is there now! He was there when I got home from the Thorntons'. Seems he and my aunt had been having a most pleasant visit."

"My father? My father is visiting with your Aunt Justine? Oh, Lance—this is all so confusing."

"I know, honey. I'm just as mixed up as you are right now. Seems like some things have been going on that neither you or I were aware of."

The four of them spent a wonderful evening together. By the time Lance had returned with Melissa, Justine had her table draped in a frosty white tablecloth and candlelight was glowing in her dining room. There was a most magnificent beef roast surrounded by carrots and potatoes resting on a massive platter. She'd sliced a freshly baked loaf of bread and served the fine wine Pascal had brought her.

Melissa was aware of the relaxed and comfortable way her father and Justine acted toward one another. It was nice to see him so lighthearted and gay! Melissa kept glancing across the table at Lance, asking herself if she was dreaming all this. Here the four of them sat eating dinner together and laughing and talking.

When dinner was over, Justine asked Melissa to help her clean up, explaining once they got into the kitchen, "I thought it would give Pascal and Lance a chance to get better acquainted, honey. He just has to like Lance once he gets to know him."

Melissa agreed and began to help her gather up the dishes. Justine asked her what she thought about Meadowbrook.

"It's beautiful out there. I love it!" Melissa told her as she turned to go back into the dining room to gather up the last of the dishes. She came back to the kitchen with a pleased look on her face, announcing to Justine that her father and Lance seemed to be engaged in a very pleasant conversation.

"Everything will be just fine, honey," Justine said.

"It's just got to be. Lance asked me to marry him,"

Melissa blurted out before she'd realized what she'd said.

Justine stopped washing dishes and anxiously asked, "And did you accept?"

Melissa smiled and nodded her head. Justine gave her a warm embrace declaring, "Oh, Melissa—I'm so happy I could almost cry! Mercy, what a day and night this has turned out to be!"

By the time the two of them joined the men in the parlor, Melissa was sure that she and Lance had his aunt's approval. Now if they would only be so lucky with her father.

Justine didn't hesitate a minute to go over to sit with Pascal on the settee, so Melissa moved across the parlor to stand beside the overstuffed chair where Lance was sitting.

Melissa was convinced that her father was smitten! She'd never seen him act like this around any other woman. Melissa could not have been more pleased.

What Melissa or Justine didn't know when they entered the parlor was that Lance had decided to speak honestly with Melissa's father and tell him that he'd asked his daughter to marry him. To Lance, it seemed like the perfect time to announce the news.

Much calmer than Lance had expected, Pascal asked him, "Did my daughter accept your proposal?"

"Yes, sir—she did. But it's important to me to have your blessing."

"Melissa's happiness is all I ever wanted. If she wishes to marry you, then you certainly have my blessing." Pascal extended his hand to Lance. Lance gave him a vigorous handshake. What a strange turn of events!

Justine's clock was chiming nine and Pascal realized that it was time they were leaving for home. The weekend was over and he had a shop to open on Monday morning.

He told Justine that it was time for them to leave and he thanked her for a most delicious dinner and evening. A sly smile came on his face as he remarked to Justine, "Looks like we've got a wedding coming up, Justine. Lance told me that he'd asked Melissa to marry him and she'd said yes."

Melissa gave out a startled gasp but Lance reached over to clasp her hand and calm her. "It's all right, honey. He gave me his blessing."

"Oh, Lance!" she said. She crossed the room and flung her arms around her father's neck. "Oh Papa, thank you!"

Justine walked over to give her nephew a big hug and kiss. She sought to tease him. "You mean I'm finally going to be rid of you? Now your little bride can keep you on the straight and narrow path!"

Lance laughed. "Guess you are, Aunt Justine. I have been a handful, haven't I?"

She grinned up at him. "Nothing I couldn't handle, young man."

Everything changed for Pascal and Melissa after that Sunday night, as well as for Justine McCall and her nephew, Lance. There were new Christmas plans to be made.

Pascal had insisted that Christmas Eve be celebrated at his home, since it was Melissa's seventeenth birthday. He'd told Justine that he would prepare his fabulous roast duck for their dinner.

"Then you and Melissa must share Christmas Day at my house, Pascal, and share the wild turkey Lance will provide for our table. I'll have all the good dishes we always had back in Texas."

Lance and Melissa were both already envisioning this time next year. Lance had told her that he'd go out and cut a fine tree that would reach the ceiling of their parlor. He grinned. "Now what will we have, Melissa? Will it be roast duck or wild turkey that I go out there in the woods around Meadowbrook to shoot?"

The cunning Melissa was ready to answer him without any hesitation. "It's very simple, Lance. We shall have both."

He'd roared with laughter and taken her into his arms to plant a kiss on her lips.

Pascal wanted everything to be perfect for this Christmas Eve, for it would be the last one Melissa spent under his roof. Renée came over to prepare delectable French desserts, but Pascal took charge of preparing the duck before he placed it in the oven to bake.

For his daughter's birthday, he purchased a lovely pearl necklace and earrings. A bride had to wear pearls on her wedding day, he felt. So soon she was going to become Lance's bride.

He bought another gift when he purchased the pearls for his daughter. Two weeks ago, he would have considered it to be extravagant and never would he have considered spending so much money on a lady other than his daughter or sister, Renée. But Justine McCall was a woman who was so warm and generous that he found himself wanting to be generous and giving of himself. The truth was, Pascal found himself in love and he had never expected that to happen to him again. But it had happened! By some miracle, it had happened and he could not deny it any longer.

Renée could not have been happier for Pascal, and now she knew that she had been right, weeks ago, when she'd told him about her friend, Justine McCall. She would be delighted to have Justine as her sister-in-law. She observed the wonders Justine had already worked on Pascal during Christmas Eve afternoon when she and Pascal worked in his kitchen. He was like a completely different man and she'd not seen him this happy since he had been married to Christine.

Justine had already invited her to come to her house on Christmas Day. Exuberantly Justine had declared, "We're to be family now, Renée. Isn't it wonderful?"

"I couldn't be happier, Justine. I'll be delighted to share Christmas Day with you," Renée told her.

Whether it was the traditions of the French or families like the McCalls and the Averys born and bred in Texas country, the joyous spirit of Christmas was the same. There were the smells of pines and evergreens mingling with the aroma of the good foods cooking in the kitchen. There was the twinkling brilliance of the many candles glowing throughout the house, along with the splendor of the tall Christmas tree colorfully decorated. Pascal had kept and cherished his decorations since the first Christmas his little daughter had entered his life. Some looked a little shabby and worn, but they were always there on his Christmas tree.

Justine chanced to come in the kitchen when Pascal was there alone. He smiled at her, declaring that it was a glorious evening and that he hated to see it end.

"Then let's not let it end, Pascal. Let's just pretend it's still the holiday." She smiled up at him. Suddenly, Justine found herself encircled in Pascal's arms and being kissed most ardently.

When he finally released her, Justine gasped, "Dear God, Pascal—you're—you're a man who never ceases to amaze me!"

"Really, Justine? Well, I'll probably amaze you again with what I'm going to ask you but I shall ask you anyway. Would you consider changing your name to Rocheleau?"

"You asking me to marry you, Pascal?"

"That's exactly what I'm asking!"

Justine's usual glib tongue couldn't work for her right

211

then, for she was too overcome with emotion. She didn't cry, but there was a mist of tears in her brilliant blue eyes. All she could manage to give Pascal for an answer was a nod of her head, but that was enough for Pascal; she'd told him she would marry him.

Pascal held her close in his arms for a while until she was ready to join the others in his parlor. When the two of them came back to the parlor, their faces were just as radiant and glowing as Lance's and Melissa's, but they made no announcement to their families.

On Christmas Day the five of them were together once again at Justine's house. Both Justine and Melissa were wearing bright scarlet gowns. Both looked so very lovely, Pascal was thinking as he admired his daughter and the lady he was to marry.

Justine had not been boasting when she'd said that nothing could compare to the Christmas feast they'd had back in Texas. The wild turkey and the dressing were delicious. Her pecan pies were so wonderful that Pascal asked for a second piece.

Justine could not have been more pleased that Pascal ate with such relish! Renée and Melissa seemed to savor her dinner, too. Before the meal ended, Pascal stood up to announce to Lance and Melissa, "You young people can have your wedding first but then there's to be another wedding in this family. Justine and I are going to be married."

Neither Melissa or Lance was prepared for this news, but neither of them could have been happier. They were both thinking that there could never be another Christmas like this.

As he kissed Melissa good night on Christmas night, Lance found himself very impatient for the next six days to pass. On New Year's Eve she would be his wife.

212

With his eyes adoring her, he told her, "But for you, Melissa, none of this would have happened. I fell in love with you, and because of that, my aunt and your father found a love that neither of them expected to know at their age. You are the miracle that made all this happen!"

Her bright green eyes sparkled as she smiled up at him. "I shall remind you of this, Lance Avery, in the years to come."

"You won't have to, honey. I'll never forget this Christmas holiday," he told her.

It was a Christmas when not one but two miracles happened!

Golden Angel

by Patricia Pellicane

Joseph Gray Wolf stood just inside the doorway to the schoolhouse. Hidden within the shadows of the narrow entranceway, he watched Miss Angel Shaw guide the children through a Nativity play, scheduled for the last day of school before the Christmas recess. A quick glance around the small room brought a scowl to his thin lips, for it was obvious that his son watched as well. Damn fool. What did the boy think he was doing getting involved with someone like her?

That was just the problem. Gray Wolf knew from personal experience that seventeen-year-old boys rarely thought before acting. And when they did, most often it wasn't their heads that guided those actions.

It was all her fault, of course. She was old enough to know better than to involve herself with a child. It wasn't so much her age that Gray Wolf objected to. He figured every young man should experience an older woman at least once. And if it had been one of the women over Lucky's place, Gray Wolf would have felt only mild amusement. It was the fact that she was the town's new teacher — the town's new white teacher — that troubled him.

Gray Wolf had nothing against whites. Most of his friends were white, and some of them mighty fine folks. He just didn't want his son to marry one.

Twenty years ago he'd done as much and that had proven to be a disaster. In love for the first time, he'd brought his adored Alice with him to settle in Clearwater, Texas. The marriage had lasted exactly ten and a half months. A month after Johnny's birth (the only good thing to come from the marriage), Alice had apparently had enough of being the wife of an Indian. One morning she'd suddenly announced, she hated ranch life and was leaving. Just like that. Leaving. It didn't matter that she'd be leaving her son as well as her husband. Nothing mattered but that she get away.

The truth of the matter was, she hadn't been accepted. In those days many hadn't taken kindly to the idea of an Indian and a white together. Of course things were better now. People were apt to be more open minded, more accepting, but Gray Wolf hadn't cared about acceptance then and he didn't care now. He wasn't about to live his life yearning for anyone's sanction. Anyone who knew him, knew that much.

Now, almost twenty years later, he was a respected member of the community. Gray Wolf's thin lips twisted into a cynical, humorless smile at the thought. Money had proven to be a powerful equalizer. A successful rancher, no matter his race, was bound to gain a degree of respect.

His dark eyes moved over the young woman he'd come to see. Judging by the looks of this one, a man wouldn't suspect she was after his money. But Joseph Gray Wolf was old enough and experienced enough to know you couldn't tell what was in a woman's heart by the looks of her. Despite the look of innocence of this one, there was little doubt that she was after his money. Why else would she have taken up with a boy? Only she'd picked the wrong family this time. John Gray Wolf was not going to marry a white.

Joseph's mouth tightened into an even thinner line. He

didn't care what he had to do. His son was never going to know that kind of pain.

Gray Wolf folded his arms across a wide chest and leaned against the wall. Half hidden in the shadows, he watched the woman. Angel. He frowned. What kind of a name was that? Gray Wolf's dark eyes narrowed as he studied her more closely. He'd noticed her the day she arrived in town three weeks ago. What man wouldn't have noticed?

He'd come into town for supplies and watched as she was helped from the stage coach. She was smaller than most. At first he thought she was only a girl, but a northerner had been blowing off the prairie that day and a gust of wind had pressed her cape against her body. No young girl had curves so lush.

Now, surrounded by a group of boisterous children, everyone of them ecstatic about the coming recess and of course the joyous festivities synonymous with Christmas, she looked every inch the innocent. What else had he expected? A painted face and low-cut gown? Not likely. At least not while she played the part of a sedate school marm.

Gray Wolf muffled a derisive snort behind the clearing of his throat, as he watched her graceful movements, her petite form, the way the children cheerfully obeyed her every order. She was beautiful. No matter how he might try, he couldn't deny that fact. Through the windows, beams of cold afternoon sunlight slashed into the room. One caught her hair and for just an instant the blond mass of curls looked like spun gold. One could almost imagine that the name "Angel" fit. One could, that is, if one didn't know better.

His son had been hanging around here for weeks. At the first sign of what was now obvious, he should have gone to the board and had her fired. He would have done just that, except he didn't want to cause his son

217

embarrassment. At seventeen, John thought he was a man. Joseph knew John would only resent his father's interference.

No. This was the best course of action. He'd speak with the woman and warn her away from his son. Pay her if need be. If that didn't work, then . . . Joseph's gaze moved over the woman's lush form with some real appreciation. If that didn't work, there just might be other ways to achieve his ends.

The children were dismissed and, after struggling into their outer clothing, ran from the building with wild shouts of glee, as if they'd been freed from prison at last. John lingered a minute longer. Joseph cursed as he watched his son and the woman. Heads together, they murmured a few intimate words, no doubt agreeing to future assignations. A moment later Johnny followed a young girl through the back door and outside.

Angel Shaw locked the door after the two and was washing down the blackboard when Joseph sauntered between two rows of desks toward the woman. "Miss Shaw?"

Angel turned, smiled, and wiped her damp hand across her dark gray skirt just before she offered her hand to his in greeting. Gray Wolf purposely ignored the extended hand. He figured it was best if they got started on the right foot. And making a pretense of civility was hardly what he had in mind.

Angel merely blinked her surprise at his rudeness, but made no comment. She knew there were men who simply didn't realize the manners that were expected of them. Odd, but by the looks of him, she would have thought this man's manners equal to the best. Angel almost smiled at the thought, knowing first impressions often proved false.

He was dressed in clean, neatly pressed work clothes. Expensive work clothes. His trousers, although perhaps a

218

bit too tightly fitted, were of the best quality. Over his blue work shirt he wore a costly leather vest. His boots were newly shined, the hat in his hand a Stetson. She knew at first glance, of course, that he was Indian. He had high cheekbones, a dark complexion, and almost blue/black hair that barely reached his collar. A very attractive man, Angel silently mused.

"I'd like to speak to you, if you don't mind. And even if you do mind," he finished silently.

"Of course." Angel smiled, moved to her desk, and sat. The moment she did, she realized her mistake. Now she had to crane her neck to see the man and he, for some unknown reason, had ignored her silent but obvious invitation to sit across from her.

There was a moment of strained silence before Angel said, "I'm sorry. As you know, I'm new to the position here. I don't know all the parents yet. You are . . ."

"Joseph Gray Wolf."

Angel frowned for just a second before a light of recognition lit up her blue eyes. "Johnny's father. Of course. I should have known. He looks just like you, doesn't he?"

Joseph cursed at the sight of her warm smile and the things it was doing to his insides. Damn all women to hell for the ability to smile like that and for the things those smiles did to men. "You might as well stop that right now. It ain't gonna work."

Angel blinked at the oddness of his response and tipped her head just a fraction to the side. Apparently she'd missed something. "Excuse me?"

"Kissin' up."

Angel frowned in confusion. Just what was this man talking about? "I'm sorry, Mr. Gray Wolf, but I fail to—"

"I doubt it, but you ought to be sorry."

Angel took a deep breath, held it for a second, and released it slowly. "Perhaps we could start again, Mr. Gray Wolf. There seems to be a problem with communication here. I don't understand—"

Again he cut her off. "You understand all right. Don't come off with that innocent act, lady. That won't work either."

Angel eyed the handsome, dark man standing before her desk. His whole body appeared tense as if he were ready to jump across the small space that separated them. Something was wrong. Something was obviously and seriously wrong. She felt a chill of apprehension. Could it be that he was dangerous? Yes, she decided. He definitely had an air of danger about him, but what Angel couldn't understand was, why should that danger be directed at her? The back door was locked. She gave a wistful glance toward the front door and wondered what her chances were of making it past him. "Why don't you sit down, Mr. Gray Wolf, and make yourself comfortable?" If she could just get him to sit, she might gain an extra half-second. That might be all she needed if it came to where she had to make a run for it.

"Said the spider to the fly?"

Angel pressed her lips together and tried to concentrate. The man was obviously upset, but after some consideration on her part, Angel decided he posed no physical threat. The real problem here was he spoke in indecipherable half-sentences, instead of clear English. She tried again. "Mr. Gray Wolf, apparently you have a problem. I'd like to help you and perhaps I could, if I knew what it was about."

"It's about you and my son."

"Johnny?" Angel's stiff smile grew warm again. "He is a nice boy. You should be proud."

"I am. And I aim to keep him nice."

Angel would have had to be deaf not to detect the obvious threat. "Meaning?"

"Meaning, keep away from him."

Angel leaned back and allowed herself a moment to

fully understand that order. It took at least that long, for she was positive no one could be stupid enough to actually believe what he was insinuating. "Are you implying—"

"I'm not implying a thing, lady. I'm tellin' you straight out. Stay away from my son."

Angel couldn't for the moment say what she felt. Astonishment, yes, but mingled with that emotion came a surge of anger so powerful she wondered how she managed to keep it under control. She couldn't remember when she'd ever been so insulted. How dare he make such wild and ridiculous accusations! Angel longed to rant, to tell this oaf just what she thought of him and his rash, idiotic conclusions, but instinctively knew no amount of denial on her part would matter. He had no proof. He could have no proof. Still, she couldn't allow the moment to pass. She had to defend herself, for to remain quiet would only further the man's erroneous suspicions. "You're not serious, of course."

"I'm damn serious, lady. If you knew me, you wouldn't have to ask such a stupid question."

"I've only this meeting to judge, Mr. Gray Wolf, but I think I can honestly say, the last thing I want is to get to know you."

"Right, they all say that, don't they?"

Angel heaved a weary sigh. "Mr. Gray Wolf. I haven't the vaguest notion as to whom 'they' are, nor to what you are talking about." He was about to interrupt her again when she cut him off with a raised hand and, "Nor do I care. You're manners are deplorable. And your common sense apparently nonexistent. I'd appreciate it if you would leave my classroom." And when he made no move to obey, she insisted with a sharp, "Now!"

There wouldn't come a day when Joseph Gray Wolf would take orders from a woman. And the sooner she got that straight, the better. "I'll leave as soon as we get

221

this settled."

"There is nothing to settle. I am at least eight years older than Johnny and I promise you there is nothing—"

Gray Wolf shot her a sly somehow wicked smirk. "Some might say they like 'em young. That way they can teach 'em the way they like it best."

Angel Lettia Shaw, being exactly the innocent she portrayed, only blinked at his last statement. "What in the world are you talking about?"

"I'm talkin' about a woman like you playin' with my boy."

Angel's cheeks grew redder than a ripe tomato as she realized his meaning. "Mr. Gray Wolf, you are the most, the most . . ." Angel was at a loss for words. She was so angry, so insulted, that she couldn't think what to call this man who was most deserving of all insults.

"So I've been told." Gray Wolf stood before her, his thumbs hooked inside the waistband of tight, low-slung jeans, his fingers hovering over, almost cupping the bulge beneath his belt. Angel's cheeks grew redder yet, when she realized her gaze was level to his hands. She came quickly to her feet, unable to imagine a stance more arrogant, or a man more insufferable. Angel knew she had to be imagining things. The man was not pressing his hips forward in an unseemly pose of male arrogance. "But you won't be gettin' any of it, darlin'. And if you're smart, you won't try to get any from my son, either. He's just a kid. He wouldn't stand a chance against someone like you."

Angel shivered her disgust. "You're insane." The moment she said it, Angel wondered if she hadn't gone too far. She knew the man had to be stark raving mad. As far as she could see, there was no other reason behind his abominable behavior and horrible accusations, but she'd once heard to accuse the insane of being insane was hardly a wise course of action.

222

Gray Wolf realized this conversation was getting them nowhere. He accused, while she simply denied. What was needed here was an even more direct approach. "How much will it cost me?"

Angel merely blinked her confusion. Now what was he talking about?

"How much?" he repeated.

"How much what?"

"Money. How much do you want to leave my son alone and get the hell out of here?"

Angel thought her cheeks had burned before, but now they felt on fire. She hated to give this beast the benefit of an explanation, but what else could she do? She couldn't allow this misunderstanding to go on. Her reputation and perhaps her job were at stake. She took a deep breath and began with, "Mr. Gray Wolf, you don't understand. The fact of the matter is—"

Gray Wolf cut her off. "Oh, I understand all right. I know how a seventeen-year-old feels when a woman like you . . ." Joseph figured it would solve no purpose to insult her more than absolutely necessary, so he cut himself off then finished with, "Just name your price."

It was too much. How dare he accuse her of something so reprehensible? Angel couldn't remember a time in her life when she'd felt half as angry. She sneered to his obvious contempt. "You don't have enough."

Gray Wolf laughed, happy to finally have her admit to the truth. "Oh, I think I might? Will a thousand dollars do it?"

Angel wondered if her cheeks would ever resume their normal color. She took a deep steadying breath. Gray Wolf didn't miss the rise and fall of her chest and cursed as he felt a stirring where he didn't want any stirrings. "Your son and I are not involved," she said flatly.

Gray Wolf ignored her statement. He knew better. "You'd better take what you can get, lady. My offer isn't

223

likely to be repeated."

"And I thank God for that. Now, if you've insulted me to the best of your ability, I'll ask you again to leave this schoolhouse."

"I haven't begun to insult you."

"You've done a remarkable job so far."

He wasn't about to apologize. If she didn't like the things he was saying, she should have thought about the consequences before she'd taken up with Johnny. "I'm not leavin' till I straighten out this mess."

"Mr. Gray Wolf, I doubt you have the ability to straighten out a straight line. If I've ever met a man more foolish, I've no knowledge of it. I'll ask you again to leave my schoolroom."

Gray Wolf watched her come around the desk. From her expression, she appeared ready to put him out by force. Gray Wolf grinned at the thought. His dark gaze moved over the length of her. She was such a little thing, but full in all the right places. He couldn't rightly blame his son for wanting her. If he didn't know better, he could almost want her himself. Gray Wolf felt his belly tighten again as he allowed the thought of taking this one to bed. Damn. He did know better and it didn't seem to matter none.

Idly he wondered how she'd react to a man a bit more skilled in the art of lovemaking. His voice grew suddenly low and silky. "Lady, if you're so set on havin' yourself a man, I reckon I could accommodate your needs."

It was then that his incredible actions became most incredible of all. Angel watched in wide-eyed, dumbfounded fascination as he moved toward her and reached an arm around her waist, drawing her body scandalously close to his. Later she would put her lack of resistance to the fact that she hadn't imagined what the man was about. And if she hadn't imagined it, how could she then be expected to stop him?

224

But the truth of the matter was, his face lowered very slowly to hers. Angel had every chance to escape his hold, to stop this catastrophic happening before it was too late.

His mouth came down hard on hers. Angel knew an instant of pain and a deep sense of degradation. His kiss held no tenderness, no gentleness. It was as if he were punishing her mouth, showing her clearly his contempt.

She began to struggle when something happened. Amazingly the kiss seemed to grow softer, more tender, and his lips sucked gently as if he were tasting something incredibly lovely. She heard a low moan as his mouth brushed softly against hers, testing for a response. Angel couldn't say if it was simply surprise or the tingling sensation of flesh against flesh that caused her to gasp. Something did. And Gray Wolf took full advantage of her parted lips.

His arms pulled her slight form forward, hard against his body. Oddly detached, almost as if she watched this impossible happening from afar, Angel felt the breath whoosh from her lungs and listened to the greedy sound of enjoyment as he breathed deeply of her.

He almost smiled at the show of virginal innocence, no doubt meant to lead a man to distraction. But he knew it wouldn't be long before she forgot her pretense and was eagerly kissing him in return.

Straining for air, Angel gasped, and took the scent of him deep into her lungs. Instead of clearing her mind, the much-needed oxygen seemed only to drag her farther into some curious debilitating haze. His lips were plucking at her mouth, pulling her lips farther and farther apart. What was he doing? What did he want?

Had he forced her, or in any way hurt her, she would have fought him like a woman gone mad. But the truth of the matter was, Angel found herself so astonished by whatever it was he was doing to her mouth that she forgot the first few moments of this kiss. She forgot to fight, forgot to step away from his now, oh so gentle hold. All she could think to do was wait and see what else he had in mind.

Angel thought she liked the slippery feel of his tongue over her lips, liked it most especially when he dipped it in her mouth and tickled the inside of her lip. She wouldn't have thought she'd like something so odd, but amazingly enough, she did. How had he ever thought of such a thing?

After all, it wasn't as if Angel had never been kissed before and she had never thought of it.

She tried to clear her mind, to think, but found herself barely capable of the feat. Through a hazy fog, she could only assume this was a kiss, of sorts. The fact was she'd never been kissed like this. In her twenty-four years, no man had ever held her so firmly to his hard body. (Were they all this hard?) No man had ever murmured words she couldn't quite understand as he discovered the dark secrets of her mouth.

Her arms had somehow gotten twisted around his neck. She didn't know how that could have happened, but as it turned out, it was a good thing it had. She couldn't breathe all that well and without air she was getting just a touch light-headed. She found herself leaning into him. Well, it was either that or fall to the floor. Oddly enough it never occurred to her to step out of his arms.

Someone moaned. It wasn't her, of course. There was no reason for her to moan just because he was kissing her lips again and again, stealing her breath, which in turn made her terribly dizzy. And the next thing she knew he was rubbing his tongue over hers. She wouldn't have believed it, but that did feel good. Actually it felt better than just good, but that was still no reason to moan.

226

She gasped as he sucked her tongue into his mouth. Lord, that was a sensation, wasn't it? And there was that moan again. She wished whoever was doing it would stop. It was annoying when she was trying to concentrate on something. The moaning stopped, but Angel couldn't remember what she'd been trying to concentrate on.

His hips pressed hers to the desk. The hands that had been around her waist edged slowly up her back, over her shoulders and down her chest.

He touched her softness then, heard her startled gasp, listened to her moan of pleasure, felt her move eagerly against him, and rockets went off inside his head.

Gray Wolf shuddered as he forced aside his need for more of this. It had been a mistake on his part. Kissing her wasn't likely to get him anywhere. Nothing would be solved by losing control. Nothing except maybe having his son hate him for the rest of his life.

Gray Wolf cursed imagining Johnny in her arms. The thought made him oddly angry. He didn't know why. All he knew was that it did. If Johnny kissed her, if he so much as touched her, the kid wouldn't stand a chance. Her kisses were too sweet, her body too soft. Gray Wolf knew Johnny didn't have enough experience to fight her allure. For just an instant he wondered if he did.

That was a damn stupid notion. Of course he did. Why he wasn't the least bit affected by her kiss. God, he couldn't count the women he'd kissed over the years. And not one of them had felt any better or worse than another.

Except maybe this one. No, damn it! Gray Wolf pushed himself from her arms, feeling a surge of emotion that in another man might have been mistaken for terror. He almost laughed in ridicule. Terror? That would be the day when a little wisp of a thing like this one could frighten him.

He was gasping for every breath, his body aching for more of this pleasure. When was the last time he'd wanted a woman like this? Jesus, he couldn't remember ever wanting like this.

Even if Angel's senses had not been devastated by his kiss, her lack of experience was enough to keep her ignorant of the fact that Gray Wolf was equally as shaken as she. She never saw the dazed look in his eyes nor heard the quiver in his voice over the pounding of her heart, the roar in her ears. "If it's a man you want, darlin', remember that I'm available. Just stay away from the kid."

He couldn't resist another quick, slightly rough, but delicious sampling of her mouth, a sampling that left her and most especially her knees dangerously weak, before he spun suddenly around and walked away without another word.

It took a good two minutes after the door shut behind him before Angel's breathing returned to normal and her mind began to clear. But when it did, she was filled with the most mortifying sense of horror. What had she done? What had she allowed him to do? And then her embarrassment disappeared as a surge of righteous anger took hold. None of this was her fault and she had no cause for self-recrimination. It was his fault. His alone. And she hated him for his evil accusations as well as his appalling maltreatment. Angel had cause to wonder if she'd live through rage such as this. All she knew was, if she didn't hit or throw something, she was going to explode.

"Peace on earth." Angel grunted out the words that were pasted to one wall of her schoolroom as she threw her globe against the wall, barely missing a gaily decorated window. "And good will to all," she sneered, repeating the words pasted to the opposite wall as she shoved her chair across the shining wooden floor, satisfied only when it clattered to its back after hitting the wall and knocking down a pine cone wreath. "Except, of course,

228

in your case, Mr. Gray Wolf. The heavenly messengers didn't mean a beast like you." Angel kicked her desk drawer shut with a loud bang and a startled cry of pain. Her fist hit against the desk's surface as she tried to control the misery she'd just delivered to her toe. Agony engulfed her brain and she danced around off balance for just as long as it took her to fall into the decorated tree, knocking both herself and the little tree to the floor. Angel blinked with some surprise at the destruction her uncharacteristic tantrum had caused.

A moment later she lifted a thick strand of golden hair from over one eye and repinned it to the knot at the back of her head, just before she came again to her feet. She limped to the tree and stood it again in the corner even as she whispered, "Merry Christmas, Mr. Gray Wolf, you swine."

"Who told you?" Johnny knew his father would find out eventually. He just hadn't expected the wagging tongues in this town to go to work so soon.

"No one had to tell me. Your horse is outside the schoolhouse every day. I know what's going on and I'm telling you to keep away from her." Joseph Gray Wolf sat in his study and watched his son's dark eyes narrow at the order, knowing he wouldn't take kindly to such a demand.

Johnny glared at his father. "And I'm telling you, mind your own business."

"You are my business, boy."

"I'm not a boy. I haven't been a boy for a long time."

"Well, you're acting like one."

"And you're acting like a crotchety old fool."

Gray Wolf slammed his hand upon his desk. "She's too old for you, damn it."

Johnny knew most girls married around the age of fourteen or fifteen. But Elly wasn't much beyond that.

229

How could his father possibly think sixteen was too old? He shot Gray Wolf a ridiculing look, knowing her age wasn't the real problem here. It was the fact that she was white. It might have been unspoken, but all his life, Johnny knew a white woman wouldn't be acceptable as a wife. That when the time came he was to look for an Indian girl. Well, it was too bad what his father thought, what his father wanted. Johnny was going to marry Elly May Clay, and if that caused an irreversible rift between them, so be it. "She is not."

Gray Wolf took a deep breath and tried to control the need to rage. If he lost his temper, he'd never accomplish a damn thing but the alienation of his son. The boy was enough like his father to do just the opposite of what Gray Wolf wanted and no amount of insisting on his part was going to stop it. All Gray Wolf could do was try to coerce him to the right direction and that could never be done with direct orders. "All right. I understand what you're going through. I can see why you find her attractive. But if you want to sleep with her, you don't have to—"

"What are you talking about?"

"I'm talking about the fact that you don't have to marry a woman just because you want her in bed."

Johnny leaned both hands on the desk. His face was inches from his father's, a picture of fury, his eyes blazing with the emotion. Gray Wolf knew the boy was on the edge of violence. He wasn't afraid of his own son, but he knew if it ever came to using fists, their relationship would never be the same again. His voice was a low husk of warning, "She's not that kind of a woman . . . and if you ever—"

"All right, all right, calm down."

Damn, this was a hell of a lot more serious than he'd first thought. Gray Wolf hadn't imagined that his son was this deeply involved. He tried another tactic. "Your mother was white, Johnny. It took less than a year and she knew, we both knew, it had been a mistake to marry."

"All white women are not the same."

Gray Wolf wouldn't have sworn to the truth of that statement. His wife had hurt him badly. After she left, he'd hated her for a long time. That hatred, although dead and buried now, had left him with a distrust of all white women. He couldn't help but imagine them all the same, for the ones he'd known since Alice were strangely intrigued and yet at the same time appalled at the thought of being touched by an Indian. Still, in this case Gray Wolf figured it best to appear to agree to his son's statement. "I know, but—"

"There are no buts. She's nothing like my mother. And I love her."

Gray Wolf sighed at the finality of those words. There was no hope . . . unless . . . If he spoke again with Miss Angel Shaw, would he be able to convince her to see his way of thinking? If he upped his offer, would that make a difference?

Damn, but he didn't want to see her again. Not with what had happened the last time. He hadn't slept last night what with thinking about the way her mouth had felt under his. She was a beautiful woman who tasted as good as she looked.

God! How could it have happened that he found himself attracted to his son's woman? It was all he needed to round out a perfectly miserable situation.

"Elly is going to be my wife, with or without your blessing."

Johnny slammed the door as he walked from the room. Gray Wolf watched the door for a long moment before he breathed a sigh of despair. He pushed aside his apprehension. He might not want to see her again, but there was no hope for it. He had to talk to—

Gray Wolf came suddenly to his feet, a look of shock

231

in his dark eyes. *Who the hell was Elly?*

A distant cloud of dust caught Angel's attention. Beneath a thickly branched tree, she sat with Mary, enjoying a break from the harsh afternoon sun. A rider was coming. Angel frowned. The lonely stretch of dirt road led only to the orphanage and was rarely traveled. Angel could only wonder who could be riding this far from town.

From atop a grassy knoll in an otherwise flat landscape, Gray Wolf had watched a horse graze on sparse grass, while still hitched to a wagon. He sat upon a black stallion, his dark gaze moving over the woman and a little girl. Even from this distance, he had no doubt who was trespassing upon his land. No one else in these parts had hair that shone like spun gold.

What, he wondered, was she doing out here? A wicked grin curved his lips. Gray Wolf figured the answer to that question was obvious. She wanted to see him again. Wanted to see him as much as he wanted to see her.

Why then had she brought a child with her? He nodded as he realized the answer. She probably didn't want to give him the impression that she was forward. Gray Wolf shrugged. She needn't have worried on that score. Gray Wolf enjoyed forward women most of all. Still, he didn't mind the games women played either, for the games only added to the enticement, the excitement of the chase, and in the end only increased the pleasure.

Mary sat across from her. With blue eyes wide, she imitated her mentor's every movement. "Show me how to act like a lady, Miss Shaw. I'm going to be a lady, just like you, when I grow up."

Angel smiled as the little girl smoothed the skirt of her new pink dress. Smoothed it in exactly the same fashion as Angel had just smoothed her own. Today was Mary's

232

birthday. She was six and Angel had given her the dress as a present. It was obvious the little girl had never owned anything half so lovely. She couldn't stop touching it. "There is more to being a lady than correct manners, Mary."

"I know. The ladies in church dip their heads behind their fans, like this"—Mary held up her hand as if it were a fan—"when they want to whisper about someone."

A fine example of Christian kindness, Angel silently mused. "A real lady wouldn't whisper about anyone."

Mary looked confused. "Why?"

"Because she wouldn't want to hurt another's feelings."

"Jane and Annabel hurt mine. Does that mean they won't grow up to be ladies?"

"I'm afraid it does, sweetheart. How do they hurt your feelings?"

"They say things about me."

"What kind of things?"

If it weren't for the pain in her eyes telling a different story, Angel might have believed the little girl's shrug of indifference. "They call me names and laugh when it's play time and everyone goes outside except me."

Angel waited a long moment before she dared to speak, for her thoughts concentrated on the two little villains in question. At the moment, she would have given much to get her hands on the Mistresses Jane and Annabel.

From the side of her eye she watched the rider's progress. As he came closer, Angel breathed a sigh of disgust. It had been a pleasant afternoon until she realized the approaching rider was Gray Wolf. She felt an almost overpowering urge to run, but forced herself to relax. He was a brute, an oaf, an arrogant impossible man, but she would not run from him. What, she wondered, was he doing out here? What did he want? "Well, if you know how it feels to be hurt, why would you want

233

to purposely hurt someone?"

"Oh, I don't want to hurt anyone. I just want to act like a lady."

"All right, then, here is the first lesson. A lady is always kind."

Gray Wolf reined in his horse and dismounted with the grace only those who spend most of their lives in a saddle could know. He couldn't resist the teasing remark, even knowing his comment would surely annoy. For some reason the thought of getting her all fired up again was damn exciting. "You talk a good story."

Angel wondered if the man ever said good afternoon or, for that matter, goodbye. She sneered in Gray Wolf's direction and said pointedly as if to remind him of his manners, "Good afternoon, Mr. Gray Wolf."

"Ladies," Gray Wolf said in return as he took off his hat and smoothed his black hair back.

He stood still for a moment. The sun reflected off his hair, his strong, manly features, his darkly tanned skin, and Angel felt a shivering response disturb the normal rhythm of her heart. Lord, but the man was good to look at. Too good to look at. If she had any sense she'd . . . what? His looks meant nothing. Less than nothing, if the truth be told. He was a horrible man and it didn't matter if his handsomeness rivaled a Greek god's.

Mary giggled, her eyes widening with pleasure at his greeting. No one had ever implied that she was a lady before. After only one lesson, was it showing already?

Angel glared at the unwanted intruder.

Gray Wolf grinned at that glare, his gaze narrowing as he remembered the passion. Uninvited, he sat and made himself comfortable, leaning his back against the thick tree. He rested one arm upon a raised knee and asked, "What are you ladies doing out here on my land?"

"Your land?" Angel hadn't known this land belonged

234

to anyone, least of all this obnoxious creature. She made a mental note, a vow in fact, never to set foot on it again.

"Yup," he said.

"We're having a party," Mary answered.

"Just the two of you?"

"I'm Mary and it's my birthday."

He smiled at the girl's obvious pleasure. "Well, in that case, I reckon you can use my land anytime you want."

"Thank you," Angel said, but if the look in her eyes meant anything, she might as well have said right out that he wouldn't be finding her here again.

Gray Wolf frowned. Now what was the matter? She had come out here to see him, hadn't she? Then why was she making out like she wished she was anywhere in the world but sitting under this tree with him? He knew she had to be haunted by the kiss they had shared. He knew he wasn't the only one who had been affected. Hadn't he felt her go all soft and sweet against him? Still, if she had been half as affected as he, she sure was doing a good job of hiding it.

Gray Wolf was a quiet man. He didn't go in much for beating around the bush and making polite conversation. When he wanted something, or in this case, someone, he came right to the point. A lady knew his interest with one look. And he understood a woman who did the same.

Gray Wolf sighed. The problem here was, this one sent out confusing signals. One minute she was returning his kiss with all the fire that he could ever have imagined and the next she was as cool as a winter breeze. He figured until she was sure of what she wanted, he was in for some rough times.

It didn't matter. The fact was, he knew what he wanted. He couldn't stop thinking about the taste and feel of that mouth. He imagined he could take just about

235

anything she had to give in order to sample it again.

Angel's gaze narrowed as she watched his tender smile. A smile that very nearly took her breath away. Was she now supposed to forgive his abominable treatment of her? Well, she could have told him it would take more than an invitation to picnic on his land and a smile. The truth was, it would take something closer to a miracle before she'd see him as anything but an arrogant oaf.

The two adults were momentarily silent, each lost in their own thoughts, when Mary said with no little pride, "Miss Shaw gave me this dress. Isn't it the prettiest thing?"

Gray Wolf had been thinking about that sweet beckoning mouth and wondering how long he'd have to wait before being allowed to kiss her again. Thankful for the opportunity to think about something else, he turned his attention toward the little girl and smiled. "I reckon it's almost as pretty as the lady wearing it."

Poor Mary, the child was in desperate need of attention. So in need, in fact, that she seemed to absorb the compliment like parched earth during a rain storm and grew instantly under his spell. Odd. Angel knew for a fact that children were the best judges of character. How then couldn't this little girl see for herself the man's puffed-up arrogance?

Mary gave the dress another loving caress. "You want a piece," she asked nodding toward the small half eaten cake. "At the orphanage, we don't get our own cake, so Miss Shaw made this for me."

Gray Wolf's dark gaze moved to Angel. He frowned ever so slightly. Apparently something had upset him. Angel couldn't imagine what it could be.

The fact was, Gray Wolf didn't much like what he was hearing. He didn't want to know that this woman spent her spare time with orphans. All he wanted from her was a few minutes of pleasure and for that he didn't have

236

to know her at all.

He looked at Mary again. "It looks mighty temptin'. And since Miss Shaw made it, I'll have to try a piece, won't I?"

Gray Wolf grinned at Angel's frown. The woman certainly appeared less than happy at giving over a piece. He sighed, knowing instinctively that no matter what passion had exploded between them, she was sure to give him a whole lot of trouble before giving over other things as well.

Gray Wolf was no longer under the misguided assumption that she had come here looking for him. Judging by her cold, almost hostile, attitude, she hadn't forgiven him for his earlier accusations. Not that he could blame her. It had been a damn stupid move on his part. Still Gray Wolf was confident he could straighten everything out once he got a chance to talk to her alone.

He nodded to himself as he watched her lips tighten in response to his smile. Yeah, getting to this woman was going to take a bit of work on his part. His gaze lowered to her breasts and Gray Wolf knew the end results would be worth any effort.

After taking a huge bite, exaggerating a moan of euphoric pleasure, then grinning at Mary's laughter, he said, "Well, happy birthday, Mary. Are you old enough to get married yet?"

Mary giggled at his teasing. "I'm only six."

Gray Wolf smiled. "Too bad, I know a few fellas that are looking for a wife. But you'd have to be at least eight, I think."

Mary thought that remark was particularly funny.

Angel's smile was obviously forced. "Well, we were just finishing our picnic, Mr. Gray Wolf," Angel said as she came to her feet and shook out the creases in her skirt.

Gray Wolf laughed at her less than subtle way of suggesting he might leave whenever he got the chance. He nodded as he came to his feet. "Good thing I came along then. I'll ride with you back to the orphanage."

"There's no need, Mr. Gray Wolf, I know the way."

"You probably shouldn't be out here alone."

"Why?" Angel stopped gathering their leftovers together and glanced in his direction. "Has there been trouble?"

"Yeah, some. A pack of coyotes took down one of my prize horses last week. I reckon two ladies out here alone could use some protection."

Angel couldn't resist. "I was under the impression that a coyote was already in attendance, Mr. Gray Wolf." She glared in his direction, ignoring first his surprise and then his wicked grin. "And I'm not the least bit afraid."

Gray Wolf bit his lower lip as laughter lit up his eyes. "Maybe you should be, ma'am. Coyotes are a strange lot. You never know when one might get to you."

Angel couldn't suppress the shiver that raced down her back at the hidden promise in those words. It was almost as if he were warning her of what lay ahead and telling her she had no choice but to give in. As she packed up the basket and placed it in the back of the wagon, she racked her brain trying to think of a way to get rid of him. A moment later she bent over the girl and grunted as she struggled to bring Mary into her arms. It wasn't until then that Gray Wolf realized the girl couldn't walk.

Immediately he took Mary from her arms and, after a long searching almost accusing look into dark blue eyes, sat the girl upon the wagon's seat, leaving Angel to wonder what that was all about.

During the ride back, Mary and Angel sang rhyming limericks. The two were laughing at one which bestowed little fondness on boys and their desire to play with things creepy crawly, when the wagon pulled up before the large house. It was nearly time for Mary's afternoon nap. After a hug and kiss, plus a promise to see her soon, Mary was carried inside.

Before she was out of sight, Gray Wolf tied his horse to Angel's wagon. He took the reins from her as he came uninvited to sit upon the wagon's seat at her side. "Does anyone ever call you Elly?"

Gray Wolf figured it wouldn't hurt none to make sure Johnny's interests lay with another. And as far as he knew, there was no way of going about it but to ask straight out. His gaze remained upon the road ahead as he urged the animal into an ambling sort of gait back toward town.

He never saw her puzzled frown. "Elly? That would be odd, don't you think? My name is Angel."

"Angel what?" There was a chance, of course, that her middle name was Elly, and where this woman was concerned, Gray Wolf wasn't taking any chances.

Angel frowned again. "Angel Lettia Shaw. Why?"

Gray Wolf forced back a grin. Damn, when had a name ever satisfied? "And no one ever uses Elly?"

Angel couldn't imagine the reason behind these absurd questions. "I told you they did not. Why?"

"No reason. I just wondered what a man usually called you."

"A man usually calls me the same thing that a woman calls me."

"What if he was your lover?"

Angel pressed her lips together, not at all happy at the direction this conversation had suddenly taken. "Mr. Gray Wolf, I suspect there is a purpose behind these questions. Why not just come right out with it?"

Gray Wolf strove for an innocence he was far from feeling. He tried not to smile, but some things just weren't possible. No one called her Elly. Johnny was in love with a woman called Elly. Obviously there had been a mistake. His son did not love this woman. "Just making conversation."

"Of course," she returned in obvious disbelief. A moment later she continued on with some real sarcasm, "I can't tell you how often I'm asked that very question." She flashed him a weak imitation of a smile and asked, "Does anyone ever call you George?"

Gray Wolf chuckled a low, oddly disturbing sound. If he noticed the sharp look she sent his way, he didn't mention it.

Did he have to laugh like that? Angel might have asked him not to do it again, if asking wouldn't have given him the false impression that the sound was somehow upsetting which it wasn't, of course. She almost laughed at the notion herself. Who would be affected by low, silky laughter? The thought was ridiculous.

A few minutes went by before he spoke again. "You like kids?"

Angel frowned. "Of course I like children. I teach them five days a week."

"You teach kids five days a week and then on one of your days off, you take an orphan on a picnic?"

"What's wrong with that?"

"Nothing. I was just thinkin' you must really like them. Ever consider having a few of your own?"

"It's usually best to marry first, don't you think?"

He shrugged as if he hadn't given the subject much thought. "So why don't you get married?"

"Not that it's any business of yours, but I haven't found a man I'd like to marry."

"You'd better hurry up. A lady's looks don't last forever."

"Meaning I'm nearing the end of mine?"

Gray Wolf chuckled.

Angel glared her resentment. Granted she had long since left behind what most considered a marriageable age but she would hardly judge herself as having one foot in the grave. The way this oaf talked one would

240

think her closer to eighty rather than her twenty-four years.

"Not yet, but the years kinda sneak up on us. And a man isn't much attracted to an old maid."

"So now I'm an old maid. Mr. Gray Wolf, please, suh," she said in the thickest Georgia accent imaginable, "you're going to turn my head with these lavish compliments."

Gray Wolf grinned at the woman beside him. She might sound all soft and sweet, but if her body got any stiffer or straighter, a slight breeze might snap her in two. "I never said you were an old maid. I said you'd better hurry and find yourself a man before you become one."

"Taking for granted, of course, that I'm interested in finding one." If this fool was an example of what this area had to offer, she'd be perfectly satisfied to remain alone for the rest of her life, thank you.

He shot her a sharp quick glance. "You're not, ah, funny, are you?"

She frowned. "I don't think so. I haven't heard you laughing much."

"No, I mean, you do like men, don't you?"

Her frown became a glare of aggravation. "Until a few days ago, I thought I did."

Gray Wolf figured she was talking about him. The thought that he could have had that kind of effect on her, actually the thought that he could have had any kind of effect on her, brought a rumble of laughter. He wanted to further investigate her answer, but he was getting off the subject. "I mean, you're not hankerin' for a woman? Women don't do it for you, do they?"

"What in the world are you talking about? A woman do for me? What does that mean?"

Gray Wolf wasn't about to tell her, if a female's interest should lie along those lines, what one woman could

241

do for another. He figured if she didn't know there was no sense saying more than, "Well, it's just that there are some that prefer women to men."

Angel knew her Bible. There was a reference to men lying down with men. Jesus had called that act an abomination, but nothing had ever been said about women. The truth of it was, Angel had never imagined such a thing. Her eyes widened in shock that he should have hinted at the possibility, especially in regards to her. "Have you just insulted me again?"

Gray Wolf couldn't believe it. Everything she said, every expression she made, brought a smile to his lips. If she wasn't the most luscious woman. "No. I just wanted to get a few things straight. How would I know if I don't ask?" He shrugged. "Besides, you ought to know there are some who would whisper about such things, if there are no men in your life."

Angel didn't believe that for a second. No one but the most evil would even consider such a thing. Her voice was almost as stiff as her body when she returned, "Let's see if I understand. You're suggesting that I take a lover, just to set some evil-minded fool straight?"

Gray Wolf chuckled again. This one was smart. Maybe too smart for the likes of him. Still, he was going to do his damndest to see to it that that beautiful face and the intellect behind it were put to the best use. The fact was, a beautiful woman was a temptation to be sure, but a beautiful smart woman was downright scary. The men around here wouldn't know the first thing about how to handle this kind of danger. Gray Wolf figured he'd be doing all of them a favor if he personally saw to it. After all, it won't be too much of a sacrifice. "Did I get you mad?"

"Mad? Like insane?" Angel wondered if he hadn't somehow done just that. Perhaps she was just a bit mad. Why else was she listening to this man and actually allowing him to upset her?

"No. Mad like pissed. Ah, I mean, you know, mad."

Angel ignored the easily spoken obscenity. "Angry?"

"Yeah, angry."

"Not at all."

"You sound like you might be."

"I'm not."

"Your voice is a little tight."

"I told you I'm not," she said, words stiffer than ever.

"That's good." Gray Wolf grinned. From the sound of that last statement he knew if she hadn't been, she sure as hell was now.

Angel almost moaned her despair. How long was this ride going to take? It seemed to her that a year had past since they left the orphanage. She couldn't wait to get back to town and away from him. He was the most . . . the most . . . Angel couldn't think what he was exactly. All she knew was she'd never felt more ill at ease in her entire life.

"How come she can't walk?"

Angel knew he was talking about Mary, although he mentioned no names. "I'm not a doctor, Mr. Gray Wolf."

Gray Wolf pulled the wagon to a stop. He wasn't about to get involved with another white. He'd made that pledge years ago and had every intention of sticking to it. But for what he had in mind, a man didn't need any real involvement.

"What are you doing?"

"We have to talk."

She shook her head. The last thing she wanted to do was to talk, especially to this man. "I think our previous conversations should last us awhile."

Gray Wolf smiled at her objection, while wondering when he was going to get another chance to hold her and touch his mouth to the sweetness of hers. "I figure if I don't apologize, I ain't likely to get what I'm lookin'

243

for."

"What?"

He took a deep breath and forced out the words. "So, here goes. I apologize for not believing you. I was out of line thinking you were sleeping with my son."

Angel moaned. Had she ever met anyone more ill-bred, or uncouth? Even if he'd thought it, how did he dare repeat such a thing to a lady?

Angel frowned as she remembered his previous statement. "What do you mean? What are you looking for?"

"I'll tell you in a minute. First, you didn't say if you accepted my apology or not."

"I accept it," she said with a careless shrug, anxious for an answer to her question. "What are you talking about?"

"Does that mean you don't hate me anymore?"

Angel breathed a great sigh, suddenly understanding. He was trying, really trying to make conversation. He might not be very good at it, but she had to give him an A for effort. She made a vow to try harder to understand. "Mr. Gray Wolf, you might never become my most favorite person, but I've never hated you."

"I could become your favorite person."

"Truly, I doubt it."

"Why?"

"It would take an entire day to get through all the reasons."

"We've got the time."

"You, perhaps, but I've got to get back to town."

"Tell me one, then."

"All right. You are crude, rude, and insensitive." The telling of one seemed to open the door for a half-dozen more. Once she got started Angel found it almost impossible to stop. "You're overbearing, arrogant, obnoxious, and thick-headed. Once you've made your mind up there's no reasoning with you. And best of all, you have a way of insulting a lady that must have taken years to cultivate."

Gray Wolf frowned. "When did I insult you?"

Angel sighed. "It seems to me that you spend far less time in polite society than with your horses."

He frowned again. "I work with horses."

"Exactly my point."

Well, if she'd made her point, Gray Wolf had missed it. He didn't know what she was talking about. All he knew for a fact was that she'd somehow gotten herself into another snit and the sparkle of anger in those blue eyes did something funny to his stomach.

Gray Wolf watched her for a long minute before he said, "Maybe it's time to show you my good side." He nodded, silently reasoning it was probably past time.

"Assuming you have one, you mean?"

He laughed at her sarcasm, thinking she was just about the most luscious piece he'd seen in a long, long time. He couldn't remember the last time a woman had mouthed off to him and he had actually enjoyed every minute of it. "Sure I have one. Doesn't everybody?"

"All right. Show me." Her eyes dared him to do just that.

Gray Wolf thought about it for a long moment and then finally came out with, "I want to go to bed with you."

Dear God! Angel's eyes widened with amazement. "And that's your good side?"

"Doesn't that sound good to you?"

"It sounds like madness."

"Why?"

"A man doesn't tell a lady something like that, straight out. It's . . . it's . . ." Angel shrugged, not at all sure what it was, and finished with a lame, "It's not the right thing to say."

"It's honest. Would you rather I lie?"

"I'd rather you gain some control."

"I am in control. I didn't do it, I just said I wanted to do it."

"Fine, now since we've had our little chat, you can start the wagon again."

"I didn't stop just to talk. I stopped because I want to kiss you again."

Her eyes widened. He saw something flash in their dark blue depths and saw as well the tremble she instantly brought under control. The thought of kissing him was exciting, even if she wouldn't admit to it. Her voice was a low warning. "Is that why you apologized? So you could kiss me again?"

"Of course." It never occurred to Gray Wolf to be anything but honest.

"Start moving this wagon." Her lips hardly moved. Gray Wolf thought that fact, and the way she glared at him, adorable.

"Why?"

"Because you didn't mean it. You had ulterior motives behind every word."

"Lady, you're no fool. You've got to know every man has ulterior motives. When a man looks at a pretty woman, he's only got one thing on his mind."

"Like I said, start this wagon."

Gray Wolf grinned, his eyes narrowing in pleasure. "I think I could get to like little, bossy women."

"Then you're going to love this. If you don't move this wagon, I'm going to kick you out of it and drive the rest of the way by myself."

Laughter filled his dark eyes as his gaze moved over the length of her, telling her without words his doubt of her ability to fulfill that particular threat.

"I mean it."

"All right." He shrugged as if his intent hadn't been all that important. "I'll kiss you the next time," Gray Wolf said as he jumped from the wagon, untied his horse, vaulted into the saddle, and set the animal into an instant gallop, leaving Angel to curse the man's rudeness, his very existence, and her insane reaction to him.

She shivered again, knowing what would have happened if he'd pressed his cause. Right now they would have been locked in a heated embrace. No matter how she might swear she didn't want it, her body didn't seem to hear a word that was said. Lord, but that man was dangerous. Very, very dangerous. And if she was half as smart as she believed herself to be, she would stay as far away from him as a woman could get.

It wasn't until he was a small dot in the distance that she realized again his efforts to make conversation. Angel couldn't stop her lips from curving into a smile. Despite the fact that he had insulted her with his outrageous comments and questions, she had somehow found the entire episode charming.

Her concentration broken at the sound of jingling spurs, Angel raised her gaze from the papers on her desk, over the spectacles perched upon her nose. Gray Wolf almost groaned at her soft smile. Damn. Was there anything about this woman that wasn't beautiful? Even with glasses perched on that little nose, she took a man's breath away. It was a good thing Johnny didn't love her. A boy wouldn't stand a chance in hell against her allure. Idly he wondered if he did?

She leaned back in her chair, her blue eyes darkening with emotion. Gray Wolf wondered if he'd ever seen this particular mixture of interest, humor, and trepidation. It looked to him as if she very much liked what she saw, but was trying not to like it quite so much. "Good morning, Mr. Gray Wolf. What can I do for you?"

God, but she was gorgeous. Every time he saw her, she seemed to grow more beautiful and, a distant voice warned, more dangerous. Gray Wolf's dark eyes darkened further. The hunger he felt was obvious. What wasn't nearly as obvious was the surprise he felt. He'd lived twenty years within the confines of the white man's world and it took only a look from this woman to bring out the urge to throw aside his supposed civilized trappings and return again to the ways of his father.

Idly he wondered what she would do if he told her exactly what it was that he wanted. Apparently his expression told enough, for she instantly sought to change a subject that had yet to be mentioned. "You've come to help, have you? I can't tell you how much I appreciate the offer."

Deliberately as if each movement were consciously planned, she placed her spectacles on the papers, came to her feet, and walked around her desk. Every inch a school marm, her blue eyes dared him to deny her conclusions.

Gray Wolf laughed a low silky sound that oddly enough sent a shiver down her spine. Angel frowned at the sensation, wondering why that should be. "Do you always ask questions and then answer them yourself?"

"Only when I'm sure I know the answer." Angel felt just a little apprehension. She couldn't forget the last time the two of them had stood this close. She knew she should ask him to leave, but the fact was, she didn't want him to leave. Also there was the obvious fact that school was not in session and Mr. Gray Wolf, like any citizen of this town, had every right to visit, especially since, according to her uncle, it was mostly because of the man's charitable instincts that the town had built the schoolhouse.

Angel had to admit to the fact that, although he was a little rough around the edges, well, perhaps more than a little rough, he did possess a few redeemable qualities.

Gray Wolf figured if he told her what he really wanted

she was likely to get mad again. He couldn't help but admit that he enjoyed her anger, but for some reason he couldn't understand, he didn't want to anger her right now. He surprised both of them by saying, "You're right. Johnny mentioned you needed help. I've come to volunteer my time." For just a moment he wondered why half the men in this town weren't here, trying to make an impression on this little bossy miss, and then he forgot the question as he watched her luscious lips curve into a smile.

Gray Wolf grinned. Angel felt her stomach lurch at the flash of white against darkly tanned skin and the sparkle of dark, dangerous eyes. The man was far too handsome for his own good. His son would one day be as handsome, she thought, but the son would never possess the arrogance of the father. Johnny was far too nice for that.

So he wanted to help, did he? Well she'd make sure he did his share and then some. "Come with me," she said as she turned and headed for the door that led out back.

Angel took a thick woolen shawl from the peg by the door, and was pulling it over her shoulders when he asked, "What happened to your tree?" The bedraggled object, slightly askew, was missing a good portion of the ornaments it had worn a few days ago.

"It fell over." Her smile had disappeared. She glared at him, as if the falling were somehow his fault. Gray Wolf, even though he could have had no part in the happening, felt the unreasonable urge to apologize for the accident.

"And the ornaments broke?"

Her response was a further narrowing of her eyes and a silent sneer.

Gray Wolf grinned again, even as he wondered at her extreme anger. He couldn't figure a reason for it except for the kiss they shared three days ago and her refusal to kiss him again. Was she sorry she'd allowed the opportunity to pass her by? Well, he figured they'd make up for it today. He wasn't leaving here without sampling that mouth again. A few kisses should put her in a better mood. He knew it would do wonders for him.

A voice came again to annoy. The same voice that had haunted him for the last few days. She was white. Gray Wolf shook aside the thought and swore it didn't matter. He didn't want anything from her except for a few hours in bed. Nothing would come of it but physical pleasure, and for that it didn't matter if she was purple.

A barn stood about a hundred yards behind the small schoolhouse. It was old and had been left unused for some time. A bit ramshackle, Angel thought, but perfect for what she had in mind. "If you want to help, clean this out."

Angel had no doubt that he'd soon make good an escape. A smile touched the corners of her mouth as she awaited the first of his excuses.

Gray Wolf shot the bossy little schoolmarm a look of surprise. "All of it?" It would take him two days to clean the barn and dispose of its contents.

"No, just this area," she said as she stepped around empty barrels and over the small discarded hand tools and broken shovels which cluttered the barn's doorway. "You can throw the stuff inside. We'll set up the live Nativity scene here and the choir will stand here," she said, pointing to the right of the wide doorway.

"Mr. Morgan is bringing over all the hay we need for the background, and I've found a manger."

Gray Wolf surprised the two of them by getting to work as he rolled two barrels to the dim interior. He was brushing his hands against his thighs when he came out and asked, "Where are you going to get a baby?" He couldn't remember hearing of any new arrivals lately.

"I have a doll."

250

Gray Wolf shot her a sharp look of censure as she tried to lift a rusted chain. Without a word he took it from her and hauled both the chain and a broken yoke into the barn and threw them into an empty corner. "What about camels?"

"Unless you have one we could borrow, I think horses will do just fine."

For a moment Angel watched him go about the business of cleaning the yard, even as she wondered why he was here. He noticed her watching him and smiled. Angel felt a strange tightening somewhere in her chest. How odd. He could say things that just about drove her crazy and then with one smile, one charming smile, she forgot all the annoyances, all his insensitivities. How was it possible that his smile brought her this sensation of happiness? No, not happiness exactly. Pleasure . . . well, maybe not pleasure either. Angel was a teacher who had mastered the English language, and yet she couldn't think of the right word to describe the things he made her feel.

It was a half-hour later and Gray Wolf was almost finished with the chore when Mr. Morgan's wagon arrived. Two ranch hands, obeying Angel's directions, set the bales of hay in place.

The scene was ready for the walk-through play when Gray Wolf asked, "Anything else?" Even as he said the words, he wondered when they would get to the good stuff. He hadn't come here for this. He hadn't even known he was coming in the first place, but once he stepped into the little schoolroom, he knew why he was here. He wanted to touch her, to kiss her. So when was she going to let him?

She pointed at both the barn and the back of the schoolhouse. "I need nails to hang lanterns everywhere."

It had taken less than an hour. All was ready for the night's festivities. Angel's mind was on the choir and the

251

songs they had practiced when her thoughts were interrupted with, "Are you going to let me kiss you now?" His dark gaze was on her profile. He couldn't imagine a lovelier sight.

Angel glanced in his direction, her eyes narrowed with warning. She shook her head. "Are you going to start that nonsense again?"

"I told you the last time, I'd kiss you later."

"So you did and of course I should be honored. After all, an old maid has to take what she can get."

"What does that mean?" His eyes narrowed, his body stiff as he awaited the final insult.

Since Angel wasn't looking into his eyes at the moment, she never noticed. "It means that it doesn't matter how old I am, I would never allow—"

"Why?" He cut her off. "Because I'm Indian?"

"Because you're what?" Angel asked with some real surprise. Her gaze moved to his. She frowned. "What has being an Indian to do with anything? I wouldn't care if you were green, yellow, or red."

"I am red."

"You are not," she muttered, her voice filled with annoyance that he should say something so ridiculous. "You're tan."

Gray Wolf grinned.

"As well as the most obnoxious and arrogant man I've ever met." He took half a step closer, before she finished with, "And I have no intentions of kissing you, now or ever." Oddly enough the latter part of her statement sounded quite a bit less determined than the former. If Gray Wolf wasn't mistaken, her voice had grown decidedly breathless.

He smiled. He might not know much about women, but he knew when he'd shaken one up. "Are you sure about that? You look like you wouldn't mind all that much."

252

Angel felt a thrill of excitement flutter to life in her chest and forced the smile from her lips. The trouble was, she forgot about her eyes and Gray Wolf saw the smile there. "Get yourself a pair of spectacles, Mr. Gray Wolf. You're obviously in need." She pressed her lips together, lest she burst out laughing.

Gray Wolf considered that smile an invitation to further a conversation that particularly intrigued. "I'm in need, all right, but it's not spectacles I want. You're adorable."

Angel didn't want to think how that compliment affected her. She forced aside a giddy sense of pleasure, knowing a smile would only urge him on to taking further liberties and said as primly as possible, "I have papers to correct."

Gray Wolf figured he could solve this whole problem if he went back to the old ways. If he took her with him to the little cabin out near the edge of his property and kept her there for a few days, maybe a week, she'd probably never stop smiling. He was almost tempted to tell her his thoughts, but at the last minute decided she'd only get all fired up again. After their last meeting had repeated itself in his mind a few times, he'd come to the conclusion that a man shouldn't be all that honest.

There were plenty of women who would admit to the wanting, but this one seemed to think something was wrong with that. Gray Wolf hadn't had much experience with her kind. But figured it was about time he did.

Still, it was one thing to say it and quite another to actually go about it. When he saw a woman he wanted, it was simple enough to convey that fact. The woman usually returned the same sentiments and that was that. But this one's lack of response left him unsure of how to go about seeing to it that both their needs were met. He figured giving her a little space wouldn't hurt, so he took a step back and hooked his thumbs in his belt as he asked, "How long are you gonna keep up this prissy act?"

Angel's laughter was mingled with surprise. "Prissy? Is that what I am?"

Gray Wolf looked at her for a long moment before he smiled. "No. I don't think so. I think you're just acting like that because you're scared."

"Of you?" she asked in some amazement. "Not likely."

"Of what you feel for me."

"The fact is, Mr. Gray Wolf, I don't feel anything for you." That wasn't entirely true, of course. She did feel something. She simply couldn't define it at the moment.

"Prove it."

Angel grinned at his wily taunt and shot him a look that told him he should have known better. "You can't trick me into kissing you. I said I won't and I won't."

"You want me."

Angel breathed a great sigh, having a time of it controlling this unsettling need to laugh. "How kind of you to let me know."

Gray Wolf shrugged. "You've got to know that I feel the same."

"All I know, Mr. Gray Wolf, is, this is just about the most ridiculous conversation I've ever had in my life."

There was no sense denying the things he felt for this spirited little beauty. He could lie from now until forever and it wouldn't change a thing. Gray Wolf sighed. He'd seen her exactly four times, spoken to her three of those times, and knew beyond a shadow of a doubt that his vow to remain uninvolved was a lie.

"My name is Joseph. I reckon you'd better use it, considerin'."

Angel's eyes widened. She wasn't about to ask, "Considerin' what?" And she wasn't about to call this man anything but his surname. Mr. Gray Wolf was moving too fast. Far too fast. "Mr. Gray Wolf . . ."

254

Gray Wolf's slow grin was the most wicked and cocky thing she'd ever seen. Angel shivered at the sight of it. She didn't think to fight him when his hand closed over her arm and without another word spoken guided her behind the bales of hay. Her back was suddenly against the wall of the barn. Gray Wolf blocked any means of escape by the strategic placement of his hands. He didn't touch her, but trapped her in place. He didn't touch her but Angel felt an ache come to life in her midsection. He didn't touch her, but her legs felt almost watery, as if she were held in the most heated embrace.

There was never any question in Gray Wolf's mind that this woman was an innocent. (Well, almost no question.) And the longer he was in her company, the surer he grew of it. He vowed to be very careful with her, but if he didn't kiss her and do it soon, he was probably going to up and die on the spot.

Angel took a few deep breaths and stared him straight in the eye. If he meant to frighten her, he was making a mistake. There wasn't a man alive who could make her cower and he might as well know it. "Mr. Gray Wolf . . ."

"Joseph."

"Mr. Gray Wolf," she insisted, "I absolutely refuse to allow you to upset me again. As far as I'm concerned, this conversation is over. I've things to do. Kindly go away."

Gray Wolf licked his lower lip as if remembering a particular delicious taste. "Meaning, I upset you before?"

Angel bit her lip. She hadn't meant to admit to it, but since she had, there was no sense holding back. "You upset me almost every time I see you."

"Why? Because I kissed you?"

"Mr. Gray Wolf." Her cheeks grew rosy at the memory.

"Joseph. Were you upset because I kissed you, or because you kissed me back?"

"Neither. And I never kissed you back."

"You're lying. You know you did."

"I didn't!"

He took a half-step toward her. Their bodies almost touched. "Why don't we try it again? Then I could tell you exactly at what point you start kissin' me back."

Angel couldn't hold back the soft laughter. He looked almost innocent. "How do you do that?"

"What? Kiss?"

"No, look so innocent."

"Do I? I don't feel very innocent." His mouth lowered a bit.

"I don't want you to do this."

"Why?"

"Because it's too soon. You're going too fast."

Gray Wolf couldn't get out of his mind the picture of how soft she grew in his arms. "Just one kiss and I'll leave."

"Promise?" Angel never realized she'd just agreed to a kiss.

"Promise."

His clean, warm breath teased her skin, especially the area around her mouth. The flesh there tingled and maybe she'd never admit to it, but more than anything she wanted to feel his mouth against hers again.

Angel couldn't quite come to grips with the emotion. First came a wave of relief and then a deep sense of disappointment at the sound of her aunt's voice. "Angel, honey. Are you in there?"

Gray Wolf sat before the fire in his study. In his lap lay a book he had long since given up trying to read. There wasn't anything wrong with his concentration. It just refused to be swayed from a certain little bossy miss. Gray Wolf sighed. When had things turned so complicated? He'd gone to a woman to warn her away from his son, only to find himself involved. He shook his head and wondered how it had happened.

The truth of the matter was, it didn't matter how it had happened. It only mattered that it had.

He tried to understand. What made her different? He had known other women — other white women — and had never felt this overwhelming need, this sense of absolute right, when holding her in his arms. She was white. What had happened to his pledge never to involve himself with another of her kind?

What had happened was, he had kissed her and he couldn't remember when a kiss had felt so good. He had kissed her and she had kissed him back. Just like that, there was no going back.

After evening prayers, Angel bid her aunt and uncle good night, took a candle, and went to her room. She shivered as she hurried into a warm cotton nightdress and wondered if she'd ever get used to these cold nights. The room was small and had no fireplace. Angel, used to the warmth of Georgia nights, comfortable even in the midst of winter, scrambled beneath the heavy quilt.

She lay there a moment waiting for the warmth. That's when it sort of snuck up on her. She should have been thinking about the coming festivities, of the play, of the children, but instead came the thoughts of a certain dark man, whose "honesty" was better left unsaid, whose smile could melt a winter freeze, whose dark eyes and low disturbing laughter left her oddly breathless and very confused.

Angel frowned into the darkness. If she was anxious for the morrow, it wasn't because she anticipated seeing him again. If she saw him, he would probably return again to what was fast becoming a boring subject. He'd only ask her for a kiss again.

He was brash, insistent, and aggravating, and she certainly would not kiss him. Angel remembered how close his mouth had been to hers when her aunt had interrupted them. How her skin had tingled in anticipation, how her lips had parted in waiting. She bit her lip trying to forget the feel of his warm, clean breath against her skin, and she then silently reconsidered. Well, maybe just one little kiss. Surely one little kiss could bring no harm.

Elly May and Angel decorated the schoolroom for the coming festivities. Elly wanted two things out of life. One was to become a teacher, just like Miss Shaw, which was why the girl often sat in on Angel's classes, and the other was Johnny Gray Wolf. Angel was rarely in the girl's company when the young man wasn't mentioned. Even now, as they looped colorful paper garlands around the room and pasted pictures of Santa the children had created to the walls, Elly May told of the hopelessness of ever getting Johnny's father to agree to the union.

Angel remarked, "Johnny is almost of age. Why not wait the six months. Mr. Gray Wolf cannot object then."

"But he can." Elly looked disheartened. "It doesn't matter how old Johnny is. Mr. Gray Wolf won't ever allow us to marry."

"Why not?"

"Because I'm white."

Angel shot the girl a puzzled look. "Elly, that can't be why. Johnny's mother was white, wasn't she?" Angel's gaze darkened with confusion. How could Gray Wolf insist that his son not marry a white girl, while he himself hinted at some very intimate happenings between the two of them? Why should it be all right for them, but not his son?

Angel shook aside the uncomfortable thought. It wasn't a very pleasant experience to feel prejudiced

258

against, even though she was sure it was all a great mistake. Angel realized she couldn't defend the man without knowing the truth of it all.

"Maybe that's why he feels like he does. Some say they didn't get along."

Johnny knocked and entered the schoolhouse before Angel had a chance to further her questioning. Angel could hardly claim surprise at seeing the young man. The fact of the matter was, wherever Elly May was, Johnny was sure to be close by. Elly often sat in on Angel's classes; therefore Johnny, whenever he had the chance, was in attendance as well.

Angel smiled as she watched the exchange of tender looks. "Your mamma wants you to come home to help with the baking."

Elly May glanced toward Angel.

Angel nodded. "Go ahead. We're finished here, and I have some baking of my own to do."

Aunt Amy, a native of Georgia, prepared her infamous peach cobbler as she remarked, "I'm so happy you decided to come, Angel. Especially now, with the holiday almost here. It wouldn't be nearly so festive if your uncle and I were alone."

Angel smiled as she slid another batch of cookies into the oven. "I thought Robert would be home for Christmas." Robert, her cousin, owned a large spread a hard day's ride south of Clearwater. Angel was looking forward to seeing him again. They hadn't seen each other since they were children, just before his parents had gone west to begin a new church in Clearwater, Texas.

Aunt Amy shook her head. "A wire came this morning. Jane is past her time and the doctor warned them not to travel."

"Well, I'm glad I'm here then. Perhaps they'll make the

trip after the baby comes."

Angel took a tray of delicious-smelling cookies from the oven and replaced it with yet another, ready to bake. "The children are going to love these." The women had been baking most of the morning. A few confectionery items, along with a huge ham, had been prepared for tomorrow night's festivities, a pot luck supper that all the townsfolk were expected to join. But the greater portion of their efforts were meant for the children at the orphanage.

Since her arrival in Clearwater, Angel had been to the orphanage many times, but this would be the first bearing gifts. It was only two days since she'd last visited and yet she couldn't wait to see the children again, most especially Mary. She could only imagine how the little girl's face would light up when these treats were served.

Even though Angel had always enjoyed working with children, no one child, until now, had come to mean so much. She'd loved Mary from the moment she'd first laid eyes on her.

To Angel's way of thinking, anyone who knew the girl couldn't help loving her. She had never met anyone half as brave.

Mary never complained of life's unfairness, but accepted her disability and the limitations it placed upon her. She was a bright child, with a good disposition. Eager to learn, usually bubbling with excitement, gentle and sweet, she was a joy. Each time she saw the child, Angel grew more sure of her intent. One day she would manage the impossible and Mary would become her daughter.

Angel sat to the right of her aunt as her uncle drove the heavy, springless wagon over the uneven ground. Ahead stood a large Victorian house set amid miles of empty land. Angel imagined the house with its thin windows and fireplaces only on the main floor most inadequate in providing warmth against the cold winter nights on the southwestern plains.

Behind the house stood a small corral and a smaller barn that housed one horse.

The wagon rolled to a stop and Angel felt something twist in her chest as children of all sizes came running. All the children ran, in fact, with the exception of one little girl who was carried to a chair on the wooden porch. There was laughter and shouts of glee, for the wagon was swollen with gifts and every child instantly understood that they would be the receiver of at least one of the gaily decorated packages.

Angel had not been raised so very sheltered from reality. After all, she had been born in the midst of a war and her family had suffered greatly in its aftermath. She realized the existence of poverty. She'd simply taken for granted that in 1885 children would have been better cared for. That if not the government, then some caring soul would have seen to their needs.

"I wouldn't have thought that an Angel could look so sad." The words were whispered for her ears alone.

Angel turned with a look of surprise and smiled. A wave of warmth settled somewhere around her heart. She never realized it was obvious to anyone who cared to look their way that the lady was very pleased to see this particular gentleman.

"Mr. Gray Wolf. I didn't expect to find you here."

Angel's aunt and uncle greeted the man in a warm fashion, and he them.

Gray Wolf, on a flimsy excuse, had stopped by the parsonage yesterday, only to find the lady had gone off with her aunt to visit with a sickly neighbor. Luckily Charles had mentioned this visit.

"Joseph," he reminded her as he helped her from the

wagon. "But you're happy you have?"

She smiled, but said nothing.

Gray Wolf chuckled, the sound delicious and far too close to her ear. "You know, you just might be the most beautiful woman I've ever seen." Gray Wolf surprised himself at the easily spoken words. He didn't often relax in a woman's company and only now realized that he'd done just that almost from their very first conversation. His heart pounded against the walls of his chest at her warm answering smile.

They joined her aunt and uncle in handing out the gifts.

The candy, sweets, food, dresses, trousers, and woolen socks were given and received with equal pleasure. The children were settled down a bit, each enjoying their treats, while boasting of their latest acquisitions. Her uncle was talking to the headmaster, Mr. Williams, a gentle man, who dressed as poorly as his little orphans, while Aunt Amy fussed over a few of the smaller children.

Angel was sitting on the porch next to Mary, having just given her a silver brush as a Christmas present. Mary, her eyes filled with awe, looked at the brush for a long time before she dared to touch it. Her small fingers moved over the intricate carvings on the handle. "Is it mine?"

"Of course it's yours."

"I never had anything so beautiful."

Angel never realized the smile as Gray Wolf came to sit at her side. "Look," Mary said as she held up her brush. "Look at what Miss Shaw gave me."

Gray Wolf's gaze moved to Angel, his eyes filled with something she couldn't quite name. All she knew was her heart suddenly began to pound. "It's very beautiful."

"I love it," the little girl exclaimed, hugging it tightly

to her chest.

They spoke for a few minutes before an aide came to take Mary, along with the smaller children, in for their naps.

Angel and Gray Wolf remained where they were. "Why doesn't she have one of those chairs, you know with the wheels?"

"She had one. It broke."

Gray Wolf made no comment, but studied the woman at his side. Angel grew slightly uncomfortable at his long look. She would have liked to ask him to stop looking at her like that, but knew should she mention it, he might very well look at her even more. "You love her, don't you?"

Angel's smile was the softest sweetest thing Gray Wolf had ever seen. One day, he promised himself, this woman would smile like that for him. "I'd like to adopt her."

"A single woman? Would they let you do it?"

"An old maid, you mean?" Then she laughed at his dark look. She shrugged. "No one else wants her. Why not?"

"It would be easier if you were married." Gray Wolf knew a moment of amazement as he realized what he'd just said. Without thought he had brought up the subject of marriage. Not that he wanted to marry her, of course. She was white and he'd vowed never to allow another white woman into his life. He tried to imagine her marrying another. For some unnamed reason, the thought annoyed him.

Angel restrained the impulse to laugh. The man appeared quite shaken at his own words. She wondered if he wouldn't suddenly jump from his seat and run. Certainly he looked as if he might. "Are you asking me to marry you?"

"No. I'm waiting for you to ask me." Gray Wolf

amazed himself at this sudden ability to tease.

Angel thought that notion particularly amusing and gave a low chuckle.

It was her laugh that did it. The sparkle of happiness in her eyes. Gray Wolf was no fool. He knew there was no sense in fighting the inevitable. He might not have wanted to become involved with a white, but it was too late. He already was. His voice lowered to an husky intimate whisper. "After we're married, promise you'll stay just as sassy."

"I haven't asked you to marry me, Mr. Gray Wolf."

"You will."

She shot him a look that told of her absolute disbelief.

"I doubt your uncle would appreciate us living in sin." Gray Wolf almost laughed aloud. Now that he was becoming accustomed to the idea, he thought he rather liked the thought of having this woman as his wife.

She shot him a threatening glare that promised untold punishment if he didn't immediately stop this nonsense. He chose to ignore it. "I didn't think so. That doesn't leave us with much of a choice, does it?"

"Let's go for a walk?"

She felt a shiver run down her spine as he touched her arm, helping her to her feet. She wondered how his presence could make her feel decidedly excited and yet oddly at ease at the same time. She'd never been particularly shy. Still there were times, especially when he looked at her the way he was looking at her now, that she suddenly suffered an almost debilitating attack of the emotion.

They walked in silence for some time before Angel shot him a sideways glance and said, "I'm embarrassed to admit to a great deal of ignorance about Indians, but I'd like to learn." She turned to look up at him then. "What kind of Indian are you?"

Gray Wolf took heart in her admitted interest. He'd known from the first that she wasn't as immune to him as she might have liked. Too bad. He hadn't any choice in the matter either. "My people were Kiowa Apache. Most of them live south of here. The minute I was old enough, I left the reservation and joined the Army as a scout. When my enlistment was up, I bought my place."

"And your family? Do they live on a reservation?"

"My family died in a cholera epidemic while I was in the Army."

"All of them?"

He nodded.

"How horrible!"

Gray Wolf nodded again. The fact was, he had planned to one day have his father, mother, and two sisters live with him, but he never got the chance. It was years before he could forgive himself for waiting so long. "It was a long time ago."

"And your wife?"

"What about her?"

"Did she die as well?"

"A few years back. I heard that a carriage she was riding in overturned."

"You heard?"

He shrugged. Gray Wolf shot her a questioning look. He thought she would have listened to the gossip and known all about it by now. "She left a month after Johnny was born."

"Left? What do you mean, she left?"

"I mean, just what I said."

"But she had a baby. How could she leave?"

"I asked myself the same thing a time or two." His eyes were cold, his mouth hard at the remembered pain.

"You loved her." Angel wondered if he didn't still? She wondered, that is, until he flashed her a warm smile. It was then that she knew whatever there had been between this man and his wife had long since died.

"Once," he easily conceded. "Looking back, I figure I

suffered more from pride than lost love when she walked." His shrug told her more than words ever could. "It's been a long time."

Gray Wolf knew as did the rest of the town that the Reverend Charles Kincaid and his wife Amy were Angel's aunt and uncle. What he didn't know was why she had left her home to come and live with them.

"What about your family? Why did you come to Texas?"

"I came because Aunt Amy wrote that Mr. Martin was retiring and the town needed a teacher."

"And there had been no reason to stay?"

Angel shot him a glance that held a sparkle of humor along with a delicious glare. Gray Wolf almost reached for her then and found he had to force his hands to his sides. "If that's your sly way of asking if there was someone special in my life, the answer is, no, there was not."

Gray Wolf choked on suppressed laughter. She was adorable. He could watch her threatening glares forever. Another of her steely looks soon brought him under control. "What about your family?"

"There was only my father. He died last year."

"You were alone?"

"No. There were cousins and an elderly aunt. I lived with her."

She changed the subject as they walked to a slight rise in an otherwise flat landscape. "Do you have a lot of money?"

Gray Wolf glanced sharply in her direction, surprised at the bold question. "Why?"

"I was thinking we could do something for them." She nodded toward the orphanage. "Compared to their needs, a wagon filled with treats, food, and few pieces of clothing is almost embarrassing."

"*We* could do something, if *I* have the money?"

Angel ignored his sarcasm. "Well, you own a ranch. I

266

thought perhaps you could give them a few horses and teach them how to care for them." She glanced his way again, her blue eyes pleading, and Gray Wolf felt his senses evaporate like the morning mist on a sunny day. "You know, how to raise them?"

"And then?" he prompted, wanting to hear more, even though he knew he would not deny her this request. The fact of the matter was, he doubted he could deny this woman anything.

"And then they could start their own business. That way they wouldn't have to rely solely on charity."

Gray Wolf decided it best not to immediately agree to her suggestion. Although giving a dozen or so horses would pose no hardship, he didn't want to appear too amicable. Women never appreciated a man they could easily control. Besides, he couldn't enjoy himself more than when talking to this woman. Well, perhaps he could, he silently reconsidered, but that would have to wait a bit. "You want me to create my own competition, is that it?"

Angel shook her head and pressed her cause. "Children are the future, Mr. Gray Wolf. Would you prefer helping now or waiting until they get into trouble?"

"And you know they'll get in trouble, do you?"

"Some will. There won't be so many doors open to them."

Gray Wolf marveled at the goodness in this woman. The fact that she was being generous with his money didn't seem to matter. She didn't want it for herself. She wanted it for these children. "You're not asking for much. There must be forty children here."

She shook her head. "They don't need a horse each. Only a few. A start, so they can help themselves."

"And what do I get for it?"

Angel's eyes widened at the question. It wasn't until she glanced his way that she realized the laughter in his

267

dark eyes. He was teasing her again, and Angel found herself a willing partner in this pleasant interlude. "A feeling of accomplishment?"

He shook his head.

"The respect of your peers?"

He shook his head again.

"A special place in heaven?"

Gray Wolf grinned. "I was thinking of something slightly more immediate."

"What?"

"A kiss. A real kiss."

He heard her soft gasp and watched as beautiful color tinted her cheeks. She couldn't quite meet his gaze. She was the sweetest, most beautiful thing he'd ever seen in his life and there was no way he was going to chance upsetting her again. Not when her eyes grew all soft and warm at his teasing. "Forget the kiss. Just call me Joseph."

It took only a moment for Angel to realize his answer. And with that realization came an almost overwhelming rush of gratitude. It was the intensity of that emotion that caused her to act so out of character.

He'd be damned if she hadn't gone and done it. Right there, out in the open, and in front of anyone who cared to glance their way. She had laughed out loud and then almost knocked him senseless when she reached up on her toes and, holding the sides of his face in delicate hands, kissed him right on the mouth.

Gray Wolf had been so startled he hadn't even thought to kiss her back, and now that the moment had past, he knew he wouldn't get the chance.

More than slightly dazed, he allowed her to lead him toward her aunt and uncle. "Oh, you'll never guess what happened. Mr. Gray Wolf," Angel interrupted herself with that awfully sexy, wicked low laugh of hers, and Gray Wolf almost groaned aloud. "I mean Joseph just promised to . . ." Gray Wolf's eyes glazed over, his hearing shut off. Later he could only hope she hadn't promised him to give away everything he owned, because he had nodded his head in agreement just as if he were a trained monkey, for all he could think about was the way she'd said his name.

He loved her, improbable though it may be. Impossible, if he'd still been in possession of half his mind. He'd known her less than a week, but he loved her, all right. There was no way that he could stop himself. She wasn't only beautiful. She was smart. She was compassionate. She had the tender heart of an angel. Gray Wolf chuckled at his thoughts. He was a goner and he knew it.

Amy Kincaid smiled as her husband came up behind her, reached an arm around her waist, and hugged her tightly against him. "I can't look in the oven if you don't let me bend over."

Charles Kincaid, the most right Reverend, was first a man and a loving husband as well. So it came as no surprise to his wife that he chuckled a low wicked sound and said, "Go ahead, bend over."

Amy swung out of her husband's arms and shot his grin a look of reproach. "Behave yourself, Charles. Angel is in the next room."

Charles Kincaid, instantly the proper gentleman again, adjusted his tie and cleared his throat, a soft blush staining his cheeks. "I thought she left for the schoolhouse."

"She did, but she came back. She forgot her wings."

It took a second, but Charles nodded, imagining his wife spoke of the costume for the angel.

Angel called out that she was leaving and that she'd see them later, just before the front door shut behind her.

Amy fussed over the finished products, placing the ham in a circle of buttered potatoes. "Charles, I've been thinking."

"Uh-oh."

"Stop teasing and listen."

"Yes, dear." His eyes sparkled with pleasure at her order.

"Do you think that Mr. Gray Wolf is sweet on our Angel?"

"Now Amy, you know how I feel about interfering."

"I've no intentions of interfering. I was just thinking, is all. He didn't take his eyes off her all afternoon."

Charles grinned at the understatement. "Yes, there was that, but I think what really gave it away was how he walked into his horse before he mounted the animal."

"Now that you mention it, his eyes did appear a bit glazed. Perhaps he is in need of spectacles."

"I imagine the man would need more than spectacles if he couldn't see a horse." Charles chuckled. "Yes dear, I'd say Mr. Gray Wolf is smitten with our Angel."

"Do you think Angel returns his feelings?"

"What I think, my dear, is that they will work it out for themselves and no amount of reflection on our part is going to matter in the least."

All was set. The children were gathering in the schoolroom, all dressed in costume. Those in the choir wore flowing white robes. There was one problem. The little girl who was to announce the birth of the Savior had come down with the chills. Her mother had come by only an hour ago to return the costume. Angel sighed, while wondering who could take the little girl's place.

Johnny and Elly May helped the Reverend and Mrs. Kincaid bring the food and pitchers of lemonade from the parsonage to the schoolhouse. It was decided that the evening was far too cool to remain outside for any length of time. Therefore, immediately after the play, all would gather in the schoolhouse for refreshments.

Most everyone had arrived by the time Gray Wolf pulled his buggy to a stop in the schoolyard. The little girl at his side looked with wide eyes over the noisy, milling crowd. Mary had never seen so many people before.

Gray Wolf noticed his lady right off. Well, maybe she wasn't his lady just yet, but if he had anything to say about it, she soon would be. He jumped from the buggy, bringing Mary with him.

A moment later he placed her in the special chair he had just picked up at the blacksmith's and grinned as she pushed it toward a little girl who appeared close to her age.

"Hello," he said as he came up behind Angel, who was bent over a little shepherd, straightening the rope that tied his headpiece in place.

Angel felt again that surge of warmth, this time accompanied by a delicious chill that raced up her spine as she turned, stood, and smiled up at the man. "Hello," she said in return and Gray Wolf wondered if he'd ever heard a sound more beautiful. God, he really had it bad.

For a long moment, they simply stared at one another. Gray Wolf felt himself lost in those dark blue eyes. "Yeah, well, ah. I'll just stand over there until you're ready." *Ready for what? What's gotten into you?* "I can see you're busy." Gray Wolf almost ran from her side. Damn, but he felt like a tongue-tied fool, totally untried in the ways of love. Every time he saw her, it was worse and yet better than the last.

He didn't know himself anymore. What had happened to the serious fellow whose entire life centered around his son and his work? He had somehow turned into a man who could bring a blush to a young woman's cheeks with a teasing comment, only now he couldn't even

271

tease. Now he babbled like some lovesick fool.

Gray Wolf had yet to get himself completely under control when he saw her coming toward him. "Where is she?"

"Who?"

"Mary. Aunt Amy said you brought her." Mr. Williams had refused to allow Mary to leave the orphanage so late at night. "Rules are rules, Miss Shaw," had been his final response. Angel couldn't help wondering how the man had managed it. But she forgot her question at his next words.

"Oh. The last time I saw her she was heading for a little girl. One of the Wilson twins, I think. They're about the same age, aren't they?"

"Heading for?" A brilliant smile lit up her face. Gray Wolf knew he was done for. Angel's gaze searched through the crowd. "You had her chair fixed?"

Gray Wolf shrugged. He hadn't done it to gain her gratitude. Gratitude wasn't what he wanted from this woman. What he wanted was something much more. . . . Suddenly she kissed him again. Damn, she had to stop doing that. He wasn't going to be worth spit if she kept that up. "That was so sweet."

Gray Wolf quickly set her from him. For the first time in his life he worried over what others might think. His eyes grew dark with warning. It wouldn't be fair to give her the wrong idea. "I'm not sweet." Gray Wolf figured she was going to find that out soon enough. He might as well tell her the truth from the first.

Angel laughed, feeling her heart swell in her chest. There was no help for it. She loved this man and his generosity only made her love him more. "You're probably right about that. Still, it was a sweet thing to do."

Gray Wolf stared at the ground, his thumbs hooked into his belt, never feeling more ill at ease. "A temporary lapse of character."

Angel smiled and resisted the urge to kiss him again. She hadn't missed his earlier look of embarrassment. "Thank you."

Gray Wolf lifted his gaze from the tips of his shining boots. Their gazes held for endless, hearthrobbing moments. Two hearts no longer afraid, but open and willing to experience this new emotion, this lovely and sweetest sensation. He managed at last in a low husky voice, "You're welcome."

The costume fit Mary exactly. And no one seemed to notice that the angel didn't fly, or even walk for that matter, but wheeled herself to one corner of the barn, before announcing to all, "On this night, a Savior is born." Angel beamed just as if she were already Mary's mother.

The play and the accompanying Christmas carols were over and all those who could fit, and many who couldn't, stood inside the schoolhouse eating and drinking their fill.

Gray Wolf found his son and the pretty young woman who hadn't been far from his side for most of the night. "Is this Elly?" he asked as he sipped from a glass of lemonade.

Johnny beamed at his betrothed and introduced his future wife to his father.

"Have you set the date yet?"

Johnny grinned, his dark eyes filled with happiness. "June."

That was six months down the road. "Why wait?"

It might have been unspoken, but Johnny realized his father was giving his permission. He wasn't about to ask why. He didn't even think what might have changed his mind. "Elly is aimin' to go back East to school. She wants to be a teacher."

Gray Wolf smiled at the thought, since having two teachers in the town might allow one of them some free time. "And you'll be going with her?"

Elly shook her head. "I'll be leaving after the holiday."

"We'll be married when she comes back," Johnny added. "Then I'll go back with her."

Gray Wolf nodded at this information and extended his hand in congratulations. "You know I wish you every happiness. If you need anything . . ."

Johnny grinned and took his father's offered hand. Neither man seemed to notice that the handshake had turned into a real hug that included a few hard pats on the back. Johnny drew his love close to his side. "As long as I have Elly, I have everything I need."

He couldn't find her. She was there one minute and gone the next. He was talking to his neighbor. Actually Tom Mason was doing all the talking, while Gray Wolf's dark gaze searched the room. Where was she? What was she doing?

Gray Wolf wondered if he'd been rude. Had he left his neighbor in midsentence? Still, he couldn't find it within himself to care. All he could think about was one particular Angel. He squeezed through the crowd. Nothing.

Outside the air was cold, but Gray Wolf didn't feel the chill. The moment he opened the door he saw a flash of velvet green skirt move into the dimly lit barn. He knew who that dress belonged to. He hadn't been able to tear his gaze from her for most of the night.

Gray Wolf never realized that he'd followed. All he knew was seconds later he was standing behind her. Behind her and another man.

He came to her side and watched a smile light up her eyes. In an instant his arm circled her waist and pulled her gently against his side. No words were needed. There was an unspoken understanding between the two men the moment his arm snaked around her waist.

274

Mr. Jaegar had been about to insist on a minute's privacy. When he saw the possessive act and Miss Shaw's smile and lack of resistance, he had an immediate change of heart.

Gray Wolf breathed a sigh of relief as Angel turned at his touch. Did she realize that she touched his chest? She didn't seem to mind that he made his intentions clear. In fact she appeared to have intentions of her own. Gray Wolf could hardly control the happiness that invaded his soul. He very nearly took her in his arms, but shot the man before them a nasty glare instead.

"Mr. Jaegar is interested in renting the barn. Until he can get his own built, he needs a place to store his extra hay. I thought the school could use the money."

Rent the barn. Gray Wolf knew better. His gaze narrowed in an obvious threat, for Jaegar had more than enough barns on his place to store anything he wanted. Gray Wolf knew the man had gotten her out here under false pretenses. It was a damn good thing he'd noticed her missing. The fact was, too many men in this town had eyes for her. Gray Wolf figured right about now was a good time to make his intentions known.

"Jaegar," he nodded in greeting. "You expectin' one of your barns to burn down?"

"No. I, ah, I just thought in case I needed more space . . ."

"Yeah, well, when you need it, let me know and I'll see what I can do for you."

His arm tightened around Angel as he spoke, drawing her a fraction closer. The man couldn't miss it. He gave a silent nod, for nothing more needed to be said.

Moments later Jaegar made a feeble excuse and walked off.

"What was that all about?"

"What?"

"If you pull me any closer, I'll be inside you."

"A very good idea. I could keep you away from all the Jaegars that way."

"Joseph," she said, insisting on an answer.

"He's married."

Gray Wolf had expected anger at his unasked-for handling of her. Instead, and to his absolute delight, he watched as she laughed and turned into his arms, her hands flat against his chest, her eyes sparkling with pleasure. "And you think he was about to . . ."

"I've no doubt of it."

"Do you think he intends to divorce Mrs. Jaegar for me?"

Gray Wolf gave her a dark look as he tightened his hold. "I think I'll break his neck if I find him within a mile of you."

"You wouldn't be the jealous sort, would you?"

"Me?" Gray Wolf grinned and then lied straight out, "I haven't got a jealous bone in my body."

"I didn't think so, but—"

"I'm just protecting what's mine."

For some it might be too soon, but Angel knew well enough what was in her heart. "And Mr. Jaegar didn't know I belonged to you?"

"He knows now."

"I'm glad."

He didn't answer her, but groaned with pleasure, both at her response and the softness of her body against his. "Oh God," he breathed. "I can't believe this."

"What can't you believe?"

"That you're standing here against me and not giving me a bit of trouble."

Angel made a soft sound of pleasure as she rested her cheek against his chest. "I wouldn't think of giving you trouble. This feels too good."

"I know." He closed his eyes, hardly able to bear the sweetness of her. "Sweetheart, you might as well know

276

right off that I'm going to be hard to live with."

A low, wicked chuckle vibrated against his chest. "I think I figured that out for myself."

"We'll adopt Mary," he said, his face lowering to her sweetly scented hair. "And as soon as we can, we'll take her to San Francisco, to see a doctor."

Angel snuggled her face into his white shirt, more than ever sure of her love for this man. "She is a darling, isn't she?"

Gray Wolf nodded. "Almost as darling as you."

Angel laughed, unable to deny her happiness. She couldn't help teasing, "Is that why you want to marry me? So you can have her?"

Gray Wolf's chuckle was low and husky. There was no need to respond to her question. They both knew the truth of the matter. "Do you realize it's only been a week since the day a certain Angel came into my life and I'm—"

Angel interrupted, "I didn't come into your life. You came into mine."

He gave her a little shake. "I'm trying to be romantic. Shut up."

Shut up? Me?" Angel laughed. "I'm afraid you have a rude awakening in store if you think—"

"I think"—it was his turn to interrupt—"I can't wait to get you into bed. You'll be a bit less sassy after that."

The light in the barn was dim, as one lone lantern hung on a high rafter, but it wasn't nearly dark enough to miss the sparkle in her eyes, nor the soft blush of her cheeks. "You'll probably notice it once we're married . . ." She hurried through the next few words, obviously embarrassed at the mentioning. "And in bed and all, but I should tell you that I'm white." She said the last as if proclaiming a fact he had not been aware of.

Gray Wolf grinned and tightened his hold. "I think I

noticed that right off."

"You know, I heard a strange story yesterday."

"Did you? What about?"

"Someone told me that you were prejudiced against whites. I told her, of course, that she had to be mistaken. I was right, wasn't I?"

"Absolutely right."

"I thought so. I told her an intelligent man like yourself would never say such a thing."

He shook his head very slowly. "An intelligent man wouldn't even think it."

"Johnny thought you wouldn't approve of Elly. I told him you would."

"I do." And he did. It took him a minute, but he suddenly realized that sometime within the last few days his prejudices and fears had disappeared. Idly he wondered exactly when that had happened.

They stood in silence for a long moment, content just to hold each other close, before he mentioned, "I lied to you before. You should know that I'm a jealous man."

Angel pulled back and gave an elaborate show of surprise. Her fingers splayed across her chest as she gasped, "No! You mean, you might look at me with murder in your eyes if you thought I was interested in another man?"

Gray Wolf laughed at her playacting. "Is that what I did tonight?"

She smiled then in a very wifely fashion smoothed his shirtfront and brushed an invisible speck from his jacket collar. "Because it's Christmas, I'll be my most magnanimous and forgive you."

"Thank you."

"You're welcome."

He rocked her against him, hugging her just a little tighter before he warned, "I'll probably give you a hard time, now and then."

"Only now and then?"

"But I love you."

"There had better be no buts about it." She advised.

Gray Wolf laughed at her response, his arms crushed her against him. "This is going to be the best Christmas of my life."

"And the last one for me if you squeeze me like that again."

Gray Wolf couldn't remember when he'd been this happy. "I love you." He shook his head, marveling at his exceptional good fortune. "God, but I do."

"Merry Christmas, darling," she said as her hands came to cup his cheeks and draw his mouth closer to the fire. "Merry, merry Christmas."

Merry

by Victoria Thompson

This was a fine thing, Joe thought, reining in his horse so the animal could blow a bit and rest. Here it was, December already, and a norther blowing around his ears, and he was in the middle of nowhere with no place to go and nobody but Ol' Blaze for company.

In the ten years that he'd been on his own, he couldn't remember ever feeling so low. Not since his mother died when he'd just turned sixteen and his stepfather'd kicked him out with nothing but the shirt on his back. A strong boy who was willing to work would never go hungry in Texas, though, so Joe had soon found a job and a new home in a bunkhouse with a lot of other boys and a few men who'd taken him in hand and shown him the ropes.

The jobs had changed through the years, but he'd always had one, and for most of those years he'd been a top hand, drawing top wages and being one of the few cowboys kept on over the slow winter months by whatever rancher he happened to be working for. In ten years, Joe had never been among the men let go to ride the grub line in the cold, traveling from ranch to ranch looking for odd jobs they could do for their keep or just spending a few days eating free off a rancher until he got tired of seeing your face and suggested you move on.

Since he'd gotten that very first job, Joe had never worried about where he'd spend the winter, at least not until this year when he'd done a really stupid thing. He'd known better, of course. Only a fool would pick a fight with the owner's son, even if the boy *was* dumber than dirt and didn't know beans from buckshot. And only a *damn* fool would pick that fight when the leaves had already fallen from the trees and the wind was blowing blue out of the north.

So now Joe was riding the grub line like some saddle tramp, with no chance of work until spring, top hand or not. Of course, he wasn't really in the middle of nowhere. He'd been riding back to his old stomping grounds, the part of Texas where he'd started and which he'd left about four years ago in search of new adventures. He hadn't found many, so he'd decided to come back. For about two miles now he'd been seeing chimney smoke coming from what should have been the Lazy S Ranch, Matt Simpson's place.

Although Joe hadn't actually worked on the Lazy S, he'd broken horses for Matt a few times when he'd been in the area. Maybe Matt would need his services again, or maybe he'd be grateful enough for past services to put Joe up for a while. In any case, the Lazy S was the first place he'd come to where he could at least hang his hat for the night and get a hot meal.

A pleasant thought, especially when Joe remembered that Matt had taken a bride just before Joe'd left the area. A real pretty girl, if Joe recalled correctly, from

282

back East somewhere. New Orleans maybe, or Georgia someplace. Nothing nicer than taking your meals across the table from a pretty woman. A man could almost pretend she belonged to him, at least for a few minutes, and dream about what it'd be like if he had his own place and his own woman.

And pretending was about all Joe could do since he'd never been farther from having his own place than he was right now. He didn't even have a bunk to put his boots under. Feeling a fresh bite of wind, he nudged Blaze into motion, hunkered down into his sheepskin jacket, and headed toward the curling smoke in the distance.

An hour later, he was riding up to the ranch buildings. He'd been able to see them for a long time before he got really close, and his practiced eye told him instantly something was wrong. The door of the barn hung crooked. A hinge had rusted through and hadn't been fixed. A pole on the corral was busted, but instead of replacing it, somebody'd just tied it up with rawhide. The corral was dirty, too, and the mare inside needed to be curried in the worst way. Matt had really let things slide, and Joe began to wonder if his old friend had fallen on hard times, too.

As he rode into the ranch yard, the door of the house opened, and Joe saw a small child peering out. The child jumped at the sight of a visitor and ran back inside piping, "Mamamamamama!"

Joe grinned, wondering if the kid was a boy or a girl. He'd caught a glimpse of a flour sack dress and long dark curls, but that didn't mean much. All children under the age of six wore flour sack dresses, and many a doting mother let her son's curls grow until the boy was old enough to demand they be cut.

A few seconds later, a woman appeared in the doorway, shading her eyes against the late afternoon sun, the child clinging shyly to the skirt of her faded calico dress. The woman was just as pretty as Joe remembered, prettier really. Motherhood agreed with her, and not just the little one at her side, either. From the swell beneath her apron, Joe could see there'd be another baby soon. He thought she looked like a rose in full bloom. Matt Simpson was sure a lucky man.

Joe reined up in front of the house and gave Blaze a reassuring pat so he'd stand. "Afternoon, Miz Simpson," he said, touching the brim of his hat politely. "My name's Joe Carpenter. Maybe you remember me. I did some work for your husband a while back, breaking horses. I was wondering if I could talk to him about a job, if he's around."

Mrs. Simpson didn't smile. In fact, she frowned, or at least that was the only way Joe could think to describe her change of expression until she stepped forward into the sunlight and he saw her more clearly. Then he recognized grief.

"I'm sorry, Mr. Carpenter, my husband . . ." Her voice caught, but she went on determinedly. "Matt . . . passed away last summer."

The hand shading her eyes gestured vaguely, and when Matt looked in the direction to which she was pointing, he saw the lone cross on the hill. He felt as if somebody'd punched him in the stomach. Matt gone. They hadn't been great friends, and Joe hadn't seen him in almost four years, but still he felt the tragedy of a young man's death and a family left alone.

Of course, no woman need be alone for long in Texas, not when there weren't nearly enough females to go around for all the men wanting wives. No sir, not even a woman with another man's baby in her belly, and for sure not when she was as pretty as Mrs. Simpson. She'd probably started getting offers before Matt was even cold in the ground. Joe knew she hadn't taken any of them, though. He knew from the way the place was so run-down. There hadn't been a man running this ranch for a long time.

"I'm sorry to hear it, Miz Simpson," Joe said. "Matt was a fine man."

"Thank you, Mr. Carpenter," she said, straightening her shoulders as if she were adjusting an invisible burden. The sun glinted off her black curls, making them shine like a raven's wing, just the way Joe remembered them shining. "You're probably looking for work, and I've certainly got some that needs to be done, but I'm afraid I can't pay wages. I've already let my men go for the winter, all except one, Rooster Andresen. Maybe you know him?"

Joe nodded and grinned at the mention of his old friend. Nicknamed Rooster for his crop of red hair that insisted on sticking straight up on his head like a rooster's comb, Andresen had always been more than ready to raise a little hell with Joe when they collected their monthly pay. "Yes, ma'am, me and Rooster go way back."

She smiled a little at this, a small curving of her lips that hinted at how much prettier she'd be if she were happier. "I'm not able to pay Rooster wages either, so he's just working for his keep. You're welcome to stay a few days and help out, too, if you like, but — and I probably shouldn't say this because it means you'll be riding on instead of giving me some free labor — you might find real work someplace else breaking horses. I remember you were very good at it. Matt was quite pleased with your work, and I know the other ranchers in the area always need help with their horses."

"Thank you, ma'am. I'm real proud you remembered me." He was, too. Something about a compliment from a pretty woman just made a man glow. Joe
was certainly glowing and not feeling the slightest urge
to move on to what might be a paying job, at least for
the moment.

"Whatever you decide, you're welcome to stay the
night," she said. "It's too close to supper to be riding
on anyway." This time she smiled for real, and Joe decided he wasn't going anywhere at all until he'd worn
out his welcome here good and proper.

She instructed him to put his horse in the barn and
his belongings in the bunkhouse, and told him she'd
call him when supper was ready. Then she ushered her
child back into the house. Only when she'd closed the
door behind her did Joe turn Blaze toward the barn.

Inside the enormous building, Joe found more evidence of neglect in the dirty stalls, and he recalled
Mrs. Simpson saying Rooster was working for his
keep. He must not think his keep was worth much if
this was how he earned it, Joe thought in disgust,
mentally listing the most pressing tasks he'd start on
tomorrow. The first one would be to light a fire under
Rooster Andresen after demanding to know how anybody could take advantage of a poor widow like this.

"I'm sorry, Blaze," he said, falling into the cowboy
habit of addressing his horse aloud. "I'll clean this
place out tomorrow, first thing. Meanwhile, you'll be
fine. I saw some oats over there which'll help make
things bearable."

When he'd rubbed Blaze down and put the horse in
the cleanest stall he could find, Joe headed for the
bunkhouse, toting his gear. He pushed open the un-
latched door with his foot and paused a moment in

286

the doorway to let his eyes adjust to the interior dimness. As soon as he could make out the empty bunk nearest the door, he dropped his stuff on it and took a long look around. That's when he realized he wasn't alone.

The figure under the blankets on the bed halfway down the long row of bunks hadn't stirred, and for one crazy moment, Joe thought . . . But that was silly. He was only thinking about death because he'd just heard about Matt dying. This fellow wasn't dead, just wasting the afternoon with a nap.

"Hey!" Joe shouted, but the fellow still didn't move, and Joe felt a slight chill. Calling himself an idiot for being spooked, he strode down the room to the fellow's bed. He was almost there before he noticed the man's red hair, now faded to a dull orange. A few steps closer and he could see the face clearly, but it wasn't Rooster's face anymore. The cheeks were sunken, the eyes shadowed, and the lips, slightly parted in sleep, were tinged a pale blue.

"Rooster?" Joe said, softly now, almost afraid to wake him and even more afraid he wouldn't be able to. But as he stared at his old friend, he saw the faint rise and fall of the blanket over his chest and realized that at least he was alive.

"Rooster," he said more loudly, laying a hand on Rooster's frail shoulder—God, he could actually feel the bones!—and giving him a slight shake.

This time Rooster's eyes flickered open, but they were dull and glazed, and Joe knew he didn't recognize his old friend.

"Time to wake up, Ol' Son," Joe said with feigned enthusiasm. "Never thought I'd catch you sleeping in the daylight. Wait'll I tell the rest of the boys."

Rooster blinked a few times, trying to focus on Joe's

face, and when he did, his faded blue eyes lighted with recognition. "Joe?" he croaked incredulously.

"That's right, and you'll never hear the end of this from me, partner. Now get your lazy butt out of this bed and tell me what on God's green earth has been going on around here since I left."

"I been some poorly," Rooster said by way of explanation, although Joe didn't need to be told that. Still, Rooster was grinning like a loon, his eyes bright with pleasure, but Joe saw how difficult it was for him to push himself upright. Without thinking, he reached to help, and to his surprise, Rooster didn't protest the assistance. Joe winced to see how thin his friend was— all except his hands, which were swollen about twice their normal size.

When Rooster was sitting on the side of the bed, he shivered slightly. "It's awful cold in here, ain't it?" he said, reaching for the blanket that had been covering him.

Actually, Joe thought the room comfortably warm, probably from the fire that had now died in the pot-bellied stove in the corner. "I'll shut the door," Joe offered, hurrying to do so, then checking the fire and throwing a dried cow paddy in to get it going again. The paddy would burn far longer than a log and was much easier to obtain than wood on the treeless prairie.

When Joe returned to his friend and took a seat on the bunk next to his, facing him, Rooster had wrapped himself in his blanket, but he was still shivering a little.

"Can't seem to get warm no more," Rooster remarked, chafing his swollen hands. "So tell me what you've been up to, Ol' Hoss," he added more cheerfully.

288

Joe briefly filled Rooster in on his activities for the past four years, including the disagreement that had him riding the grub line. "So what happened to Matt? An accident?" he asked when he'd finished his own tale.

"No, appendix burst. It was pretty bad." Rooster shook his head sadly, and Joe had no trouble at all picturing how Matt Simpson had spent his last days, writhing in agony until the poison of his own body killed him. There wasn't even anything a doctor could do, if there'd been a doctor at all, which seemed unlikely.

"This was last summer?" Joe asked.

"Yeah, July. We buried him up on the hill. Did you see?"

Joe nodded.

"We tried to keep the place together, best we could. Matt had three of us working then, but I was already getting sickly. Miz Simpson was in a bad way at first, as you could expect, but she come around right enough. Couldn't make it work, though, not like Matt could, and she's real worried about money. Sent the others away when it turned cold." He smiled then, a disturbing sight for Joe to see his blue lips stretched tight. "She should've sent me off, too, but she could see I was sick. Nobody'd take me on like this. Some days I can't even set a horse. So she says to me, 'Rooster,' she says, 'I'm afraid to be here all by myself, so I was wondering would you stay on. Can't pay you wages, mind,' she says, 'but I'd consider it a personal favor if you'd help me out.' Can you feature it, Joe? She's saving my life, and she says it's a *personal favor* to her."

"She's a fine lady," Joe said, thinking how inadequate the words were. Not many folks would've done for

289

Rooster the way she had. And now he understood why the place looked so bad. She'd been doing it all herself. Heaven only knew what things were like on the range, too. He'd take a ride out first chance he got and check out the cattle, make sure they were faring well. "How come she's not remarried, though?" he asked, still not quite able to work it out in his mind. "Is it because of . . . her condition?" Joe felt awkward discussing such a delicate subject, one he never would have dared mention in Mrs. Simpson's presence.

Plainly, Rooster felt just as uncomfortable. He shrugged beneath his blanket. "No, I don't think it's that, or at least there's been plenty of men around asking her, even when they could see plain as day what they'd be taking on. I think she's still grieving for Matt, so she turns them all down. Now, she don't tell me what's in her mind, you understand, so I'm just guessing. But it's mighty hard on her. She sure could use a man to help out around here, and if that's all she wanted, she's had her pick."

"What do you suppose she wants then?" Joe asked, for some reason a lot more interested in the answer than he had any right to be.

Rooster shrugged again. "How should I know?" He grinned slyly. "Maybe she's been waiting for some no-good saddle tramp like you to come along."

To his dismay, Joe felt his face redden, and when Rooster snorted with laughter, he knew his friend had noticed, too. The worst part was knowing it really was a joke, though. Mrs. Simpson had her pick of men, even if she was looking, which she obviously wasn't. And when she did, she'd never look twice at the likes of Joe Carpenter.

"So, are you going to put yourself in the running, Joe?" Rooster teased.

Joe managed a grin. "Sure. Why not?"

"Then you're staying?" Rooster asked, delighted.

"For as long as she'll have me," Joe replied.

Merry Simpson ushered her tiny daughter inside, out of the cold. "Where are your slippers?" she scolded, seeing the child's bare feet.

"I don't know," little April replied with an ingenuous smile.

"Well, you'd better find them and put them on before your toes turn blue and fall off!" Merry planted her hands on her hips and scowled until April reluctantly marched over to her small bed in the far corner of the room and pulled the knitted slippers out from where she'd hidden them under the bed.

Poor April. She'd never had shoes and couldn't understand the necessity for them. Now, with Matt gone, she might never own any either, Merry thought in despair. How could she let her daughter grow up with nothing? And what would happen to them and the new baby with nobody to take care of them? Merry couldn't do it all alone, she knew.

She was an idiot, she told herself as she watched April plop down on the floor and grudgingly put on the slippers. She should have swallowed her pride and gone back to her family when Matt died. Sure, they'd disowned her when she'd run off with a wild Texan, but they'd be only too glad to take her in now that they'd been proved right about him never amounting to anything. The only condition they would impose for her return would be making her listen to them reminding her of it day in and day out. The prospect of their I-told-you-so's had been too daunting to face last summer when Matt's death had been so new and raw upon her soul. Now, with the baby so close, it was too late to go even if she *had* been willing to trade her pride for shoes for her children.

At the very least, she should have accepted one of the marriage proposals she'd received since Matt's death. Instead of facing a bleak winter all alone with a child to care for and a baby coming, she'd have a home and a husband and security and . . .

She sighed. If only that were all she needed. If only *any* man could fill the hole Matt's passing had left in her heart, then she would be settled by now.

But marriage was more than just a home and security. Marriage was sharing, sharing your hopes and your dreams and your future and your life and, yes, your bed with one special person. Matt had been her special person, and Merry hadn't yet met another man she wanted to share those things with. Especially a man she wanted to share her bed. The mere thought of another man's hands touching where only Matt had touched made her blood run cold.

"Who's that man, Mama?" April asked when she'd finished putting her slippers on.

"What man?" Merry asked absently.

"The one on the horse? Who is he?"

"Oh, he's . . ." What had he said his name was? "His name is Joe Carpenter. He did some work for your father once, a long time ago."

"Before I was born?" she asked.

"Yes, dear. Now hop up here and wash your hands so you can help me with supper."

Merry helped her little daughter onto a stool in front of the sink and the pump Matt had installed before he died. He'd wanted only the best for his family, and he'd made sure they got it. Her parents had been wrong about him, and he'd proved it more than once.

Now none of that mattered, not without him.

When April's hands were clean, Merry helped her roll out the dough and cut the neat, round biscuits. Then Merry put them in the oven of her cast iron stove, the one Matt had bought her last year after he'd sold some cattle. No more cooking over an open fire, he'd said proudly, and Merry had been so pleased.

"Be careful," she warned April for the thousandth time.

"I know," the child said with elaborate boredom. "Hot."

Merry smiled in spite of herself. "Yes, hot, and you'll be real sorry if you touch it."

"What's he want?" April asked suddenly.

"What does who want?" Merry replied, confused.

"The man. Joe. What does he want?"

She opened her mouth to tell April he was just looking for work, but when she pictured him the way he'd looked sitting his horse out there in the yard, the words died on her lips. She'd been so upset at having to tell yet another passing stranger about her husband's death, she hadn't even noticed the stranger himself. Or at least she hadn't realized she'd noticed him until just now.

What was it about him that had suddenly brought his image so clearly to her mind?

"Mama?" April prompted, impatient for an answer to her question.

"He wants a job," she said quickly. "And I suppose he wants some supper."

"You said he could eat with us," April reminded her. "Will he?"

"I expect so." Merry hadn't felt the emotion for so long that she almost didn't recognize the pleasant tingle along her nerve endings as excitement at the prospect of having Mr. Joe Carpenter sit down at her table.

"Mama, why are you smiling?" April asked.

Merry quickly stopped smiling. "Don't be silly. Now, we're having company for supper, so we'd better get ourselves cleaned up a little, hadn't we?"

"Why?" April asked. As she had approached her third birthday, this had become her favorite word.

"Because . . . well, because, that's what you do when you have company."

Oh, dear, she thought, glancing down at her faded work dress. Had she really gone to the door looking like this? And what a mess her hair must be. She hadn't even thought about her hair in weeks. It was bad enough she was as big as a barn. The least she could do was keep herself neat.

"Why are you taking your dress off, Mama? It's not time for bed. We didn't eat supper yet!" April protested, following her mother behind the curtain that separated Merry's bed from the rest of the room.

"Hush, now," Merry scolded, opening the chifforobe that held her meager wardrobe and wondering what might still fit. "No more questions! And if you're real good, I'll read you a story after supper."

April jumped up and down and clapped her hands. Then she stopped, considering. No, plotting, Merry realized when her daughter's brown eyes lit up. "Maybe Joe'll read me a story. I'll ask him!"

By the time supper was ready and Merry went outside to ring the dinner bell to summon Joe and Rooster from the bunkhouse, she was fairly tingling with excitement. Something was wrong with her, she knew. Simply having another man to cook for or another person to talk to at supper shouldn't have caused

294

so strong a reaction. She'd been alone too long, that was it. She was getting cabin fever or maybe it was because of the baby. Women who were expecting often got strange notions. That must be it, she thought, as she clanged the bell.

That *had* to be it, since she certainly wasn't excited about a visit from some saddle bum who was down on his luck. Her life must be even duller than she'd suspected if she was able to take pleasure from such a little thing.

Still, she found herself lingering on the porch, in spite of the frigid wind, until she saw Joe and Rooster coming. They'd taken a while to respond, and Merry knew it was because Rooster was moving so slowly these days. Joe matched his pace to Rooster's, holding the other man's arm as if it were perfectly natural to do so, and Merry could see they were talking and smiling as they came, Joe telling Rooster something that made him throw his head back and laugh once. How long since she'd heard laughter around the Lazy S?

Or seen someone as full of life as Joe Carpenter seemed to be. Standing next to Rooster, stooped and shrunken as he was, Joe seemed a giant, tall and straight and strong in his worn Levi's and sheepskin jacket, his battered Stetson pulled low over his eyes. Had she noticed this before? Was that what had made her nerves jump at the possibility of welcoming him into her house?

Or was it simply the prospect of being around somebody who wasn't dead or dying? Merry didn't know and didn't care. The important thing was that tonight would be different from last night and all the other nights since Matt had died. Tonight she had something to look forward to.

She ducked back into the house, not wanting Joe Carpenter to think she was so anxious she couldn't even wait for him to come inside. April followed her, but not without a protest, having caught her mother's enthusiasm for their company.

Merry busied herself dishing up the beans and fatback and wishing absurdly that she'd had something a little fancier to serve.

" 'Evening, Miz Simpson," Joe Carpenter called when April let the men in.

"Good evening," Merry replied, unable to keep from returning his smile and not even trying. She nervously smoothed her apron over the mound of her stomach. "You can hang your coat and hat there by the door and wash up in the sink." She pointed toward the pump.

"Thank you, ma'am. Real nice place you've got here," he added, glancing around at all the conveniences Matthew Simpson had provided his family.

"Yes, my hus . . ." Merry began, then decided she wasn't going to dwell on the past any longer. "Thank you," she amended and watched as Joe Carpenter hung up his coat and hat after helping Rooster into a chair.

Merry had thought it must be the bulky coat that made Joe look so big, but he looked almost as big without it, broad shouldered and muscular. He seemed to fill the room with his presence, or perhaps it was just the force of his personality, which he suddenly turned on April, who'd been staring up at him with unabashed interest.

"Hello, there," he said with a grin and hunkered down until he was as close to eye level with the child as he could get. "What's your name?"

"April," she replied shyly, delighted at the attention.

"That's a girl's name," Joe informed her solemnly.

296

"Are you a girl?"

"You're silly!" April said, giggling.

"Well, are you?" Joe insisted.

"Yes," she said, tilting her head and flirting outrageously. Where had she learned to *flirt?* It must be something girls were born knowing, Merry thought, and she wondered if it was also something they forgot. She, for example, couldn't imagine herself ever doing it again.

Quickly, she said, "April, say 'How do you do?' to Mr. Carpenter."

"How do you do, Mr. Carpenter?" April parroted in a singsong voice that made Joe Carpenter smile again. He had the most wonderful smile, Merry thought, big and full of energy. He seemed to charge the very air around him, and Merry was beginning to feel that charge.

"I'm fine," Joe Carpenter replied. "And I'm very pleased to meet you, Miss April."

She giggled again, and this time she hid her face in her mother's skirt. The skirt of the dress Merry had changed into, a red flowered calico wrapper and the nicest thing she owned that would still fit over her stomach.

Joe rose to his feet, and once more Merry was struck by how enormous he seemed, even though she judged he wasn't even quite six feet tall. Still, he towered over her five feet, two inches, and made her feel tiny in spite of her bulging stomach.

For a minute she just looked up at him, taking note of how brown his eyes were, so dark she couldn't even see the pupils, and of the way his sun-streaked brown hair had been mussed a little by his hat and of the white laugh lines around his eyes that stood out against his deep suntan, and of the firmness of his mouth and jaw. He wasn't handsome in the traditional sense, but he had so much vitality, Merry didn't even notice the lack.

"What're you staring at, Mama?" April asked, breaking the spell that had held Merry. She jumped guiltily and hurried to finish putting supper on the table while Joe went to the sink and washed his hands.

Joe took the chair Merry indicated — Matt's chair, although she didn't let herself think about that — and they all bowed their heads as Merry said a brief grace. Then she started to pass the food, stopping to serve both April and Rooster, neither of whom was able to handle the large serving dishes.

When she passed the bowl of beans to Joe, their eyes met, and she saw the questions in his dark eyes. He'd be wondering why she'd kept Rooster on when he was clearly helpless. Maybe he even thought she was a fool for doing so. Well, if he did, so what? Everything she'd done lately had been foolish: refusing to go back to her family, keeping Rooster on, refusing to marry again, trying to run the place alone with a baby coming. If Joe Carpenter thought so, he wouldn't be the only one.

They ate in silence, as was customary in the West, and when they were done, Joe Carpenter got up to help clear the table.

"You don't have to do that, Mr. Carpenter," Merry protested, although she was absurdly pleased by the gesture.

"Just call me Joe, Miz Simpson. I might not remember to answer if you call me Mr. Carpenter," he said, ignoring her protest and carrying more dishes to the sink for her to scrape.

Smiling, she took the plates from him and accepted his help, trying to remember when such a simple kindness had pleased her so much.

While they worked, Rooster excused himself and shuffled out, heading back to the bunkhouse, obviously exhausted. When the table was clear, Joe stood for a moment at loose ends, apparently uncertain whether he should sit down again or return to the bunkhouse, too. Merry was trying to think of some reason to ask him to stay when April said, "Will you read me a story, Joe?"

"His name is Mr. Carpenter," Merry reminded her gently, but April frowned impatiently.

"He said he wouldn't answer to that, remember?" April reminded her right back.

Merry was about to scold her when Joe chuckled. "She's right," he said, "and you *can* call me Joe, Miss April. Now what kind of a story did you have in mind?"

"I've got a storybook Mama reads to me," she explained. "I'll get it."

"Uh, how about if I *tell* you a story, instead?" he suggested.

"Yes!" she cried, jumping up and down and clapping her hands. "But you have to sit in the rocking chair and hold me on your lap," she added.

Merry opened her mouth to tell him he didn't have to do everything April commanded, but Joe was already picking her up and heading for the old, battered rocker, which was the only really comfortable chair in the place.

When they were settled, with April snuggled into the crook of Joe's arm, he said, "Do you know the one about Moses in the bullrushes?"

This time Merry's mouth opened in surprise, since Joe Carpenter didn't look like the type of man who went around telling Bible stories, but she swallowed

299

her surprise and kept on quietly doing the dishes so she wouldn't miss a word.

"What're bullrushes?" April asked.

"Darned if I know," Joe chuckled. "I figure they must be something grows in the water, like cattails."

"Cat's tails don't grow in the water, silly! They grow on cats!" April informed him, giggling at his joke.

"Oops, you're right," Joe admitted. "Well, anyway, there was this mean king in Egypt—"

"Where's Egypt?" April demanded.

Merry would've told her to stop interrupting, but Joe said, "It's a place real far away from here. And this mean king was killing all the babies . . ."

Merry lingered over the dishes, stretching out the job until Joe Carpenter's story was finished and savoring the sound of his rich, masculine voice softened for the ears of a child. Even the baby inside her seemed soothed by the sound and lay still in her womb.

". . . and the princess adopted him and raised him as her own son," Joe said, finishing the story.

"Did he grow up to be a king?" April asked, obviously awed by the tale.

"Well, not exactly, but that's another story," Joe said.

"Tell it to me!" April begged.

"Not tonight," Merry said, drying her hands. "Joe's done his duty, and it's time for bed."

"Awwww," April whined, but Joe tickled her and made her giggle.

"I'll tell you the rest of it tomorrow, if that's all right with your ma," he promised.

It was more than all right with her ma, Merry thought, but she said, "I thought . . . that is, won't you be riding on, looking for work?"

Joe seemed a little embarrassed and wouldn't quite meet her eye. "Well, there's plenty to do around here for a few days, if you don't mind putting up with me."

"No, not at all," Merry assured him. "I'd . . . I'd be grateful if you'd stay." And for the first time since she'd buried her husband, Merry found herself looking forward to the morrow.

By suppertime the next night, Joe was bone tired from trying to do six months' work in ten hours. The place looked a sight better, though, even for the little bit he'd been able to accomplish. He'd need materials from town to do some of the jobs properly, however, and knowing how worried Mrs. Simpson was about money, he hesitated to ask her how good her credit was at the store.

Of course, he had some money of his own, the wages he'd had coming when he'd been fired from his last job and a little he'd been saving. He could buy the things for her, but some people were funny about that, considered it charity, and he didn't want to offend her. He'd just have to give the matter some thought, he decided. Maybe Rooster would know what he should do.

Joe spent a little time getting cleaned up before supper, changing his clothes and scrubbing down with the hot water he'd asked Mrs. Simpson for. Rooster teased him some, but not much, especially after Joe asked him what to do about the things he needed to buy.

"I sure as hell don't know," Rooster said. "Maybe you should just ask her. She's not like a lot of women, all silly about money and such. She'll say if she can afford it."

"And what if she can't?"

"She'll say that, too."

"I mean, how would she take it if I got them for her

myself?"

But Rooster didn't know the answer to that either.

When the dinner bell rang, Joe still hadn't decided what he was going to do. He and Rooster made their way over to the house, and they found little April waiting eagerly for them in the doorway.

"Joe!" she cried happily, reaching for him to pick her up.

"What about me?" Rooster demanded, pretending to be offended.

"Hello, Rooster," she said perfunctorily, then reached for Joe again.

Joe couldn't have resisted her even if he'd wanted to. She was the cutest thing he'd ever seen with her glossy black curls and her dancing brown eyes, and except for her dark eyes, she looked so much like her mother, it sometimes stopped his breath.

He scooped her tiny body up into his arms and gave her a hug, which she returned enthusiastically. She smelled sweet, and she felt so small, he just wanted to hold her like that forever so nothing bad could ever get her. Just the way he'd like to protect her mother, too, if he only had the chance.

"Let Joe take off his coat at least, April," Mrs. Simpson called from across the room.

Her voice reminded him of a music box he'd heard once, tinkly and gentle, and when he finally allowed himself to look over at her, he saw she was wearing the red dress she'd had on the night before, the one that showed off her dark hair so nice. Her cheeks were flushed from the heat of the stove, and her blue eyes shone as brightly as her daughter's dark ones, as if she was as glad to see him as April was.

After April let Joe take off his coat, they sat down to eat just as they had before, and when they'd finished, Rooster once again excused himself and got up to leave. This time, however, he gave Joe a surreptitious wink, as if they'd agreed he was to leave Joe alone with the Widow Simpson.

Flushing, Joe glanced at Mrs. Simpson and was relieved to see she hadn't noticed.

"Can I have my story now?" April asked as she helped Joe and her mother clear the table.

"When we finish helping your ma," he told her, carefully timing his trips to the sink so he would pass Mrs. Simpson. On each trip, he got a whiff of her scent, a musky, feminine smell that made his blood run a little hotter and his nerves twitch with delicious anticipation. Too bad that was as close as he'd ever get to her, but Joe was willing to savor what little bit of her he could have.

When Mrs. Simpson started the dishes, Joe settled into the rocker again and took April into his lap. She curled up like a kitten, feeling almost as soft and a lot more precious, and looked at him with the kind of adoration he'd thought only kings enjoyed. He had to clear his throat before he could start, and April listened raptly as he told her about Moses and the burning bush and turning his staff into a snake and the seven plagues of Egypt and the parting of the Red Sea.

Somewhere in the middle of the plagues, Mrs. Simpson finished the dishes, pulled up a chair beside them, and started to knit by the flickering light of the fire in the stone fireplace. He watched her out of the corner of his eye, absorbing the blissful contentment of the scene. This was what it would be like every night if he had a home and a family of his own, he thought. The knowledge was bittersweet.

When the children of Israel had crossed the Red Sea

and Pharaoh's soldiers had drowned, Joe paused, waiting for April's inevitable questions. "No questions, little one?" he asked the top of her head when she said nothing.

"She's asleep," her mother said softly.

Joe looked down and discovered she was right. "Why didn't you tell me?" he asked, feeling a little foolish for going on and on when his audience was gone.

Mrs. Simpson smiled. "Because I wanted to hear how the story ended myself," she said.

The sight of her smile made Joe's mouth go dry, and for a moment he could almost believe . . . But that was crazy. She was just a nice lady, being nice to somebody who was helping her out.

"What should I do with her?" he asked, whispering now because he was afraid of waking April.

"I'll get her," she said, setting her knitting aside and using both hands to push herself out of the chair.

Joe found himself watching in alarm at her awkwardness and wondering just how close that baby really was to coming. Being no judge of such things, he still couldn't help realizing it wouldn't be much longer, maybe no more than a few weeks, if that. By Christmas, even. What would she do then? She couldn't take care of this place and Rooster, too, not with a new baby to do for.

Reluctantly, he let her take April from him, too disturbed even to react when her hand brushed his in the process.

"I don't wanna go to bed, Mama," April protested sleepily when her mother lifted her away from him. "I wanna hear more about the children."

"Tomorrow, sweetheart," her mother murmured, carrying her off to her bed in the corner. "Now wait just a minute while I wash you off," she said, setting the

304

child on the side of her bed and hurrying to the stove, where she drew a basin of warm water from the boiler.

"I'm sleepy," April complained when her mother began to wash her face and hands.

"We can't put those dirty feet into bed, now, can we?" her mother replied, swiftly wiping the feet in question, then with an efficiency that amazed Joe, stripping off the child's dress and slipping her nightgown over her head. In an unbelievably short time, April was tucked beneath the covers, fast asleep, her mother's kiss on her forehead.

Mrs. Simpson pulled the curtain around April's bed and smiled at Joe again. His heart might have skipped a beat if it hadn't already been lodged firmly in his throat. He swallowed it down as best he could and rose from the rocker.

"I reckon I'd better go," he said hoarsely.

"Oh, no," she protested, as if she really meant it, then smiled again. "I mean, it's early yet. Unless you're tired . . ."

"Oh, no, ma'am," he assured her, not quite able to believe she was as anxious for his company as he was for hers but willing to be convinced.

"Then stay awhile. I . . . I'm a little starved for grown-up company."

He nodded, thinking he understood—*anybody* would do—then quickly stepped aside, offering her the rocker. "It's more comfortable," he explained, taking the chair in which she'd been sitting and turning it around so he could straddle it.

She sat down in the rocker and picked up her knitting bag, digging in it as she talked. "You know a lot of Bible stories, Joe," she observed.

"Yeah, well, my pa was a preacher. He died when I was thirteen, but by then I already knew the stories all by heart." He didn't tell that to a lot of people. He felt the heat in his face and hoped the light was too dim for her to see it.

"You're awfully good with children, too. Did you have lots of brothers and sisters?"

"No, ma'am. I just . . . I don't know, they like me and I like them. Always been that way."

She smiled knowingly, as if he'd just explained a mystery to her, although he didn't think he'd said anything even interesting. Then he noticed what she'd pulled out of the knitting bag.

"Is that a doll you're making?"

"Yes, it's for April, for Christmas." She held it up. "What do you think?"

It was a rag doll with an embroidered face and black yarn hair. "It looks like April," he said in surprise.

"Do you really think so?" she asked, pleased. "I tried to get it to, but I wasn't sure I'd succeeded. I'm knitting some dresses for it, too."

"She'll be tickled."

"I hope so. I can't do much for her this year . . ." Her voice trailed off and her smile disappeared. Joe would have sold his soul to see it again. But maybe he could at least share her burden.

"I know it ain't none of my business, and you can tell me so if you want, but just how bad *are* things with you, ma'am?"

She sighed and fiddled with the doll a moment before she said, "We'll make it through the winter just fine. It's the future I'm worried about. We'd planned . . ."

He waited, willing her to go on and afraid to speak lest he remind her he had no right to be nosing into her affairs.

306

"We'd planned everything so carefully," she said at last. "We could afford hired hands in the summer, and Matt could handle things himself in the winter for the first few years so we could save on wages. This place is small, but we were making it fine until . . . Well, without Matt to do the work for free . . ."

She shrugged one shoulder helplessly, and she looked so sad and lost, Joe had an overwhelming urge to take her in his arms and comfort her. He closed his hands into fists and glared into the fire as he fought it.

"Don't you have some family you could go to?" he asked when he trusted his voice again.

"No," she said in a tone that invited no questions.

The news shouldn't have pleased Joe, but somehow it did. "Well, I been a little worried about where I'd spend the winter this year. I know it's kind of bold of me to ask and all, but maybe you wouldn't mind putting me up for a while. I can work for my keep and—"

"Oh, Joe, that's awfully kind, but I couldn't ask it of you. I can't do more than feed you, and you could probably get wages someplace else if you tried."

Joe studied her lovely face, trying to gauge the sincerity of her protest. Was she just being polite or was she politely telling him to move along? "If you don't want me to stay, you're going to have to say so, ma'am," he told her finally.

Her pretty blue eyes went wide with surprise, and she said, "Oh, but I do want you to stay!" Then she must've thought that sounded too forward because she added, "I mean, I'd be grateful, like I said." Color came to her cheeks, and she lowered her eyes, embarrassed.

Joe was so happy, he wanted to hug her, although how he could have explained his delight, he had no

307

idea. He'd just committed himself to weeks of back-breaking labor for a woman he hardly knew who wasn't going to pay him a dime. And of course, if he *did* hug her, all bets would be off. So he just grinned. "Thank you, Miz Simpson. You won't regret it."

She raised her eyes again, surprised once more. "I'm the one who should be thanking you, and Joe, I . . ."

"What?" he prompted, when she hesitated.

"Well," she said, nervously fiddling with the doll again, "since I must call you Joe, I think you should call me Merry."

"Mary? That's your name?" he asked, so shocked by this evidence of her favor, he didn't know how to react.

"Yes, only it's *Merry,* M-E-R-R-Y, as in Merry Christmas. It means happy." Her smile was sad, though, and once again Joe had to resist the urge to take her in his arms. If he was going to stay, he'd have to be mighty careful not to do anything to let her know how he really felt about her.

Joe had to clear his throat again. "All right, ma'am, I mean, Merry." Her name was sweet on his tongue, like a treat he didn't really deserve.

This time her smile wasn't the least bit sad, and Joe knew he'd better get out of there fast before he made a fool of himself. "It's getting late," he murmured and rose from his chair, lifting it from between his legs and setting it aside.

"Before you go, I . . ." She jumped up, too, hastily putting the doll down. "I've been wanting to ask you about Rooster," she said, concern darkening her eyes.

"What about him?" he asked warily.

"Is he . . . ? I don't think he's getting any better, do you?"

Joe shook his head. "I haven't seen him in a long

308

time, but he don't look too good to me."

She bit her lip uncertainly. "Maybe you think I'm foolish to keep him on like this when he can't work."

"Oh, no, ma'am," he assured her hastily. "I think . . . Well, what I think don't matter, but it's a fine thing you're doing. He'd probably be dead now if you'd let him go."

"I just couldn't send him away," she said earnestly, as if she were trying to make him understand, although he already understood perfectly.

"I know," he said, and instinctively, he lifted his hand and laid it on her shoulder reassuringly.

Instantly, he felt her heat through the thin fabric of her dress, and the soft roundness of her woman's body. His own body went weak with longing for what he might touch but never possess, and his breath snagged on the stabbing pain of loss in his chest.

Her eyes widened at his touch and her breath caught, too, as if she also felt the impact of his reaction. But before she could shrug him off, he jerked his hand away and stepped back, stuffing his hands in his pockets so he wouldn't be tempted to touch her again. If he hadn't already worn out his welcome, he wasn't going to press his luck any harder.

"I guess I'll be going," he managed, taking another backward step and colliding with the table.

"Be careful," she cautioned when he almost stumbled.

His face was on fire by the time he'd lurched around the table and struggled into his jacket. If she didn't think he was a masher, she'd certainly think he was an oaf, he thought, jamming his hat onto his head.

"Well, good night," he managed, mortified.

But when he made himself look at her one last time,

she was smiling an oddly satisfied smile. "Good night, Joe," she said. "See you tomorrow."

He hurried out, closing the door carefully behind him. When he was gone, Merry reached up and touched the shoulder Joe Carpenter had touched just moments before. She imagined she could still feel the warmth of his hand and the momentary surge of comfort he'd brought her.

He'd felt something, too, something more than comfort if the expression on his face was any indication, and Merry smiled at the thought. Maybe he didn't find her burgeoning figure completely repulsive. Maybe he wouldn't even mind that she was carrying another man's child. He certainly seemed fond enough of April, and he was so good with the child. He'd probably be good with the new baby, too.

And Merry couldn't help wondering if he'd be good with the baby's mother, given the opportunity.

That night, for the first time since her husband's death, Merry began to imagine what it might be like to have another man in her life.

For the next week, Joe worked harder than he'd ever worked for anyone, and to his surprise, Rooster rallied and began to help him for at least part of each day. But nobody'd ever labored the way Joe did. Part of him was working to fix things up for Merry and make her life a little easier. The other part of him was working himself into exhaustion so he wouldn't have the energy for imagining what his life might be like with a wife like Merry Simpson.

The exhaustion didn't seem to help, though, because no matter how tired he was when he crawled into his bunk at night, he still met her in his dreams, dreams that made him blush in the light of day. Seeing her at every meal didn't help either, since she seemed to get prettier every time he saw her, and friendlier, too. It was only appreciation for the way he was helping her, he knew, but still, he couldn't stop himself from caring more and more about her every day. If he wasn't careful, he'd be in love with Merry Simpson, and then what would he do?

Heaven knew, he was already in love with little April, who followed him everywhere, asking questions about what he was doing and "helping" when he'd let her. Of course, a man would have to have a heart made of solid stone not to love a kid who hollered his name and ran into his arms every time she saw him.

After a week of being lavished with such attention, Joe knew he'd better get away for a little while or risk taking it to heart.

"I reckon I'll go into town today," he told Merry after breakfast the next morning. "Do you need anything?"

"Can I go?" April asked, clinging to Joe's leg and giving him a look he knew he'd never be able to refuse.

Fortunately, her mother refused for him. "You've got to stay here and help me, sweetheart," she told her, then turned back to Joe. "I do need a few things. I'll make you a list," she said.

Joe had his own list of things he needed to finish fixing up the ranch buildings, but he didn't ask Merry if he could charge them to her account at the store. He'd finally decided how to handle it. He'd pay for the stuff himself and let her think he'd charged them. By the time she found out, he'd probably be long gone, so she'd never have to feel beholden.

The only thing he hadn't decided was what to do

about Christmas. He'd pick up some tobacco for Rooster and a toy for April, but what should he do about Merry? He'd never bought a present for a lady before, and he wasn't even sure it was proper for him to give her one. Then again, that's what Christmas was all about, wasn't it? He dearly wished he knew somebody to ask about the situation.

As soon as he got to town, Joe started running into old friends who were a lot happier to see him again than he'd ever expected. It took him an hour to get from the street where he'd parked Merry's wagon into the mercantile, twenty feet away. Along the way, he had to explain to about a dozen folks where he'd been for the past few years and what he'd been doing and let some cowboys buy him a beer so he could tell everybody in the saloon, too, before he could finally go back to the store to fill his order.

Even then, he spent another ten minutes telling the storekeeper his story before the man would accept the list of supplies and begin to fill the order. While Joe was waiting, he started wandering around the store, idly examining the merchandise on display. In the very back corner, he found what appeared to be a chair covered with an old sheet. A sign pinned to the sheet proclaimed the chair was covered with silk brocade and was for sale for the princely sum of ten dollars.

Curious to see what could make a chair worth so much, Joe lifted the sheet. He saw at once. The silk brocade was richly red and upholstered the back, the arms, and the spring seat of a platform rocker. The rest of the chair was carved mahogany which gleamed with a lustrous sheen even in the dimly lit store. It was a chair fit for a queen.

And Joe could picture her in it, her dark curls dancing, her lovely face smiling as she rocked her new baby. It was the perfect chair for a new mother, and it would be the perfect gift for Merry.

Joe didn't even bother to wonder whether she would accept such a gift from him. He'd just tell her Santa Claus had brought it and deny any knowledge of where it had come from. The only problem he considered was how to pay for it.

He had some money, of course, but he was already spending part of it on materials to fix up the ranch, and a long winter loomed ahead during which he might need to help Merry out some more. Ten dollars would take too big a bite out of his reserves to leave him feeling comfortable.

Considering his problem, Joe didn't notice the lady who had just come into the store, but she noticed him right away.

"Joe Carpenter, is that you?" she demanded, striding right up and looking him square in the face. She was a stout, middle-aged woman in a gingham dress and a drooping bonnet.

"Miz Holling?" he asked, peering under the bonnet, not quite certain he recognized the wife of his former boss.

"The very same! Joe, you're a sight for sore eyes. How long's it been? Three years?"

"Nearer to four, I'm afraid."

"I declare! Where've you been all this time?"

So Joe had to go through the whole story once again, ending it with an explanation of how he came to be staying out at the Lazy S.

"How's Merry doing?" Mrs. Holling asked, frowning her concern.

"Seems to be fine," Joe said, "although the place was mighty run-down. Say, don't the menfolk around here believe in doing for widows and orphans anymore?"

313

This was a question he'd been wanting to ask but until now hadn't encountered anyone from whom he could expect a straight answer.

As he'd guessed, Mrs. Holling's answer was straight as an arrow. "It's a sin the way they neglect her, it's true. I've been trying to figure it out myself, and I'm of two minds on the subject. Either they're trying to make her sorry she didn't marry one of them, or else each one of them's afraid to do any work on the place for fear she'll up and marry somebody else and another man'll get the benefit of their labors."

Joe had to chuckle at the picture she painted. He could easily imagine a man feeling such a hesitation. Shoot, he might well end up in that very situation himself. The thought gave him a momentary qualm, but before he could linger on it, Mrs. Holling distracted him.

"Can't understand why you didn't come on out to our place, Joe. Mr. Holling'd love to see you, and so would our girls. They always did have a soft spot for you, and they're all growed up now. The twins've been receiving gentleman callers for almost a year now, and little Edith will be starting in the spring. They'd be pleased as punch to see you again. In fact," she recalled after a moment's thought, "Mr. Holling was just saying the other day how he wished he could find somebody as good as you to break some horses he's rounded up. I'll bet if you ask him, he'd hire you on for the job in a minute."

"Well, I sorta promised Miz Simpson I'd stay on at her place and help out. Rooster's been feeling a mite poorly and . . ." Feeling his face redden, Joe stammered to a halt while Mrs. Holling smiled knowingly.

"So that's the way things are," she said, and Joe

314

didn't dare deny or confirm, since he didn't have any idea how she thought things were. "Well, now, nobody said you've got to leave Merry permanent. Mr. Holling prob'ly don't want to take on another hand for the whole winter anyways. But if you'd like to pick up a little extra money to tide you over until spring, Mr. Holling is over to the livery stable getting a harness repaired, and I'm sure he'd—"

"Thank you kindly, Miz Holling," Joe said, already on his way.

"Joe!" she called, stopping him. "Have you heard about the dance?"

"Dance? What dance?"

"On Christmas Eve. We're having a dance here in town, at the schoolhouse. Everybody's invited. Be lots of pretty girls here for you to dance with, mine included . . . if Merry'll let you come, that is," she added slyly.

Joe knew his face must be scarlet, but he pretended he hadn't understood Mrs. Holling's implication. Instead he tipped his hat and thanked her again and fled the store, calling out to the storekeeper that he'd be right back to pick up his order.

Mr. Holling was indeed glad to see Joe and offered him the job breaking horses before Joe could even ask. No more than three or four days' work, Mr. Holling had said, and he'd pay him a dollar for every horse he broke. Since a rancher's idea of "broke" was gentling a horse only enough so he would tolerate the weight of a saddle and rider on his back, Joe figured he could easily earn enough money for the chair and then some.

When he returned to the store, he picked out a little doll cradle that would be perfect for April's new baby doll and a pouch of tobacco and a pipe for Rooster and asked the storekeeper to hold them for him until

315

Christmas Eve.

"And I'll be wanting that rocker you've got in the back, too," Joe added, trying to appear nonchalant. "Can I pick everything up when I come into town for the dance on Christmas Eve?"

"Sure can," the storekeeper told him. "I'll be mighty happy for that rocker to find a home. Fellow who ordered it couldn't pay for it when it come in, and I thought I'd be stuck with it for good."

Grinning, Joe loaded the supplies into the wagon and headed back to the Lazy S, the place he was starting to think of as home. This sure was going to be some Christmas, he thought happily. He'd take Merry and April to the dance in town, and Rooster, too, if he felt up to it, then he'd take them home and surprise them with his gifts. For the first time since he could remember, Joe felt like he was in charge of his life and that things were going just the way he wanted them to, which was why he couldn't understand Merry's reaction to his good news.

He'd waited to tell her until after supper, when Rooster had gone back to the bunkhouse and April had gone to sleep, the time he'd started to think of as "theirs."

"I told you I saw Mr. and Mrs. Holling in town," he started when she'd settled herself back into the worn rocker where he always insisted she sit unless he was telling April a story. As usual, Joe was straddling one of the straight-backed chairs and sat facing her.

"Yes, you did," she said, smiling over the tiny doll dress she was knitting.

"Did I tell you Miz Holling asked about you?"

"Yes, you did, Joe," she repeated, still smiling.

"And you already knew about the dance?" he continued.

316

"Yes, and I've already told you I was sorry for not telling you about it myself. It should be a lot of fun." Her smile shone. Joe could have looked at that smile all night.

"Well, Mr. Holling offered me a job breaking some horses for him."

Her smile vanished. "Did he?" she asked carefully, lowering her gaze to her knitting.

"Yeah," he said, a little startled by her lack of enthusiasm. He tipped his chair forward a little in an effort to close the gap he'd sensed had suddenly developed between them. "It'll be a good way for me to earn some extra money. What with Christmas coming and all," he added lamely, wondering what he'd said to make her frown like that.

"Oh, yes, of course, I told you somebody'd pay you wages," she said stiffly, concentrating harder on her knitting than he'd ever seen her do before. Maybe she was doing some particularly difficult stitch. Joe could think of no other reason why she would refuse to meet his eye. "I suppose you've got gifts to buy for . . . for somebody special," she said. "The Hollings have daughters, don't they? Real pretty girls, too."

Joe didn't want to discuss his gifts, and he didn't have the slightest idea what the Holling girls had to do with any of this. "I don't like leaving you alone, but the work's mostly caught up, the important stuff, anyways," he tried, thinking this might be what she was worried about.

"I'm very grateful for everything you did," she told him, still not looking up. "I never really expected you'd stay all winter." Her voice sounded so strained, Joe almost missed the implication of what she'd said.

When he did, he blinked in surprise. "I ain't going anywhere," he said.

She looked up at this, a little impatiently, he thought. "You just said you were going to work for Mr. Holling."

Now he understood. "I'm just going to break some horses for him," he explained quickly. "Won't take more'n a few days. I'll be done and back before Christmas."

This time *she* blinked in surprise, and her sky blue eyes widened with understanding. "Oh," she said, looking relieved and a little embarrassed. "I see. I . . . *ow!*" she cried suddenly, clutching her side.

Joe's heart stopped dead in its tracks. "What is it?" he asked in alarm, ready to fling his chair aside, jump to his feet, and run for help.

"Just the baby kicking," she said absently, rubbing her bulging stomach. Then she realized what she'd said and to whom, and the color blossomed in her cheeks. "I mean . . ." she stammered, obviously mortified, but she couldn't seem to think of any way to correct herself without making things worse.

Joe was flushing, too, embarrassed because no gentleman would consider mentioning a woman's delicate condition, most certainly not in her presence. He'd never even imagined discussing such a thing with a lady. He supposed a married man might have to talk it over with his wife, although Joe couldn't picture doing so himself, any more than he could picture actually being married.

Still and all, she'd been the one to bring it up, and after a minute he thought maybe he'd figured out why she seemed so unhappy about him going to work for Mr. Holling. Swallowing down hard, he forced himself to say, "Maybe I shouldn't be leaving you just now. If . . . if it's going to be soon, maybe . . . maybe I should . . ."

"No," she said quietly, still staring intently at her knitting, although she hadn't taken another stitch since the baby had kicked her. "It's not for another month or so."

Joe's face was so hot he thought it might actually burst into flames, but fortunately, Merry didn't look at him so she didn't notice. His shoulders sagged in relief. At least he didn't have to worry about *that* happening while he was gone, although he certainly didn't want to be anywhere near when it did. The thought of Merry giving birth absolutely terrified him.

But of course no one would expect him to be anywhere near. Riding for help when the time came, that's the most anybody'd expect, which was a good thing because that was about all he'd be good for.

Which made him think of another problem. "You . . . shouldn't you have some womenfolk to help? I mean when . . ." He gestured helplessly.

"I will. We . . . we arranged for someone to be with me during the last few weeks before . . . The ladies'll take turns, and they'll start coming after Christmas. Nobody wants to be away from their families on Christmas, and there's still plenty of time and . . ." Her voice trailed off in renewed embarrassment.

He swallowed again, this time with relief, and cleared his throat. "Well, then, Mr. Holling said he had about three, four days' work. Christmas is six days off, so I'll be back in plenty of time to take you and April to the dance. Rooster's been doing a lot better lately, and he can look after things in the meantime. And if you do need me for anything, all you have to do is holler," he added, thinking nothing would keep him away if Merry sent for him.

The offer didn't seem to please her, however. "Thank you, Joe, but you know you don't owe me anything.

319

I'm the one who's indebted to you, so you mustn't feel any obligation to come back if somebody offers you a real job." When she looked up, her lovely eyes were clouded and troubled, but Joe couldn't begin to guess what was troubling her.

"I'll only be gone a few days," he insisted.

She nodded as if she understood, but if she did, the understanding gave her no comfort. "April will miss you," she said.

"I'll miss her, too," he replied. "I'll miss . . . everything here," he added lamely, wishing he dared tell her the truth, that he'd probably be thinking about Merry every minute he was gone and how the days would feel more like weeks until he got back to her again. But if she looked worried now, she'd be plumb scared to death if she knew how Joe felt about her, so he kept his mouth shut and his true feelings to himself.

"I reckon I'll leave first thing in the morning, right after breakfast," he said after an awkward silence.

She nodded and looked down at her knitting again, although her hands lay still in her lap.

When she didn't respond, Joe said, "It's late. I guess I'll hit the hay."

"Good night, Joe," she said a minute later when he opened the door to leave. He murmured his reply and was gone, closing the door softly behind him so as not to wake April.

Sitting there alone in the sudden silence, Merry watched the tears fogging her vision and made no move to wipe them away when they began to trickle down her cheeks. Well, what had she expected? That Joe Carpenter would find her attractive with her stomach sticking out a mile from another man's baby? That he'd want to be tied down with a ready-made family? So what if he liked telling April stories. So what if he

320

was the hardest worker she'd ever encountered. So what if he was the only man she'd felt comfortable with since Matt. None of those things meant he wanted to settle down with her here and fill her lonely life with his gentle sweetness and strength.

A few days with the Holling girls fawning all over him was all it would take. And Merry was certain they would fawn on him, too. What red-blooded woman could resist him? After that, Merry would be lucky if she ever even *saw* Joe Carpenter again.

Well, it wasn't the end of the world. It wasn't as if she was in love with him or anything. She'd only known him a week, for heaven's sake. You couldn't fall in love with somebody you'd known for only a week, even if he *was* the sweetest, most handsome, most charming man alive.

But if she wasn't in love with him, why couldn't she stop crying?

Joe had been right to think the days away from Merry would be the longest of his life, and when he knew he wouldn't be finished with breaking all the horses on the third day, he felt lower than a snake's belly at the thought of staying at the Hollings' bunkhouse one more night.

Not that it was bad at the Hollings'. Just the opposite. Several of his old buddies were wintering there, and the Holling daughters were mighty pretty and remembered Joe fondly from when they'd been much younger. Now all they wanted to do was flirt, though, and Joe had no time for such things.

"We're saving you a dance," one of the twins had said at supper that evening, referring to the Christmas Eve shindig in town. He wasn't sure which one of them had said it, since he couldn't seem to tell them apart, but since she was speaking for the both of them, he figured if he danced with both girls, they'd be satisfied. Joe was only interested in dancing with one particular girl, though, a real pretty girl with dark curls and sky blue eyes. The rest of the time, he'd just be going through the motions.

So he went to bed that night thinking about Merry Simpson and fully expecting to dream about her as he often did. Instead he encountered Rooster.

"You're supposed to be looking after Merry. What are you doing here?" Joe asked in the dream, oddly aware of how silly the question was because he knew he was dreaming and Rooster wasn't really there at all.

"Remember when you told me you was coming over here for a few days?" Rooster asked. Joe noticed he looked the way he used to look before he took sick and got so skinny. His hair was bright red, the way it used to be, too.

"I remember," Joe said.

"And I told you not to worry, that if anything happened, I'd send for you."

"Yeah?" Joe prompted.

"Well, something's happened, something bad. You've got to get back right away. Merry needs you."

Joe felt annoyance at hearing Rooster calling Merry by her given name. He was just going to say something about it when Rooster began to fade away, reminding Joe this was just a dream.

Even still, he couldn't seem to shake the memory of Rooster's summons when he woke up the next morning, and although he wasn't quite finished breaking all the horses yet, he told Mr. Holling he'd have to leave after the noon meal and get home to the Lazy S. "I'll come back after Christmas and finish up," he promised.

322

"We'll see you at the dance, though, won't we?" one of the twins asked later as he was rising to leave the table.

"For sure," he replied, smiling to conceal his eagerness to be gone. "And you'd both better save me a dance."

"Now you wait a minute, Joe Carpenter," Mrs. Holling said. "I've got a fruitcake I want you to take to Merry for me." So Joe had to delay for what seemed an eternity while Mrs. Holling wrapped the cake for him.

Only when he was riding Blaze toward the Lazy S did he admit the hard lump in his stomach was apprehension over what he was going to find there.

Although the past few days had been pleasantly warm, the wind began to pick up as he rode, stirring up dust devils and pushing dark clouds across the sky. The lowering weather matched his mood and compelled him to kick Blaze into a ground-eating lope to cover the distance between him and Merry as quickly as possible.

The wind tugged at his hat and his coat, trying to slow him down, but Joe rode on, his face stinging from the icy blast, his heart leaden with a growing sense of dread.

He saw her from a mile away, standing on the hill beside her husband's grave, the wind whipping her skirts and lashing her hair. His first response was relief to see she was all right; his second was jealousy to think she still mourned her husband's loss enough to brave the cold. But after a while, when she didn't move, in spite of the biting wind, but continued to stand on the hill, he forgot to be jealous, and his sense of foreboding blossomed into alarm.

Why was a pregnant woman standing out in this

wind when she could be inside where it was warm and safe? A visit to her husband's grave was one thing, but not on a day like this and certainly not for so long.

As he closed the distance between them, he saw she wasn't simply standing there. She was doing something, and when he realized what it was, his heart turned to stone.

"Merry!" he called, panicked now, but the wind snatched the word away, and she didn't turn, didn't respond. She just kept digging. Dear God, she just kept digging at her husband's grave!

Joe sawed on the reins and vaulted off Blaze's back before the horse even had a chance to stop. He hit the ground running, letting Blaze go, racing for where Merry wrestled with the shovel. She'd made little progress, he saw in the first split second, and in the next, he saw she wasn't really digging at Matt's grave at all.

"Merry!" he cried, grabbing her and turning her toward him. Her eyes were swollen and her face blotched with weeping. For a moment she didn't even seem to recognize him. "Merry, what are you doing?" he demanded, shouting over the howling wind.

"I . . . I didn't think . . . you'd come back," she said weakly.

The shovel slipped from her hands and landed in the dirt with a clunk. Then Joe realized the howling wasn't all the wind. Some of it was little April, who sat next to the cross marking her father's grave, crying her eyes out. She hadn't noticed Joe yet, either.

"Merry, what's going on? What are you doing?" he demanded.

"I'm digging . . . a grave . . . for Rooster . . ." With that, her eyes fluttered closed and she went limp in his arms.

324

"He didn't come for breakfast this morning," Merry explained hours later, after Joe had carried Merry into the house and seen to her and April's comfort. After he'd found Rooster's cold body resting in his bed where he'd died in his sleep. After he'd chopped a grave out of the stubborn earth and carefully placed Rooster's body in it. After he'd recited the appropriate scripture verses he remembered from his youth over Rooster's final resting place. And after Joe had rustled up some supper for them all and made sure Merry ate it because she still looked as if she might keel over again at any minute.

Now she sat in the rocking chair, April curled in her lap, snuggled up against the bulge of the new baby. April sucked her thumb, something Joe had never seen her do before, and he figured it was because of the shock of the day.

"I didn't think anything of it," Merry was saying, her gaze fixed on the fire, as if she could find the answers to her questions there. "Rooster often slept in when he didn't feel well, but when I rang the bell at noon and he didn't come, I got a little worried, so I sent April over to fetch him."

April pulled her thumb out of her mouth. "He wouldn't wake up," she informed Joe solemnly. "I shook him and shook him, but he wouldn't wake up."

"I know," Joe said, reassuring her in case she thought she'd done something wrong. "It's all right. You couldn't help it."

Placated, she put her thumb back in her mouth and laid her head against her mother's breast. Joe noticed her eyes were drooping and figured it was time to put her to bed.

"She's almost asleep," he told Merry.

Merry nodded and made a move to get up, but Joe instantly saw she didn't have the energy to lift her daughter. Merry's face was gray in the firelight, her eyes red-rimmed and shadowed. Instinctively, Joe jumped up and plucked April from her lap. "I'll take care of her," he said without thinking, and the fact that Merry didn't protest told him he was right about the extent of her exhaustion.

Only when he'd carried April over to her bed and set her down did Joe realize what he'd gotten himself in for.

"You have to wash my face and hands," April told him, her dark eyes wide and expectant.

Well, he'd known that, he told himself. He'd seen Merry put her to bed often enough, so he knew the procedure. And he could certainly perform it. It was a lot easier than breaking a horse, for heaven's sake.

Or so he thought until he got soap in April's eye and made her cry. And when he'd got her settled down again, she reminded him of the next step. "I can't put these dirty feet in bed, now, can I?" she said, mimicking her mother.

Then he had to remove her little dress and put on her nightdress.

"Why is your face so red, Joe?" April asked when he'd finished the process.

"Taking care of you is hard work, little one," he explained, hoping Merry wasn't paying too much attention. He pulled back the covers and helped her crawl underneath them, then tucked her in as he'd watched her mother do.

"Now you have to kiss me," April informed him, smiling expectantly.

He leaned over and touched his lips to her tender

326

cheek, inhaling the sweet, little girl smell of her. Her dark eyes shone with such love and trust, Joe's throat closed up with a lump as big as a fist. He couldn't speak for a few seconds, and before he could, he had to clear his throat twice.

"Go to sleep now, little one," he murmured, pulling the curtain closed around her bed.

When he turned back to Merry, he saw she was crying silently, the tears glittering on her cheeks in the firelight. He hurried to her, not knowing what to do but wanting to make things better for her. Awkwardly, he hunkered down beside her and took one of her hands in his, remembering the feel of her body as he'd carried her back to the house this afternoon when she'd fainted.

He wanted to hold her now, too, but didn't dare, so he just held her hand. It was like ice in his.

"I'm sorry, Joe. He was your friend, wasn't he?" she whispered.

"I never should've left you here alone," Joe said, taking the blame on himself. "I knew he was sick—"

"But he'd been so much better," she argued, trying to convince herself as much as him.

"You was the one I was worried about, too, not him," Joe insisted.

Her fingers tightened on his, although she was still staring into the fire. "I wanted you to come, but I didn't know how to get you here. There wasn't any way," she said helplessly.

"Rooster called me," he said, remembering the dream and knowing Rooster must have been dead when he'd appeared to Joe. "He said he would if anything happened, and he did."

Plainly, she didn't understand, but she was also plainly too exhausted to question him about it. "I'm so

327

tired of death and dying," she said, the tears coursing freshly down her face. "I'm just so *tired*."

"You better get to bed, too. Everything'll seem better in the morning," he said, quoting his long-dead mother. "Or at least not quite so bad," he added at Merry's disbelieving look.

He rose and took her other hand to help her from the chair, but her legs weren't quite steady, and she almost fell. Once again Joe caught her.

She murmured a faint protest as he lifted her to his chest, but he ignored it, savoring the feel of her softness against him and inhaling her sweet scent. Her hair brushed his cheek as he carried her to her bed, the feather touch like a kiss, and for that moment Joe could almost believe she was truly his.

With great regret, he laid her on her bed, knowing she was much too weary to undress herself and not daring even to think of helping her, much as he might like to. Gingerly, expecting a shocked reprimand at any moment, he removed her shoes and set them carefully on the floor beside the bed, pretending he hadn't noticed her slender ankles or anything else about how pretty she was everywhere and not just her face.

But she didn't seem to mind, didn't even seem to notice his ministrations, and when he'd removed the only articles of her clothing he could, he pulled the covers down and back up over her, tucking them in as he'd tucked April in a few minutes ago.

By then she was asleep, her face pale against the pillowcase, her breathing slow and regular. She looked so beautiful, Joe thought his heart might burst from wanting her.

"I'll take care of you, Merry," he promised in a whisper. "I won't let anything bad happen to you ever again."

He held his breath, waiting for her to open her eyes in shocked surprise, but she didn't stir, so he knew she was sound asleep. That was the only reason he was bold enough to bend down and kiss her, touching his lips to her cheek for one blissful second before drawing guiltily away.

Then, not wanting to leave her alone and not wanting to spend the night in the bunkhouse where his friend had so recently died, Joe rolled up in a blanket and fell asleep on the floor in front of the fire.

Merry awoke when the first faint light of dawn was peeping over the horizon. The cabin was still dark, so at first she was disoriented, wondering what was wrong. Then she remembered.

Rooster's death. Her own futile efforts up on the hillside. April crying and Merry not knowing what to do. And just when she'd been about to give up, Joe had come. The answer to her prayers. He'd come back without even being called.

Vaguely, she remembered a conversation with him last night. He'd said something about Rooster sending for him, although Merry hadn't understood it at the time. She still didn't.

The baby kicked, bringing her fully awake and creating an urgent need to visit the outhouse. Cautiously, she sat up, reluctant to leave the warmth of her blankets and wondering why her robe wasn't at the foot of her bed where she usually left it.

Could she have slept in it? she wondered, then realized she was still fully dressed. How could she have gone to bed in her clothes? But when she tried to remember, she drew a blank. All she recalled was Joe being there when she needed him. For everything.

Could he have . . . ? But that was impossible. Although she didn't remember putting April to bed last night either.

Awkwardly, she shifted her bulky figure and heaved herself out of the bed. The floor was cold through her thin stockings, but she didn't wait to find her slippers or shoes. Pushing aside the curtain separating her bed from the rest of the room, she was about to hurry across to check on her daughter when she saw something that startled a cry from her throat.

Joe Carpenter stirred in his blankets and blinked a few times before focusing on her. " 'Morning," he mumbled sleepily, pushing up on one elbow. "How do you feel?"

"I . . . fine," she managed, still trying to make sense of everything. "What are you . . . I mean, is anything wrong?"

"You mean, why am I sleeping on your floor?" he corrected her, grinning the grin she'd come to love. "You were mighty tuckered out last night. I figured I oughta stay in case April woke up or anything." He sat up completely, rubbing the sleep from his face. "And . . . well, I didn't cotton to the idea of sleeping in the bunkhouse just yet, if you know what I mean."

Merry nodded, remembering other things she'd like to forget. She couldn't blame him for not wanting to share the bunkhouse with Rooster's ghost, and the idea that he'd stayed with her all night made her feel warm all over, in spite of the morning chill. "Is April all right?"

"Snug as a blood tick on a fat hound, last I saw," Joe said, grinning again. "I reckon I'd better build up the fire, though, so she don't catch a chill when she wakes up."

Merry nodded, suddenly recalling her urgent need

330

to visit the outhouse, and muttered something incomprehensible before finding her shoes and her shawl and hurrying outside.

She really shouldn't be so happy, she told herself. Not with Rooster hardly cold in his grave and a baby coming and winter looming before her along with all the other uncertainties of the future. It wasn't seemly. But still, Joe was back, and she couldn't seem to smother the glow of joy smoldering somewhere very close to her heart.

Shortly after breakfast, Joe reminded her and April that it was Christmas Eve, another reason for them all to feel unreasonably happy, no matter what the circumstances.

"There's a party in town tonight, and everybody's invited. There'll be dancing and food and lots of kids to play with," he told April.

The little girl jumped up and down and clapped her hands. "Can we go, Mama? Can we?"

"Of course, we can, sweetheart," Merry said, thinking she'd love to go to a party with Joe beside her. Not that he'd stay beside her for long, though. She knew he'd much prefer dancing with pretty young girls instead of an old married lady, even if she hadn't been pregnant and unable to dance at all anyway. But at least they'd go together and come home together.

So she let herself feel April's excitement as Joe went out to cut a mesquite bush for them to use as a Christmas tree. While he was gone, she and her daughter popped popcorn and strung it for garlands, the way Merry had always done as a child. For the first time, she shared with April the memories of Christmases past when she'd lived in her parents' house, before she'd had to choose between them and the man she'd loved: apple cider with cinnamon sticks

331

simmered over the fire, stockings hung beside the chimney for Santa to fill, candles on the tree.

They had no cider or candles, but Merry got out the tiny box where she stored her precious, handmade ornaments and explained to April how she'd come to make each one. Then they hung April's small stocking from the mantel.

Merry supposed it was all that leaning over to string the popcorn that made her back ache, but the ache didn't go away when she stood up again. By the time the tree was decorated and crowned with the star she'd carried with her all the way from Georgia, she was in real pain.

Must've slept on it wrong, she told herself as she prepared the noon meal for the three of them. But Joe noticed the way she kept pausing to plant her hands in the small of her back and arch to relieve the pressure.

"Is something wrong?" he asked, looking up from where he'd been using the porcelain figures in the crèche to explain the Christmas story to April.

"No, not a thing," she lied, forcing a smile, but she saw him watching her more carefully as the afternoon lengthened and the pain continued. As bad as she felt, she savored Joe's concern. It had been so long since she'd had a man to look after her, being uncomfortable was almost worth indulging herself in this novel luxury.

But by midafternoon, Merry had to accept the fact that she felt too ill even to think about riding into town, much less attending a dance.

"We oughta be getting ready to go," Joe told her, but the uncertainty in his voice told her he already suspected what she would say.

"I think I'd better stay home," she told him reluctantly. "I wouldn't be much company anyway."

"We don't have to stay long," he said, trying to convince her, but his dark eyes were clouded with concern.

"I . . . I just don't think I could stand that long ride," she explained apologetically, absently rubbing the ache in her back. "April will be so disappointed . . ."

"About what?" April inquired, running in from outside where she'd been playing in the afternoon sun.

Merry winced at the thought of her reaction but steeled herself against it. "Mama's not feeling very well, so I don't think we'll go to the party tonight."

April's small face wrinkled up, preparing for a howl of protest, but then she thought of something. "I can go with Joe," she said, smiling again.

"Don't be silly," Merry said, thinking she knew what Joe was going to say. If she wasn't going, he wouldn't want to go either. Not her Joe, not the man who'd come back when she needed him so desperately. Not the man who'd been so sweet to her. No, he'd never go off and leave her and April alone on Christmas Eve. But still she had to go through the motions of allowing him to say it. "Joe doesn't want to be taking care of you. He wants to have a good time."

"He won't mind," April insisted, although her eyes were growing suspiciously moist. "Will you, Joe?"

Joe opened his mouth to reply, but Merry didn't give him a chance. "April, we aren't going and that's that," she said sternly. April started to howl, and Merry picked her up, ignoring the nagging ache in her back, and tried to comfort her.

After a few minutes the child calmed down, pushed herself out of Merry's arms, and went over to her bed to pout, in a last futile effort to make her mother change her mind. Merry sank wearily into her rickety rocking chair. Joe was still standing there, looking nonplussed over the whole situation. Merry smiled at him.

"Now Joe, you mustn't worry about us," she told him perfunctorily. "We'll be fine. You go along and have yourself a good time at the dance."

She watched, still smiling bravely, ready to hear him insist he'd much rather stay here with her. Instead he frowned.

"You not feeling good, is it because . . . ?" He gestured helplessly, his face growing crimson with embarrassment.

Merry understood instantly, and her own face grew warm, too. "Uh, no," she hastily assured him. "I told you, that's . . . that's not for weeks yet." Why was it that as soon as a woman's stomach started pushing out the front of her dress, everybody got a little crazy, worrying she'd drop the baby right in front of them or something?

"Oh, good . . . I mean . . ." he stammered, mortified. Merry smiled inwardly but didn't embarrass him anymore by letting him see her amusement.

"I told you," she said, "you don't have to worry about us. Everything is fine." Except for the fact that he hadn't told her he wasn't going to the dance, which he was going to do any minute now. She waited expectantly.

"Well, if you're sure. I mean, I don't want to leave you, but if . . . if everything's all right . . . I mean, I've got to go into town tonight. I've got to . . . to see someone."

Merry felt as if the bottom had dropped out of her stomach. She stared at him in disbelief, knowing he could plainly see her abject disappointment but unable to do anything to conceal it. "I . . . I see," she managed.

334

"I really don't want to leave you all," he insisted, but Merry knew he was only being polite. What a fool she'd been! How could she have thought a man like Joe Carpenter would want to spend Christmas Eve with a pregnant widow and a child when he could have a dozen pretty girls flirting with him — especially that special someone he had to see tonight — and maybe even steal a few kisses from her under the mistletoe?

She felt the hot sting of tears, but she resolutely blinked it away. "I understand," she said stiffly, certain she did. "You go and have a good time. You . . . you deserve it."

"If you're sure . . ." he said again, but Merry wasn't going to beg a man to stay with her. She didn't want Joe Carpenter's pity.

"I'm sure, now go on before you get April to crying again," she said more sharply than she'd intended.

Joe frowned again, but he left, heading for the barn. Merry didn't dare look at April because the sight of her daughter's frustration would most certainly reduce her to tears herself. Instead she stared at the fire, listening. Listening for sounds of Joe returning to say he'd changed his mind.

Instead she heard him driving the buckboard out of the barn. Why he wanted to fuss with taking the buckboard when he could just ride his horse, she had no idea, but she wasn't about to ask him about it. She squinched her eyes shut over the threatening tears as she heard the wagon rattle to a stop before the door.

In the next second, Joe stuck his head inside the door. "I'm leaving," he informed her rather uncertainly.

"Have a good time," she said through stiff lips, unable to look at him lest the sight of him shatter her resolve and force her to swallow her pride and tell him how very much she wanted him here, with her.

"I . . . I won't be late," he said. "I don't want to miss Santy Claus."

She could hear the smile in his voice, there for April's benefit, but April was still pouting and refused to be charmed. Merry refused, too. "Stay as late as you like," she said, wanting to bite her tongue off as soon as the words were out. What was wrong with her? She was practically driving him away.

"I won't be late," he said again, more firmly this time, as if he were trying to tell her something. But she was too upset to guess what that something might be. Instead, she pouted like April and refused to look at him until he left.

But as soon as she heard the wagon start up again, she lurched from her chair and hurried across the room as fast as her bulk would permit to gaze out the window at the sight of him driving away.

Hours later, after she had finally put a still-unhappy April to bed, Merry again sat in her rocker, staring at the fire and trying to find a comfortable position to ease the aching in her back. She'd put on her night-dress and robe, knowing she should go to bed but un-willing to face her empty bunk just yet. She should also put the gifts under the tree before she retired so April would think Santa Claus had come, but she couldn't seem to make herself do that either. If Joe were here, she couldn't help thinking, how much fun they'd have whispering and giggling over April's doll and the small parcels she'd prepared for him. And for poor Rooster, too. She supposed she'd give Joe the gift she'd made for Rooster.

At the thought, she could no longer hold back the

336

tears she'd been fighting all evening. Silently, bitterly, she wept for the dead, for Matt and Rooster, and for the living, her and April, and for the loneliness she'd been silly enough to think some fiddle-footed cowboy could salve, and for the burdens she was too weak to bear alone, and for the love she'd foolishly fallen into with Joe Carpenter.

Now she'd have to marry someone she didn't love, because she'd have to marry *someone,* sooner or later, and she now knew Joe Carpenter wouldn't be that someone. Shoot, she'd be lucky if he even came back here at all. More likely he'd return to the Hollings', where three pretty young girls would moon over him day and night. Or else he'd go someplace else even more inviting.

A sob rose in her throat, and she was just about to surrender to it when she heard what sounded like sleigh bells. *Sleigh bells?* In the middle of Texas with no snow within a couple hundred miles?

Swallowing her sob, she strained to listen and heard the sound again. She must be losing her mind. It wasn't sleigh bells. It was the jingle of trace chains, and in another second she could hear the rattle of the wagon to which they were attached. It was just a wagon driving up to her house.

A wagon driving up to her house?

Merry jerked up out of her chair and hurried to the window. She couldn't make out much in the darkness, but her ears told her someone had just delivered her very own buckboard to her door. Throwing open that door, she peered into the shadows, trying to make out the driver.

"Joe?" she called softly, uncertainly.

"Ho, ho, ho, Merry Christmas," Joe called back, not at all softly.

337

"Shhh! You'll wake April," she cautioned, pulling the door closed behind her. Her heart was racing, but whether from surprise or pleasure, she didn't bother to decide, and she swiftly wiped the tears from her face with the back of her hand. "Joe, what are you doing back so soon?"

"I told you I wouldn't be late," he reminded her, hopping down from the wagon seat and landing right in front of her. His clothes smelled of fresh air and outdoors and of Joe himself, and Merry had to resist an overwhelming urge to throw her arms around him.

"You said you wouldn't be late, but . . ." She did some fast figuring. "You couldn't have spent more than five minutes at the dance to get back here so soon!"

"I said I had to see someone, that's all. You didn't think I'd go to the dance without you, did you?"

Since that was exactly what she *had* thought, Merry ignored the question. "Who was so important that you had to drive all the way into town to see him on Christmas Eve?" she asked instead.

"Santy Claus," he replied happily. "He had some presents he wanted me to deliver, so of course I had to pick them up. Otherwise, they wouldn't've been here on Christmas morning."

Merry gaped at him, trying vainly to make out his expression in the feeble moonlight. Was he serious? "Presents?" she echoed uncertainly.

"Yeah, here, you can help me carry them in. This one's for April." He reached into the back of the wagon and pulled out an oblong object wrapped in an old rag. "Take it on inside. I'll get the rest."

Burdened with Joe's gift, Merry stumbled awkwardly through the door and set it down on the table so she could examine it in the firelight. Pushing the cloth away, she saw instantly what it was. "A cradle!" she

338

cried aloud before she caught herself. "Oh, Joe, April will be so happy!" she whispered to him as he maneuvered a huge object bundled in an old sheet through the narrow doorway.

"I figured it would go good with the baby doll," he said, smiling at her over his load.

Merry was so excited over the cradle, she didn't even think to notice what Joe was carrying, and while he brought it into the house and set it down, she scurried around, retrieving all the other Christmas surprises from their hiding places. Finding the doll, she laid it carefully into the cradle and draped the extra dresses over the side.

"I'll make some bedclothes for it first chance I get. April will be so happy!" She looked up and saw Joe standing beside the other gift, smiling expectantly.

"Don't you want to see what Santy Claus brought you?" he asked.

"Me?" she echoed stupidly, glancing at the object under the sheet.

Slowly, clumsily, she rose to her feet and took a few uncertain steps toward it, toward Joe, while she tried to figure this out. It was a chair. She could see that much from the shape of it. But why on earth would Joe have brought her a chair?

Impatient with her hesitancy, Joe pulled the sheet off it, revealing the chair in all its glory. Merry gasped and covered her mouth with both hands. "Oh, Joe, it's *beautiful!*" she cried when she could speak. The wood glowed in the firelight and the red brocade seemed to undulate.

"Don't you want to try it out?" Joe prompted when she didn't move.

Of course she did, so she carefully lowered herself down onto the spring seat. "It rocks!" she cried in sur-

339

prise, giving the chair a gentle push.

"Yeah, I figured . . . well, pretty soon you'll be doing a lot of rocking."

Instinctively, Merry laid a hand on her swollen stomach and smiled with all the joy and contentment she imagined the Madonna must have felt on Christmas Eve. If Merry'd had any doubts left, they were gone now. She loved Joe Carpenter, pure and simple.

Fighting tears of happiness, she pushed herself out of the chair, threw her arms around his neck, and kissed him on the cheek. "Thank you, Joe," she whispered. "You've made me happier than I ever expected to be again!"

If she'd shocked him, he recovered quickly, and when she would have pulled away, his arms slipped around her, holding her fast. "Merry, I . . ." he started, but plainly he couldn't think of the right words to say.

Merry didn't need any words, though. She just needed Joe. So she waited, lifting her face to his and letting her love shine in her eyes while he overcame his shyness, and finally, after what seemed an eternity, he lowered his mouth to hers.

His kiss was infinitely sweet, and Merry felt herself melting into his embrace. She wanted him close, closer than the baby would allow him to get, but she held him as tightly as she could for now.

When they were both breathless, Joe lifted his mouth from hers and smiled a little uncertainly. "Merry Christmas, Merry," he said hoarsely.

"Merry Chris—*oh!*" The pain was like a knife slicing across her belly, and she doubled over with it. Then she felt the warm gush of liquid running down her legs.

At first Joe thought he'd hurt her somehow, and

340

then he heard the splashing sound. "What is it? What's wrong?" he asked, terrified.

"My water . . . broke . . ." she gasped, carefully straightening up.

Joe could plainly see the puddle forming around her slippered feet, but, "What does that mean?"

"It means . . . the baby's coming . . ." she told him.

Joe jumped back a foot in abject terror. "But you said a few more weeks!"

"It's early, then."

Joe was as near panic as he'd ever been. "I'll . . . I'll ride straight back to town! All the ladies are there for the dance. They'll know what to do!"

He was almost to the door when Merry's cry stopped him. "No! Don't leave me! There isn't time!"

Joe was about to ask what she meant when she doubled over again with another pain. This wasn't good. It wasn't good at all. He rushed to her side, not knowing what to do but knowing he had to do something.

"You need some ladies to help you," he tried when the pain had passed and she straightened up again.

"No time," she said, panting slightly, her eyes glazed now, looking past him to some secret place he couldn't see. "When I had April it . . . it only took a few hours. By the time . . . you get to town . . . it'll be all over."

Which meant, of course, that Joe was in this all by himself. "I can't help you!" he insisted. "I don't know the first thing about it!"

This time she squeezed his hand when the pain took her, and he slid his other arm around her, supporting her weight until it passed.

When she'd caught her breath again, she said, "You've helped with calves, haven't you?"

Of course he had, whenever a cow got into trouble,

341

but he didn't imagine she'd want him to tie a rope around the baby's foot and pull it out. And when he thought about where the baby would be coming out of Merry, his knees turned to jelly. "It's not the same!" he insisted, but Merry ignored him.

"There's an oil cloth in the trunk at the end of my bed," she told him. "Strip the bedding off my bed and put the oil cloth over the mattress, then cover it with a sheet."

She sank down onto one of the kitchen chairs while he worked, and he stopped and held his breath each time a pain took her. When he'd finished with the bed, he helped her into it, then did the rest of her bidding, gathering string and scissors and towels and all the other necessities. Joe had no idea what it was all for, and he was too terrified to ask.

"The backache, I should have known," she muttered once when he was stuffing a pillow behind her as she had instructed. But he didn't ask her what she meant. He didn't think she'd been talking to him anyway.

Joe thought once that he should probably be praying, and he would have, too, except he didn't have the time. Everything went too fast, even faster than Merry had predicted, and before Joe could catch his breath from gathering up everything she'd wanted him to have ready, Merry was grabbing her knees and bearing down in no uncertain terms.

Joe had already seen more of her bare legs than he'd ever in his wildest dreams expected to, and now he could see a lot more than that.

"The baby's coming!" she gasped between contractions. "I can feel it! Can you see the head?"

It took Joe a minute to realize that's exactly what he was seeing, the top of a head covered with damp, black curls. "Yeah, yes, I can!" he cried, forgetting for

342

a moment he didn't want to wake April.

"You have . . . to catch it," she told him as the next pain convulsed her.

He was going to ask what she meant, but then he *saw* what she meant as the tiny body slipped from hers. He caught it and lifted it carefully, mindful of the cord. For one amazing second, he stared down at the tiny, perfectly formed child in his hands. Then he realized something was terribly wrong.

"It's not crying!" Merry gasped. "Grab it by the feet! Hold it upside down and slap its bottom!"

Joe was sure she'd lost her mind, but one glance at her face told him she was perfectly serious. Gingerly, he took the minuscule, slippery feet in one hand and lifted them until the baby hung upside down. Then, fighting every instinct he'd ever known, he slapped the little bottom.

"Harder!" Merry cried.

So he slapped harder and was rewarded by the sweetest sound he'd ever heard, a baby's howl of outrage. Instantly, the little body grew rosy with life and the little arms began to flail. Joe gladly surrendered the baby to Merry's eager arms.

"It's a boy," she told him, but he was too busy with the scissors and string to pay much attention. It was alive, and so was Merry. That's all Joe cared about.

The next morning, Joe awoke to the sounds of April's delighted laughter. "Look what Santa brought me, Joe!" she cried, shaking him and holding the rag doll right up against his nose.

He was stiff from sleeping on the floor again, but he rubbed the sleep from his eyes and dutifully admired April's baby before he remembered the other baby.

343

"She has a bed and dresses and everything!" April was telling him. He nodded perfunctorily and scrambled to his feet, listening for sounds of life behind the curtain that hid Merry's bed from him. Not wanting to wake her if she was asleep, he went to the curtain and pulled it aside. For a second he thought his eyes might pop right out of his head.

Merry was awake and smiling up at him like he'd hung the moon, which was shocking enough, but she was also nursing the baby at one beautiful, white breast which he could see in its entirety, or at least all but the little bit the baby had in his mouth. He knew he shouldn't be staring like that. He knew he should drop the curtain and turn away, but he couldn't seem to move.

So Merry, seeing his predicament, removed her nipple from the baby's mouth and pulled her nightdress closed. To his surprise, she didn't seem the least bit embarrassed, which was good because he was embarrassed enough for both of them.

"April," Merry called. "Come and show me the baby Santa Claus brought you."

April came running but stopped dead when she saw the little bundle lying beside her mother. "What's that?" she demanded.

Merry smiled beatifically. "Well, it looks like Santa brought us both a baby. Yours is a doll, and mine is a real one."

April squealed ecstatically and asked a dozen questions about where the baby had come from, which her mother deftly avoided answering.

"It's just like the baby Jesus, born on Christmas!" April declared when she'd asked everything she could think of. "Can we name him Jesus, too?"

"I think that would be disrespectful to the real Jesus,

344

don't you?" Merry said.

April nodded in solemn agreement. "What *is* his name, then?"

Funny, that was just about the only thing Joe hadn't thought about last night when he'd finally had Merry and the baby tucked into bed, safe and snug and warm. He'd thought about everything else, though, and he was going to tell Merry what he'd decided just as soon as they were alone again. She might not like it at first, but he'd make her see things his way. She'd have to.

And when she looked up at him, her beautiful blue eyes shining like a Texas summer sky, she said, "I'm going to name the baby 'Joe.' "

By the time Joe had fixed them a makeshift Christmas dinner and they'd put a small dent in Mrs. Holling's fruitcake and April had fallen asleep on the floor, worn out from all the excitement, they were already calling the baby "Little Joey."

Which made Joe bold enough to raise the subject of the future. As soon as Merry had finished nursing the baby again, he pulled a chair up beside her bed and straddled it. She eased the sleeping baby over to her far side and tucked him in, then folded her hands on her much flatter stomach and smiled expectantly.

"Merry," he said after he'd cleared his throat twice. "We need to talk."

"We certainly do," she said to his surprise.

Joe had to clear his throat again, and he sent up a silent prayer that he would remember the speech he'd prepared. "I know Matt hasn't been dead too long, but it's not good for you and April and now the baby to be on your own. You need somebody to take care of

345

you." There, so far so good, and she was still listening. Still smiling, too. He took a deep breath and plunged back in. "I know this is sudden, and you haven't known me very long, but I think you know me pretty well."

She nodded solemnly, although her eyes were dancing with silent amusement. "And you know me pretty well, too, especially after last night."

Joe felt his face catch fire, but he valiantly ignored his embarrassment and hoped the winter light was too dim for her to see him flushing. "Yeah, uh, which is why I think . . . I mean, it's only proper and all, after what happened, that we should . . ."

"Should what?" she prompted when he ran out of steam.

He swallowed down hard and squared his shoulders, bracing himself for the refusal he had every right to expect. "Why, we should get married."

He'd been ready for just about any reaction, stunned amazement, outrage, even laughter. Instead, she just stared at him calmly for a long moment. Finally, she said, "Is that the only reason?"

"The only reason what?" Joe asked, thoroughly confused.

"The only reason you think we should get married, because you helped deliver my baby."

"Well, no," Joe assured her, flustered. "There's lots of reasons."

"Like what?"

Joe's face started burning again as he remembered the way she'd let him kiss her last night, but he didn't think he ought to mention it in case she'd forgot. "Oh, like because I'm a hard worker, and I could really make something out of this place. You'd never have to worry about anything again. I'll take good care of you,

346

all of you. And a boy needs a father, too. I figure since I helped bring him into the world, it's sort of like my duty to see he makes out all right."

She nodded, but she said, "What else?"

What else? Joe thought, feeling the first stirrings of panic. He'd expected he'd have to convince her, but not like this. "Well, April seems to like me," he said lamely. "And I like her fine."

"And what about me?"

"What?" Joe asked, more confused than ever.

"Do you like me fine, too?"

"Well, sure," he said uncertainly.

"And is that all?"

"All what?"

"Do you only *like* me? I mean, when people get married, they usually have feelings for each other, strong feelings. They usually love each other, Joe. Do you love me?"

Joe was so mortified, he thought he might just go up in smoke, but he wasn't going to back down now, not if there was still a chance. "Yes, I do," he said, his throat tight, but he forced the words out, one by one. "I reckon I've loved you since, oh, I don't know when. I always admired you, even when you was married to Matt, and when I came back and you was free . . . I know you've got your pick of men, and you don't have to settle for some saddle bum, but nobody'll love you more than I will, Merry. I can promise you that. And I know you don't feel the same, at least not yet, but maybe you will someday. In the meantime I'll sure do everything I can to see that you won't have much choice *but* to love me."

She looked funny, like she was going to cry, and Joe wanted to bite his tongue off for saying something to make her sad, but to his surprise, she smiled.

347

"I do love you, Joe. I don't know when it started either, but you're an easy person to love, so it might've been since the first day you rode in here."

Joe was shaking his head in disbelief, and Merry misunderstood the gesture.

"It's true, and if you'll pull off your boots and come under these blankets with me, I'll show you."

Joe had his boots off in less than a second.

"Now we can't do anything but kiss for a few months," she cautioned as he slid into the bed beside her, "because of the baby. So maybe we should put off getting married until spring."

Joe took her in his arms and pulled her close, much closer than he'd been able to last night, until every inch of her touched every inch of him. Inhaling her sweet scent, he kissed her long and lingeringly. He could wait for the rest. In fact, he figured he'd die of pure pleasure if he had all of her at once. No, he'd work up to it, a little at a time.

And meanwhile . . .

"I think we'll get married right away. We'll tell April that Santy Claus brought her a new daddy, too."

DISCOVER DEANA JAMES!

CAPTIVE ANGEL (2524, $4.50/$5.50)
Abandoned, penniless, and suddenly responsible for the biggest tobacco plantation in Colleton County, distraught Caroline Gillard had no time to dissolve into tears. By day the willowy redhead labored to exhaustion beside her slaves . . . but each night left her restless with longing for her wayward husband. She'd make the sea captain regret his betrayal until he begged her to take him back!

MASQUE OF SAPPHIRE (2885, $4.50/$5.50)
Judith Talbot-Harrow left England with a heavy heart. She was going to America to join a father she despised and a sister she distrusted. She was certainly in no mood to put up with the insulting actions of the arrogant Yankee privateer who boarded her ship, ransacked her things, then "apologized" with an indecent, brazen kiss! She vowed that someday he'd pay dearly for the liberties he had taken and the desires he had awakened.

SPEAK ONLY LOVE (3439, $4.95/$5.95)
Long ago, the shock of her mother's death had robbed Vivian Marleigh of the power of speech. Now she was being forced to marry a bitter man with brandy on his breath. But she could not say what was in her heart. It was up to the viscount to spark the fires that would melt her icy reserve.

WILD TEXAS HEART (3205, $4.95/$5.95)
Fan Breckenridge was terrified when the stranger found her near-naked and shivering beneath the Texas stars. Unable to remember who she was or what had happened, all she had in the world was the deed to a patch of land that might yield oil . . . and the fierce loving of this wildcatter who called himself Irons.

Available wherever paperbacks are sold, or order direct from the Publisher. Send cover price plus 50¢ per copy for mailing and handling to Zebra Books, Dept. 3975, 475 Park Avenue South, New York, N.Y. 10016. Residents of New York and Tennessee must include sales tax. DO NOT SEND CASH. For a free Zebra/ Pinnacle catalog please write to the above address.

LET ARCHER AND CLEARY
AWAKEN AND CAPTURE YOUR HEART!

CAPTIVE DESIRE (2612, $3.75)
by Jane Archer

Victoria Malone fancied herself a great adventuress and student of life, but being kidnapped by handsome Cord Cordova was too much excitement for even her! Convincing her kidnapper that she had been an innocent bystander when the stagecoach was robbed was futile when he was kissing her until she was senseless!

REBEL SEDUCTION (3249, $4.25)
by Jane Archer

"Stop that train!" came Lacey Whitmore's terrified warning as she rushed toward the locomotive that carried wounded Confederates and her own beloved father. But no one paid heed, least of all the Union spy Clint McCullough, who pinned her to the ground as the train suddenly exploded into flames.

DREAM'S DESIRE (3093, $4.50)
by Gwen Cleary

Desperate to escape an arranged marriage, Antonia Winston y Ortega fled her father's hacienda to the arms of the arrogant Captain Domino. She would spend the night with him and would be free for no gentleman wants a ruined bride. And ruined she would be, for Tonia would never forget his searing kisses!

VICTORIA'S ECSTASY (2906, $4.25)
by Gwen Cleary

Proud Victoria Torrington was short of cash to run her shipping empire, so she traveled to America to meet her partner for the first time. Expecting a withered, ancient cowhand, Victoria didn't know what to do when she met virile, muscular Judge Colston and her body budded with desire.

Available wherever paperbacks are sold, or order direct from the Publisher. Send cover price plus 50¢ per copy for mailing and handling to Zebra Books, Dept. 3975, 475 Park Avenue South, New York, N.Y. 10016. Residents of New York and Tennessee must include sales tax. DO NOT SEND CASH. For a free Zebra/ Pinnacle catalog please write to the above address.

WAITING FOR A WONDERFUL ROMANCE?
READ ZEBRA'S

WANDA OWEN!

DECEPTIVE DESIRES   (2887, $4.50/$5.50)
Exquisite Tiffany Renaud loved her life as the only daughter of a wealthy Parisian industrialist. The last thing she wanted was to cross the ocean on a cramped and stuffy ship just to visit the uncivilized wilds of America. Then she shared a kiss with shipping magnate Chad Morrow that made the sails billow and the deck spin. . .

KISS OF FIRE   (3091, $4.50/$5.50)
Born and raised in backwoods Virginia, Tawny Blair knew that her dream of being swept off her feet by a handsome nobleman would never come true. But when she met Lord Bart, Tawny saw at once that reality could far surpass her fantasies. And when he took her in his strong arms, she thrilled to the desire in his searing caresses . . .

SAVAGE FURY   (2676, $3.95/$4.95)
Lovely Gillian Browne was secure in her quiet world on a remote ranch in Arizona, yet she longed for romance and excitement. Her girlish fantasies did not prepare her for the strange new feelings that assaulted her when dashing Irish sea captain Steve Lafferty entered her life . . .

TEMPTING TEXAS TREASURE   (3312, $4.50/$5.50)
Mexican beauty Karita Montera aroused a fever of desire in every redblooded man in the wild Texas Blacklands. But the sensuous señorita had eyes only for Vincent Navarro, the wealthy cattle rancher she'd adored since childhood — and her family's sworn enemy! His first searing caress ignited her white-hot need and soon Karita burned to surrender to her own wanton passion . . .

Available wherever paperbacks are sold, or order direct from the Publisher. Send cover price plus 50¢ per copy for mailing and handling to Zebra Books, Dept. 3975, 475 Park Avenue South, New York, N.Y. 10016. Residents of New York and Tennessee must include sales tax. DO NOT SEND CASH. For a free Zebra/ Pinnacle catalog please write to the above address.

JANELLE TAYLOR

ZEBRA'S BEST-SELLING AUTHOR

DON'T MISS ANY OF HER
EXCEPTIONAL, EXHILARATING, EXCITING

ECSTASY SERIES

SAVAGE ECSTASY	(3496-2, $4.95/$5.95)
DEFIANT ECSTASY	(3497-0, $4.95/$5.95)
FORBIDDEN ECSTASY	(3498-9, $4.95/$5.95)
BRAZEN ECSTASY	(3499-7, $4.99/$5.99)
TENDER ECSTASY	(3500-4, $4.99/$5.99)
STOLEN ECSTASY	(3501-2, $4.99/$5.99)